C000055515

SHERLOCK HOLMES

The Shadow of the Rat
The Tangled Skein

SHERLOCK HOLMES

The Shadow of the Rat
The Tangled Skein

David Stuart Davies

with a Foreword by
Peter Cushing

WORDSWORTH EDITIONS

In loving memory of
MICHAEL TRAYLER
the founder of Wordsworth Editions

I

Readers interested in other titles from
Wordsworth Editions are invited to visit our
website at www.wordsworth-editions.com

For our latest list and a full mail-order service contact
Bibliophile Books, Unit 5 Datapoint,
South Crescent, London E16 4TL
Tel: +44 020 74 74 24 74
Fax: +44 020 74 74 85 89
orders@bibliophilebooks.com
www.bibliophilebooks.com

This edition published 2010 by
Wordsworth Editions Limited
8B East Street, Ware,
Hertfordshire SG12 9HJ

ISBN 978 1 84022 652 2

Typeset in Great Britain by Roperford Editorial
Printed by Clays Ltd, St Ives plc

CONTENTS

THE SHADOW OF THE RAT
A Sherlock Holmes Adventure

To the Smarden Crew
Lynne, Auberon, Freda, Tony,
Elaine, Jonathan and Richard
Happy days and nights

An Old Friend

When recollecting the great number of investigations in which I have been involved with my friend Sherlock Holmes, the consulting detective, many and varied are the vivid moments that immediately spring to my mind. Some are amusing, some dramatic, some life-threatening, and some emotionally draining; but all are remembered, now that those days have passed, with a kind of nostalgic affection. All, that is, with one exception – a nightmare episode that haunts me still in my unexpected dreams and bleak waking moments. The sensations are so powerful that I live that time again when I was trapped in the darkness with the creature. I hear the scuttle of its clawed feet and smell the overpoweringly nauseous stench of its breath. I remember with fear and loathing the terrible threat that it carried with it. I see again those large, ferocious eyes and sharp yellow teeth. It was a rat. But no ordinary rat. It was the Giant Rat of Sumatra.

However, I see that I am falling into the way of telling stories that Sherlock Holmes criticised so: relaying information illogically and out of sequence. To begin at the beginning we must return to the year 1895 and a period when I was living in Baker Street. At this time, Holmes and I had known each other some twelve years or so. During those years I had been married and widowed and Holmes had spent three years out of the country, presumed dead, after the Reichenbach incident. So in the year in question we were now middle-aged bachelors, comfortable with each other and in each other's company. My friend's rather *outré* habits no longer surprised or irritated me in quite the same way as they had in the early days of our association and, similarly, Holmes was more tolerant of my mundane habits. He had become more deferential, more considerate and, indeed, more companionable.

If I have to pinpoint precisely when the shadow of the rat began to throw its pall over us, it was the night we had a late supper at Simpson's and encountered Stamford again. Earlier we had attended the Wood Green Empire for an evening of frivolous entertainment.

Top of the bill was the Great Salvini, an extraordinary hypnotist. He interested me very much, as mesmerism was slowly being introduced into some branches of medicine. There had been a recent article in the *Lancet* on the subject and I was intrigued by its power and potential. However, Holmes was more dismissive of Salvini's talents. 'The use of planted assistants in the audience easily explains away all the magic,' he observed nonchalantly during our cab ride back to the West End. In this instance I believed my friend to be wrong. Although my knowledge of the subject was very limited, I was convinced that a skilled practitioner could take control of a willing subject's mind for a brief spell, without the need for trickery and subterfuge. Subsequent events proved that even this simple assumption greatly underestimated the terrible power of hypnotism.

By the time we reached Simpson's our topic of conversation had moved on from our evening's entertainment and we were discussing Holmes's recent cases. He had just concluded a neat little investigation concerning a baronet's will, a quantity of iron filings, and a topiary manual, and he was in fine form. Uncharacteristically, he had ordered a second bottle of wine, a fine burgundy, and we sat back smoking cigars in a very mellow mood. It was at times like this when Holmes dropped his guard a little and, on this occasion, he had begun to talk of his childhood in Yorkshire. He recalled a treehouse which he and his brother Mycroft had built in the garden; and how they had taken it in turns to 'own' the house, whilst the other brother plotted schemes and strategies to oust the tenant. 'It was not a very sophisticated pursuit,' said Holmes grinning, obviously enjoying his childhood reminiscence. 'It usually ended in fisticuffs. Mycroft and I had our fair share of black eyes and bruised knuckles over that tree-house.'

At that moment a man bumped into our table as he was passing. The fellow turned awkwardly and apologised. 'Sorry about that, gents. My mistake.' His speech was slightly slurred and his eyes had the glazed appearance of the inebriate. Glancing at his blotchy features, I recognised the fellow immediately. It was Stamford, who had been a dresser under me at St Bartholomew's Hospital. I had heard that he had completed his medical studies and was now a junior doctor on the wards there. But the man I saw before me this night held little resemblance to the young, fresh-faced chap who, all those years ago, had introduced me to Sherlock Holmes. Dark, unruly, curly hair tumbled over his face, which bore an unhealthy pallor and was shiny with perspiration, while the fleshy, pink nose gave testament to his regular over-indulgence in drink. His clothes were dishevelled and his whole demeanour was one of personal neglect.

On turning to apologise, a light of recognition flamed in his eyes and then his face split into a cheery grin. 'Watson, old fellow. And Holmes. What on earth are you doing here?' He shook his head and giggled. 'You're having a meal, of course. Well, well, Holmes and Watson. Do you mind if I join you for a couple of minutes?'

Before we had an opportunity to respond, Stamford had hailed a waiter to bring him a chair. When the chair arrived, our friend pulled himself up to our table, and asked the waiter to bring him a brandy and soda.

'Well, well, well,' he grinned, leaning right over the table. 'Good old Holmes and Watson. What a surprise. Of course I read about you all the time in those splendid yarns of yours, Watson.'

'They are hardly yarns,' I replied stiffly. 'They are records of Holmes's investigations.'

The idiotic smile dropped from Stamford's face and he appeared suitably chastened. 'Of course. And very good they are.' He paused to light a cigarette, his shaking hand having some difficulty holding the match steady. 'By the way,' he continued, through a haze of smoke, 'I was sorry to hear about Mary. Very sad.'

'Thank you. Yes.'

'And how is the world with you, Stamford?' cut in Holmes, in an obvious effort to channel the conversation in another direction.

Our drunken companion shrugged. '*Comme ci, comme ça.*'

'I was wondering if you were celebrating this evening – or drowning your sorrows?'

Stamford leaned further forward onto the table and stretched out his arm, pointing his cigarette at Holmes. 'Up to your little tricks again, Sherlock Holmes? Surely you don't have to ask me? You can tell me.'

'I can tell,' said I, interrupting, 'that you have had too much to drink.'

At this point the waiter arrived with Stamford's brandy and soda, whereupon he sat up in his chair and raised his glass. 'You're wrong, Watson. I've not had too much to drink . . . yet.' So saying, he downed the brandy in one gulp and then slumped forward onto the table in a dazed stupor.

'We had better get this fellow home, Watson, before he does himself any more damage,' said Holmes; and leaning forward, he removed the smouldering cigarette from Stamford's limp hand, and stubbed it out in the ashtray.

An examination of Stamford's jacket soon produced details of his address: 32 Tunnacliffe Road in Chiswick. With some effort, wecarried our inert companion through the dining-room, to the amusement of some diners and the disgust of others. Once out into the cool night air, Stamford rallied a little, but it was clear that he was not capable of seeing himself home. Holmes hailed a cab and we set off for Chiswick.

Our drunken associate fell asleep on the journey and purred contentedly in his slumbers. 'What makes a man treat himself in this way?' I said. 'When I worked with him he was sober and reliable.'

'Well, it is not for lack of money. In searching for his address I noted that his wallet was bulging with cash; and a meal at Simpson's is not cheap – especially for a junior doctor. However, it is clear to me that something is preying on his mind, frightening him so much that he feels the need to drown it out of his consciousness.'

'What, for heaven's sake?'

'I cannot tell at present. There is insufficient data on which to build a clear hypothesis, but when I see a junior doctor with a full wallet, spots of blood on his cuffs, and a desire to escape from reality, I begin to suspect that he is involved in some illegal practice.'

Tunnacliffe Road proved to be a shabby, tree-lined avenue and we discovered that number thirty-two was a 'guest house for discerning gentlemen'. By now Stamford was aware of his surroundings and he began searching for his key in his pockets. 'Mrs Sanderson mustn't see me in this state,' he rambled, the words emerging thickly and indistinctly, 'or she'll have me out on the street.'

'Obviously this is not the first time that you have arrived home in such a condition,' said Holmes.

'Another brilliant deduction,' cried Stamford sarcastically, almost losing his balance.

'Let's get him to his room and leave him to sleep off his stupor,' I snapped, snatching the door key from Stamford's feeble grasp. I really was losing patience with him. I could hold no respect for a man who allowed himself to become so incapable through drink, for whatever reason.

'First room on the right at the top of the stairs. Number six,' he mumbled as I opened the main door. Holmes virtually carried Stamford through the entrance and up the stairs, his boots scraping along the carpet. We reached the landing without being seen but, just as we were about to enter our companion's room, a door opened on the ground floor, throwing a yellow shaft of light into the hallway. 'Is that you, Mr Stamford?' came the shrill cockney voice from below.

Stamford had the presence of mind to utter a cheery goodnight before stumbling into his quarters. At times I have complained about Holmes's untidiness, but the bed-sitting-room in which we found ourselves was in such a state of disarray that, at first glance, it looked as though it had been ransacked. Clothes were draped carelessly over the furniture, drawers were left open with the contents spilling out, and there were books and papers everywhere. However, on closer inspection, it became clear that this indeed was how the man lived. My disgust towards him grew the stronger. Stamford staggered into the room and collapsed face down on the bed. I turned to leave, but Holmes stopped me with a wave of his hand. 'Let's see what we can learn of our friend's plight,' said he, closing the door quietly. 'I fear that he is in some terrible trouble and in desperate need of assistance.'

With quick, easy movements, Holmes removed Stamford's jacket and rolled up his shirtsleeves. On both arms the pale skin between the elbow and wrist was dotted with several dark scarlet scabs. My friend gave a grunt of solemn satisfaction.

'Drugs,' I said. 'That would explain his wild behaviour.'

'Drink explains his wild behaviour. It is what drove him to drink that concerns us. These marks are not the simple souvenirs of drug taking. Before you make the point, Watson, yes, I am one who should know and, indeed, I do. When he lit a cigarette this evening, I noted that Stamford is left-handed. The fact that both arms are desecrated in this manner suggests that these injections have not been self-administered.'

As I looked down at my old acquaintance, his pallid flesh frosted with perspiration and his mouth agape in a silent snore, I wondered what strange train of events had led him to this demoralised state. For a brief moment I remembered the lively and dedicated medical novice whom I had known in my days at Bart's. The pathethic, drunken creature we had encountered tonight was a base travesty of the real Stamford. My heart felt heavy to see such promise abused.

My feelings must have been as apparent as print on a page, for Holmes placed a comforting arm on my shoulder. 'There is nothing we can do for the poor wretch tonight, old boy, but we must make enquiries about our friend, for it is quite clear that he sorely needs our help.'

As though in a perverse response to my friend's sympathetic words, Stamford shifted in his stupor and, with his mouth still wide open, emitted a rasping snort.

'Come,' said Holmes, 'let him sleep it off.' Moving to go, something caught his attention on the bedside table. He leaned closer and examined the surface.

'What is it?' I asked.

Rather than reply, he pointed to some letters scrawled in the dust on the top of the table. They looked like idle scribbles.

'Bart,' said Holmes softly, for those were the letters inscribed in the dust.

'What does it mean? Bart's Hospital?'

Holmes shrugged. 'I am not sure. But a sober man may tell us many things. We shall return tomorrow. For now let us leave him to his drunken slumbers.'

CHAPTER TWO

The Body from the River

Little did I know as we rattled away from the environs of Chiswick that we were never destined to see Stamford alive again. I was also unaware that the strange chance encounter in Simpson's with this figure from our past would trigger off a series of bizarre and life-threatening events, which would finally bring us under the dark shadow of the rat.

On returning to Baker Street, Holmes and I felt little disposed to retire for the night, so we sat up with our pipes and a brandy and soda apiece, staring into the dying embers of the fire, each of us locked in our own private thoughts. Mine were of Stamford, but what exactly was running through Holmes's brain, I could not tell. Whatever it was, it prompted a stern expression to settle on those fine chiselled features, furrowing deep lines on his brow. For myself, I relived the events of the evening's encounter in great detail, attempting to determine if there was anything that Stamford had said or done which could provide us with clues as to why he was in such a desperate state. There were so many conflicting pieces of evidence: he was obviously well off, but he was unhappy; he had strict medical training, yet he and his quarters were so squalid. Then there were the strange pinpricks of blood on his arms. It was most mystifying.

At length, Sherlock Holmes gave a low moan, stretched his arms, and, without a word to me, headed for bed, leaving me alone with my wretched thoughts in the amber gloom. I succumbed to temptation and poured another brandy. Whether I wanted it to aid my sleep – an aid I really did not need – or to help me blot out the image of my friend Stamford as he lay, bloated and drunk, on his bed, I cannot now remember. Whatever reason, the alcohol was successful on both counts. So it was that I found myself emerging from an uneasy slumber some hours later with a wretched stiff neck, still sitting in my chair in total darkness, the fire now but a dull, smouldering heap of ashes. With stiff and weary joints I pulled myself awkwardly to my feet and, noticing with some dismay that it was now three o'clock in the morning, made my way to bed.

I paid for my over-indulgence the following morning for, as Holmes roused me by tugging back the curtains to allow bright, searing sunlight into my room, I felt little devils with anvils start hammering in my brain. Infuriatingly, Holmes was bright and lively. 'Come on, Watson,' he cried with unnatural cheeriness, 'we have demands upon our services and all you can do is lie there and snore like a Berkshire pig.'

'Demands on our services,' I repeated groggily, pulling myself up in bed and screwing up my eyes against the fierce light that shafted in from the window. 'What on earth are you talking about? Do you mean we have a client?'

'Not exactly, unless you regard Inspector Giles Lestrade as such. We have been summoned to the Yard.'

Half an hour later, after I was dressed and had consumed a head-ache powder and several cups of coffee, Holmes bundled me into a waiting cab while the impish anvil chorus continued its tattoo in my head. Until that morning I had never realised how noisy a hansom cab could be. At every jolt and shudder of the journey it creaked alarmingly, thudded incessantly, and boomed like a kettledrum as it ran over the cobbles. I felt myself sinking in a sea of noise. In his irritating way, Holmes sat back, a smile of contentment on his face, apparently deriving some pleasure from my discomfort.

'I hope that you have your notebook with you, for this promises to be an intriguing case,' he grinned at me.

Sullenly, I tapped my breast. 'It is always with me. Anyway, what does the matter concern? Has Lestrade explained?'

Holmes raised his eyebrows and threw over a crumpled telegram. 'This is our summons and that is all I know,' he said.

Holding the telegram towards the window, I read the following:

PLEASE COME TO YARD THIS MORNING. NEED YOUR ADVICE ON
VERY STRANGE AND PUZZLING MATTER. URGENT. G. LESTRADE

'The rhetoric is certainly a touch dramatic and the tone is strangely earnest for Lestrade,' I observed, passing back the telegram.

'Quite so,' said Holmes. 'Our friend the Inspector usually reserves the use of hyperbole for the accounts of his successes and, as a general rule, hates to admit that he is out of his depth and requires our services. That is why I think this could be a most interesting excursion.'

It was a very grim-faced Inspector Lestrade who greeted us in his office at Scotland Yard some fifteen minutes later. The shadows under his eyes bore witness to a sleepless night, his brow was furrowed, and his shoulders bowed. 'I won't beat about the bush, Mr Holmes, Dr Watson,' he said wearily, after a perfunctory shake of our hands. He indicated that we should take a seat, while he sank into a chair behind his cluttered desk. 'A body was fished out of the Thames last night – throat cut and with no identifying marks on, or in, the clothing.'

'Not a particularly unusual event, I should have thought,' observed Holmes, matter-of-factly.

'That's right,' agreed the policeman. 'The river police pick up two or three bodies a week – suicides, petty criminals, and the like. But this one – this one . . . ' He shook his head gravely. 'I've never seen anything like this one.'

'What is unusual about it?' I asked.

'You're obviously tired and upset, Lestrade,' observed Holmes. 'You're not making much sense at the moment. I think it would be a useful idea for us to view the corpse.'

Lestrade rose instantly. 'Indeed. That's why I asked you here.'

Without further deliberation, the Scotland Yarder led us into the depths of the building to the morgue area. Here the lighting, and indeed the heating, was minimal, and the walls glistened with condensation. At the far end of a dingy corridor we came upon a door which was guarded by a burly young constable. He saluted the Inspector and, without a word, unlocked the door for us to enter.

It was a small, dimly lit chamber, containing a stone sink and a wooden cabinet. In the centre of the room was a raised stone slab on which the body was laid, covered by a heavy green sheet. Lestrade went around the room, turning up the gas mantles. 'I want you to be able to see this thing clearly,' he said ominously. 'If you are able to explain how a man could get into this condition, I'd be eternally grateful.'

Holmes glanced furtively in my direction, raising his eyebrows in surprise at Lestrade's emotional behaviour. It was so incongruous in such a down to earth individual, the most flat-footed of police officers. He was a man whom Holmes had always intimated lacked any real imagination, which was why he had never risen above the rank of Inspector. Yet here he was behaving like a character from a music hall melodrama.

'I recommend that you clasp a handkerchief to your mouth and nose, gentlemen. The smell is very bad,' he said.

We did as he suggested. Then, after copying our actions, he gave a tug to the heavy cover, which fell to the floor revealing the body on the slab. It took just one glance to appreciate what had caused such erratic and emotional behaviour in an unimaginative man like Lestrade. It was a sight I should not care to see again.

That the body was human and of the male gender was reasonably clear, but the features and the flesh were covered in the most obscene excrescence and pustules, which had erupted with a foul green putrescence. These were so disfiguring that many of the human features were hidden or obliterated. The remaining skin was marked at irregular intervals with purple blotches. The stench emanating from the open sores was almost overpowering.

The legs and arms in particular were swollen to nearly twice their normal size, and there were traces of gangrene in both legs. One side of the creature's head was swollen and this fearsome growth had crusted with a hard, plate-like surface completely covering the left eye. One of the hands had apparently dropped off and had been placed at the end of the ragged stump of his wrist.

Holmes, braver than I, clamped his handkerchief tightly to his mouth and examined the body with his magnifying glass, being careful not to actually touch the flesh. After but a few minutes he pulled back, perspiration dampening his brow, his eyes screwed up with distaste. It was clear that he could not stand to remain in such close proximity to that rotting corpse any longer.

None of us spoke for some time, but I felt my eyes misting with tears. I mourned for this creature, whoever he was, whatever he had been, and whatever his biography, for, be he devil or saint, no man deserved such an end. It was as if all the plagues of hell had been visited upon his body, corrupting it from within.

Plagues of hell. The phrase echoed in my brain and my body tingled with a strange recognition. Chords of memory vibrated and momentarily I was back at the University of London staring at an illustrated textbook while Professor Lindstrom spoke, with ringing tones, and in gratuitous detail, about the main illustration on the page. 'It is like a satanic visitation, is it not? Like all the plagues of hell.'

'My God!' I said softly, as the chill fingers of understanding gripped my heart. 'My God!'

Both of my companions stared at me with concern. 'What is it, Watson?' asked Holmes gently.

I looked at him steadily. 'It is bubonic plague.'

'What!' exclaimed Lestrade, adding, 'and what . . . what is that?'

'It is a contagious bacterial disease thought extinct, character-ised by the presence of buboes – inflamed swellings,' I replied, reciting almost word for word from the textbook I had studied in my younger days.

'It ravaged the city in 1665 and decimated the population. It was only eradicated successfully by the Great Fire of London the follow-ing year,' said Holmes.

Lestrade surveyed the diseased corpse with even greater horror, and repeated the one word that had struck him like a knife. 'Con-tagious,' he said. 'You say it's contagious?'

I nodded grimly. 'Yes. Less so in this cool temperature, but even here, close and prolonged proximity to the thing could prove dangerous.'

Lestrade gave a gagging sound and took a step back from the slab. 'Are you certain?' he asked, all the colour draining from his face.

I nodded. 'Yes, I am. You must burn it – consign it to the furnace. Destroy it straight away before it has a chance to infect others. Once it does that, this insidious disease spreads at great speed. Once it takes hold, it is like a bush fire in the Australian outback: there is no stopping it. It consumes all within its path.'

The policeman nodded vigorously. 'I'll take your word for it, doctor. You have convinced me. I will arrange for it to be done straight away. Come gentlemen, let's leave this place. I am already starting to itch.'

Some fifteen minutes later we were ensconced once more in Les-trade's office, drinking hot, strong tea. The policeman had given orders for the corpse to be destroyed, and instructed that those involved with its destruction should wrap scarves or handkerchieves around their nose and mouth and wear gloves. He sat opposite us now, fiddling nervously with his teaspoon, his face ghastly white. 'The plague . . . ' he said in disbelief, more to himself than to Holmes and me.

'Where on earth did it come from? And why kill the man in such an advanced stage of the disease?' I asked.

'What do you mean?' asked Lestrade.

'His throat was cut,' said Holmes. 'He was murdered. From what I could detect, it was clear that the corpse had not been in the water for long, so the murder was quite recent. The blood around the throat had only recently congealed. Most likely it took place last night when the fellow was in the advanced stages of this wretched disease. He must have been on the verge of death anyway, so why take the trouble to murder him? What was the motive?'

'To put him out of his misery,' I suggested.

'It is a possibility. But that would suggest a caring action. Dumping him in the river is not. If the slashing of the throat was to bring his suffering to an end, why did the killer not just bury him somewhere, rather than disposing of him in the Thames where eventually he would be found?'

'Perhaps the act of murder robbed the killer of his capacity for rational thought,' I ventured.

Holmes nodded. 'You are probably right, Watson.'

I smiled to myself. Whenever Holmes agreed with me that easily, I knew that he had his own preferred version of events.

'What concerns me, gentlemen,' said Lestrade, 'is whether we have seen the last of the matter. One unsolved murder in London will go unnoticed. But another plague victim will not. What if the perpetrator of this murder was also a carrier? What am I to do?'

Holmes shook his head sadly. 'My advice will bring no comfort I am afraid. There is nothing you *can* do at present. There are no clues, or leads to follow, so you will have to be patient and wait for further developments.'

Lestrade ran his fingers through his hair. 'I . . . I feel so helpless.'

Holmes rose and beckoned me to do likewise. 'When there are fresh developments – as there most surely will be – inform me immediately. Whatever the hour, I will drop whatever investigation I am conducting to come to your aid.'

The policeman's tired face softened into a sad smile. 'Thank you, Mr Holmes. That is some comfort at least.'

We left the inspector alone in his gloomy office staring blankly at the papers that littered his desk. It was a great relief to leave that claustrophobic building and emerge into the fresh air once again; to be able to cast off the awful stench of death which still seemed to cling to us. Also the raucous, bustling normality of London, with its clip-clopping horses and noisy vendors, helped dispel from my mind the unsettling thoughts generated by the rotting corpse. My morning headache was completely forgotten.

'Let us walk a while by the river. I need time to think,' said Holmes quietly.

We crossed the road on to the Victoria embankment and walked a while in silence. I was conscious of the great leaden-grey Thames floating by us, carrying a varied array of large and small craft upon its seething swell, some setting forth for foreign climes, some bringing with them strange cargoes to be unloaded at our docks. Maybe not only strange but deadly also. I shuddered at the thought.

As he walked, Holmes's chin rested upon his chest and his brow was contracted in deep thought. Autumn was in the air and already the early victims of the changing season had begun to fall from the trees to be teased into small piles by a sprightly breeze. From time to time Holmes swung his cane absent-mindedly and sent the brown and yellow leaves spinning around his feet. After a time we stopped and leaned on the parapet overlooking the river.

'This is a very dark business,' he said at length. 'This city could be in great danger unless the source of this malignant disease is found.'

'As a doctor, I am well aware of the consequences of an outbreak of bubonic plague,' I replied, starkly.

'Of course you are, my dear fellow. I apologise if my summation seemed arrogant and overly dramatic. I was merely thinking aloud. Something must be done.'

'I agree, but what? As you told Lestrade, we have no clues, no leads. We have to wait until we have something tangible to work with.'

Holmes gave a weary sigh and, turning his back on the river, leaned against the parapet, his cane over his shoulder. 'I was not quite honest with friend Lestrade. I do have one tenuous lead.'

'What!'

'Well, it is so *very* tenuous that I want to follow it up first before involving the professionals. It may lead us nowhere and then again it may guide us to the truth. Whatever, a quiet and subtle approach is necessary. Lestrade may be diligent, but quietness and subtlety are not amongst his virtues.'

'I see,' I responded, non-committally. 'And am *I* to be allowed to know your secret?'

'Of course. In this matter, as in so many others, your help will be invaluable.'

I waited for my friend to continue, but once more he seemed caught up in his own thoughts, and his eyes took on a faraway look.

'So,' I prompted, dragging him from his reverie, 'what is your lead, your tenuous clue? Where on earth did it come from?'

'The body, my dear Watson. That wretched corpse. You will remember that I examined it rather more closely than you.'

I nodded, and shivered involuntarily as the hideous image of the plague victim flashed into my consciousness once more.

'It was a most unpleasant task, but it did reveal to me something which I found most interesting. I observed that both arms were dotted at regular intervals with small dark scabs – needle marks – as though they had been injected with something. Both arms, mind you. Very much in the same manner as . . . '

'Stamford! My God!'

'Yes, Watson, very much in the same manner as Stamford.'

CHAPTER THREE

The Mystery of the Disappearing Doctor

It was mid-morning when Holmes and I alighted from a hansom cab at the corner of Tunnacliffe Road in Chiswick. My friend had reasoned that, due to the state Stamford had been in the previous night, he would only now be surfacing from his inebriated slumbers and rejoining the land of the living with 'a head so fragile that any sudden movement or noise may cause it to fall off'. Therefore we were more likely to catch him at his lodgings rather than at Bart's Hospital.

'If by some miracle he has managed to rouse himself and has dragged himself into the hospital this morning, we can take the opportunity to scrutinise his room further,' Holmes explained as we approached number thirty-two, 'Mrs Sanderson's Guest House for Discerning Gentlemen'. In the bright glare of daylight the house looked even more down at heel than it had appeared the previous night. It was certainly not the kind of establishment one might expect a respectable doctor to frequent.

'What about his landlady, Mrs Sanderson? She may not take too kindly to two strangers "scrutinising" his room.'

Holmes sighed. 'In all your accounts of our cases, you never give me sufficient credit for my persuasive charm, a commodity as useful to a detective as his lens or knowledge of poisons.'

'I only write from real life. I do not write fiction. Your persuasive charm is elusive. Perhaps it is a figment of your imagination.'

My friend's features lightened and he smiled for the first time since we had seen that wretched corpse. 'You grow more acerbic with age, my friend. I shall have to guard myself against your sharp tongue.'

We had arrived at number thirty-two and without hesitation Holmes knocked loudly on the shabby door. In due course a young woman, aged somewhere in her early twenties, answered the door. She had a plain, but not unpleasant, face, but its features were marred by a plastering of gaudy make-up: her cheeks were heavily rouged and her lips a rich scarlet, while her eyelids were smeared with blue paint. It was as though she was made up for the stage, but in the morning light the effect was garish and rather sad. Dressed in a cheap blouse and grubby skirt, she was a tragic creature indeed. The girl gazed at us indolently for some moments before speaking.

'Sorry, gents,' she said eventually, in the broad accent of east London, her face void of expression, 'we're full up at the moment. Mrs Turpin at number fifty-seven might be able to accommodate you.'

Holmes removed his hat and smiled at the young woman. 'Good morning, Miss Sanderson. We are not in search of accommodation. We are here to call upon a friend of ours: Dr Stamford.'

'Who?' It was a challenge rather than a query.

'Dr Stamford. Robert Stamford. He is a resident here.'

'No he ain't. You got the wrong shop, mister.'

The girl was about to close the door but Holmes firmly placed his hand upon the outer handle.

'No, we have *not* got the wrong shop,' he said, steel finding its way into his voice now. 'Dr Stamford lives at this address. There is no mistake. We brought him home here last night.'

The young woman's face suddenly grew animated. The horribly tinted eyelids fluttered wildly with annoyance. 'I don't know what your game is, but I tell yer there ain't no doctor here or any geezer called Stamford. So if you don't hoppit, I'll call the police.'

Holmes smiled sardonically. 'That won't be necessary. We *are* the police. I am Inspector Holmes of the Yard and this is my assistant, Sergeant Watson.'

So much for the persuasive charm, I thought.

At Holmes's announcement of our bogus professional police status, the young woman's demeanour hardly changed, although the eyes registered a sign of unease. She gave a shrug. 'You could be Mr Sherlock Holmes himself for all I care,' she snapped, 'it don't change cases. We ain't got nobody as you describe.'

'He is lodging in room six,' I said over Holmes's shoulder.

'Room six? That's empty now. Last person who had that room was a fellow called Birdie Evans. He's on the halls. Trained canaries. He got me mother and me seats at the Chiswick Empire. Bit of a duff act if you ask me. He left about a week ago.'

'You say room six is unoccupied?' said Holmes.

'That's what I said.'

'But when you first opened the door you informed us that you had no rooms available.'

'S'right. Number six is empty now, but it's booked for tonight by one of our regulars, Mr Duddridge. Now then, if that's all there is...'

Holmes shook his head. 'I am afraid that my sergeant and I will need to take a look at the room – just to set our minds at ease.'

'I'm not sure,' replied the young woman warily. 'My mother's out just now. If she knew I'd let the coppers in, I'd be for it.'

'We will be in and out in no time, I assure you,' said Holmes, gently brushing past the belligerent young woman. 'And I should not have to remind you that obstructing the police in the pursuit of their duties is a very serious matter.'

'Just be quick, will yer. There's nothing to see.'

Holmes stood on the first step of the stairs and turned to face our reluctant hostess with his hand outstretched. 'To aid the speed of our investigation we shall require a key.'

The girl scowled, gave a gasp of impatience, and disappeared into the front room, returning moments later with the key, which she handed over to Holmes. 'Follow the landing round and you'll come to it. There's a big six on the door. Five minutes and no more, see,' she snapped. 'And don't you be touching things or taking things away "as evidence" for you to flog at Coules's pawnshop.'

'From the girl's demeanour it seems quite evident that she has had dealings with the police before,' said Holmes under his breath as we reached the landing. 'I have my doubts as to the respectable nature of this lodging house. There are "discerning gentlemen" in the criminal fraternity too.'

Within seconds we were inside room six; and what a surprise greeted us as we closed the door behind us. It was indeed the same room in which we had left our friend Stamford the previous evening: the dingy brown wallpaper was the same, the faded cream curtains were the same, and, indeed, the rickety chest of drawers, wardrobe, and iron bedstead were the same; but there was no sign that the room had been inhabited recently. The bedspread was fresh and tidy. The drawers and wardrobe were empty. There were no clothes, luggage, or any other personal effects whatsoever in the room.

Holmes whipped out his lens and began a thorough examination of the chamber. For some time he crawled about on the floor inspecting the carpet, before turning his attention to the wardrobe and drawers. I also checked the drawers to see if I could glean the slightest clue, but, apart from a discarded newspaper, there was nothing to be seen.

'Well, we didn't dream it, did we? We were here with Stamford last night . . . so what's afoot?' I asked, mystified.

Holmes, who had been examining the tiny washbasin, spun round, a broad smile lighting his face. 'It is a pretty puzzle, isn't it? Certainly I can confirm that we did not dream our visit here last evening and that the room, until very recently, has been occupied by a dark-haired man – some of his whiskers are visible around the rim of the plughole. Also, that newspaper bears yesterday's date, and yet Miss Sanderson maintains the room has been empty for a week. It is unlikely anyone would leave a newspaper in this room, especially in a drawer, unless he were the occupant.'

'Why deny that Stamford stayed here?'

'Money. No questions asked. That is my surmise. Mrs Sanderson and her lovely daughter are too simple to be in charge of this deception. They are merely willing puppets following orders. There is a clever agency behind this business, Watson, some force that needed to silence Stamford because he was becoming a threat.'

'In what way?'

Holmes shrugged. 'I do not know, but it is clear now that our friend was involved with some activity that was not quite proper. Remember his wallet crammed with money, money that he could not have earned in the hospital. He was someone's paid servant – and an unhappy one at that. With his reckless drinking and erratic behaviour, he was clearly in danger of becoming indiscreet and was therefore a threat to his paymasters. He obviously knew things which were meant to be secret.'

'You don't think he's dead?'

Holmes's face darkened. 'It is a possibility we cannot rule out, I'm afraid. I sense that Stamford's disappearance is only a minute part of a much greater mystery, a much greater threat, which in some way is linked with that scabious corpse fished from the Thames.'

'Then we had better interrogate the girl and her mother. They are obviously mixed up in this matter,' said I.

My friend shook his head. 'There is no point. They know nothing. If they did they would not still be free. No, they have been paid to keep quiet about Stamford's occupancy here, that is all. Coin will have answered all their questions. It is clear to me that three men have been in this room today and that there was a struggle of some kind: the scuff marks and indentations on the carpet area by the bed indicate as much, and also that Stamford went unwillingly. He even left behind a little clue. I found this stuck between one of the cracks in the bedhead.' Holmes held up a little matchfolder from Simpson's. It contained several broken matches.

* * *

There was nothing further to be learned from the room other than the details that my friend had gleaned, so we made a hasty retreat. The young girl remained tight-lipped as we left the house, but I sensed her relief that we had not stayed longer. The door shut behind us with a resounding bang. On reaching the end of Tunnacliffe Road, Holmes suddenly pulled on my arm, steering me from the pavement and behind one of the large plane trees growing by the roadside.

'Look,' he exclaimed in a hoarse whisper, his eyes lighting with excitement.

I observed a hansom cab pull up outside number thirty-two and a plump, flaxen-haired woman alighted.

'Mrs Sanderson,' hissed Holmes. 'Money has obviously been burning a hole in her pocket.' He was referring to the large number of brightly wrapped packages that the cab driver handed to her before she disappeared into the house.

'Spending her ill-gotten gains,' I observed.

'Indeed,' agreed my friend. 'Spending the money before it can be taken away from them. Their crime is a very minor one in the great scheme of things – just a simple lie – but it does establish the fact that our friend Stamford is mixed up in something serious and dangerous, and if, as I suspect, it is connected with the plague victim we saw this morning, it is imperative that we find out exactly what it is as soon as possible – for all our sakes.'

CHAPTER FOUR
Reunion

It was not difficult to surmise that our next move would be to visit Bart's. As we passed through the portals of this great hospital, I could not help but be reminded of my time working there, although a great deal of that time was now shrouded in the mists of failing memory. So much had happened to me since I left Bart's to serve in India, that images of my salad days in medicine had been superseded by the more vibrant memories of war and adventure.

However, there was one occasion connected with the hospital that will be forever etched in the table of my fond records. It was the occasion when Stamford brought me here to meet a strange acquaintance of his who was in search of a fellow lodger to share comfortable rooms in Baker Street. It was my first introduction to Sherlock Holmes, a man who has been an integral part of my life ever since. It is therefore thanks to Stamford that I have been able to share the extraordinary exploits of this remarkable man whom I am proud to regard as a close friend. The day we met, a world away now, remains still rich and vivid in my memory.

Holmes made enquiries at the registration desk about Stamford's likely whereabouts, and we were soon traversing the gloomy corridors with their dun-coloured doors, heading for the surgical ward. As we approached the swing-doors we were met by matron, who viewed us with some suspicion. She was a plump lady of middle years but her round face, framed by silky blonde hair which spread down from her cap, was still pretty, and her bright blue eyes sparkled with intelligence and charm. She was twice the age of the Sanderson girl, but there was something more youthful and spirited about her demeanour than that of the miserable creature we had encountered at the guest-house in Chiswick. My friend explained our errand in simple terms. The matron eyed us up and down sharply. 'And who might you be?' she asked in a pleasant voice which still held traces of her Scottish roots.

'I am Sherlock Holmes, and this is . . .'

'Dr Watson.' The words were summarily snatched from Holmes by the matron, who took a sprightly step towards me with a wide grin upon her face. 'Dr John Horatio Watson, late of the Northumberland Fusiliers, who once upon a time had a partiality for ship's tobacco and a glass or two of Beaune with his lunch,' she announced, gently prodding me in the chest with her outstretched finger.

'Why yes . . . ' I stammered, taken aback by this personal summary.

'I say all that and you still don't recognise me, John. I know it's over twenty years and I have put on some weight since those days, but surely I haven't changed that much.'

I gazed in utter surprise as a fine veil was lifted from my memory. 'Nurse Mellor,' I gasped. 'Alice.'

Her grin broadened. 'The same. Matron now,' she said with some pride, before leaning forward and kissing me gently on my cheek. 'It is good to see you after all these years. I always felt sorry that we lost touch with each other when you went off to that nasty business in Afghanistan.'

Holmes stood by, totally bemused by this unexpected reunion. Alice and I had been good friends when I was a junior doctor at Bart's after my graduation. She had been a great help in aiding me to find my feet as a doctor. Paper qualifications were one thing; actually dealing with the sick and dying was something very different. The road from academia to reality is a hard one. Nurse Alice Mellor had eased my rite of passage. Indeed, some of our acquaintances of those far off days assumed, or hoped, that a romance would develop between us, but I was a shy fellow then and Alice was being wooed by another doctor, Alec Callaghan, whom I later learned she had married.

I held her hand and squeezed it warmly. 'I had no idea you were still at the old place. I thought you had gone back to Edinburgh.'

'That was the plan, but Alec was offered a consultancy in London, so we stayed. I stopped nursing for a time when I had my daughter, Bella, but when Alec died, I returned to my duties at Bart's. It was like coming home.'

I shook my head sadly. 'I'm sorry. I didn't know that you had lost your husband, Alice. I am so terribly sorry.'

She gave a resigned shrug of the shoulders and, momentarily, some of the sparkle left her bright eyes. 'It happened five years ago. He developed a brain tumour. It was a cruel death, John, but as time has gone by I have learned to live with it and cope. I have Bella and my memories – that is more than some people have.'

I opened my mouth to tell her of my own loss, but the moment passed.

Taking a pace back, she looked me up and down.

'Well, apart from a few grey hairs,' she said playfully, 'you look very much as you did when you used to walk these wards in fear and trembling of Sir Randolph Dowson – as did all the junior staff. Do you remember?'

'Indeed I do. He was a tartar. A brilliant man, but a tartar.'

'But, of course, I know all about your more recent adventures from your written accounts of your exploits with Sherlock Holmes.'

At the mention of my friend's name we both suddenly remembered his presence. While we had been talking, re-establishing links with, and from, the past, Holmes had remained silent, an abstracted look of amusement on his face. Now he stepped forward, inclining his head in a brief nod. 'I am always pleased to meet an old friend of Watson's,' he said graciously.

'And I am pleased to meet you, Mr Holmes.'

They shook hands.

'Now, if I may press you concerning the purpose of our visit. There is a certain amount of urgency connected with our enquiry.'

'An investigation? How exciting.'

Holmes did not reply.

'You wish to see Dr Stamford?'

We both nodded.

Alice shook her head. 'He is off duty today, I believe; but quite honestly, gentlemen, he has been giving the staff grounds for concern.'

'In what way?' I asked.

Alice hesitated as though she had said something she wished she hadn't. She wrinkled her nose. 'Nothing definite – just erratic behaviour, I suppose.'

'And what form did this erratic behaviour take? Pray be precise as to detail,' said Holmes darkly.

Alice looked uneasy. 'I don't really think it's my place to talk about it, especially in the hospital. Perhaps I have said too much already. I have no notion of the nature of your enquiries, and I certainly do not want to say anything which might get Dr Stamford into trouble. After all, he is a colleague and has duties on my ward. Perhaps you had better have a word with Dr Stamford's senior.'

'Very well,' said Holmes, 'I appreciate your dilemma.'

'Thank you. If you will come with me, I will introduce you to Dr Karswell.' Alice glanced at her watch. 'He will have finished his morning round and most likely will be in his office.'

*   *   *

We arrived outside an anonymous room, midway down a dimly lighted corridor. Alice held up her hand to us to stay outside. 'Leave this to me,' she said softly. 'I will go in first and explain who you are. Dr Karswell can be . . . a little difficult at times.'

Holmes nodded his understanding and Alice knocked sharply on the glass panel of the door. After a brief pause, there came a response from within. 'Come,' cried an imperious voice. Alice threw us a conspiratorial smile and entered. A short time later she emerged, her soft features somewhat flushed. 'Dr Karswell is a very busy man, but he says he will grant you a few minutes of his valuable time,' she announced breathily, obviously repeating the doctor's own words.

'Thank you,' said Holmes, opening the door. As I was about to follow, Alice held me back and whispered something in my ear.

In my experience, Karswell's office was typical of the cluttered and dingy hidey-hole from which most senior doctors had to operate. It seemed that, in certain areas, there had been little change or improvement since my days in the hospital. The man himself was seated, with his back to us, at a tiny desk that was covered with large piles of case notes. As I closed the door behind me, he turned around and greeted us, a smile lighting his features. He was a pale-faced man in his late thirties with a bald head and a dark, tidy beard. He wore gold-rimmed spectacles, through which his black eyes glittered with an unwavering stare.

'Sherlock Holmes, the detective?' The voice was deep and mellifluous.

My friend gave a curt nod.

'I am Dr Simeon Karswell. I gather you are seeking Dr Stamford? Well, as I believe you have been informed, he is not on duty today or tomorrow, so I can't really say where you will find him. I presume you have tried his lodgings.'

'We have, and he has left there without providing a forwarding address.'

Karswell looked dismayed. 'I see. Oh dear, oh dear. This is most worrying.' He removed his glasses and ran his hand over his forehead. 'You see, Stamford has been acting somewhat . . . irrationally of late. Look . . . I know of your reputation, Mr Holmes, and I believe you to be a man of integrity and discretion, so perhaps you ought to know . . . For some months now Dr Stamford has been leading rather a dissolute life. I suspect that he has fallen in with a bad crowd. I have heard of his visits to unsavoury clubs, bouts of reckless gambling, drinking sessions . . . '

'Have you any idea how he has funded this wayward existence?'

Karswell shook his head. 'Not really . . . unless . . . unless he has been supplying drugs. He has access to vast supplies within the hospital and, if the truth be known, I have begun to suspect that he was himself turning into an addict.'

'But this picture you present is not one of the Stamford I know,' I cried, realising as soon as I spoke that my last view of my friend had been of him laid across his own bed in a drunken stupor.

'Drugs can soon change a personality. Over-indulgence can wreck a noble brain. But, as I say, I have only suspicions. However, I am worried for Stamford, and for the patients under his care. Now that you say he has left Mrs Sanderson's today, my concern grows for his safety. I fear he may do something rash to his own person.'

'Have you any evidence for this supposed addiction?' asked Holmes.

Karswell shook his head. 'Nothing but the usual signs of lethargy: dilated pupils, sudden mood swings . . .'

'A great deal of which could be the result of too much alcohol or depression,' I suggested.

'That is true, Dr Watson. I am sorry to be so vague but you know, as well as I do, that in the medical profession one so often has to rely on past experience and assumptions when making a diagnosis.'

'As a detective, I need facts,' stated Holmes, pithily. 'Can you supply me with any names – members of this "bad crowd" with which you suggest he may have been involved?'

Karswell shook his head again. 'Stamford never mentioned names. In fact he kept very quiet about his private life outside the hospital. I have only pieced together what I assume to be the truth from my own observations and some common-room gossip.' He paused, his eyes narrowing as though he had suddenly thought of something. 'I do recall . . . yes . . . there was one occasion when he received an urgent note while he was on the ward with me. When he read it, he went white in the face and excused himself for some moments. I did observe some part of the message, as it was scrawled in large ill-formed capital letters.'

'The signature of the sender?' I asked eagerly.

'I was not as fortunate as that. But I caught the words "bridge of dreams". I don't know if they mean anything to you, Mr Holmes.'

'I am afraid they do,' replied my friend. 'I am afraid they do'.

*   *   *

'Well,' said I, after leaving Simeon Karswell's office. 'That wasn't an awful lot of good. He wasn't terribly helpful.'

'He was just helpful enough. I shall reserve my judgement as to whether his information is beneficial to our investigation.'

'What about this phrase "the bridge of dreams"?'

'Ah, I see your lady friend has waited to find out how you got on,' observed my friend coolly, indicating the figure of Alice Mellor in her blue matron's uniform waiting at the head of a staircase. 'I will leave you to chat with her, Watson, but say nothing of what we know of this case, nor mention "the bridge of dreams". Take your conversation back to those good old days when there were no grey hairs in your moustache, eh?' He stopped and gripped my arm. 'I do not speak idly. Do as I say. Invite the lady to take tea with us tomorrow afternoon. I have some work to do now. We have a busy and possibly dangerous night's work ahead of us. I will see you back at Baker Street before nightfall.'

CHAPTER FIVE

The Bridge of Dreams

'The Bridge of Dreams is a club of sorts, run for the enjoyment of certain members of society who prefer their pleasures on the seamier side: drugs, women, and gaming. The activities are all technically within the law, of course, but only just.'

It was dusk, the gas lamps had been lighted in Baker Street, and our own jets had been turned up, bathing our sitting room in a warm yellow glow. Holmes was in his favourite seat by the fire, wrapped in his purple dressing-gown, his long legs stretched out before the grate, his feet resting on the fender as he puffed on a gnarled old briar. I sat at our dining-table finishing off my evening meal with a cup of tea and a slice of Mrs Hudson's Dundee cake.

'If you cast your mind back to last night,' my friend continued languidly, 'when we left Stamford to sleep off his carouse, you might recall that I noticed letters written in the dust on his bedside table.'

'Yes, I had forgotten that. "Bart".'

'You assumed that the word referred to the hospital.'

'Of course,' I replied with a certain hesitation. No doubt Sherlock Holmes was about to prove me wrong.

'A very sensible assumption, too,' said he. 'Last night, I could see no reason to contradict such an interpretation . . . except . . . '

'Except . . . There is always an "except", Holmes. What is it this time?'

'Well it seemed to me that the word, obviously scrawled when our friend was drunk or in a bemused state, was not complete. There was a streak where the finger wandered off at the letter T, as though there were more to come.'

'There's another monograph here: Analyses of writing in the dust.'

'Don't be brittle, Watson.'

I grinned. 'So there was a longer word and now you know what that word was meant to be.'

'Quite right. I did a little ferreting around after I left you at the hospital with your charming lady friend . . . '

'Holmes . . .'

' . . . And discovered that The Bridge of Dreams is currently managed by a certain Josiah Barton.'

'It could be a coincidence.'

'So it might – but a strange one, Watson. Think of it: Stamford turns to a dissolute way of life. His name is linked with The Bridge of Dreams. The manager is a fellow called Barton, a name our friend appeared to be writing in the dust at his lodgings in an idle moment – a name that was obviously preying on his mind. Consider also that Stamford may, in some roundabout way, be involved with the corpse with bubonic plague. Now, tell me: what creature is responsible for the spread of this dread disease?'

'The rat?'

'And the latest sporting craze at The Bridge of Dreams, arranged by Josiah Barton, is . . . ratting.'

A tingle of fear raised the hairs on the back of my neck. 'Great heavens,' I exclaimed.

Holmes gave me a stern look. 'The disparate strands are slowly weaving themselves together into a very dark fabric indeed.'

* * *

Later that night we found ourselves in the environs of Mayfair. The streets were quiet, with only the occasional top-hatted pedestrian passing us by. Holmes led me down into a smart mews, at the end of which was a large town house. A very stout fellow in dark livery guarded the entrance. At our approach he stepped forward, barring us from the door.

'Good evenin', gentlemen,' he said in a gruff voice which struggled to be neutral, but which could not prevent the natural aggression of his nature from breaking through.

'Good evening, Baldwin. Not sparring tonight?'

'Who wants to know?' came the guarded response.

'You mean to say you don't know me?' Holmes sidestepped nimbly and brought his right hand up, so that his fist scraped Baldwin gently on the chin. 'You're still too slow with that protective right, my man.'

'Sherlock Holmes,' croaked the man in a gush of recognition. 'Well, knock me down if it ain't the fighting 'tec.'

Holmes grinned at me. 'Mr Baldwin and I have engaged several times in the gentle art of fisticuffs. It was in my younger days, Watson, before I had such a scrupulous biographer.'

Baldwin nodded his head enthusiastically at the memory. 'Down at Hennigan's, Lambeth way. Mr Holmes beat me each time, 'cept on one occasion when I caught him with his guard down.'

'Not boxing tonight, eh?' I asked politely.

'Nah. It's ratting night tonight. Those little bleeders get more customers than a good honest fight these days.' Suddenly the brute's features darkened. ''Ere, Mr Holmes, you're not about to cause any mischief are you? It's more than my life's worth to let you in if you're going to upset things like.'

Holmes shook his head. 'Such ideas are the furthest from my mind, my dear Baldwin. No, no, it is Dr Watson here – he is so intrigued by the sport of ratting that he has persuaded me to accompany him to an evening's entertainment.' As my friend spoke, he slipped a sovereign into the old boxer's hand.

Baldwin gazed at it for a moment, and then his great rough fingers closed over the coin and he slipped it into his pocket.

'As long as you promise to be on your best behaviour,' he said, and opened the door.

'We do,' said Holmes, bowing.

'Actually, you've come on a good night. We've got some extra special rats on tonight. Should see quite a lot of blood.' Baldwin's face broke into a grin, revealing a row of rotten, and broken, teeth.

Without further ado we entered The Bridge of Dreams and found ourselves in a brightly-lit hallway with a brilliant chandelier shimmering above our heads. A short, lithe fellow appeared at our side. He was dressed in smart evening clothes, with his black hair plastered down like shiny leather. He gave us an empty smirk. 'Good evening, gentlemen. Welcome to The Bridge of Dreams. I am George. What is your pleasure this evening? You may like to know that Katarina is back with us in the Orchid Room . . . '

'We come for the ratting,' said Holmes brusquely.

The fellow beamed. 'Oh, gambling gents, eh?' He looked us up and down as though we were suspects in the police cells. 'There'll be some good business tonight. Special consignment of rats.' He coughed gently. 'That will be ten guineas apiece, gentlemen'.

It was my turn to cough and splutter. Holmes, on the other hand, nonchalantly handed a bag of coins to the lackey, who took some moments to examine the contents closely. Finally he pocketed our admission fee and led us through to the back of the house into a room, which at one time would have served as a conservatory. The contrast between the quiet and opulent hallway and this chamber was most marked. For a start it was crowded and noisy, with a rich fog of cigar smoke hovering in the air. The majority of the men were in evening dress, wealthy sporting types who were here for the gambling, while a small knot of fellows, dressed in rough costermonger's corduroy, lolled by the bar. This latter group consisted of dog men, and most had a mutt with them. Some of the hounds were tied to the foot-rail of the bar, others were sleeping in their owners' arms, while others still were being inspected for fractures, and having their mouths peered into as though a dentist were examining their teeth. Nearly all the animals were marked with bites and scars. 'Pity to bring him up to rat-killing,' said one fellow, stroking a particularly fierce-looking bull terrier.

George clicked his fingers and another similarly attired lackey appeared at our sides. He could have been George's twin. 'Eric, see to it that these gentlemen are provided with drinks and that they get a good view.' Eric nodded and, without a word, led us through the throng towards the centre of the room and 'the pit' – which consisted of a small circus some ten feet in diameter, fitted with a high wooden rim up to elbow height. Over it, suspended from the ceiling, was a gantry of electric lighting which illuminated the white painted floor of the arena. With practised ease, our guide elbowed his way forward and cleared a space for us by the rim. We slipped into the space just before the tide of spectators flooded back, pressing up against us. Within moments Eric had produced a bottle of champagne and two glasses and extracted another exorbitant sum from Holmes in payment.

It was not long before the grisly entertainment began. Standing on a box at one end of the arena, a stocky fellow with a great drooping moustache, who introduced himself as 'The Captain', called the room to order. 'Gentlemen, please place your bets on the first match of the evening between Tom Herrick's Grasper' – at this point a large bull terrier was held aloft to cries and cheers – 'unbeaten yet and taking on twenty-five rats.' There were more cheers, and then a flurry of betting activity commenced, both between individuals and also the accountants of the house.

'It is appalling and degrading,' I said.

'Indeed it is. Instructive, too. It reveals that, even with the benefit of education and money, certain men naturally regress. Nobility and sensitivity of Nature have little to do with situation or breeding. And then there is the matter of greed.'

As he spoke a large basket was dumped into the arena. The Captain stepped forward and, wearing a large leather gauntlet, dipped his hand into the black, writhing mass to pull out the first victim of the evening. Again there was a clamorous cheer. One by one he pulled out the remaining twenty-four rats. He laid hold of their tails and jerked them into the arena. Some of the creatures ran about the painted floor investigating their new surroundings. One of the spectators leaned over the barrier and poured a glass of champagne over one of the frightened creatures. They were sewer and water-ditch rats, and the pungent smell from them was like that from a hot drain. Many of the spectators held handkerchiefs to their noses.

Then slowly a chant began with the gamblers. It started almost as a whisper and grew in volume and ferocity: 'Bring on the dog! Bring on the dog!' At last the owner, Tom Herrick, introduced the dog to the arena.

Within seconds the rats were running around in panic. With practised ease, the dog methodically attacked the rats one by one, snapping their little bodies in his slavering jaws. Gobbets of blood sprayed the white floor like red dew. Some of the rats braved the dog's attack; one dauntless creature clung to the hound's nose, its beady eyes flashing wildly in the electric illumination. The dog shook his head furiously, but the rat stayed put. In final frustration, the dog dashed it against the side of the arena, leaving a patch of blood, as if a strawberry had been squashed there.

Some of the rats collected in an obscene mound, huddling together as if for mutual protection. The cry went up, 'Blow on them!' at which many of the spectators waved their handkerchiefs vigorously over the arena.

'It's a ploy to split them up,' Holmes whispered in my ear. 'The rodent does not like a cold wind on its back.'

The waving of the handkerchiefs had the desired effect and the creatures were sent fluttering like so many dark feathers about the arena, whereupon Grasper recommenced his bout of killing, seeking out each rat individually and snapping its neck. Within a short time the arena was littered with the bleeding bodies of dead, or dying, rats. There were great cheers around the room, and coins and notes were exchanged as wagers were settled. The arena was swept and mopped by two attendants; the rats were gathered up by their tails and slung into a great sack.

We had to endure three more of these disgusting spectacles, each one involving more rats than the previous match. Finally, a dog, aptly named Butcher, dealt with a hundred of the more esteemed country-caught barn rats before The Captain announced an interval before 'the spectacle of The Grand Match'.

'Haven't we seen enough?' I said, sharply. 'I have no appetite for this kind of grotesque cruelty.'

Holmes shot me a sympathetic glance. 'Neither have I, Watson, but it would be foolish to leave now, just before the big bout of the evening involving the gentleman we have come here to observe.' He nodded his head in the direction of the bar area, where I saw The Captain in deep conversation with a tall, bald-headed Negro, who wore a large brass earring in his right ear. 'That,' said my friend, 'is Josiah Barton.'

Some ten minutes later, The Captain stepped into the arena once more and called for silence. The room immediately fell into a hush. The crowd knew that the really exciting moment of the evening had arrived.

'Can I ask Abe Chapman to bring up Bobby.'

'Aye aye, sir,' came the raucous response from the back of the room, and a beefy fellow came forward holding his dog above his head so that the crowd could catch full sight of him. Bobby was a hefty mutt, a crossbreed with a great deal of terrier in him. The dog wriggled in his owner's arms, already excited by the cheering and the smell of the blood. At the same time, with the aid of four men, a large wire cage was lifted into the arena. A tarpaulin sheet hid the occupants from view, but the frantic activity within, and the occasional flash of a furry brown body between the gaps in the sacking, brought an unexpected hush from the spectators.

Josiah Barton, replacing The Captain as master of ceremonies, stood on the box and held his hands up for silence. 'Gentlemen,' he said in a deep, rich voice, smooth and educated, 'you are about to witness a remarkable event. On the one hand we have Bobby, the unbeaten scrapper from Wapping. Bobby is a veteran of thirty-seven bouts and has killed over two thousand rats.'

A cheer went up and the dog's owner held him aloft to encourage the cheering.

Barton waited patiently for the noise to subside.

'On the other hand we have no ordinary vermin as opponents for Bobby. There are only twenty of them but they are a particularly vicious, and a particularly large, strain of killer rodents, specially shipped here from the Dutch East Indies. Gentlemen, if you please?'

This request was to the four handlers, who pulled back the sacking to reveal the contents of the cage. As they did so, there was an audible gasp of horror from the crowd. Before us, squirming and scuttling around their prison, were the largest rats I have ever seen. They were the size of a young puppy. But it was not the size alone that raised the hair on the back of my neck; it was their ferocious, demonic appearance. They bore the most startling, beady, red eyes and possessed two large, prominent, yellow teeth, which constantly gnashed in a frenzied fashion. The dog's owner appeared hesitant. Even the dog was less boisterous than he had been.

'Let battle commence,' said Barton quietly, more to Abe Chapman than to the crowd. Chapman still appeared nervous and unsure and then the cry went up, 'Bring on the dog. Bring on the dog!'

Reluctantly he passed over Bobby to one of the handlers, while the other three made a rapid departure from the arena. The dog stood uncertainly for a moment, gazing at the cage of shrieking giant rats. And then they were released.

What followed was a most disgusting and depressing spectacle. To the roars of delight from the crowd, the rats, showing no fear or apprehension, swarmed over the dog, smothering him with their foul brown bodies. Within seconds the hound toppled over with squeals of pain. Rivulets of blood seeped from the vicious wounds on his contorting body and collected into one amorphous, scarlet pool on the white floor of the arena. The carnage was over in less than a minute.

Once the dog was dead, the vermin seemed to lose interest in their prey and began to wander around. Some attempted, in vain, to scamper up the sides of the arena. Instinctively the crowd pulled back with disgust, and a certain amount of fear. I looked down at one of these creatures, whose bulky body was over a foot in length. It looked back at me with a malevolent, baleful glare from its bright red eyes. The four attendants had re-entered the ring and began driving the rats back into the cage with the aid of large sweeping brushes, the heads of which had been covered with thick sacking. Most of the rats returned to the cage without problem, but one or two attempted to escape the brushes and had to be chased.

Abe Chapman was kneeling down by the tattered corpse of his dog in some state of distress. The man's body heaved with emotion and he wept unashamedly. 'Oh, Bobby,' he wailed. 'Oh, Bobby, what have they done to you?' As he leaned nearer to the dog, one of the rats leapt upon him, sinking his teeth into the man's neck.

With a cry of shock and horror, he staggered to his feet, the foul brown creature still scrabbling at his neck. One of the attendants leapt forward and yanked the rat by the tail, pulling him free. The creature, his bloodied teeth constantly gnashing, writhed and twisted in a furious effort to escape. It was with great fortitude that the attendant swung the rat into the dark recesses of the cage. Abe Chapman sank to his knees, attempting to stem the flow of blood from the vicious wound at his throat with a large handkerchief. A small group of the dog men came to lead him away.

'That man needs medical attention, Holmes. Perhaps I should help,' I said.

'No,' came the unequivocal reply. 'Leave him to his own. We have far more important business here tonight.'

Attack!

The wire cage containing the monster rats was covered once more with tarpaulin and taken from the room. There was a general sense of relief when the thing containing its foul cargo disappeared from our view. I could tell from the expressions etched on the faces of the crowd, even the rough and sturdy features of the dog men, that the sight of the unnatural carnage had made them very uneasy. It was clear that it was a greater horror than they had witnessed before.

Josiah Barton, his bald head gleaming under the lights, climbed into the arena and addressed us. 'Gentlemen, that little *divertissement* concludes the sport for tonight. However, the bar will remain open and, of course, there are further entertainments on offer in the other rooms. Please ask our waiters for details. I bid you a good evening.'

'Hah!' I hissed in furious indignation. 'He calls that barbarity sport!'

'Steady, old fellow. Whatever our personal feelings regarding this inhuman activity we must sublimate them, especially if we wish to leave the premises unharmed.'

'Therefore,' said I stiffly, 'I would appreciate it if we could take our leave now.'

'Oh no, not now, Watson. I need to have words with Josiah Barton. It is imperative to our mission. See, he's over by the bar at this moment and alone. Now is the time to strike.'

'What are you going to say?'

'Time for a little subterfuge, I think. Come with me, but don't speak unless spoken to directly.'

After Barton's announcement the room had emptied fairly rapidly. Now there were only about a dozen men left, some leaning idly by the bar drinking, others involved in a card school. All the dog men had gone. Josiah Barton was standing at the far end of the bar, with a drink in hand and a wide grin on his face. He was a tall man with broad shoulders, dressed in a flamboyant evening suit with lace cuffs and a bright red silk waistcoat. The smile faltered somewhat as Holmes approached. My friend gave a little bow and held out his hand in greeting. When he spoke it was, to my surprise, with an American accent.

'That was a mighty fine show, sir,' he said. 'I ain't seen nothin' as fascinatin' before. You are to be congratulated on puttin' on such a unique entertainment, Mr . . . ?'

At the paean of praise, the grin returned to its former brilliance and the Negro shook my friend's hand. 'Thank you, sir,' he replied graciously. 'I am Josiah Barton, the manager here.'

'Mighty glad to know you. My name's Hennesey, Claude Hennesey. I could do with a fellow like you at one of my joints. I own a couple of places on the Barbary Coast, 'Frisco, y'know: The Hennesey Palace and The Golden Bear. Ever heard of 'em?'

Barton shook his head. 'I don't recall their names, sir, and I have travelled widely in the United States of America.'

'Well, if you're ever in the neighbourhood make sure you drop in.'

Barton nodded uninterestedly and was about to turn away, when Holmes stepped nearer and dropped his voice. 'I've come to talk to you about rats, sir. The big ones. They were mighty pleasin' to see. Quite an attraction. I reckon you might be the guy to put me on to a supplier of the brutes. Quite like to ship a brood over to the States and try 'em out at the Palace. I reckon my clientèle would go for them in a big way.'

Barton's eyes glittered darkly. 'Those rats are specially bred for us and are not for sale.'

Holmes chuckled. 'Why, everything has its price, sir. I'm not after spoiling your livelihood here; I just want a bunch for my place in the States. No competition – to you. How about it?'

'I say that they are not for sale.'

'Well, I don't want to be greedy. How about a mating pair – then I can breed my own pack?' Holmes chuckled again.

Barton smiled back at my friend, but it was a smile dipped in frost. 'Have another drink sir, on the house, then I suggest that you leave the premises never to return. If you do, it might be detrimental to your health.'

Holmes appeared unaffected by this thinly veiled threat and continued to chuckle. 'Well, it appears I've ruffled your feathers sir, for which I apologise, and I will press you no further. But as my pappy used to say, there are more ways than one to trap a rabbit. I will bid you goodnight, Mr Barton.'

With a smile he turned to me. 'Come on, Johnny,' he said, tugging my sleeve and leading me from the room. Before our exit I caught a final glimpse of Barton. He was not smiling.

*   *   *

'And what good did that little interview do you?' I asked brusquely, as we collected our coats. 'Apart from nearly getting us thrown out, that is.'

Holmes did not reply until we had emerged into the cool night air once again. 'I ascertained how closely Barton and the club are associated with these rats and I made the man nervous. That will do for now.'

'But we have no evidence to connect those rats with the plague victim.'

'No evidence, but we have a link: Stamford. Tell me, Watson, have you ever seen rats like those brutes this evening?'

'Never. The fellow said something about them coming from the East Indies.'

'Sumatra.'

'How can you be so sure?'

'One of the rules in the art of detection is never to discount anything as a possible clue or aid to the investigation. That newspaper we found in Stamford's room – did you read it?'

'It was a day old.'

Holmes sighed. 'Not for the content, for any clues.'

'You know I didn't.'

'But I did, and it revealed one tit-bit of information which I filed away until I could make sense of it; and tonight it did.'

'What was this tit-bit?'

'In the shipping column, listing the docking and embarkations in London this week, Stamford had underlined the arrival at Christopher Dock of the cargo ship *Matilda Briggs*.'

'From Sumatra . . .'

'In the East Indies. You know, Watson, we hold so many little pieces of this puzzle, and yet the overall picture is not yet clear. For the moment I cannot quite trace the links that connect these disparate elements. But, as Hamlet observed, "if it be not now, yet it will come".'

Having eschewed the idea of a hansom cab, we were returning to Baker Street by a series of side streets. Holmes's exact knowledge of the geography of London was a great aid in allowing our journeys on foot to be as direct as possible. In the distance Big Ben was striking two in the morning, and its lugubrious chimes floated out on the still night air. There was a bright moon in a clear sky and our elongated shadows shot out in front of us like stealthy guards.

We had just turned into Cooper Street when Holmes stopped suddenly and held his finger to his lips. 'I think we are being followed,' he said in urgent, hushed tones.

How he came to this conclusion I had no idea. I had neither heard nor sensed anything untoward. We stood for a moment straining our ears to catch any sound. Apart from the faint rattle of a lone cab in a nearby street, there was no other noise.

Holmes gave a reluctant shrug. 'I am rarely wrong in these matters, but perhaps I am being over sensitive this evening after Mr Barton's dark threats. However, let us quicken our pace and leave nothing to chance.'

'I should have brought my revolver,' I said, 'but I had no idea this evening might turn into a dangerous occasion.'

'Fear not,' said Holmes, glancing over his shoulder, 'I have mine with me.'

We made rapid progress, and although now all our senses were on the alert, we registered no indications of pursuit. It was when we were within half a mile of home, on Muswell Road, that we spotted the solitary cab which we had heard several streets away. It swayed down the road towards us as though the driver was asleep.

'Why don't we avail ourselves of this cab,' I suggested, 'then we can be at home in no time and throw off anyone who might be trailing us.'

Holmes did not reply at first, but he stopped in his tracks, his whole body visibly tensing, as he gazed strangely at the cab. As it rumbled towards us, a dark imposing silhouette, Holmes suddenly cried out. 'Run, Watson! Run!' Before I could react, he was dragging me round and pulling me with him, back in the direction from which we had travelled. But it was too late. From the unlighted interior of the cab there appeared three burly figures that leapt to the pavement and gave chase. Two of them were carrying weapons – wooden staves. There was nothing for it now but to stand and fight our ground.

Holmes fired his revolver and hit one of the fellows in the shoulder. He fell to the slimy pavement clutching his wound. As I fought off one of the other ruffians with my fists, I caught sight of Holmes receiving a vicious blow on the back of the head. He dropped to his knees, the gun flying from his grasp and landing in the middle of the road. However, he seemed to recover quickly and, clutching his attacker by the arm, flipped him on his back using the ancient art of baritsu.

Meanwhile my assailant had grabbed me by the throat, and I was desperately trying to haul the fellow off. Despite my frantic efforts, his brutish fingers fastened tighter around my neck and I began to gasp for air. He brought his grinning face closer to mine. He had a large bulbous nose, wicked staring eyes, and a sallow skin, but these features soon began to dissolve in front of me as consciousness ebbed away. Grey swirls clouded my vision and I felt my knees buckle under me. My head began to throb as I gasped for air. Just before I floated away from this spinning, conscious world, I thought I heard another shot ring out, and then there was a black void of numbness.

When I regained my senses I was lying in a darkened shop doorway some twenty yards from where I had been assaulted. Slowly, painfully, I dragged myself to my feet and immediately slumped against the door as my brain tried to readjust itself to a waking state. I rubbed my throat where I could still feel those fingers clamped, squeezing my flesh. At length I consulted my watch. When my eyes focused on the dial I saw that it was nearly five o'clock in the morning. I had been unconscious for almost three hours. I staggered out of the doorway on unsteady feet, like a drunken man, and waited a few moments for both my brain and my eyes to focus. My neck was sore and my throat was as dry as dust. Wearily I surveyed the empty street, grey and eerie in the first glimmerings of dawn. There was no sign of our assailants and more importantly, I realised with heart-stopping clarity, there was no sign of Sherlock Holmes either.

I moved forward to the spot where we had been attacked. There were two dark patches of blood, still damp and shiny, blotching the pavement. These were the only signs that there had been any kind of a fray. I looked about me, peering into other doorways to see if Holmes had been dumped there in the same manner as I had. However, the doorways, like the street, were empty.

'Holmes!' I cried. 'Holmes!' My voice rang hollowly down the street and was swallowed up by the ensuing silence.

What had happened to my friend? I shook my head in a desperate attempt to clear it. Surely he would not have left me in such a fashion if he had had the freedom of choice? There was only one awful conclusion to be drawn: he had been abducted. If the devils had killed him they certainly would not have bothered to take him away with them. So, I reasoned, at least he was alive. But what did they want with him, and why did they leave me behind? I realised that these were not questions which would immediately answer themselves. What I needed to do now was return to Baker Street, refresh myself, and take food and a little medication to set me up for the day. Then I could begin to consider the matter carefully and decide which course of action should be taken. With one more cursory glance around, I made my weary way back to our lodgings.

On climbing the stairs up to our sitting-room I held the irrational hope that, on opening the door, I would find Holmes seated at his chemical bench conducting some malodorous experiment. He would give me a wave, beckon me to a chair, and explain the purpose of the bubbling retorts and foul odours. Sadly, this was not the case. An empty apartment, somewhat colourless in the pale light of morning, was all that greeted me.

I determined that for the present I would tell no one of Holmes's disappearance, not even Mrs Hudson or Lestrade, not until I had had a chance to try and solve this riddle myself. Certainly Mrs Hudson would not question Holmes's absence at breakfast. He was forever staying away for days and nights on end when on a case. The wonderful Mrs Hudson always took him as she found him; it was one of her great qualities.

By eight-thirty I had bathed, dressed, and taken a powder for my throbbing head. After a full breakfast and coffee I began to feel like my old self again. I then sat by the fire with my pipe and tried to map out my plan of action. It seemed clear to me that the men who attacked us were the minions of Josiah Barton. It may be that they had taken Holmes back to The Bridge of Dreams, but that would be too obvious. Surely they would be aware that I could easily arrange a police warrant and have Lestrade and his men search the premises. Perhaps they were hoping I would do that in order to provide proof of their innocence in the matter. I thought of Barton's grinning face and self-satisfied manner and became convinced that this was exactly what he expected me to do. Therefore it was my task to disappoint him.

Of course, the problem remained as to where to start looking for my friend. Then I remembered the conversation I had had with Holmes on leaving The Bridge of Dreams, and his mention of the cargo ship *Matilda Briggs* at Christopher Dock, which had been marked out in Stamford's newspaper. Here was a most promising location and, as no other presented itself to me, I had to place my hopes on it. Certainly Barton and his gang would have no idea that we held this information and so they would feel very safe hiding Sherlock Holmes on board the vessel. I felt rather satisfied with this observation and decided that a visit to Christopher Dock might well clear up part of this mystery very quickly. On this excursion I *would* take my revolver with me. However, there was one point that puzzled and concerned me, and that was the nagging question at the back of my mind: what on earth did these villains want with Sherlock Holmes?

I was just about to put on my coat when Mrs Hudson announced that I had a visitor.

'For me?' I asked, with some surprise.

'Yes, doctor, for you. It's a young woman.'

'I really do have the most pressing business at the moment. Would you be kind enough to ask her to return tomorrow.'

Mrs Hudson pulled a face. 'Now, doctor, that is not like you. Surely you can spare ten minutes of your time for her. She seems most upset and told me that the matter was a very important one.'

'What is the lady's name?'

'Mrs Callaghan; but she said you would know her better as Alice Mellor.'

'Alice!' I said with great surprise. 'Oh, by all means show her up.'

I threw my coat over a chair and waited with some apprehension for Alice's arrival. Within moments she entered the room, her face flushed with concern. 'Oh, John,' she cried, distractedly, 'I've made a terrible discovery at the hospital.'

The Hungry Dragon

It was quite clear from her demeanour that Alice was in a mild state of shock. As I led her to a seat, her whole body shook with emotion and her eyes began to moisten with tears. Despite the early hour, I poured a brandy and encouraged her to drink it. Whatever tale she had to tell, its nature had brought about a severe change in my friend. There were shadows under her eyes, and the healthy pallor of yesterday had evaporated, replaced by a grey hue.

'Oh, John,' she sobbed softly, her head bowed, the tears falling freely now.

I sat beside her and squeezed her hand in mine. 'Come now, my dear, nothing can be as bad as that. And I will do all in my power to set things right.' As I uttered these words I realised how empty and meaningless they were. Here I was doling out expressions of comfort while I was embroiled in a nightmare mystery, and the only man capable of solving it, my friend Mr Sherlock Holmes, had disappeared.

With remarkable fortitude, she wiped away her tears and gave me an embarrassed smile. 'You have not lost your bedside manner, Doctor John.'

I returned her smile. It was good to see some of the light return to her eyes.

'I think I should tell you what brings me here to weep all over your carpet.' For the first time since she entered the room she seemed to take note of her surroundings. 'Isn't Mr Holmes here? I am sure he would wish to hear my tale also.'

'I am sure he would,' I replied awkwardly, 'but I am afraid he is unavoidably detained elsewhere at present.'

She gave an understanding nod. 'Well, you alone shall be my audience then.'

'Tell me all.'

'After your visit to the hospital yesterday, I was called into Dr Karswell's office and asked a number of questions about the reason behind your enquiries. I told the doctor that I knew no more than he did. He was quite brusque with me. "What does Sherlock Holmes want to come snooping around here for? This is a hospital, not a prison," he snapped. He was quite unlike his usual self. I don't think he believed me. As I left he gave me a most curious look.'

'In what way curious?'

'It is very hard to explain, but it made me feel uneasy. It was rather menacing in a way. By this morning, I had almost forgotten about the incident. Then I was about to deliver some fresh sheets to the old morgue – you remember the old morgue down in the basement.'

Indeed I did. A grim place it was, too, even in my day. It was little more than a vaulted cellar where the bodies of dead patients possessed of contagious diseases were dumped, awaiting cremation in the great Bart's furnace – the hungry dragon, as we called it.

I nodded to Alice to continue her narrative.

'I was just approaching the door to the morgue when it swung open and Dr Karswell came out. On seeing me he seemed to start. "What are you doing here?" he asked in an angry manner. "Why aren't you about your duties?"

'"I *am* about my duties," said I. "I am just about to deliver these sheets to the morgue."

'He glanced at the sheets over my arm and virtually tugged them from me. "I'll take them," he growled. "Now get back to the ward." With that he turned on his heel and went back into the morgue. He had never behaved like that to me before. It was as though he had become someone else – another person. As I reached the end of the corridor and turned back, I observed Dr Karswell leaving the morgue again. He looked around him furtively before departing.'

Alice took another sip of brandy before resuming her narrative. Gradually the colour and life were returning to her face.

'I waited a few minutes to make sure that Dr Karswell had gone, then I crept along the corridor and tried the door of the morgue. Not only was my curiosity aroused now, but also I feared that something was greatly amiss in the hospital that I love so dearly. Because part of my duties includes "servicing" this gloomy chamber, I have a key. Without hesitation I let myself in, shutting the door behind me. I don't know how well you remember it, John, but it is quite a small room, arched as a vault, with two meagre gas jets for illumination. And it is cold, so very cold.' Her face almost broke into a smile as she made this final observation, and she hugged herself in a mimic demonstration.

Alice's description of the morgue stimulated my own memories of this grim receptacle for the waiting dead. Corpses were laid on a series of stone slabs, covered with sheets, in readiness for their final journey to the 'the hungry dragon'. As young men, my colleagues and I used to play cards in an attempt to avoid officiating at this ugly cremation ceremony. In those days it was deemed appropriate by the hospital authorities that one member of the medical staff be present at each cremation. Being nimble with the pack, I avoided this duty more than most, but, on the occasions when I failed to come up with an ace, I experienced feelings of nausea as the diseased body slid into the inferno.

'There was just one body in the morgue, covered by a regulation green sheet. Apart from that, the room looked as normal. What, I wondered, had Dr Karswell wanted to hide from my sight? For this is surely what he had tried to do, barring me from the room and then locking it. I determined that the answer must lie under the sheet. In the dim light I pulled it back and received the shock of my life.'

Alice's features had grown tense again and her eyes widened in terror, as though she were re-living this moment with great clarity. She paused, her mouth slack but unmoving, as though she were unable to speak further of this incident.

'What did you see, my dear?' I prompted.

'It . . . it was Dr Stamford. Under the sheet. It was Dr Stamford.'

'What!'

'There can be no doubt. His face was swollen and badly bruised as though he had been in a fight, but I had no difficulty in recognising him.'

'My God,' I cried, my own blood chilling at this news. 'How on earth did he meet his death?'

'That's the worst of it, John. He was not dead.'

'You . . . you're sure?' I asked in a hoarse whisper, my mind beginning to reel at this macabre scenario.

'Instinctively, I felt his pulse. It was weak and irregular but it was still there. As you can imagine, I was horribly confused. I did not know what to do. Why was this man here? What did they intend to do with him? The answer to that question was too terrible to contemplate. Do *you* know, John?'

I shook my head, sadly. 'Not in any coherent fashion. What did you do next?'

'I thought of you and Mr Holmes. If I could not trust Dr Karswell, there was no knowing who else I could trust in the hospital. Some evil conspiracy is at work there. I had to talk to someone who could help. I came straight here.'

'Then there is not a moment to lose. We must return to Bart's at great speed and pray that we are not too late.'

* * *

I can never remember such a terrible journey as I made that morning in the cab from Baker Street to Bart's. In a way the normality of it increased its nightmare quality. The cabman drove the horse as fast as he could, but this was mid-morning and the streets of the capital were choked with traffic, making our progress infuriatingly slow. At one point we were held up on Caulder Street by a wagon with a broken wheel. Traffic either side of the damaged vehicle, narrowed into one thoroughfare, pushed its way through, rarely giving way to the oncoming queue. For the whole course of the journey, Alice sat on the edge of her seat saying nothing, though her strained, pale face and anxious eyes spoke volumes.

After an eternity the cab pulled up outside the hospital. Alice led me in through the staff entrance. The corridors were quiet but we did encounter several nurses and two doctors on our way to the morgue. Fortunately, they seemed too fully occupied with their own concerns to question, or even notice, our presence. As we descended to the basement of the hospital, an overwhelming sense of foreboding settled on my soul. I was conscious that I was out of my depth in this matter, and sorely missing wise words from my friend, Sherlock Holmes.

Cautiously we approached the door of the morgue. 'It's best if I go first,' whispered Alice. 'At least I have authority to be here.'

I nodded in agreement and watched as she went ahead of me and tried the door. Apparently it was unlocked. She opened it, glanced into the morgue, and then beckoned to me. Together we entered this grim chamber. It was as I remembered it. Untouched by time or improvement, my view of it at this moment fitted exactly the image I held in my imagination: the vault-like ceiling, glistening with damp, the rough uneven stone floor, the dull flickering gaslight, and the protruding stone slabs. On one of the slabs lay a body covered by a sheet. My heart leapt with joy. I rushed forward and pulled back the sheet to reveal a wizened old man with an amputated arm. I gazed down at him in horror, then glanced wildly about the room.

With a strangulated croak, Alice spoke the words that were thundering through my head. 'We are too late. They have taken him.'

Without hesitation we fled the room and hurried in the direction of the great furnace. At the end of the corridor we descended yet again, this time by means of an iron ramp and then through two large metal swing doors into the furnace room. Once inside one was immediately conscious of the sudden rise in temperature and the dull roar of 'the hungry dragon'.

We moved forward to the closed furnace doors. On the floor by them was a crumpled blanket.

'Not brought another so soon, 'ave yer?' The voice came from behind us and we turned to see a short, elderly man in a scruffy boiler suit.

'Hello, Bill,' said Alice sweetly. 'This is Bill, Dr Watson; he's our very efficient furnace man, aren't you, Bill?'

Bill grinned. 'Well, it ain't for me to say nor agree with them sentiments, but it's nice o' yourn to say so anyway.'

'You've just had a client I see?'

Alice's query was matter of fact and conversational. Her use of the word 'client' for corpse was typical of the way those who deal with death every day try to distance themselves from the gruesome reality.

Bill nodded and sucked on an empty pipe. 'Not more'n fifteen minutes ago.'

'Did you get a name?'

Bill shook his head and smiled in a strange patronising fashion. 'No names here, Matron. They've gone past the name stage when they gets to me.'

'Did you get a look at the . . . client before he . . . '

'That I did do, sir. I always do and I always has a little word with 'em. I wishes 'em luck on the other side and asks 'em to say hello to my Sarah if they bumps into her.'

'What was he like? Your last client?' I asked with more urgency in my voice than I intended.

Bill didn't answer immediately, but donned two enormous asbestos gloves and pulled back one of the furnace doors. The room suddenly filled with orange light reflected from the incandescent glow of the furnace. Waves of dry heat rolled out like a scorching wind. Instinctively, Alice and I took a step back, but Bill retained his position. No doubt years of tending to the 'dragon' had made him somewhat immune to the ferocity of the heat. His tight leathery complexion gave evidence of this.

He peered into the throbbing amber heart of the furnace and shook his head. 'Nah, he's just a black shape in there now. Youngish chap he was. Pity that. Don't so much mind feeding the old ones to the dragon. Sometimes we get little nippers here and that fair breaks my heart.'

'Did you notice anything unusual about him?' I asked, disconsolately.

'Unusual?' The word seemed to challenge him. 'Can't say I did. No, nothing unusual about that feller. Mind you, his face was fairly black and blue. He looked as though he'd been beaten up shortly before he'd snuffed it. Bruised and swollen he was.'

The Thing in the Hold

With leaden hearts, Alice and I left Bart's by the way that we had entered, taking care not to be noticed. If ever I felt the desperate need of my friend, Sherlock Holmes, it was at this hour. I was confused and dispirited, lost down some dark alley with no percept-ible way of escape. I had no notion of what to do next.

Once outside the gates of the hospital, I hailed a cab and we made a silent journey back to Baker Street, each of us wrapped in our own wretched thoughts. Questions upon questions revolved around in my brain with ever-increasing rapidity. Why had Stamford been murdered, for murder it certainly was? What dreadful secret had he harboured? How did his death tie in with the abduction of my friend? What part did Josiah Barton play in this bleak affair? And where on earth was Sherlock Holmes? I prayed with all my heart that he had not met with the same fate as Stamford. The contemplation of this made my gorge rise, and a deep-seated pain gnawed away in the pit of my stomach. Never had I felt as bewildered and out of my depth as I did on that cab journey.

'I appreciate that you will want to hear what Mr Holmes has to say about this matter, John, but in the end, surely, we must go to the police.'

We were back in the sitting-room at Baker Street and these were the first words Alice had uttered to me since we had left the grounds of Bart's.

I shook my head slowly. 'I really do not think the police will be able to help us in this matter. We need to know more and have more evidence – positive proof – before we can involve them. Having said that, I am at a loss as to what to do.'

'No doubt Mr Holmes will have his own theories.'

'No doubt,' I agreed bleakly. I knew then that it was no use keeping up the pretence concerning Holmes's whereabouts. I could not deceive Alice any longer. She deserved to know the truth. So, in an awkward and halting fashion, I broke the news to her of my

friend's disappearance. I recited a simplified version of the events
that occurred the previous night, ending with my discovery that
Holmes had disappeared.

Shock and amazement clouded Alice's features. 'Why, this is
terrible! I cannot believe all this is happening. Since yesterday I have
become involved in a situation that seems horribly unreal.' She
shivered and clasped my hands. 'I am suddenly very frightened,' she
cried in a hoarse whisper. I put my arm around her to comfort her,
and gave her a kiss on the cheek. I had no words of succour to offer.
For a moment, I held her tight and she surrendered to my embrace;
then, somewhat embarrassed, we pulled apart. She gave me a coy,
understanding smile. 'I am sorry,' she said. 'I am not usually this
emotional. On the ward I can be a bit of a tartar, but I am sailing in
somewhat strange waters at present.'

Her words had an electric effect on me. They pierced the fug in my
mind. 'Of course,' I said, starting forward, 'I am forgetting that I
have at least one clue, one lead to follow up: the ship *Matilda Briggs*
berthed in Christopher Dock.'

Alice's puzzled frown prompted me to explain this detail, which I
had omitted from my account of the previous night.

'What do you intend to do?' she asked when I had finished.

'Investigate.'

'On your own?'

'Certainly,' I cried with some excitement, a plan already forming
in my head. 'I will take a leaf out of Holmes's book and disguise
myself as a sailor to be less conspicuous. There must be something I
can learn about this wretched business on the dock.'

'And what if they capture you as they have done Mr Holmes? Oh,
John, is it wise to go alone?'

I grinned for the first time that day. 'You're not suggesting that you
come with me, are you?' From the expression on Alice's face I could
see that this possibility had crossed her mind but, with some passion, I
soon dissuaded her of the practicality of such an endeavour. 'For a
start,' I explained, 'it may be very dangerous and, if something should
happen to me, you are the only person who has full knowledge of the
facts to pass on to the police. I must go alone.'

Wisely, she accepted my reasons without further protest.

It was agreed that she should return to her own home, where I felt
she would be safer. 'At present your involvement with this affair is
unknown. These rooms will be the first port of call if our antagonists
should decide to round up all those considered to be Holmes's

accomplices. When I have finished my business, I will come to your address. If I have not arrived by first light tomorrow morning, contact Inspector Giles Lestrade of Scotland Yard and tell him all that you know.'

Alice nodded with some reluctance and gripped my hands once more. 'You will be careful, won't you, John?' she said.

* * *

Two hours later I was in the east of the city. Having passed through Poplar, I had reached Blackwall, a district of narrow, squalid streets and mean houses, inhabited by a poor and densely crowded population. It is here one encounters the dark and deprived tail-end of the spiral of wealth that runs through London. It is also where the great East India Docks are to be found. One of these was the Christopher Dock. With some help from Sherlock Holmes's wardrobe of disguise costumes, and a certain amount of ingenuity of my own, I hoped that I fitted in with the sailing fraternity milling around the streets. I was dressed in a dark blue reefer jacket and a peaked cap, with a striped neckerchief at my throat. I had daubed my features with some dark greasepaint to give myself a swarthy complexion, and a final touch was Holmes's old clay pipe filled with pungent ship's tobacco.

· The sky had clouded over. Amorphous blotches of grey loured above me, mirroring my own gloomy mood, as I trudged towards the great iron gates of Christopher Dock. I grunted an indistinct 'good afternoon' to the watchman, who barely raised his eyes from the '*Pink 'Un*' he was gleaning, and I slipped by him without scrutiny.

I came upon an idle group of four sailors squatting on up-turned tea chests, playing cards. 'Where'll I find the *Matilda Briggs*?' I asked gruffly, leaning against the wall with as much nonchalance as I could muster to observe their game. None of the players took their eyes off their cards, but one blond-haired fellow responded in the same off-hand manner I had adopted. 'Looking for work?' he growled, slapping a pair of kings down in front of his fellow gamblers. Before I had a chance to answer, he added, ''Cause we're looking for extra hands. Lost a few on our last voyage, we did, matey.' Now he turned his fierce blue eyes on me and studied me, as a breeder would potential stock. 'Well built sort of a feller. Yeah, I reckon Cap'n Rogan could use you.'

I nodded my head.

He grinned a wide, mirthless smile. 'Take yourself down here a while, a couple of hundred yards, and you'll see the old *Matilda*. Ask for Cap'n Rogan. Say Gunson sent you.'

'Much obliged.'

At my response, the fellow roared with laughter and returned to his game. Warily I made my way in the direction indicated and, when I was a good distance away from the gamblers, I turned back to look at them and met eight hostile eyes staring straight back at me. Then they broke from this frozen tableau and resumed their game with noisy enthusiasm.

Quickly I moved on and, as I passed around the rusty metal base of a crane, I saw the *Matilda Briggs*. She was a typical three-masted cargo vessel, some two hundred feet in length. The dark lines of her masts and the rigging were silhouetted against the grey light of the gloomy sky. There was no sign of life above deck and an aura of stillness and silence emanated from the vessel. It seemed unreal, like a ghost ship, an illusion shimmering before me, and I was reminded of some lines of Coleridge:

> As idle as a painted ship
> Upon a painted ocean.

I stood for some moments by the gangplank – hesitant and unsure of what to do. Should I board noisily, call out Captain Rogan's name, and come up with some tale about wanting to sign on for the next voyage, or should I risk a covert investigation? Overall, I believed the latter option would be more likely to reveal information that I needed, but it would be the one that placed me at the greatest risk. Was Sherlock Holmes on board? I had to find out. Of course, I could call out his name, but if he were held prisoner he might well be unable to reply, and such a cry would announce me as the enemy to all who heard it.

I looked about me. The dockside was deserted, as were the decks; and the only sound I could hear was the creaking of the timbers as the vessel shifted gently in the water. Quickly and quietly I scurried up the gangplank and dropped onto the deck of this mystery ship. I moved towards the stern where the cargo hold would be located. On reaching one of the hold doors that was battened down, I crouched and, like a hunted animal, sensed the air for danger. With some effort, I forced the batten through the metal handles, thus releasing the hold doors. Slowly, I pulled one of them open. It creaked, the noise seeming unnaturally loud in the stillness. I froze and held my breath. Silence returned. I moved the door again, just enough distance to allow me to pass through. Gingerly, I found my footing on the stairway that led below.

Before allowing the door to close, drowning me in darkness, I fumbled for the bull's-eye lantern. The feeble beam carved a thin strip of light into the blackness. The air was hot and oppressive, and there was a strange cloying smell in the atmosphere. I had just reached the bottom of the stairway when I heard a noise. There was a rustling and a strange, deep rasping sound like the angry grunt of a pig. The icy hand of fear clasped my heart as I was suddenly reminded of the large rats from The Bridge of Dreams. No doubt this was the vessel on which they had been transported to this country, and there might be more of the foul creatures on board. My instinct was to turn and run. With some effort I quelled my fears and, stepping further into the darkness, swung the beam of my lantern around the hold to discover the source of the sounds. I could discern nothing but blackness. However, there was something moving in the void before me.

'Holmes,' I called, praying I would receive a response, but expecting none. 'Holmes,' I called again.

Whatever responded to my cry was not human. It was that strange, strangled, rasping sound again. I withdrew my revolver from the pocket of my reefer jacket and progressed further into the hold. Then I saw something. The finger of light from my lantern picked out what appeared to be a large crate covered by a tarpaulin. It was some six feet high and eight feet long. And it seemed to be occupied.

Now I could smell it. A foetid stench attacked my nostrils, causing me to retch involuntarily. Quickly and deliberately, without reasoning the outcome of my actions, I pulled the tarpaulin away from the front of the crate to reveal the bars of a large cage. What was contained within the cage made me drop my revolver in shock. There, blinking at the light, with hatred in its bulbous eyes, was the largest brown rat I have ever seen.

The creature was the size of a large dog and was covered in rust-coloured, shaggy fur. It sat on its haunches, its front paws hanging, immobile like talons, before its great chest. Dark whiskers quivered at the end of its cruel snout. It was a living exhibit from Dante's *Inferno*!

When it saw me, the creature threw itself against the bars of the cage with great ferocity in a feverish attempt to get at me. The whole construction shook and the bars rattled. Its great orange teeth gnashed at me from its prison, and it emitted a weird half-scream, half-growl that filled the darkness around me. I responded with a gasp of terror as I visualised the beast breaking free, and its great incisors slashing my flesh.

It was at this moment that my nerve failed me. Not waiting to search for my revolver in the darkness, I turned on my heels and scrambled up the stairs to the door of the hold like a drunken man, my feet tripping on the rungs in my frantic haste. With sweating palms and thumping heart, I fumbled in the darkness for the handle, while the cry of the frenzied beast still rang in my ears. Once I secured a grip, I gave a mighty push, swung the door open, and clambered out on to the deck of the ship. I sprawled forward in an undignified manner. I did not care. I had got away from the giant rat. I do not consider myself a coward; but the sight of that unnatural, venomous thing in the hold had frightened me more than all the bullets I had faced in Afghanistan or all the dangers I had encountered with Holmes.

Waiting but a moment to capture my breath, I pulled myself to my feet, only to find myself facing the angular features of a blond-haired sailor; it was Gunson, the man who had given me the directions to the ship. This time he looked far from friendly, and he had an iron bar in his right hand which he smacked rhythmically into the open palm of his other hand. Standing just a little way behind him was another figure I recognised. It was Sherlock Holmes.

Before I could move or speak I received a blow on the head from behind, and the black hole of unconsciousness swallowed me up once more.

CHAPTER NINE
Crescent Lodge

Even before I opened my eyes, I became aware of gentle movement and the sensation of my body swaying in an almost regular rhythm. Then my nostrils were assailed by the smell of strong tobacco; the familiar dark shag smoked by Sherlock Holmes. As my consciousness returned gradually, and my brain began to reassemble the fragile structures of thought, logic, and memory, I felt the throbbing pain at the back of my head where I had been struck. Recognition of this pain triggered my memory, and I relived the moments just before I was rendered unconscious. These vivid images brought me sitting bolt upright with my eyes wide open.

What I saw gave me a further shock. I was sitting in a carriage with the blinds down, travelling at a fast pace. Sitting opposite me, smoking his old briar, was Sherlock Holmes. He was smiling at me as though he did not have a care in the world.

'Welcome back, Watson. You have been in the land of nod for some considerable time,' he said, puffing contentedly on his pipe.

Instinctively my hand strayed to the back of my head and felt for a wound. There did not appear to be an open one, but my fingers discovered a lump, the size of a quail's egg, protruding through my hair.

'How are you, old boy?'

'I'm not sure,' I replied shakily, pulling myself up into a proper sitting position. 'I suppose I'll live, but at present a herd of buffaloes is stampeding across my brain. Do you have a hip flask? . . . A brandy . . . '

'Of course, my dear Watson.' Holmes flapped open his coat, dug into the side pocket of his jacket, and retrieved a silver hip flask, which he passed to me after unscrewing the top. I took a good slug of the brandy and soon felt the fiery liquid at work.

'What is happening?' I asked, passing the flask back after taking a second gulp. 'Where are we going?' I realised my questions were very simplistic, but I had not yet fully assembled the details of my last few waking hours into a coherent series of facts on which

I could base slightly more complex questions. In reality, given the rhythmic movement of the coach, the warming effects of the brandy, and my throbbing pate, I would have been more than happy to just slip back into sleep again. As always, Holmes was cognisant of this situation.

'Are you sure you are up to the rigours of dealing with the complexities of the case in your current condition?' he asked smugly.

'Probably not,' I replied tersely, 'but I would like to know who hit me on the head and, more importantly, how you managed to effect our escape.'

Holmes smiled broadly. 'The fellow who floored you on the *Matilda Briggs* is a sailor called Fraser, but he merits little attention. He does not figure in this case.'

'My head says otherwise. It would give me the greatest pleasure to return the compliment,' I observed gruffly.

Holmes continued to smile, but ignored my taunt. 'As to the matter of your escape . . . well, you did not escape, old fellow.'

'What do you mean?'

'You are my prisoner.'

I shook my head – a painful action – wondering if I had heard my friend correctly. 'Please don't talk in riddles, Holmes. I'm not quite up to following you round those particular mazes at present.'

'You never are, Watson, with or without a cracked skull. And it seems that when the simple truth is placed before you, you are still unable to comprehend it.' As he spoke these words, my companion was still smiling at me, but his voice had the cold, sharp edge of a well-honed razor.

'But it doesn't make sense. How can I be your prisoner? I just don't understand.'

'Perhaps this will help you to understand a little better.' So saying, Holmes pulled a revolver from his overcoat pocket and aimed the barrel at my heart. 'One false move and I shoot you. It is as simple as that.'

'Is this some kind of joke?' Even as I uttered these words I could tell by the icy glint in Holmes's eye that he was deadly serious.

'Don't be naive.'

'Then you are not well,' I said. 'You cannot be in your right mind. Why on earth would you want to kill me? I am your friend. We have shared many dangers together. We began investigating this damned case together.'

'Circumstances alter cases.'

'What circumstances, for Heaven's sake?'

'Watson, Watson, you are so limited in your vision. You cannot see beyond the expected and the predictable. I have always prided myself on the flexibility of my thinking and my moral philosophy, even to the extent of admitting that I have been wrong on certain occasions. And now I am prepared to see my past life as one massive mistake. I was working in the wrong channels.'

This was patent nonsense, and was recited as though it had been learned by rote. I leaned forward in my seat and as I did so, Holmes stiffened and thrust the gun nearer to me. 'No silly acts of spont-aneous bravery, please.'

I gazed into his eyes. The pupils were heavily dilated and cloudy. This was not the alert face of Holmes the detective; this was the face of Holmes the drug addict. He wore that dreamy, distracted countenance I saw when, fighting off the boredom of inactivity, he resorted to the needle and a syringe of cocaine. But now there was a serious difference. Never had I seen him aggressive or irrational in these fits. Dreamy, lethargic, and sometimes loquacious, certainly, but always amiable. On this occasion, there was something very strange and sinister about his behaviour.

'What *are* you thinking, Watson?' he asked.

'You usually tell me without my needing to explain,' said I in a relaxed fashion. I had realised that it was necessary for me to play along with this bizarre charade, in order for me to find out exactly what was happening, and so that I might discover a way to bring my friend back to his senses.

He gave me a mirthless grin. 'You think that I am not quite myself and I need a good rest to come round, eh?'

'Something like that.'

'Ah, well, you are wrong, doctor. This *is* my real self. I have come round after a long time in the darkness.'

'I see. So now that you are involved in this devilish rat affair, you have decided to side with the enemy.'

Holmes gave an unsteady laugh. 'You can always be relied upon to describe events in the most emotive language. However, in essence you are correct.'

My heart sank at these words. How, and in what manner, this change in my friend's personality and behaviour had been brought about I could not guess, except for my notion that drugs had been involved, but what frightened me was how successful the transformation had become. I was contemplating a situation in which Sherlock Holmes was working for evil ends, and was my enemy.

Suddenly the coach juddered and slewed to a halt. Holmes lifted the blind, pulled down the window, and looked out. 'Ah, we have reached our destination.'

I could see that it was already evening, so I had been asleep for five or more hours. I heard what sounded like large iron gates being opened and then the coach began moving again. I saw that we passed a large stone gatepost and drove into what appeared to be a broad driveway before the window was raised and the blind drawn again. 'There is no need to strain your eyes, Watson. I will tell you where we are. We have just passed into the grounds of Crescent Lodge, the home of my new friend.'

Moments later the coach stopped again. This time Holmes flung open the door and, pointing with the barrel of his gun, indicated that I should leave the carriage. I did so and he followed me. I stood before a great old house, the pale stone of the frontage darkened in places by the ivy that clung like a strange form of decay. There were four Palladian pillars, standing like sentries, two either side of the stone steps leading up to the front door, which was ajar. Framed in the doorway, silhouetted against the light streaming from the brightly-lit hallway, was the tall, imposing figure of a man. Even in the gloom I thought I recognised him. He came down the steps to greet us.

'My dear Holmes,' he cried enthusiastically, 'it is good to see you. I observe you have brought us a gift.' He nodded in my direction. I did indeed know this man. It was Josiah Barton.

Holmes stepped forward to shake his hand. 'When a fool will not leave well enough alone it is best if he is removed from the action.'

'Of course. You acted quite correctly. I am sure the Baroness will be most interested to meet him. Come.'

Holmes thrust the gun in my back and urged me forward up the steps and into the house, and then the massive door of Crescent Lodge swung to behind me with a loud bang. We were in a high hallway, lit by a single, sparkling chandelier. To our left a broad marble staircase swirled round, leading to the upper quarters of the house, while to our right a long corridor, sparsely illuminated, ran off into the heart of the building. Barton bade us wait, then disappeared down the long corridor, his figure merging with the shadows before vanishing from sight.

'For heaven's sake, Holmes,' I hissed turning to my friend, 'if this is some ploy to worm your way into the enemy's lair, please let me into your plans.'

Holmes's features lightened and he inclined his head to my ear. 'Take heed, old fellow. One silly move and I shoot you.'

I turned sharply to face him and he raised his gun to my heart again. There was nothing but a blank coldness in his eyes. I felt as wretched as I have ever been in my life.

Barton returned, beaming. 'The Baroness will see you now,' he said.

I was led down the corridor towards the rear of the house and taken into a sumptuous, heated conservatory. Once Holmes and I were inside, Barton left us, closing the door behind him. The room was filled with great fan-like green palms and exotic plants with vibrant blossoms. For all the world, it resembled an artificial jungle. Brightly coloured butterflies fluttered in the warm, moist air and there was a small fountain trickling gently to the left of the door, while in the centre of the room a woman reclined on a cushioned bamboo couch. She was dressed in a long, black gown and was reading a sheaf of papers through a lorgnette as we entered. She looked up, a half smile touching her face fleetingly. As she lowered the lorgnette, I could see she was a beautiful, pale-faced creature with high cheekbones and dark, feline eyes. Indeed, there was something very cat-like about this woman both in her appearance and movements.

'Ah, Sherlock, you have brought your friend.' Her English was tinged with an accent, but I was as yet unable to place it. She put her papers to one side and, with a curl of her long forefinger, beckoned us nearer. Holmes, who still held the gun, prodded me in the back and moved me closer to the woman.

She was indeed a fabulous creature. Her shiny, raven hair framed a face that, while irregular of feature, was both hypnotically beautiful and yet strangely cruel. She extended her hand to me. 'I am so glad you have come, Dr Watson.'

'I had little choice in the matter,' I replied curtly, ignoring her hand. 'Perhaps you will be good enough to explain what this charade is all about, and why my friend is behaving in this alien manner.'

She gave a purring chuckle in response, her eyes closing in the process, only to open wide again and flash in my direction. 'Alien manner,' she said softly, the smile still on her lips. 'What can you mean?' She leaned back on the couch and eyed me with amusement. 'You find your friend different in some way? How strange.'

It was clear that the woman was playing with me in the taunting fashion that a cat plays with a mouse. My temper snapped. 'This is intolerable. I demand an explanation.' In my anger, I took a step forward, and, as I did so, I heard the cocking of a pistol.

'That is far enough, Watson. One further step and I shoot.'

I chilled at these words, for I believed him. I knew for certain now that this was no act and he meant exactly what he said. He would kill me. With this frightening realisation came a further wave of despair which rolled over me, swamping my spirit. Great heavens, he really was on their side. He was one of them!

'Take a seat, gentlemen, and then perhaps, Sherlock, you will explain to the doctor the rules of our game.'

Holmes dragged two cane chairs over and placed them some four or five feet away from the couch. It was as though there was an invisible barrier around this woman that must not be breached. Holmes indicated that I should sit. I did so and, as he followed suit, I noticed a fine sheen of perspiration cover his brow. Although the chamber was unnaturally warm, I had never seen my friend perspire in such a fashion before. I was completely baffled as to how he had got himself into this state and as to what exactly was going through his mind.

'First, introductions,' he said stiffly, the face betraying no emotion. 'May I introduce Baroness Emmuska Dubeyk.'

The Baroness gave a nod of greeting.

'And are you responsible for the giant rat?' I asked, bluntly.

'He thirsts for knowledge, your friend,' she said softly, with a raise of the eyebrow. 'And I so believed the English were the masters of polite conversational gambits. Instead, I find they are like ravenous terriers on seeing a bone.' She turned to me. The smile had gone and the eyes, those fascinating dark eyes, glittered coldly. 'Very well, since you wish to know, I will tell you. It can do no harm now, and I do try to give pleasure to my guests. Yes, doctor, I am responsible for the giant rat. The giant rat is my weapon. I . . . how shall I phrase this? I engineered its development. Although I was born in Hungary, I spent many years in Sumatra, where I observed these strange, vicious creatures. The size of a puppy they are, but in a pack they can overpower a man and savage him to death within minutes. How much more threatening one would be, I pondered, if it were larger and the carrier of a deadly bacillus. What power that would bring. I have studied many things in my life and I have a great facility for learning, understanding, and developing what I have learned.

Taking my knowledge a little step further – throwing light into the shadows – has always been my goal. Medicine, science, the occult – I have studied them all. I have mastered them all.'

'The occult!' I exclaimed involuntarily.

'The small mind never questions beyond what is already known. One must go further to develop . . . to gain control.'

'So that is what it is all about – control?'

'Of course. It is the *raison d'être*. Control is power and power is freedom. I now control Sherlock Holmes and therefore I am free from his interference in my plans.'

I glanced at my friend. His face was in repose. The eyes were glazed and, although he still held the gun pointed at me, I could tell that he was not really seeing me. He heard but apparently did not comprehend. He seemed entranced by the Baroness and her melli-fluous words.

'And,' our hostess continued, 'I will soon control you, Dr Watson. Do not protest, or believe you will escape my influence. You are now a helpless little fly caught in my web – never to escape. You shake your head, but it is just a desperate . . . a futile bravado. Let me demonstrate my powers to you.'

Suddenly she sat bolt upright on the couch and, for a fleeting moment, I observed a glint of metal and realised that one of her legs was encased in a calliper. She was lame. Nature, who had given her such beauty and a remarkable brain, had cheated her with a damaged body. She seemed not to notice my observation, or at least was not prepared to acknowledge it. Doing so would only be a reminder of what, in her eyes, was her one defect. For all her knowledge, and her supposed ability to go beyond the known in medical science, there was no cure for a withered limb. It must have made her very bitter.

She sat on the edge of the couch, her long fingers pressing in on either side of her forehead. For a moment she closed her eyes and whispered one word: 'Babaska'. Then suddenly her eyes shot open and she smiled. 'He will come.'

Somewhere at the back of the conservatory there was a rustling of leaves, and then the heavy pad of feet on the marble floor. I was conscious of what sounded like claws clicking on the hard surface. The sound grew louder and then, emerging between the fronds of a low growing palm, there appeared what at first seemed to be a large black cat; but as the creature drew nearer, I saw that it was far larger than any domestic animal. It was in fact a fully-grown black panther. It was sleek and glossy and moved with fluid, feline grace, the muscles rippling beneath its smooth coat. Occasionally it would open its mouth in a gentle snarl, revealing its deadly white teeth.

I felt myself grow numb with apprehension and now I, too, began to perspire: thin rivulets of sweat trickled down my neck. If the creature chose to pounce I would have no chance of survival. Those vicious teeth could tear me to pieces in seconds.

The panther padded round and sat at the feet of his mistress just like a trained pet. The Baroness stroked its jet-black head and it purred and leaned against her leg. 'One of the wildest creatures of the jungle, Dr Watson, a natural killer, and yet, with me, as tame as a kitten.' So saying, she prised open the panther's jaw and placed her hand inside, gently pulling the animal's great incisors in a playful fashion. The creature gave a throaty roar and its eyes rolled wildly, but it still sat demurely, leaning against its mistress.

'I am sure, Dr Watson, you will be cognisant of the point I am making. If I can control this fellow, what chance do you have of resisting my powers?'

She leaned over, bringing her face close to that of the great cat, whispering to it in her native Hungarian as a child might address a fluffy kitten.

Holmes watched this bizarre scene impassively. I noticed that his grip on the pistol had slackened and that the gun's barrel was no longer pointing directly at me. Obviously, his level of concentration had lessened. If I were going to act at all, in some desperate bid to escape from this intolerable situation, it had to be now – now while the Baroness was lavishing her attention on her deadly pet, and Holmes had relaxed his surveillance of me. Yes, I convinced myself, it had to be now. But, what on earth was I to do?

CHAPTER TEN
The Man of Action

There are moments in life when you realise that you must grasp the nettle and risk the consequences. I knew I had reached one of those moments. I held no scheme in my befuddled mind, only an overwhelming urge to extricate myself from a perilous situation. I knew that death might result from my actions, but I reckoned that the alternative was just as fearsome. Holmes frequently referred to me as a man of action, but my army training had always alerted me to the fact that action without planning could lead to disaster; and here I was about to strike out into that unplanned unknown.

The Baroness continued to make cooing noises to her ferocious pet, her long fingers scratching the fur on its head. The creature purred and nuzzled closer. If I were to be presented with a moment – this was it. And so, with my heart thundering in my breast, I took my chance. It was, as I analysed the situation, my *only* chance.

Since the appearance of the panther I had been, for all the world, apparently frozen to the spot with fear, immobile like a statue. Suddenly, I leapt from my seat and, before Sherlock Holmes could react, delivered a direct blow to his jaw. He only just registered my movements before my fist made hard contact with his chin. There was a hefty smacking sound. His eyes flickered, the pupils rolled upward revealing the whites of his eyes, and he fell backwards off his chair, crashing to the floor. As he did so, I grabbed for his gun, snatching it from his inert fingers. For the moment I had gained some control – the concept the Baroness held so dear. Certainly a gun gives one some control but, in my circumstances, perhaps not enough.

Seeing what had happened, the Baroness uttered some words of her native tongue into the panther's ear. They had an immediate effect. It sprang to its feet and loped towards me, its pink tongue lolling over treacherous white teeth. The panther's green eyes were focused on me. I backed away as the creature crouched down ready to pounce. My brain pounded and my mind revolved. Fear and total desperation forced a wild plan into my mind. I had to act – now!

Without hesitation, I fired my gun at the animal – but with the intention of shooting wide. With the barrel aimed at it from my outstretched arm, the panther hesitated for a spilt second as though it sensed the danger it was in. Then came the deafening report. The bullet ricocheted off the marble floor and hit one of the glass panes of the conservatory. This diversionary tactic gave me just enough time to make for the double doors behind me and wrench one open. As I did so I could hear voices in other parts of the house roused, no doubt, by the gunshot. I knew I had only seconds before the black beast would be upon me. I raced into the hall and then slewed myself backward with force and speed, pinning myself flat against the closed double door. As I did so, two things happened at once. The figure of a man appeared at the far end of the corridor, and the panther bounded from the conservatory. On spying the distant figure, whom I now recognised as Josiah Barton, the big cat emitted a wild blood-curdling roar and raced towards him. I had no time to wait and see what happened. Quickly I slipped back into the conservatory, slamming the door shut and bolting it. I grimaced as, beyond in the hallway, I heard frantic cries of pain mixed with the guttural roars of the jungle beast claiming its prey.

I now found myself locked in the room with my unconscious friend and the Baroness. She was still sitting on the bamboo couch in some state of shock, bearing an expression that indicated she did not fully comprehend what was happening. Ignoring her for the moment, I dashed to the rear of the conservatory and, with the aid of a chair, smashed one of the great panes of glass. Immediately I did so, I felt a blast of cool night air wafting into the warm, damp atmosphere. This, I hoped, was to be my escape route.

By now the house was in uproar. There were shouts and screams and several shots. No doubt the Baroness's deadly pet was the main reason for the furore. Then there came a hammering on the conservatory door. The Baroness was struggling to her feet when I returned. I played the same trick with the revolver, firing at her, but aiming to miss. The bullet embedded itself in one of the cushions on the couch.

'Stay exactly where you are if you want to live,' I barked, while dragging Sherlock Holmes to his feet. He was regaining consciousness now, but still groggy. The Baroness glowered at me with blazing eyes and her hands twitched with frustrated passion, but she obeyed my instructions and remained seated on the bamboo couch. I smiled inwardly. For a brief moment she had lost her power – her control.

I shepherded Holmes to the smashed pane, my makeshift exit, and with some effort pushed him through it. He fell into the shrubbery in the darkened garden beyond. By now the hammering had grown louder and I realised it would not be long before the door was broken down. I fired another warning shot and then slipped from the room. Holmes was scrambling to his feet in the darkness. 'You won't get away with this,' he muttered in a slurred fashion, his brain not fully conscious. It was clear, despite all that had happened, that he was still my enemy. There was only one thing I could do in the circumstances, for both our sakes, one thing that would help to avoid us being recaptured. I clubbed my friend on the back of the head with the butt of the revolver. He gave a little groan and fell into a comatose heap. Slipping the gun back into my pocket, I hauled him up and over my shoulder like a sack of produce. I was never more glad that his appetite was meagre and that he was excessively lean. The lights of the house enabled me to see that we were in a spacious garden bordered by trees, large shrubs, and rose bushes, with a fence at the far end which appeared to lead on to some meadowland.

Without hesitation I headed for the thickest shrubbed area and made my way as far as I could into the dense undergrowth. Unceremoniously, I dumped the body of Sherlock Holmes beneath a rhododendron bush, making sure he was hidden from sight. Returning to the lawn, I ran to the fence and climbed over it, ensuring that my muddy shoes left traces on the crossbars. Next, I deliberately caught my jacket on a protruding nail, so that it left a portion of material attached to its rusty head. Then, with as much speed as my throbbing heart would allow, I retraced my steps and threw myself down by the inert body of my friend, in the depths of the shrubbery, and waited.

There were still noises from the house. I deduced that the conservatory door had now been broken and then, suddenly, there was a female cry of despair. No doubt this was the Baroness wailing for the death of her pet, for surely someone within the household would have had to destroy the creature. Its bloodlust had been up, stimulated by the Baroness herself, and, although I had been its original prey, it would have turned on anyone in its path.

Within minutes a group of six men emerged through the broken window, each of them carrying a flaming torch.

The chase was on.

The men traversed the garden, searching for us with their illuminated torches. On more than one occasion the burning brands were thrust into the shrubbery near to where we lay but, thank heaven, no

one attempted to penetrate the thick foliage. One of the searchers
eventually crossed to the fence and found my tracks. 'Over here!' he
cried. 'They've gone this way.'

The men seemed to be under the instruction of a short, stout
ruffian with a rasping voice who one of them addressed as Parker.
There was no sign of Josiah Barton, and I wondered how severely
he had been wounded by the panther. Perhaps it had gone beyond
wounds.

I caught sight of Parker's broad face illuminated by the flickering
yellow flames of the torches, his brow creased, his eyes hard and
unblinking. He deployed three of the men to search for us on the
heath, sending the other two around the front of the building. Remarkably, it seemed that my plan had worked. These ruffians had no
conception that I was still within a hundred yards of the house. It is
always assumed that an escapee will want to place the greatest distance
between himself and his place of incarceration in the shortest possible
time. But that is often the quickest way to be recaptured. I surmised
that Holmes and I were safe where we were for the time being.

I waited some three hours, lying on the cold damp ground. Thankfully Holmes remained unconscious. He had, in essence, now drifted
into a deep sleep. Not only the blows I had dealt him, but also the
strain which had been placed on his brain in the past few days – a
strain that had caused him to act completely out of character – had
no doubt assisted in propelling him into a sleep where his mind could
not be troubled or manipulated.

The searchers had returned dejected some time ago. No one had
picked up a trail and, straining to catch snatches of their disappointed
exchanges, I concluded that the general assumption was that we were
miles away by now. The broken window in the conservatory was
boarded up and the lights in the house were extinguished. Then, just
as I thought the inhabitants of Crescent Lodge were about to retire
for the night, I witnessed the strangest of ceremonies.

It was around midnight. The moon was high, bathing the house in a
thin, creamy light. A small group of men came out into the garden.
Some were brandishing torches, burning sticks that threw long, harsh
shadows which danced grotesquely against the wall of the building. I
recognised the leader of the party: it was Dr Simeon Karswell. I felt
my body stiffen and my hands clench in anger. It was as Alice and I
had suspected. Not only was Karswell involved in this damnable affair
but he was also, directly or indirectly, responsible for the death of my
old friend, Stamford. There was no excuse upon Earth for a doctor to

betray his oath. To do so reduced him to the lowest level of humanity. Karswell was vermin! I cursed the fiend's name under my breath. To do more at this time would have resulted in my immediate exposure and recapture. But I vowed, there and then, that I would not rest until Karswell was brought to justice and made to pay the heaviest penalty the law would allow for his treachery.

Four men carried the body of the dead panther on a makeshift stretcher. The creature's vicious claws hung limply over the edge and its black face was innocent, doll-like in the stillness of death. Some way behind the group, moving unsteadily across the damp lawn, was the Baroness, her face strained, tear-stained, but motionless in the moonlight.

Parker and two other men began to dig a grave. The company remained silent while they did so. At last the creature was lowered into the shallow pit. The Baroness knelt down by the grave and whispered some words of Hungarian, which floated softly on the night air. Her slender body shook with emotion as she attempted to stifle her sobs of grief. After a time she grew still and then, with Karswell's help, rose from her knees and ordered the men to fill in the grave.

As they were patting the earth flat with their shovels, the Baroness broke free of Karswell's support and raised her arms to the heavens; her hands were tight black fists, silhouetted against the mid-blue of the sky. She cried out in her native tongue. I could make no sense of the words but it was clearly a kind of vengeful oath, rather than a wail of mourning. There was fire and fury in that cry, and the hairs on the nape of my neck prickled as it echoed in the midnight garden. It was obvious to me that death would be a comfortable alternative to falling into that lady's clutches again.

Slowly the funeral party, including the Baroness, returned to the house. Within half an hour or so the Lodge was in total darkness. Now was the moment to escape, I told myself, and the escape had to be successful. There certainly would be no second chance. Holmes still slumbered. He snored gently from time to time, but not enough to be heard unless one was within a few feet of him. It was time for action. After the events of this evening, I was learning the benefit of taking risks. I left him lying beneath the rhododendron bush and went in search of the stable.

Keeping as low as possible, I raced across the lawn and skirted around the back of the house. The moon was still bright in a cloudless sky, which was helpful to me, but it was also helpful to anyone watching from within. Conscious of this, I clung to the shadows as best I could until I eventually reached a six-foot-high wall with a latticed wooden door set in the middle. Through the diamond-shaped apertures I could see a yard beyond. It contained the carriage that Holmes had used to transport me to the Lodge the previous evening. The shafts were empty, but I surmised that the horse must be stabled nearby. Perhaps my luck was on the turn, for surely here was our possible means of escape. However, I realised that where there were stables there were likely to be stable hands also. Whether one or more of them had been ordered to keep an overnight vigil, I knew not, but this thought increased my caution.

I tried the door. To my relief it swung open easily. Closing it behind me, I tiptoed into the yard and, from a distance, studied the surrounding buildings. None gave the appearance of a stable. I crept closer and listened. The air was still: not a sound rippled upon it. Then, in the distance, I heard some village clock strike the hour: two o'clock. I remained still until the melancholy chimes faded. As I stood there in the shadows, I glanced down to the far end of the row of outbuildings and thought I caught sight of a glimmer of light in the end section, the furthest from the latticed door. The building was low, with a sagging roof and a solitary, begrimed window.

Crouching down, I moved along to the window and, slowly raising my head just above the sill, peered inside through the murky pane. Sure enough, there was a light burning. An oil lantern hung from a hook in the wall, but the illumination was dim. It was like looking at a scene through a yellow fog. There was a fellow inside sitting on a small stool under the lantern. He was smoking a clay pipe, which hung loosely from his lips, and reading a newspaper in a desultory fashion. Four empty ale bottles lay at his feet. Beyond him in the gloom was a pair of horses, each in a stall of its own.

I had got thus far, I reasoned, by being reckless and relying on my own resources. I had to continue in the same manner if I were to get Holmes and myself away from this dreadful place. I looked around for a weapon, and found it easily. There was an empty, decaying barrel standing nearby. It took no effort to wrench a stave free from its moorings. I felt it. It was soft and pliable, but still stout enough to deliver a sound blow. Grabbing a handful of pebbles, I threw them at the stable door and then flattened myself against the wall to the far side of it and waited.

After a moment I heard the fellow rub the pane of the window, as though he was looking out into the yard to discover the source of the noise. 'Robin, you devil? Is that you, Robin?' he croaked.

I mumbled a soft unintelligible response. The door opened slowly and the fellow slouched out into the yard.

'Where the devil be ye?' he said, his words slurred through the effect of drink. As he turned to face the carriage, I hit him with the barrel stave. I tried not to make the blow too hard: my purpose was to render him unconscious, no more. At first he fell to his knees with a surprised, strangled cry, and then mumbled, 'Why d'you do that, Robin?' before he fell face downwards onto the cobbles. Quickly checking his pulse, I determined that he was both alive and unconscious.

Wasting no further time on the inebriated groom, I led one of the horses from the stable and had her between the shafts of the carriage as quickly as I could. I then sped back through the wooden door into the garden to where Holmes still lay still sleeping. Hauling him over my shoulders once more, I staggered to the carriage and, with a great heave, managed to dump him on the seat inside. He stirred in his slumbers and, for an instant, his eyes flicked open, the pupils rolling wildly, as though he were about to propel himself into consciousness. Then the moment was over, the eyes closed again, and his breathing fell back into the regular breathy rhythm of sleep.

I pulled the window blinds down and shut the carriage door and then, with some trepidation, led the horse from the yard around to the front of the house. Here we moved from cobbles on to gravel and I was conscious of every squeak and lurch of the carriage and the crunch of its wheels. I held my hand over the nag's mouth to prevent it from making a sound, and gazed up at the house, fully lit by moonlight, the black shiny windows staring down, like vicious eyes spying on me. I felt totally exposed as I directed the horse and carriage past the steps leading to the front door and into the broad open drive, at the end of which I spied the great iron gates that I had passed through but a few hours previously. It seemed like a lifetime ago.

In the milky light, the gates glimmered before me like a mirage. They were the gates that led to freedom. Once beyond this portal, with its forbidding dark iron tracery, I believed I had a strong chance of making a successful escape. But not until then.

As I neared the gates, I glanced back at the house. It was still in blessed darkness. So far I had not been detected. And then my heart sank. I spied a thick iron chain looped around the middle portion of the gates, at the end of which dangled a large padlock. They were locked. What did I do now?

Frantically I considered my options. If I could not get out through here, it would be impossible to use the carriage for my escape. What other options were open to me? Should I release the horse, try to lead it to the garden at the rear, and attempt to jump the fence with Holmes straddled across her, as if she were a pack mule and he was my baggage? That contingency seemed both dangerous and farcical. It would also take time, which was in very short supply. I did not know how long it would be before the groom regained consciousness and raised the alarm. I reasoned that there was absolutely no point in searching the grounds for another exit, as this would also be time-consuming, and might turn out to be fruitless.

I could not believe I had come so far, or that it was my lot to fall at the final hurdle. I had to escape. There was far more at stake than my own insignificant life. I gazed once more at those high gates, the implacable metal barriers to my freedom and, as all seemed lost, a fresh thought struck me. I still had Holmes's gun. I pulled it out of my waistband and held it tight, so that the metal of the handle dug into my flesh. I could shoot through the chain to release the gates. It was possible that it might work. It *must* work. The noise would certainly rouse the household, cutting down my head start to a dangerous minimum – but at least it would be some kind of start. Should I take the risk? Then something occurred which made the decision for me. One of the windows in the lower portion of the house became illuminated and, very dimly in the distance, I could hear raised voices. Perhaps the groom had raised the alarm, or maybe Robin had gone to relieve the fellow of his night watch duties and found him unconscious with the carriage and one of the horses missing. There was no time to waste on such musings. People were being roused and my escape was threatened.

I blasted the lock and chain with two bullets. Thankfully the shattered lock fell with a heavy thud to the ground, releasing the gates. With an effort I swung them apart and then leapt aboard the carriage and, cracking the whip with some ferocity, set forth into the night. The carriage raced past the gateposts and I shook the reins furiously, encouraging the horse to gallop as fast as she could. The greater the distance I put between Crescent Lodge and myself the better. I did not glance back. I did not want to see if the Devil was closing in behind me.

CHAPTER ELEVEN
The Man of Mystery

The drive that night was like some wild hallucination. Everything about the experience seemed unreal. I sped down moonlit, twisting roads, with overhanging branches that appeared to lean forward in the breeze to snatch me away or unseat me. The carriage bucked and swayed wildly as I urged the horse on. Periodically, I cast a furtive glance back at the grey ribbon of road to see if my pursuers were in sight. But, strangely, I seemed to be alone in that dark landscape. There was no sound of hooves or angry cries in the distance – just the ghostly, anonymous countryside. What added to this mad, dreamlike state of unreality was that I had no conception where I was or in what direction I was travelling. As the cold night air beat against my face, causing my eyes to mist and water, I realised that, for all I knew, I might be racing down the narrow lanes away from London, rather than towards it – travelling away from any kind of security.

And then, about half an hour into my journey, I reached a little village, Buddington, and, to my great delight, saw a signpost to the capital. My heart soared. London was but a mere twenty miles away. My instincts had been correct after all and I had been heading in the right direction. However, by now the horse, its sleek flanks iridescent with perspiration, was already tiring. She could not maintain the pace I had set her thus far and I knew that, before long, the Baroness's men would be hard at my heels. I reasoned that to continue my journey now would lead inevitably to capture. Therefore, I decided to conceal myself, hide myself away, hoping that my pursuers would pass me by and then, when it was safe, I would resume my journey to London.

I pulled the carriage into a yard at the rear of a darkened hostelry, The Cross Keys, and waited. Here, in the shadows and out of sight of the road, I hoped I would not be detected. As it turned out, my period of waiting was short. Some five or ten minutes later I heard the distant rumble of hooves on the night air. The relentless drumming grew ever louder. They were catching up on me.

It was not long before my enemies clattered through the empty streets in hot pursuit. The noise of their hooves echoed on the cobbles, but the still, eyeless houses failed to respond to this sudden cacophony. As quickly as the horsemen had arrived, they were gone, and sweet silence descended once more upon the village. I afforded myself a brief smile. My ploy seemed to have worked, but I knew I must not grow incautious after this apparent minor success. I must ensure there was a goodly distance between this Devil's posse and myself before I made another move. With tingling nerves and enforced patience, I waited another half an hour before resuming my journey.

Soon the sky began to lighten and bleeding red streaks materialised in the east. The stark silhouettes of trees and hedges gradually gained colour and detail. I could not guess what my enemies' plans were but I knew that, once they had reached the outskirts of the city and were presented with several routes into the metropolis, they would either have to give up the chase or split up into smaller groups. Whichever decision they took, it increased the odds in favour of my escaping capture. I felt now that I had a good chance of avoiding them altogether. I allowed myself a brief grin, my first for many a long hour.

My estimations proved to be correct. I saw no more of the Baroness's men that morning. Mercifully, the rest of my journey was uneventful and, to be honest, it now remains but a vague memory in my mind. After the traumas and exertions of the night I was both physically and mentally exhausted, and I drove the carriage through the streets of the waking city as though I were an automaton, my normal faculties in some kind of fatigued suspension. Buildings of various sizes and hues passed by me in a blur, as though my eyes refused to focus on reality.

I felt sure that my pursuers would expect me to head for Baker Street, and I knew that, for the moment, this address was the most dangerous in London for my inert passenger and me. To return to 221B would mean immediate capture. There really was only one place where I could go.

On opening her door, Alice Mellor gave a gasp of horror, her eyes widening in disbelief. In my tired brain I had forgotten that she was not seeing the respectable John Watson, her old friend, standing before her on the doorstep, but a dirty, bedraggled, and somewhat disreputable-looking sailor with a day's growth of beard. Thankfully, it took only a few moments for her to recognise me beneath the alien clothes and hirsute adornments, although the expression of incredulity remained, tinged somewhat, I thought, with an affectionate smile. And then came a flood of questions.

'Later,' I said, rather more brusquely than I intended, glancing back at the carriage in the road. 'I have not come alone.'

With Alice's help we carried the still unconscious Sherlock Holmes from the back seat of the carriage into her dainty, and well-ordered, parlour and laid him on a *chaise longue*. With a cup of strong tea in my hand I tried to clear my head in order that I could recount my adventures in some coherent fashion. Alice sat opposite me and I began. She was engrossed in my tale, her face reflecting her increasing amazement as the narrative progressed. When I finished she remained silent for some moments, then rose and stood by the window, staring through the nets into the street outside. 'It is all very strange, John,' she said at length. It was clear that my story had both frightened and disorientated her. 'If they can get the better of Mr Holmes . . . ' She shook her head. 'What can it all mean?'

'I'm not sure. There is an infernal plot, and I am aware of certain elements of it, but I have no comprehension as to the whole. That is for Sherlock Holmes to inform us.'

'Holmes?' she said, turning to the prone figure of my friend. 'How can he tell you? He looks barely alive. Anyway, you say that he has been indoctrinated by these people. He has changed sides . . . '

'But not voluntarily. Of that I am sure. Nothing natural on Earth would cause Holmes to behave as he did.'

'Nothing natural! Then what?'

I knelt down by Holmes and pulled back the eyelids to reveal two grey, misted, static pupils, which stared back sightlessly at me. 'I believe I know and I also believe I know someone who can help us.'

'I think you had better explain, John.'

Some two hours later I was making my way to the Wood Green Empire in south London. I had bathed and shaved, and Alice had been able to provide me with one of her husband's old suits which, while not fitting me exactly, certainly gave me more of an air of respectability than the sailor garb in which I had arrived at her house in Courtfield Gardens. At first I had been apprehensive about leaving Alice alone with Holmes. If he regained consciousness he could easily effect an escape, and that would be disastrous. But she convinced me that she could cope. 'I have a small phial of chloroform,' she told me, 'and, if I see Mr Holmes begin to rouse from his slumbers, I will administer a pad soaked with the drug to his mouth.'

I travelled to Wood Green by Underground. I reasoned that if I were being followed it would be more difficult to keep up with me on public transport. However, I thought it unlikely that my whereabouts were known, but after the events of the last twenty-four hours I had begun to suspect even my own shadow.

The Empire Theatre was situated close to the Green and was very much in the style of a hundred other provincial Empires and Palaces. There was an extravagant façade with slim Palladian columns covered with posters advertising the various acts performing at the venue that week. It seemed strange to me that Sherlock Holmes and I had been ensconced in the front stalls of this very theatre but a few nights ago – the night we encountered Stamford – enjoying the show, oblivious of the great shadow which was soon to darken our lives.

I made my way down the side of the building to the Stage Door. I entered and was immediately challenged by a grey-faced, balding rake of a man. He popped out of a minuscule office to the left of the door. His tangled hair stuck out horizontally from the side of his head and his pale blue, watery eyes flashed with indignation.

'Oi, mate, can I help you?'

'I am here to see the Great Salvini.'

'Are you now? You got an appointment?'

'Not exactly . . . '

'Sorry, mate. Mr Salvini don't see no one without an appointment. He's resting in his dressing-room at the moment. He has a matinée this afternoon and he don't want to be disturbed. You from the press?'

'No.'

'Well, if it's a signed programme you're after . . . '

'I am from the police and this is a matter of great urgency,' I snapped, pushing past the officious fellow and making my way down the dimly lighted corridor where I assumed the dressing-rooms to be. Surprisingly the door-keeper did not attempt to follow. Instead he called after me in a strangled, peevish voice: 'From the police are we? Well, we'll see about that . . . !'

At the far end of the corridor there was a green door, which bore the name 'The Great Salvini' scrawled in white chalk. I knocked.

'Who is it?' came the muffled response.

I opened the door and entered.

The room was quite tiny and untidy. There was a large mirror and dressing table, a wardrobe, a clothes rack with several lurid costumes hanging on it, and a small bed. A wicker basket full of props took up most of the remaining floor space. The occupant of the room was lying on the bed. His eyes were covered with a black mask, which he tore off when I entered. 'What is the meaning of this? Who are you, sir?' he cried. 'How dare you interrupt my meditation?'

'I come on an errand of mercy, sir. I am Doctor John H. Watson, a friend of Sherlock Holmes . . . '

I got no further. At the mention of Holmes's name, Salvini's eyes widened with interest. 'Sherlock Holmes, the detective. You . . . you are the one who writes his cases.'

I nodded.

'Fascinating. I would love to meet such an unusual man. He would make a wonderfully challenging subject.' He grinned and pulled the chair from the dressing table and, with a gesture, bade me be seated. He was a lithe and nimble man, much smaller in height than he seemed on the stage, possessing doll-like, almost feminine, features with bright dark eyes which glittered unnaturally. Dropping down on to the bed, he perched on the edge, staring at me with great interest.

'An errand of mercy?'

'I believe my friend has undergone a deep hypnosis which has effected a change in his personality.'

'Really?' He shook his head. 'That is unlikely. With a character like Sherlock Holmes the detective – the reasoner – with a brain so sharp, independent, he would fight against any such changes. However strong the practitioner, you cannot make a subject do anything under hypnosis which is against his own in-built ethical or moral code.'

'I believe the hypnosis was facilitated by drugs.'

'Drugs!' The little man's face coloured with indignation. 'That is cheating. No self-respecting hypnotist would resort to drugs. Hypnotism is a science which uses brainpower and auto-suggestion. It is the meeting, and the combat, of two minds. Using drugs is a denigration – it is an abomination!' The colour rose in the little man's face as he expressed his anger.

'The person who did this to Holmes is unscrupulous and will go to any lengths, as long as the desired results are achieved.'

'A criminal?'

'Worse. Trust me when I say that I cannot go into detail. The situation is too delicate and time is of the essence . . . '

Salvini waved his hands in the air vigorously. 'My dear sir, I have no desire to compromise you. And I certainly do not wish to press you on these matters, but I shall need some information if I am to try and bring your friend back to his own self again. That is what you wish me to do, is it not?'

'Then you will help?' I asked, my heart warming to this little man with the extraordinary eyes.

'Of course. I will regard it as a privilege to help one of this country's greatest men.' He consulted a silver watch which he pulled from his waistcoat pocket. 'I have a matinée late this afternoon. However, I do not make my entrance until the second half. That should give me just four hours to be of service to you.'

'Then come with me now,' I said, standing up and moving to the door. 'I will take you to Sherlock Holmes and recount all the relevant information, scant though it may be, on our journey.'

'Excellent,' cried Salvini, jumping from the bed and retrieving his coat from the clothes rack.

As we left the theatre, the doorkeeper poked his head round the door of the little office. 'Hello there, Mr Salvini,' he called in an over-familiar fashion and then, glancing at me, added, 'so he was from the police then?'

Salvini eyed the man shrewdly. 'From someone much more important than the police.'

On our journey I gave Salvini a much-edited, prudent version of the events that had prompted me to seek his help. He came to know that, while on an important investigation, Holmes had been kidnapped by his antagonists and in some way they had indoctrinated him, so that he had willingly joined forces with them. In doing so, he was rejecting his previous lawful and moral stance and adopting that of the criminal world. I was fairly convinced that this incredible transformation had been brought about through hypnosis and a clever use of drugs. Salvini's sharp face was attentive throughout my explanation. When I had concluded, he nodded thoughtfully and sat back in his seat with a gentle sigh. 'We shall see,' he remarked quietly. 'We shall see.' That was all he said, and he fell silent for the remainder of the cab ride.

On reaching Courtfield Gardens, I discovered that the situation was much the same as it had been when I had left. After brief introductions, Alice showed Salvini into the parlour where Holmes still lay on the chaise longue. He had shifted in his slumbers but he remained in a deep sleep.

Salvini knelt beside Holmes and felt his pulse. 'Very slow,' he said faintly, to himself rather than to us. With remarkable gentleness he ran his fingers over my friend's brow. 'He is in very deep, friend Watson. It will take a great deal of effort to pull him back.'

'But you can do it? Surely?' There was a note of desperation in my query that caused the little man to smile.

'I can try,' he replied matter of factly. 'Now, I shall need a bowl of cold water, a sponge, and some smelling salts.'

Without hesitation, Alice bustled off to obtain these items. Meanwhile, Salvini threw off his coat and began pacing the floor, his head upon his chest, his brow deeply furrowed.

When the water and the smelling salts arrived, he began. At first he bathed Holmes's face in the icy water. The shock of it caused my friend to stir, the face muscles twitching awkwardly, but his eyes remained resolutely shut. Salvini continued the cold water treatment for some five minutes and, with each fresh application of the cold sponge, Holmes responded with greater awareness. Then Salvini thrust the smelling salts under his nose. This had dramatic results. Holmes burst out in a violent attack of coughing, his body rising up and his arms flailing wildly. As he did so, Salvini shook him and cried out his name at the top of his voice, 'Sherlock Holmes!' The eyelids flickered and seemed about to open, and then the body slumped back against the cushion. Salvini carried out the same procedure three or four times over the next five minutes. Each time, my friend rose closer to consciousness. And then as Holmes began coughing violently, Salvini threw the cold water over him, completely drenching his face. He followed this action with a series of sharp slaps across my friend's cheeks.

With a cry of annoyance, Sherlock Holmes gulped for air and his body stiffened. Suddenly he opened his eyes.

CHAPTER TWELVE
The Threat

Sherlock Holmes sat up with a start and gazed around his strange new surroundings with a sense of alarm. He moved like a badly-controlled marionette, arms and legs jerking in a stiff and awkward fashion, as though they had been newly fitted. He was obviously completely disorientated. His brow wrinkled in consternation and, turning in my direction, he looked at me blankly, showing no recognition whatsoever. It was not simply that he did not know where he was, but it also seemed clear that he was not quite sure *who* he was. Gently, Salvini placed his hands on Holmes's shoulders and eased him back down onto the chaise.

'Sherlock Holmes, Sherlock Holmes, Sherlock Holmes,' Salvini chanted in a lilting fashion as he stared into the detective's puzzled eyes. 'It is time to bring you back, Sherlock Holmes, to bring you back from the darkness into the light. Trust me and you will be yourself again. Look into my eyes and listen to my voice. Put all other thoughts, sights, and sounds from you. I am going to ease your mind and bring you back, so look, look into my eyes and listen to my voice. Do not stir. Do not fight against me. Relax, Sherlock Holmes. Do you understand me?'

Hesitantly, Holmes nodded his head.

'You will now close your eyes and sleep briefly. You will sleep and your mind will be filled with who you are. Sherlock Holmes, the detective. Sherlock Holmes of Baker Street. Sherlock Holmes, the friend of Dr Watson. Sherlock Holmes, the enemy of evil doers and criminals. Sleep now. Sleep now.'

Obediently, Holmes closed his eyes immediately.

Salvini rose to his feet. 'We will let him rest for half an hour before I attempt to untangle his thought processes.'

'But he has been asleep for eight hours or more already,' I cried impatiently.

The hypnotist gave me an indulgent smile. 'Of course. But you see, Dr Watson, that was not neutral sleep. As he slept he was still under the influence of the drugs and suggestions of the enemy. His mind must spend some time in limbo before I can have a chance to coax him back to himself. In doing so, he must reject the influences that have corrupted his thoughts and actions. It will be a battle, but one I will definitely lose unless I give Holmes a respite from *all* influences.'

'I'm sorry,' I said. 'I did not mean to question your knowledge. It is just that I am so eager to see my friend back to his old self again.'

'I understand. You know, doctor, I do believe that you would benefit from some sleep yourself. You look worn out.'

'I am rather. I have been too preoccupied to realise how exhausted I am,' I said, suddenly feeling terribly weary.

'Mr Salvini is right, John,' said Alice, coming forward and placing her hand on my arm. 'You seem as though you're about to fall over with tiredness. Come and lie down on the bed in the guest bedroom. You'll be no good to Mr Holmes unless you get some rest.'

She led me away like a lamb. I did not have the energy to resist. Within five minutes I was lying down on a soft counterpane and the world was swimming away from me.

* * *

'Come along old fellow, the game's afoot.'

I had been dreaming, dreaming in a deep sleep in which large rats featured along with the Baroness, Stamford, and Sherlock Holmes. He appeared now before me, leaning over me, his image shimmering like a reflection in water, the ripples distorting the features. The face was paler and more gaunt than usual, but the eyes were bright and piercing as of old. In my slumbers, he shook my shoulder as though to rouse me. 'Watson, this is no time to take it easy. We have work to do.'

'Holmes,' I mumbled in my dreams.

'Yes, I am here,' he said, shaking me harder.

My body rocked and I was propelled into wakefulness. Instinctively I sat up and then my jaw dropped, for there in front of me was indeed the figure of Sherlock Holmes, and he was smiling.

'Holmes!' I croaked, rubbing my eyes to convince myself that I was indeed awake. 'By all that is wonderful. It *is* you!'

'A slighter version of my former self.' He gave a feeble bow.

'You . . . you are all right?'

'It would be mendacious of me to say that I never felt better, but I am on the mend thanks very much to you and this gentleman here.' He gestured to a figure in the shadows by the door.

Salvini took a step forward and bowed. 'Your friend is returned to you, Dr Watson,' he said with a smile. 'His mind will remain a little fuzzy for some time, but rest assured that the man you see before you is your old friend, in mind as well as body.'

I shook my head in wonderment. 'Why, you have performed a minor miracle,' I cried.

'I have practised my art,' he replied solemnly. 'Now, I would love to stay and speak further with you but I am already very late for my matinée, so I must take my leave. Should you need my assistance again, you will find me either at the theatre or at my hotel.' He handed Holmes a card.

'Thank you.'

'And,' said the little man, stepping to the door, 'I beg you that when this affair is over, you will both come to the theatre to see my show and we shall have supper together afterwards.'

'It is the least we can do, Signor Salvini,' said Holmes. 'Watson and I will be more than happy to accede to your request.' It was a joy to hear those familiar self-assured tones once again. Salvini had indeed worked a miracle.

The three of us shook hands and I expressed my deep gratitude to Salvini for his assistance. Then the hypnotist departed to make his way back to Wood Green and the Empire Theatre.

As we returned to the parlour along with Alice, I touched my friend's arm. 'We have a lot to discuss and you have a great deal to tell me,' I said with some urgency.

Holmes nodded. 'This has been a remarkable adventure. There is nothing quite like it in our annals.'

'You talk as though it is all over,' said Alice, her features clouded with worry.

Holmes gave her a grim smile. 'It is far from over, and we have to move swiftly. When are you due back on duty at Bart's?'

Alice looked puzzled by his question. 'Later this evening. Why?'

'Karswell. You must go on duty as normal this evening. It is imperative that you do not arouse his suspicions. If he thinks that you are involved with us, your life would not be set at a pin's fee.'

'If that is the case,' I protested, 'Alice will be placing herself in the greatest danger by returning to the hospital.'

Holmes shook his head. 'Karswell has no reason to think that Mrs Callaghan is in league with his antagonists, and at present he and his unholy crew have enough to trouble them now that I have been rescued from their clutches. Karswell's mind will be distracted.'

'I believe Mr Holmes is right,' agreed Alice.

'I see the logic of the argument, but I am uneasy at the thought of you being in close proximity to Karswell.'

'He is a fairly small cog in the Baroness's machine. Mrs Callaghan has nothing to fear if she behaves normally.'

'Baroness! I had forgotten about her,' said Alice, her brow furrowing. 'You were sketchy in your account, John. I don't believe you fully explained who she is and what her motives are.

I shook my head sadly. 'My account was sketchy simply because I am only partly aware of what this business is all about. Holmes holds more pieces of the puzzle.'

My friend nodded. 'Indeed I do, but even I do not see the full picture clearly. One thing is for certain, however: if our enemies knew that I had been brought back to my senses, none of our lives would be safe.'

'I can well believe it,' I shuddered, as I recollected my encounter with the beautiful and cruel Baroness Dubeyk.

Alice gave a frustrated sigh. 'Well for goodness' sake, don't you think you had better explain to me what on Earth is going on? Whether I like it or not, it appears that I am mixed up in your investigation and, therefore, that places me in some danger too.'

'You are quite right, but really it is Holmes who can do that better than I.'

'I will try my best,' Holmes responded with a weary sigh. 'But first may I have a glass of water?' He ran his thin hand down the side of his face and closed his eyes momentarily. It was clear that he was quite weak and still suffering from the effects of his hypnotic ordeal.

Alice nodded kindly. 'I think what both you gentlemen need is a hot cup of tea and some sustenance. I suspect it is quite a while since food passed your lips. Am I right?'

We responded to her query with muttered agreements.

'Sit yourselves down,' she said, taking on the tone of the matron. 'I am sure I can find some bread, cheese, cold beef, and pickle in the larder.'

So it was that some fifteen minutes later Holmes and I were indulging in our first meal for quite some time. It was simple fare but, after our exploits and hardships, it was like a banquet. As I pierced the last piece of cheese with my fork and slipped it into my mouth I felt something like my old self again. And from Holmes's expression and the pale flush on his hollow cheeks I could tell that the food and drink had been medicine to him also.

'Now then, Mr Holmes, I have provided the victuals; will you provide an explanation?'

My friend dabbed his napkin to his lips and smiled. 'I shall do my best, but it is not an easy tale to tell. I do not have all the details and parts of the overall picture are still in shadow, but I shall endeavour to present what I know in coherent fashion.' He took a final sip of tea, lit his pipe, and sat back in his chair.

'There is a plot afoot to blackmail the British government,' he said, simply and quietly.

The words in themselves were innocuous enough, but the meaning behind them stabbed me to the heart like the ice-cold blade of a stiletto knife, leaving me speechless. Alice gave a startled gasp, nearly dropping her cup and saucer.

'Baroness Emmuska Dubeyk is the power behind the plan. She has been cultivating it for many years. She possesses a brilliant brain. She has studied medicine to a very high level and, following in the footsteps of Mendel, studied hereditary characteristics in animals. She is also a strong, resourceful woman with incredible powers. As Watson knows, it was she who hypnotised me. Rather than have me killed, as she so easily could have done, she wished to control my brain, to use it as a resource. She believed that, with me effectively on her side, there would be no real opposition to her machinations. The Baroness is already a rich woman and, although her plan would increase her wealth, she has a love of power too. She needs to dominate, to control. You saw how she enjoyed manipulation, Watson.'

'But what is this plan?' cried Alice. 'How on Earth can this woman blackmail the British Government? The whole idea is preposterous.'

Holmes responded to this outburst with a bleak smile. 'The fact that it is preposterous only increases its appeal for the Baroness. She has lived in Sumatra for some years, a country that boasts one of the world's largest, and most ferocious, species of rat. Through a course of experiments, she has created a monster version of this indigenous rodent – a giant rat as big as a large dog. It is the female of the species and is capable, by means of injection, of spawning others of its kind. No mate is required. The Baroness's plan is to release a pack of these foul creatures into the city unless the British Government pays her price.'

'Great heavens,' I cried.

'Her cruelty does not stop there. She intends that each of these rats should be a carrier of the bubonic plague. If the pack is released, within weeks the city and its environs will be in the grip of this insidious disease. It will be a repeat of the Great Plague of 1665.' He paused, and then added softly: 'I almost believe she would prefer that to receiving her money.'

'Then the British Government must pay,' cried Alice, her face pale and drawn.

'In the last resort it will have to. At present I suspect the Government has yet to be contacted by the Baroness. The plan is, or rather was, in its early stages. I suspect our escape has accelerated matters somewhat. One diseased corpse has been released into the Thames to alert the authorities to the potential dangers and, in time, there will be another body.'

The image of the corrupted cadaver that Holmes and I had examined in the morgue at Scotland Yard flashed into my mind; an image that was vivid and repugnant, and I grimaced at the thought of it.

'Once the Baroness has created fear and panic, alerted the authorities to the power and seriousness of the situation, then the threat will be made.'

'It is hardly believable. It's like a horrible fairy tale with this Baroness woman as the wicked witch,' said Alice.

'Indeed it is,' affirmed Holmes. 'As I say, our escape will have thrown out their timetable somewhat. They will now have to move the mother rat from Christopher Dock to safety and abandon Crescent Lodge. That gives us precious time.'

'What is our first move?' I asked with some urgency.

The question seemed to baffle Holmes for a moment. His brow furrowed and he shook his head as though to clear his thoughts. My heart sank. It was obvious that my friend was still suffering the ill effects of his ordeal, and that his intellectual processes were slow. What had Salvini said: 'His brain will remain a little fuzzy for some time.' How long? I wondered. Then the terrible thought struck me that there might be permanent damage and that Holmes may have been robbed of his peculiar bright genius. I gritted my teeth and wiped the idea from my brain. I could not entertain such a possibility. I knew that if we were to be saved from the terrible threat that threw a black shadow over all our lives, then Sherlock Holmes was the only man who had the ability to do it. If his brain was in any way crippled, then we were doomed.

I repeated my question with more force: 'What is our first move?'

Holmes pursed his lips and narrowed his eyes. 'I would have thought that was obvious.'

CHAPTER THIRTEEN

Council of War

Sherlock Holmes once described the Diogenes Club as 'the queerest club in London'. It was an establishment that ostensibly supplied comforts to the most unsociable and unclubbable gentlemen in the metropolis. No member was allowed to take the least notice of another. To the outside world it was an oak-panelled haunt of affluent city hermits, who found respite from the hurly burly of life within its hushed environs. To a large extent this was true, but the club's stellar member was my friend's brother, Mycroft Holmes, who was so influential in government circles that I believe that, when things came to a crisis, his opinion counted more than that of the Prime Minister himself. Mycroft had a remarkable brain and, in looking back over the years, I am convinced that the British Empire would not have reached the heights it did in that period leading up to the turn of the century without his influence and guidance. Therefore the Diogenes Club had rather a more potent and covert purpose than merely that of a gentlemen's club: it was for all intents and purposes an adjunct of the cabinet room.

This remarkable establishment was our destination after we left Courtfield Gardens. Already the autumn day was fading and dusk was ready to descend on London. Gas lamps were lighted, and the inhabitants of the great city bustled about their daily business, innocent of the dark shadow that was waiting to fall over their lives.

Holmes ignored the first two cabs we encountered and hailed the third. 'I really do not believe that our enemies have an inkling of where we are,' he muttered, climbing aboard, 'but I prefer to err on the cautious side. It has long been a maxim of mine, Watson, that it is always prudent to overestimate your opponent's abilities. That way, all your surprises will be pleasant ones.' This sentiment was delivered in those confident, self-assured tones I had come to know so well, yet I was not fully convinced that my friend was back to his old self. There was still a noticeable reserve and uncertainty in his behaviour that unsettled me.

However, as we travelled in the hansom cab he seemed comparatively relaxed, and spoke more of this strange affair in which we were embroiled. 'I managed to glean many small pieces of information during my captivity, Watson – some directly and some indirectly. I learned, for example, how Stamford was recruited to aid the Baroness. Sadly, he had turned into a dissolute gambler and an alcoholic. His career had not developed as he hoped and, in his disappointment, he had taken to drink and playing cards for high stakes, with the result that he found himself floundering in debt. Karswell came to the rescue. He offered Stamford financial help for various services in return.'

'Various services?'

'They are too ugly to detail. Let it suffice if I say that he allowed his blood to be used for the experiments concerning the rat.'

'The puncture marks!' I cried, remembering the livid red scabs on both of Stamford's lower arms.

'Precisely. He had other duties aiding the Baronesses's machinations, which indicates the depth of the pit into which he had fallen. There indeed was "a noble mind o'erthrown".'

I nodded grimly, a deep depression cloaking my spirits. Stamford had never been a remarkable individual, but he had been a decent and a good man, and in the final judgment that is all that is required of any of us.

Some thirty minutes after our journey began, we turned into Pall Mall and pulled up outside the discreet entrance to the Diogenes Club. Sherlock Holmes was known to the doorman and we were allowed entry without delay. My friend announced our arrival to the clerk on the desk and requested to see his brother. The clerk informed us in whispered, sibilant tones that, 'Mr Mycroft has another visitor with him at present. I shall have to ascertain if he can see you.' Without further words, he disappeared into the sepulchral recesses of the club. Within less than a minute he returned, gave a brief smile and a nod, and indicated that we should follow him. We passed through a large room where several members hid behind copies of the evening paper, or slumbered contentedly; and then were led up a dimly lighted staircase and ushered into the strangers' room.

The clerk announced us and quietly departed. As we moved into the room, I gave a gasp of surprise, for I saw that Mycroft's visitor was none other than Inspector Giles Lestrade of Scotland Yard. The policeman's face grew animated when he saw my friend. 'Well, well, Mr Holmes, we were just talking about you. I thought you had disappeared from the face of the Earth. I have my men scouring the city for you – and you too, Dr Watson.'

Holmes threw out his arms in a theatrical gesture. 'Well, here I am now. I have returned from oblivion.'

Mycroft stepped forward and clasped his brother's hand in his. 'I trust you are well, Sherlock.'

'I am.'

'Good, for it is clear you have recently undergone hardship and a change of tailor.' He smiled warmly, but the eyes remained serious and concerned. 'And you, Watson,' he added, turning his ample form towards me, 'you have been in the wars too, I see.'

'I'm fine,' I replied, as easily as I could.

'Good. You certainly arrive at a most opportune moment.'

'Most opportune,' repeated Lestrade, in a strange, self-satisfied way.

'You've had the ransom note then?' said Holmes quietly.

This utterance brought differing reactions from the two men. Lestrade's jaw dropped in amazement and his eyes widened in disbelief; while Mycroft smiled sardonically and helped himself to a pinch of snuff.

'There is very little that escapes my brother, Inspector,' explained Mycroft, gesturing for us to take a seat. The room was oak-panelled and contained a large rectangular table, around which six chairs were arranged in a formal manner. Holmes and I hung up our outer coats and joined Mycroft and Lestrade around the table.

'You know all about the ransom then?' asked Lestrade; his voice still tinged with surprise.

Holmes shook his head. 'Not all. I suspect that each of us in this room holds parts of this terrible puzzle unknown to the others. It is time for an exchange of information.'

'Excellent idea,' cried Mycroft, rising to his feet. 'I will arrange for some drinks and sandwiches, then we can pool our knowledge to see how we can move towards resolving this affair.'

And so it was, some ten minutes later, that we sat around the table, an array of sandwiches upon a silver platter before us, each with a large glass of claret, holding a council of war. Holmes began. He gave a precise and detailed account of all our adventures, including the relevant details regarding Stamford's involvement in the mystery, our visit to The Bridge of Dreams, and his own enslavement by the Baroness. As he spoke, Lestrade, his face white with horror and dismay, made hurried notes, while Mycroft sat perfectly still, like a wooden Indian, an enigmatic expression on his face. At times during my friend's narrative, Holmes broke off and asked me to make a contribution, filling in the details that his experience lacked. When I described my encounter with the giant rat, a strange hush descended on the room. When we had finished, it was some time before anyone spoke. Eventually, it was Mycroft who broke the silence.

'That is quite an incredible account, and yet I know it to be true, for the details more than fit the facts as I understand them; they illuminate them.'

'I think it is now time for you to throw some of that illumination in our direction, dear brother.'

Mycroft took a sip of wine. 'Certainly. You know of the first body found in the Thames – and Watson here was quite right, it was infected with bubonic plague. Well, a second body was discovered by a constable early this morning, in an alley in Limehouse.' He looked at the inspector for elaboration.

'The corpse was not so advanced with corruption as the first,' Lestrade said, 'but was heavily disfigured. A sailor, one would say.'

'Why?'

'Nautical tattoos and his manner of dress.'

'Murdered?'

Lestrade nodded. 'Exactly like the first: throat cut from ear to ear. I should say that the fellow was killed elsewhere and then his body dumped in Limehouse later. What made this corpse really different from the first is that he had a letter on him. A letter addressed to the Prime Minister.'

Holmes showed no sign of surprise at this declaration. Instead, he leaned back in his chair and brushed an imaginary crumb from his jacket. 'What did it say?'

'I have no doubt you can hazard a guess, Sherlock.'

My friend frowned. 'I never guess. You know that very well. Besides, an approximation of the message is almost worse than useless. I need to know the exact wording.'

Mycroft drained his glass, gave a mock indulgent sigh, felt inside his jacket, and pulled out a sheet of crumpled paper. He passed it to his brother. 'Here is a copy. The original was destroyed for fear of contamination.'

Holmes read it quickly and then passed it to me. It ran thus:

Dear Sir

Please accept this corpse as the second medical exhibit giving you proof of the power I hold over you, your government, and your city. Both men have the plague. Both men acquired this dread disease by being bitten by a giant rat from the isle of Sumatra. Not only is that rat now resident in London, but at present many brothers and sisters are being bred in readiness.

You will appreciate the chaos and disaster that would result should these rats be released. The plague would sweep through the metropolis in a matter of weeks and, like a seeping wound, would eventually spill out, spreading further afield. It is not just your city but your country, sir, that is at the crossroads. Only you and your government can bring salvation. This threat can be eradicated – for a price.

The price is a high one, as you would expect. My friends and I require a payment of five million pounds. Payment is to be made within a week of receipt of this letter. Keep an eye on the agony columns for further instructions.

Any attempts to foil our plans will result in our precipitating the threat.

You have been warned.

THE PIPER

'Five million pounds!' I exclaimed, letting the note fall from my hands onto the table. 'Why, it's outrageous. Surely you do not intend to pay?' I fired my question at Mycroft.

'Of course it is outrageous,' he replied evenly. 'And of course we cannot pay it for, once we did, what real guarantee would we have that we would not be threatened again; or that the threat would not be carried out anyway?' He gave a weary sigh and continued. 'And yet, Dr Watson, we cannot afford *not* to pay. We cannot gamble with our citizens' lives.'

'They must be stopped. This Baroness and her unholy crew must be stopped,' I cried, my desperate words filling the room.

Mycroft nodded slowly. 'We shall do our best, eh, Sherlock?'

My friend seemed totally preoccupied with his own thoughts, and the mention of his name broke through his reverie. 'Tell us what you know of the Baroness,' he said simply.

Mycroft shrugged. 'Little more than you. Our secret service knew of her existence only as an alien of dubious qualifications. She was born in Hungary of noble blood. A brilliant child, she excelled at all her subjects. In her early twenties she was crippled in a riding accident, which robbed her of a promising career in the theatre. So she turned her mind to the study of medicine, and genetics in particular.

She married a planter from Sumatra, where she lived for several years before he died under mysterious circumstances. Already a rich woman, she inherited her husband's wealth and property. After his death, she sold up and came to England three years ago, bringing her considerable fortune with her. Since then she has invested on the stock market very successfully, and has rented a string of large country houses, never staying in one of them for very long. She has a penchant for exotic pets and has been known to entertain some of the more affluent felons from our criminal fraternity, but has not herself committed any offence that we know of.'

'Until now,' piped up Lestrade. 'If I could get my hands on her!'

'As always, Lestrade, you hit the nub of the problem. Indeed, arresting the Baroness would bring all our worries to an end, for I am convinced that, without her, the rest of her organisation would be like a headless chicken, running around useless and directionless. However, we have no notion where the good lady is. Already all trails will have been wiped clean. Search Christopher Dock, The Bridge of Dreams, and Crescent Lodge and you will find no trace, no whisper, no scent of the Baroness, and that goes for her lieutenants too.'

Lestrade nodded his head wearily. 'Yes, I know. The Bridge of Dreams was razed to the ground by fire this morning.'

'So where does that leave us?'

'Very much in the dark, I fear, doctor,' said Lestrade.

'Let us not be too despondent,' said Holmes. 'We have a few days in which to track this creature to her new lair, and we have certain information that could be useful in helping us to this goal.'

'What information?' queried the Scotland Yarder.

'Of that I'm not certain. I need to ponder the situation. If ever there was a three pipe problem, this is it.'

Mycroft gave a little cough. 'I must add that our quest is not merely to find the Baroness. We must also discover this nest of giant rats and destroy them. As long as they exist no one is safe.'

'I need time to think and a good night's rest,' said Holmes, his voice sounding weary. 'I am not sure where Watson and I can lay our heads tonight. To return to Baker Street at such a time would be a foolish act.'

'I'll find you accommodation here in the guest-rooms. That is no difficulty and it will mean that you are able to report back to me as, and when, you are able. And that is something I must stress, Sherlock. This is not one of your private investigations; this is a matter of national importance. Your client is the British Government and we must be kept up to date on all matters. And there must be none of your holding things back until you deem it fit to tell us. Is that understood?' Mycroft was all but wagging his finger at his brother by the end of his speech.

Holmes flashed a brief smile in response.

'You can be assured that any request for assistance, in any shape or form, will be granted immediately if it is humanly possible.'

'That goes for Scotland Yard, too,' said Lestrade. 'My men are available to you at any hour of the day or night.'

'Thank you gentlemen. I appreciate your offers and will bear them in mind. However, I do believe that, if we are going to succeed in this matter, cunning and brainpower are the tools that will win the day, rather than force. Now, Mycroft, if you will be so good as to show us to our quarters, I think that a good night's refreshing sleep will help to put a sharp edge on the intellect.'

Making Contact

The guest-rooms in the Diogenes Club were spartan, but the clean, crisp bed sheets and the soft, down pillow soon dragged me into the arms of Morpheus where I drifted into a deep, and thankfully dreamless, sleep. However, I was awakened abruptly sometime around five in the morning when the sky was slowly beginning to lighten, nighttime's tarry black already shading to light grey. A sharp, inarticulate cry came from the next room, the one in which Sherlock Holmes was resting. Without hesitation, I pulled on a robe over my borrowed nightshift and burst into my friend's quarters.

A strange sight met my eyes. Holmes was lying on the bed, the bedclothes tossed aside and, although his eyes were closed, he was mumbling and shaking his head in agitated fashion. A sheen of sweat covered his brow. Suddenly he raised himself into a sitting position, his face twisting into a weird grimace, and then his eyes shot open. He gave another strangled, fevered cry. It seemed as though he were trapped within a horrible nightmare and was unable to break free of it.

I stepped forward and shook him by the shoulders. This had no apparent effect on him: he continued to mumble in an unintelligible fashion while shivering with fear. I called out his name, and slapped him across the face in an effort to release him from his trance. Like an underwater swimmer breaking the surface, he opened his mouth wide gasping for air; and then, remarkably, I saw consciousness returning to his wild eyes.

'Holmes,' I cried. 'Holmes, are you all right?'

He turned his head from side to side vigorously, as though shaking it free of bad thoughts. 'Watson,' he gasped, his voice finding words at last. 'Thank God, Watson. She was reaching for me. Reaching into my idle brain.'

This seemed further gibberish, and my dismayed expression halted Holmes in his tracks. He sighed heavily and wiped the sweat from his brow. 'I'm sorry, Watson, I must sound like a candidate for

Bedlam.' A feeble grin touched his gaunt features. 'Light me a cigarette, old fellow, while I bring myself round, and then I'll attempt to explain.'

I did as requested while he staggered from the bed and wrapped a robe around himself. Holmes pulled desperately on the cigarette as though it were his last, taking deep lungfuls of the tobacco. At length the nicotine seemed to steady his nerves and he turned to me with the same weak smile. 'Thank you. Rescuing me from unpleasant experiences is becoming rather a habit with you at present.' He took a final puff of the cigarette before flinging the stub into the grate.

'But what actually was the nature of this "unpleasant experience"?' I asked with some puzzlement.

'I haven't shaken her off fully. She's still here.' He tapped his head with his long forefinger.

'The Baroness?'

Holmes nodded. 'Having taken control of my mind and my will once, it appears that she still has some power over me when my brain is at rest – when I am asleep. It is as though she has her own private telegraph wire along which she sends messages to my mind. The creature called to me in my dreams. I saw her face, her eyes.' With shaking hands he reached for another cigarette.

'What does she want of you now?'

Briefly his face was enveloped in clouds of tobacco smoke. 'She wants to know where I am – what our plans are.'

'Then we are not safe here?'

Holmes shook his head. 'For the moment there is no danger. I fought against her, against those dark, penetrating, persuasive eyes. She learned nothing from me – on this occasion. But it is something we must guard against. Her hypnotic powers are so strong that they may even be able to overtake me when I am awake.'

'There must be some way you can cut off this communication.'

Suddenly Holmes froze in mid action, the cigarette held motionless two inches from his face. And then softly he said, 'Communication. Yes, communication.' Without warning, he jumped from the bed and slapped me on the back. 'Watson, you often are my torch bearer – illuminating the obvious which I sometimes fail to observe.'

I smiled in amusement at this grandiose praise, but also shook my head in bewilderment.

'Communication. It was the word you used. Communication,' Holmes attempted to explain.

'I still don't see.'

'Communication suggests a two-way interchange, does it not? The passing of an idea, conversation, a message from one to another with appropriate responses. If the Baroness has this "telegraph wire", as I called it, to my mind, then cannot messages be sent both ways? Is it not possible to learn of her plans and her whereabouts?'

'But how? She has great hypnotic powers. You do not.'

'That is true, although I have no doubt that, given the time, and the appropriate tuition, I should be able to develop the skill quite easily. However, we do not have the time – but we do have the ability to enlist the help of a master of the art.'

'Salvini.'

'Yes. He has been of great use to us already and I believe that, with his assistance, I may be able to find my way into the consciousness of Baroness Emmuska Dubeyk and learn things to our advantage.'

Fantastic as the idea was, I suddenly felt strangely confident that it would work. 'Then we must waste no more time in contacting the fellow,' I cried.

'My thought entirely,' agreed Holmes, rubbing his hands with enthusiasm. He then glanced at his watch and threw off his dressing gown. 'It is now just before six o'clock. I will see you down in the lobby in thirty minutes, ready to make an early call on Signor Salvini at his hotel.'

It was nearing eight o'clock when our cab dropped us outside the Adelphi Hotel in Enfield, some three miles from the Wood Green Empire. Holmes and I approached a sleepy clerk at the desk and requested the number of Salvini's room. Once furnished with this information, we moved to the lift to reach the fifth floor where the little hypnotist had a suite, but, as the gates of the lift slid open, there, as if by magic, was the man himself. His face beamed in recognition. 'Why, gentlemen, this is an unexpected pleasure. I did not think that we should meet again so soon.' And then he paused, the smile fading. 'You are here to see me? There is further trouble? You seek my help?'

'Indeed we do,' said Holmes.

Salvini's smile returned. 'Good. It will be a pleasure. I was just about to take my morning walk in the little park across the road, as I do every day before breakfast. Perhaps you would care to join me and, as we stroll, you can explain your dilemma and how I can be of assistance to you.'

We entered the park, which was deserted, apart from a tramp huddled up on a bench under a pile of newspapers from which heavy snores could be heard. The day was mild, but cloudy, and the sky loured gloomily over our heads like a veiled threat. Salvini walked with a bright spring in his step and at a sprightly pace. It was obvious that his morning constitutional was not meant to be a relaxing affair. Holmes explained his dream and how, despite Salvini's efforts the previous day in returning him to his rightful mind and memory, the Baroness still had the power to reach him. As he explained, the hypnotist nodded sagely. By the time my friend had concluded his narrative, we had reached a pond, at the centre of which was a small island where several ducks were congregating. At the sight of us standing on the edge of the pond, the birds waddled into the water and began swimming towards us, stirring the still surface with the ripples of their wake. Salvini took a paper bag from his pocket, retrieved several small chunks of bread, and threw them into the murky water. 'Good morning, my children,' he cooed softly as he propelled more bread towards the ducks. 'See what your papa has for you.'

Obviously this was a morning ritual with him, and he was not going to allow our presence to disrupt it. As he came to the end of the supply of bread, he held one piece up towards Holmes, a sly grin on his face. 'I wonder if you can perceive certain parallels here, Mr Holmes. These birds reacted mystically to my presence. They responded to me because I have power over them – because I have bread, something that they desire greatly. If I moved to the other side of the pond there is no doubt that they would follow me without hesitation. That is part of the secret of hypnosis. Influence that controls without question. Thank Heavens you are now in a position to question, to reject certain requests. That is why you were able to fight off this woman when she came to you in your dream. You have power too.'

'But it is a fragile power. I may not be able to resist next time.'

'Possibly. But now your mind knows instinctively to reject her power, she will have to try very much harder next time. Before then, if we can combine our minds, with your intellect and resistance and my power, perhaps we can, as you request, invade her mind and learn from it.'

Holmes grinned. 'That's it exactly.'

The little hypnotist threw the last piece of bread and it was caught by an eager bill before it hit the water. He turned and faced Holmes with a stern expression. 'I believe it is possible. But, it is something that even I, the Great Salvini, have never tried before.

It could be dangerous. However, I am willing to try, Mr Holmes, if you are.'

*   *   *

Salvini drew the curtains of his hotel room, so that only a very fine shaft of light penetrated the darkened chamber. Holmes lay on the bed, a flickering candle on the bedside table the only other form of illumination. Salvini stood by him, breathing heavily, as though involved in some preparatory exercise. His face was solemn and his brow furrowed with concern.

'Are you ready, Mr Holmes? Are you prepared to travel down that dark tunnel of unconsciousness and make contact with your enemy?'

'I am.'

'Very well, we will begin. I beseech you, Dr Watson, remain still and, whatever happens, do not utter a word unless I ask you. Is that understood?'

I nodded. 'It is, sir. But I will make notes of all that Holmes says while he is hypnotised.'

Salvini nodded. 'A wise move, doctor. It is most likely that Mr Holmes will remember nothing when he surfaces. So, then, let us begin.'

He held his pocket watch before Holmes's face, swinging the bright gold orb to and fro. 'Let your eyes follow the watch, follow the watch. Observe the brightness in the candlelight. Follow the watch. If your eyelids grow heavy, do not fight against them. Just follow the watch as long as you can. Follow the watch, until you need the darkness. Until you need sleep.'

Even I found Salvini's recital soporific and, after a short time, Holmes's eyelids did start to droop. I noticed, also, that his hands, which had been clenched, began to relax and unfurl.

Salvini continued to speak in soft crooning tones for some time, even after my friend's eyes had closed and his breathing slipped into the heavy rhythm of sleep. As he stopped talking, he picked up a pin from the bedside table. 'Now, Holmes, you are truly asleep but in my power. I can control your mind and your body. For a while you must surrender to me. Will you surrender to me? Nod your head if you will surrender to me.'

Slowly, Holmes nodded his head.

'That is good. That is good. Now you have surrendered to my will, I can tell you that until I say otherwise, you body will not feel pain. Do you understand – will not feel pain.'

Again Holmes nodded.

Salvini took the pin and pushed it into the back of Holmes's hand. I winced as the sharp point pierced the tender skin but, from my friend, there was no reaction whatsoever. Holmes's face remained still and mask-like, while his hand lay immobile as if it were that of a mannequin.

'So far, so good,' said Salvini for my benefit. 'Now comes the difficult part.'

The Game is Afoot

The hypnotist looked heavenward and crossed himself, before leaning over Sherlock Holmes and whispering softly in his ear: 'It is time, my friend, to travel. Free your mind, open up your subconscious, and we shall travel.'

Holmes's eyelids flickered momentarily and his tongue moistened his dry lips.

'In your mind I want you to reach out for the Baroness. Call her. Let your senses reach out for her. Travel down the dark corridor she has created. Enter her mind. See what she sees. Hear what she hears. Call! Call with your mind.'

My friend's face seemed drawn tight with concentration, his lips puckered and his brow furrowed. Indeed, his whole body stiffened with the effort of will.

'Breathe deeply, breathe deeply,' instructed Salvini gently. 'And tell me what you see.'

Holmes shook his head. 'Nothing.' His voice emerged as a thin dry croak. 'Dark – dark.'

'Try harder, my friend, you must try harder. Force your senses further. Push hard against the door.'

Holmes shook his head. 'Too dark.'

Salvini looked glumly at me. 'She is too strong. Too powerful.'

Suddenly Holmes began to move. Raising his head from the cushion, so that his neck muscles tightened like knotted rope, and pulling himself into a half-sitting position, he spoke. This time his voice was louder and more urgent. 'A tower – There is a tower. I can see . . . '

'What kind of tower?'

'I cannot – too dark . . . '

'Try. You must try!'

'Crooked steps – water – white letters on a wall.'

'What letters?'

'What letters?' There was a long pause and then: 'A large L – and a large E . . . '

'Give me details . . . '

'I cannot. Too dark. A chain – rusty links. A bird – a bird of prey.' And then suddenly my friend fell silent. His head dropped back on the cushion and his arms fell limply at his sides.

'You must tell me more. Give me more details,' implored Salvini, leaning closer to his subject.

'It is growing darker – growing – darker.'

By now my friend's forehead was awash with perspiration, and his knuckles were chalk white as he clenched and unclenched his fists in controlled agitation. Suddenly he gave a sharp cry and his body shuddered in an uncontrollable spasm, while his face contorted with pain.

'My God,' I cried, unable to stop myself. 'What is it?'

'Dr Watson!' hissed Salvini urgently, silencing me with a wave of his hand.

'She is aware of me,' muttered Holmes. 'She knows there is someone there . . . '

'Do not let her know it is you. Pull back now. Pull back.' Salvini leant over my friend and whispered further words into his ear, words that I could not quite distinguish, but I gathered that he was helping to bring Holmes slowly back to consciousness. At length, Holmes's body seemed to relax, and his breathing grew less laboured. The hypnotist ran his palm in a soothing gesture over Holmes's moist brow and then he turned to me. 'I am sorry I was so abrupt with you Dr Watson, but I did ask you not to say a word.'

I shook my head sadly. 'I am entirely at fault,' I confessed. 'I just hope my outburst has done no permanent harm.'

'I doubt it. I was able to draw him away from the Baroness before she could wield her full influence over him.' He gazed down at Holmes, whose face was now in total repose. Salvini gave a little smile. 'Soon our friend will be with us once more. He is now travelling back, and his normal senses are gradually returning. But I am afraid we have learned as much as we are likely to from the Baroness. She is a very strong opponent. She was able to break through my protective barrier and inflict a certain amount of pain on Holmes. That is why I called him back. It is possible she could have damaged his mind forever if he had stayed.'

I gave an involuntary shudder at the thought. 'The woman is in league with the Devil.'

'That is too simple an explanation, doctor. It is true she has developed her mind and her hypnotic powers to a remarkable degree, but that in itself is not evil. It is the use to which she puts her tremendous skills that is the Devil's work. So strong is she that she has, it would seem, steeled herself, prepared herself, for such an experiment as we have tried to perform today. It is as if the Baroness has built an invisible protection around her mind, so that no one can enter. Holmes did remarkably well to go as far as he did.'

I glanced at my notepad. 'Sadly, there is little here in payment for your joint exertions. References to a black tower, water, rusty chain, a bird of prey – and large white letters on a brick wall – whatever they may mean. I think that even Sherlock Holmes will find it impossible to construct much out of those fragments.'

Salvini shrugged. 'We both did as well as we could. Who knows, there may be something there that triggers off an idea?' So saying, he turned and spoke to his subject once more. 'You are resting after your journey, Mr Holmes. In a few moments, I will recall you to consciousness. Do you understand?'

Holmes, his eyes still closed, nodded wearily.

Salvini gave a heavy sigh. Moving away from the bed, he threw his arms wide into the air and stretched his body, releasing it from the tension it had been under. Then with two nimble strokes he pulled back the curtains, filling the room with muted daylight.

'Be a good fellow, doctor, and call for the maid and order tea. I am sure our friend will need some refreshment after his arduous journey.'

Within twenty minutes Salvini, Holmes, and I were sitting around a cosy fire in the hypnotist's suite, drinking tea like three old friends at a reunion. The reality, of course, was far more serious. Thankfully, Holmes appeared to have suffered no real ill effects from the hypnotic session, but his mind retained little memory of it.

'I can vaguely remember seeing the black tower. A tall dark finger reaching into the sky,' he said slowly, gazing off into the middle distance as though the vision of the tower were there. 'I've never seen it before, as I recall, but I certainly would recognise it again.'

'What of the references to water, and a rusty chain, and the large white letters L and E painted on a wall?' I asked.

'There was also a reference to a bird of prey,' added Salvini.

Holmes gave a dismal shrug of the shoulder. 'My mind is blank on those at the moment. I certainly don't remember their significance.'

'Tell me, Holmes,' Salvini said, leaning forward in his chair, 'do you retain any peripheral memories: smell for example?'

The detective thought for a moment, his eyes glazed in introspection, and then he wrinkled his nose. 'The smell of bitter almonds,' he said, eventually. 'And – yes – the reek of stagnant water. Or at least I think so.' He put both hands to his head. 'I'm not sure what I think at the moment. I have a thundering headache. I think the second battle of Maiwand is being conducted in my brain.' He flashed me a grim smile.

'You have had a very extraordinary experience,' said Salvini. 'Both your mind and body will be drained. Avail yourself of my couch for a few hours' natural sleep, and then you should be back to your old self.'

'I am not one for taking mid-morning naps in general, but on this occasion I believe you are right. If, of course, you think I am safe to do so.'

'Indeed. We shall be here and, if you exhibit signs of unease or distress, we shall waken you.'

'Good; then excuse me while I lie down and rest for a few hours.'

While Holmes slept, Salvini questioned me about the affair. Understandably he was curious as to who Baroness Dubeyk was, and what threat she posed to Holmes and others. I could see that having crossed mental swords with this woman, so to speak, Salvini was somewhat in awe – or perhaps simply jealous – of her remarkable talents. I knew that I could not reveal the truth surrounding our investigation, and yet I thought it inappropriate to spin our friend a thin, mendacious tale after he had been so helpful to us. I explained the delicate and confidential nature of the case but filled him in on a few details surrounding the Baroness, explaining that it was vital that we discover her whereabouts within the next few days. The hypnotist was fascinated by my recital and, although I could see that he was desperate to learn more, the natural discretion of his nature prevented him from attempting to press me further.

It was just after noon when Holmes stirred from his uninterrupted slumbers. Refreshed by sleep, his face bright and eager, he requested that I recount once more in detail what had happened, and, more particularly, what he had said during his hypnotic trance. While he puffed away on his old briar, I did as he asked, referring to my notes to give him a verbatim record of his utterances.

'They are vague small features of a large picture,' he observed when I had concluded. 'Each feature is apparently unrelated; and yet, they must be related. A black tower, uneven steps, water, a rusty chain, and those large white letters L and E.'

'There is no proof that these things are really connected with the Baroness. They may just be ideas or thoughts that came into your brain,' I said.

Salvini shook his head. 'No, doctor. He was travelling down that corridor that led to the dark lady. What Holmes experienced was directly related to the Baroness and her current surroundings. I am certain of that.'

'We must start,' said Holmes, rising from the couch and pacing the room, his head bent in thought, 'by making some educated assumptions and see if that leads us anywhere. The Baroness is unlikely to have travelled far from the city. She needs to be close to the action and the giant rat.'

At the mention of 'the giant rat', Salvini raised his brows in surprise and a question quivered on his lips, but a glance from me made him hold his tongue.

'She also needs to be close to a means of escape.'

'Water!' I exclaimed.

'Possibly.'

'So what we are looking for is a large house which resembles a black tower, near London, probably on the coast.'

'That is a logical assumption,' my friend responded, slowly, 'but water is not necessarily sea, and a black tower does not have to be a house.'

'Well she needs somewhere large to accommodate her gang, and – '

'Of course!' cried Holmes, clapping his hands together. 'Of course!' Whatever new thought had flashed into his brain, it had changed his whole demeanour. His body stiffened like a wiry dog ready for the chase, and his eyes sparkled with renewed brightness. 'We must return to London, Watson,' he continued with vigour, snatching up his coat and hat. 'I have a theory to test.'

Before I had a chance to reply, he had leapt forward and grabbed the little hypnotist by the hand, shaking it warmly. 'I really cannot thank you enough, my dear sir, for your remarkable efforts on my behalf. You have been of invaluable help and you have my deepest gratitude.'

'Mr Holmes,' stammered Salvini, taken aback by Holmes's sudden effusions.

'Not another word, please, I beg of you. If I am able to bring this case to a successful conclusion I can assure you that you will receive thanks from much higher quarters than Baker Street. Now sir, time is of the essence. Come, Watson, the game is afoot.'

CHAPTER SIXTEEN
Find the Lady

Once Sherlock Holmes and I were settled in a hansom on our way back to the heart of the city, he explained the thoughts which had suddenly galvanised his actions. 'I am sure that in this affair you will consider that I am reneging on my proud boast that I never guess. You may well have a point, but I will defend myself by saying that there are guesses and there are informed assumptions, and when one has so little data to work with one has to fall back on the latter. Assemble the scraps of knowledge you have and connect them by intuitive and practised means into a reasoned scenario. Certainly playing about with the various known elements in this way may lead to the truth.'

'And what are your assumptions?'

'Well, I have already stated them. The Baroness needs to be near London and near an escape route, while, at the same time, her lair needs to be somewhere safe, secret, and well hidden. One immediately thinks of a large house halfway between the city and the coast, a property like Crescent Lodge.'

'Indeed. As Mycroft informed us, she has lived in a series of similar houses in the last five years.'

Holmes nodded. 'But logic tells me that now she knows the authorities are on her track, she will not wish to repeat patterns. Patterns can be traced. Knowing the way her mind works, I am certain that her new bolt-hole would have been already prepared in the event of such an emergency as our escape created. All we have done is to precipitate a move she would have made anyway.'

'To go underground as it were?'

'Yes, Watson. The lady was well aware that, as soon as her machinations were set in motion, she would not be safe. She knew that the might of Scotland Yard and the British Government would be working all out to discover her whereabouts and, therefore, she would be in great danger.'

'So if she is not in a large house in the suburbs somewhere, where is she?'

'I am not absolutely sure, but as the children say in their game, I am getting a little warmer. Certainly, I am warmer than I was first thing this morning, thanks to our friend Salvini.'

I shook my head. 'I am not sure I understand.'

'Return to our educated assumptions. We have little to play with, but we must work on those fragments that I retrieved during my hypnotic trance. We must make some sense of them. Now, water, stagnant water it was, and rusty chains suggest docks or a canal somewhere. I will plump for a canal.'

'Why?'

'Because I think we are looking at a warehouse or a factory somewhere in London.'

'A factory?'

'Deserted, of course. Owned by a firm that has gone out of business.'

'But why a factory?'

Holmes leaned forward, his eyes gleaming with excitement in the dull light of the cab. 'Think about it, Watson, a black tower reaching up into the sky – a round black tower.' He lifted up a solitary finger of his gloved hand and held it before my face. 'Think of a skyline, my friend.'

'Great heavens, Holmes, I see what you mean: it's a chimney – a factory chimney.'

Holmes gave a harsh guffaw of pleasure and sat back in the cab. 'A factory owned by a company, the name of which begins with the letters L E. Or those are the main initials of the company.'

'Why, this is marvellous!' I exclaimed in my excitement.

'Marvellous assumptions, maybe. They may all turn out to be built on shifting sand. However it is all we have for the moment. I have not yet deduced where the bird of prey fits into this uncertain picture.'

'What are our plans?'

'We shall return to our temporary base, the Diogenes Club, and check if there are any messages there for us from Mycroft or Lestrade, and then I suggest we take a spot of lunch. It has been a long morning, and we set out without breakfast.' He smiled and gazed out of the cab window.

'Don't be infuriating, Holmes. What then?'

His smile broadened. 'Then we shall carry out some research at Companies House.'

There were messages from both Mycroft and Lestrade. Mycroft's was brief, stating that the Prime Minister had been informed of our involvement in the matter and that he had given us his blessing. He also reminded Holmes that it was essential for him to keep in touch with regular reports.

'I will,' said my friend, almost to himself. 'When there is something to report, I will report it.'

The message from Lestrade was more pertinent to the case. The police had raided Crescent Lodge at dawn to find the place empty apart from the body of a black man, who appeared 'to have been mauled by a wild animal'. Alice had been taken into police protection and Dr Karswell had disappeared.

Holmes read the messages without comment before passing them to me. 'The fellow mauled by a wild animal is obviously Josiah Barton,' I observed.

Holmes nodded. 'A fitting end for the scoundrel who took great pleasure and large profit from the infliction of pain on other animals. There is enough savagery in the wild without the need to create it artificially for the entertainment of the depraved.'

For a moment the image of the rat arena, awash with blood, flashed into my mind. 'However, his death is no great loss to the Baroness,' continued Holmes. 'His usefulness was over anyway. He only provided a testing ground for the mutant rats as they developed in size and ferocity. Now the testing is over, Karswell is the dangerous one. It is he who has the knowledge regarding the plague bacillus, which is to be injected into the rats before their release.'

'How many of these damned creatures are there?'

'I don't know. There is the giant brute of a mother, the creature you encountered on the *Matilda Briggs*. It was clear that she was due to give birth to her monstrous litter within a few days. A normal rat usually has about five or six offspring, but this species may be different. Once they are born it can only be a matter of days before they are ready, and lethal enough, to be released on to the streets of London.'

'And they are lodged in this warehouse where the Baroness is to be found?'

'For all our sakes let us pray that is the case.'

'You talked earlier of lunch, but this conversation has robbed me of all appetite,' I remarked glumly, my heart heavy with dark foreboding.

Holmes grinned. 'Nonsense, old fellow, once I propel you through the door of Marcini's and you catch a whiff of their excellent spaghetti bolognese, the old hunger pangs will return in double measure. Trust me.'

As always, I did trust Sherlock Holmes and, although my mind was swirling with gloomy apprehensions, once I was seated in the restaurant with a pre-prandial glass of sherry, my spirits rose as my companion had predicted. Holmes now seemed remarkably relaxed. The lines of recent tension, and the dark circles beneath his eyes, had all but disappeared, and he chatted easily and casually on a stream of diverse topics, never once mentioning the dreadful business in which we were embroiled.

At the end of the meal, during which we quaffed a half-bottle of Chianti, I felt almost sanguine, until it struck me that Holmes's exhibition of apparent good spirits was perhaps all an act, performed specially for my benefit. He was attempting, quite successfully, to buoy me up, to prevent me from dwelling on the almost impossible task that lay before us. As the waiter presented us with our coffees, I smiled at Holmes and patted his arm. 'It's good to have you back to your old self again,' I said earnestly.

My friend lit a cigarette and returned my smile. 'It's good to be back.' Then suddenly his face grew serious and he looked directly into my eyes. 'This is a tight corner, Watson. The tightest. But we'll fight our way out of it, don't you worry. We'll fight our way out. We have to.'

After lunch we took a cab to City Road near Moorgate where Companies House was located. It was a dreary part of London, where both the traffic and pedestrians were scarce and the streets had a strange melancholy air about them. We entered the age-weathered offices and Holmes made enquiries concerning firms that had gone out of business in the last twenty years. We were led by a sprightly young clerk to a dingy cell where he removed a very large ledger from a row of sagging shelves. He blew a coating of dust off the spine and placed it on a table near to the grimy window, which, apart from a solitary gas lamp that flickered feebly, was the only source of illumination.

'This contains records from 1850 to 1859,' said the clerk quietly, as though he were in a church or some other holy place. 'The remaining years are in the subsequent volumes along the same shelf.' He pointed. 'Please replace the volumes carefully after use. Good hunting, gentlemen.' He flashed a mechanical smile and left us to our own devices.

We pulled a couple of rickety chairs up to the table in preparation for our search. 'Now remember,' said Holmes, 'we are looking for a firm whose initials are L E or one that begins with those letters. Two pairs of eyes are better than one, Watson, especially in this dim light. So we'll scan each volume together. It should not take us too long.'

He pulled open the first ledger and groaned. Looking at the tight scrawl on the first page, I saw the reason for his dismay. The firms were not listed in alphabetical order but by the date they ceased to trade. There was going to be no short cut in our search. Placing his long forefinger at the top of the column on the first page he slowly drew it down: Page's Boot and Shoe Rejuvenators Ltd.; Taylor's Carriage Co.; Ambrose of Houndsditch, Medical Suppliers; The Empire Button Co. Ltd.; Sackville's Fruit Salts Works; Jerkins, Gun and Rifle Manufacturer; and so the list went on, with all the names etched on the white page in the same crabbed hand.

'We shall go blind before we discover anything,' I muttered.

'*Nil desperandum*, Watson,' responded Holmes, whipping the first page over with a flourish, only to reveal an almost identical page: Connolly Tyres Ltd.; Barrington's Soaps; Caldicott, Suppliers of Hemp and Jute Ltd.; and Harvey's Ceramics of Islington. There were hundreds of names, companies that for one reason or another had fallen by the wayside on that great thoroughfare of profit and success – but none revealing a suitable L or E. After an hour we had completed the first volume and moved on to the second. By now the handwriting had changed and the new author had kindly placed the company's name in upper case letters. With this bonus and our growing expertise at reading the information, we were able to speed up, with the result that we were on to the 1870s in less than forty minutes.

And so we ploughed on, reading line after line, page after page. The handwriting changed approximately every seven years, while the variety of the casualties seemed to increase; but there were no firms with the letter L or E that fitted our requirements. Within three hours we were reaching the end of the last ledger and I turned the final page with a sinking feeling. The daylight had almost gone and our search was carried out by means of the meagre erratic flame of the gas mantle. Half way down the page the entries came to an abrupt stop with Benson's Mattress Company (Clapham) Ltd.

I sat back in my chair with a heavy sigh. 'We must have got it wrong. Either L E does not stand for the name of the firm or they do not use a warehouse near a canal or the docks.'

Holmes did not reply, but stared at the gas flame as though he was hypnotised. 'The fact that the letters were painted on a brick wall certainly supports that hypothesis. We are missing a link, that is all,' he announced softly. 'Just one link – and it is staring us in the face.'

'Well what about this bird of prey?' I pondered. 'What was it? A hawk, an eagle, or a kestrel maybe?'

Holmes shook his head. 'The image was not clear, a mere outline – but wait a minute.' Suddenly his voice sounded full of excitement. 'It was *obviously* an eagle.'

'How can you be so sure now?

'Because the fact has been staring me in the face and I failed to recognise it. An eagle. Of course! Think, Watson, the last two letters of the word are L and E. Whatever company we are searching for, their name is Eagle. Heavens, Watson I was so stupid as to assume that L E were the first letters of the name. They are in fact the last letters.'

I looked at the row of ledgers. 'So we begin again.'

'We begin again.'

Thankfully, this time we did not have to search for long. We reversed the process by starting on the most recent volume and working backwards. By 1876 we had struck gold.

'We have it, m'boy, we have it,' Holmes cried in triumph. He drew his long forefinger along the line which read 'Eagle Printing Co., Solomon Wharf, Solomon Road, Deptford'.

'That will be near Rotherhithe by the Deptford Reach.'

'On the Thames – only a few miles from Christopher Dock.' Holmes gave a barking laugh. 'Ha! See how brazen the lady is. It is as though she has just moved next door, while the authorities are seeking very far and very wide for her, never thinking that she would remain in the same vicinity.'

At this moment the door opened and the young clerk entered. He gave a little cough to attract our attention. 'I am afraid I shall have to ask you to leave, gentlemen. We are about to close for the day.'

'Of course,' said I, rising to my feet.

'I hope you have found what you wanted.'

'Indeed we have,' announced Holmes, replacing the ledger on the shelf with a theatrical flourish. 'Indeed we have.'

I had fully expected my friend to make his way to Scotland Yard with the newly gleaned information regarding the Baroness, but I suppose I should always expect the unexpected from Sherlock Holmes. However, I was more than a little shocked when, after successfully hailing a cab, he gave the driver our destination in clear ringing tones: '221B Baker Street, and step on it, cabby!'

'Are you mad?' I cried. 'Surely that is the last place on earth we should go?'

'Oh, Watson, I am tired of living the gypsy life, and I am tired of wearing borrowed clothes. I crave the comforts of home.'

'Those comforts may include a murderous attack upon you. And me.'

'Possibly,' he replied, with infuriating smugness. 'However, I really do think you over-dramatise the situation. By now the Baroness will have firmly established that I have not returned to my quarters – have not *dared* to return to my quarters for the very reason you suggest – and she will have called off most, if not all, of her men watching the address. In any case I wish to play her at her own game. Baker Street is the last place the dark lady expects to find me and, therefore, that is where I shall be. In essence it is the safest of locations.'

'I am not convinced.'

'Well then, to placate you and to ensure our safety, we shall indulge in a little subterfuge on our arrival.'

On nearing our destination, Holmes instructed the cab to drop us at the corner of Marylebone Road and Baker Street. As we stood on the crowded pavement, my friend pulled me to him and whispered in my ear: 'Now, Watson, I want you to walk on to 221B. Be as nonchalant in your approach as possible. Be as unsubtle as you wish: whistle, swing your cane with aplomb – that sort of thing. Be noticed. Meanwhile I'll hold back and keep my eye out for any suspicious-looking fellows who take particular interest in your arrival. I will be with you very shortly, all being well.' So saying he pushed me forward down the street, while he fell back into the myriad of passers-by, and slipped out of sight.

I did as instructed. Whistling a melody from *Iolanthe*, I swung my cane casually and gazed about me with a relaxed smile upon my face. As I did so, I scrutinised the faces of those I passed. None seemed suspicious or dangerous in the slightest. Nor did anyone seem the least bit interested in me. Perhaps, I pondered, I had over-estimated the danger involved in our return to Baker Street, and this little charade was Holmes's way of demonstrating the fact.

I approached 221B and experienced a pleasurable inner glow as my hand reached the knocker on that familiar door. It was a sentimental glow, I admit, but it cheered me and lifted my spirits. Within moments I was admitted by a flustered Mrs Hudson.

'Am I glad to see you, Dr Watson?' she said, closing the door and shutting out the noise of the street. 'You are a sight for sore eyes and no mistake.' She gave a gentle laugh. 'I don't think I'll ever get used to you and Mr Holmes disappearing for days on end while you're off on one of your investigations, leaving me here to wonder when I'll see you again – *if* I'll see you again. Indeed, I had hoped when you returned that Mr Holmes would be with you.'

'He will arrive shortly,' I reassured her.

'Thank goodness. This place has been like a circus in the last few days. There have been visitors galore. The police, Mr Holmes's brother, numerous clients, and some strange fellows who wouldn't state their business – all wanting to see Mr Holmes.'

'Well don't fuss yourself any further. We have returned.'

'Indeed we have,' came a voice from the top of the stairs.

Both Mrs Hudson and I turned our gaze to the landing and there, standing before us, partly in shadow, was Sherlock Holmes. He came down stairs to join us, a broad grin wreathing his features.

'Oh, Mr Holmes, you are one for surprises. How on earth did you get in?'

'The back way.' His eyes twinkled mischievously.

'There isn't a back way,' our landlady observed.

'I am afraid I exercised my joint skills of shinning up drainpipes and breaking and entering.'

'Really, Mr Holmes. I hope you did no damage.'

'Nothing very substantial.'

Mrs Hudson clicked her tongue in disapproval, but a gentle smile of amusement lit her face.

'And I suppose all this was in aid of some investigation or other.'

'As always. Now, Mrs Hudson, pray return to your quarters, for I am expecting a rather unpleasant visitor at any moment, and Watson and I will have to deal with him in a none too decorous fashion. Ah, this must be the fellow now.'

A loud knocking broke into Holmes's speech.

'Now, go along with you,' said my companion, gently shooing Mrs Hudson into her sitting-room.

'Whatever you do, take care not to damage my china ornaments,' she said as a genuine entreaty, before disappearing behind her door.

The knock came again, resonating in the high hallway.

'Impatient fellow,' Holmes observed languidly, and with neat, precise movements he turned to me, the gentleness fading rapidly from his features. 'Now, Watson,' he said in a harsh whisper, 'if I am not very much mistaken our caller is Gunson, one of the Baroness's thugs, eager to discover why you are here and where I am. Let him in while I position myself behind the door with my revolver.'

The harsh knock came yet again, louder and more insistent this time.

I nodded my head in understanding and called out 'Coming' to the impatient visitor outside.

Holmes slipped to the side and flattened himself against the wall as I opened the door. Standing before me was a tall, blond, brawny fellow in seaman's garb. I had seen him before. He was the sailor from Christopher Dock.

'Hello, Dr Watson,' he said with a cold arrogance, his blue eyes glazed in an unblinking stare.

'What do you want?'

'To start with, I want to come in.'

'For what purpose?'

'I don't intend to discuss the matter on the pavement,' he snarled, producing a pistol from his belt and pushing it into my stomach. 'Shall we move inside?'

I stepped back, allowing the fellow to cross the threshold. He slammed the door behind him and leaned against it. As he did so, Holmes stepped forward and clapped his revolver to the side of the intruder's head.

'Drop your gun, and please do not make any sudden movements; this trigger is somewhat sensitive and I am rather on edge today.'

Without a word the fellow allowed his gun to drop from his grip.

'Now follow Watson up the stairs into our sitting-room, where we can have that chat you wanted – but it will be on my terms.'

It was an especial pleasure to enter our sitting-room once more. Those shabby but cosy quarters had all the attraction of a royal palace to me after the wild events of the last forty-eight hours. And it was as if we had never been away. Everything was in its place, with a fire burning low in the grate.

Holmes pushed our antagonist over the threshold and ordered him to take a seat by the fire, while he remained standing. 'I want the answers to some very important questions, Gunson. Where is your mistress, Baroness Dubeyk? And where is the giant rat?'

'You do not imagine that I will tell you, do you?' our prisoner replied without emotion, the words uttered in a mechanical fashion.

'I am of a mind that you can be persuaded,' replied Holmes, cocking the pistol.

He gave a dull laugh. 'Shoot me if you wish – if you dare.'

I saw a flicker of uncertainty light Holmes's eyes. I knew that he couldn't – wouldn't – shoot, or even wound, the fellow in cold blood. That sort of violence was not his moral way, no matter how desperate our situation.

'If you will not tell me willingly, then I shall have to resort to other means – like hypnotism.'

At this, Gunson's smug smile evaporated immediately and he shifted uneasily in the chair. 'What do you know of hypnotism?' he said, attempting a sneer.

'Enough.'

'Then you should know that you cannot make a subject reveal what he doesn't want to.'

'Oh, yes. Unless, of course, his will is weakened by drugs.'

'By drugs?'

'By drugs.'

The sailor looked decidedly concerned now. With startling accuracy, Holmes had discovered his Achilles heel: hypnosis. As a disciple of the Baroness he would know all about the powers of this particular practice. It struck me then that, with his dilated pupils and stilted speech, and his apparent lack of fear of Holmes's gun, he was already under a hypnotic spell, programmed never to cooperate with the enemy. As soon as I thought of this possibility, I knew I was right. He was, for all intents and purposes, the Baroness's puppet, controlled at a distance like an automaton.

'I reckon I shall have to call your bluff,' snapped the sailor suddenly with feigned bravado, but I observed a trickle of perspiration emerging from his side-whiskers and rolling down his cheek. This man was frightened.

Holmes shrugged nonchalantly and handed me his revolver. 'Keep an eye on our visitor, Watson, while I make the appropriate preparations for my "bluff".' He moved to his chemical bench, threw off his coat, and bent over a rack of small bottles neatly labelled in his own precise hand, his face a mask of concentration. 'A strong percentage, I think,' he muttered, almost to himself, as he located his hypodermic syringe. 'That should speed matters up and quickly eliminate our friend's reluctance to cooperate.' With a bottle of cocaine in one hand, he lifted the syringe up, the fine needle glinting in the dim gaslight, and returned his gaze to our prisoner. 'As you can see, this is no bluff. We shall soon have the truth out of you.'

At the sight of the needle, the sailor gave a groan of despair, gripping the sides of the chair in desperation; and then suddenly, without any warning, the fellow jumped to his feet, flinging the chair back behind him. His eyes widened into a terrified stare like that of a trapped animal.

'Watch him, Watson,' cried my friend, dropping his apparatus onto the bench and moving forward.

Like a drunken man, the sailor lurched towards the fireplace and then turned round to face us. His eyes were glazed and unblinking as he spoke: 'You will never find out. You will never find out anything from me.' So saying he thrust his hand into his jacket pocket. It looked to me as though he was attempting to retrieve a concealed weapon, and I fired my gun, wounding the fellow in the shoulder. A small badge of red, identifying the location of the wound, appeared on the rough material of his jacket. With a gasp of pain, he stumbled backwards, his left arm flailing to steady himself. It took purchase on the mantelpiece, scattering papers and small items, sending them cascading into the hearth. In his other hand he held not a weapon but a small white pill which, with a defiant glance in my direction, he popped into his mouth.

'Stop him!' cried Holmes, who flung himself at the man, bringing him down upon our hearthrug in a rugby tackle. His hands reached for the fellow's jaw, pulling it open, frantically trying to retrieve the pill, but it was too late. Already Gunson's sturdy frame was convulsed in the agony of death throes. In less than a minute he lay still, all life having left his body.

Holmes gave a cry of frustration and pulled himself to his feet. His face was white with anger – anger directed at himself. 'I should have suspected such a thing.'

'He has committed suicide?' I asked, a mixture of uncertainty and incredulity clouding my mind.

Instead of replying, Holmes knelt by the body and extracted another white pill from the sailor's jacket. Placing it in the palm of his hand, he held it out to me to inspect. 'The last resort,' he said, his voice charged with emotion. 'Innocent looking thing, isn't it? Probably cyanide. Such is the power of that woman.'

'You mean to say that he was so scared of her he would prefer to die rather than reveal her secrets?'

'Artificially scared. The idea had been planted in his brain.'

'By hypnosis?'

'Yes.'

Holmes was interrupted by a sharp staccato knock on our sitting-room door, and the muffled cry of distress from our landlady, obviously concerned by the sound of the pistol shot. 'Mr Holmes, Dr Watson, are you all right? For Heaven's sake, what is going on?'

My friend moved to the door and, without opening it, responded to Mrs Hudson's queries. 'There is nothing to worry about, Mrs Hudson. Watson and I are just carrying out a small experiment.'

'Experiment!' The note of apprehension had been replaced by one of indignation. 'There was a gunshot! You could warn a person!'

'Our apologies. You will be pleased to learn that our little experiment is completed now.'

'Well, I hope you clear up after you,' came the final retort as we heard our landlady retreat down the stairs, back to her own quarters.

Holmes gave me an embarrassed grin, but his features darkened immediately as his glance fell upon the dead man on our hearthrug.

'Through my own laxity, we have lost a wonderful opportunity, not only to confirm our theory regarding the whereabouts of the Baroness and her foul mutant rat, but also to learn more about her plans.'

'You cannot blame yourself. What we have witnessed here is the most remarkable example of the power of fear and hypnotic control. Surely it is unique in the annals of crime?'

Holmes nodded. 'I believe so; but I should have been prepared for such a possibility. I have experienced first hand the incredible force of this woman. I should have been able to predict the full scope of her hypnotic influence.' He gave a great sigh and rubbed his face with his long narrow fingers. It was as though he was trying to clear his mind, wipe away the regret, the lost opportunities and possibilities. 'Let us hope it is as Tennyson has it, that "sorrow makes us wise".'

'What is our next move?'

Holmes looked at the dead man. 'A proper disposal of this fellow will have to wait. We have more urgent business to attend to.'

'I agree, but we cannot leave him here. What if Mrs Hudson comes in?'

Holmes gave an unstable chuckle. 'Indeed. I think we should be in search of new quarters in that eventuality. He can lie in my bedroom for the time being. I shall certainly not require its benefits this night. Come let's "lug the guts into the neighbour room".'

Once the body was safely stowed in Holmes's bedroom, I poured brandies for us, which we drank quickly and in silence.

'Now for tonight's activities,' said Holmes at length. 'I must ascertain that we have been on the right track in supposing that our enemy has decamped to the empty premises of the Eagle Printing Company by paying a visit to Rotherhithe.'

'You cannot go alone. It is too dangerous and our time is short.'

'I am glad you said that, Watson. Another pair of eyes and an extra gun would be most useful. Come with me, by all means. I did not automatically include you in my plans because there is certain to be great danger in such a venture and you have already risked your life on more than one occasion during this investigation – but, if the truth be known, your help will be invaluable this evening.'

'I am not talking about myself. You must inform Lestrade and he'll get a body of men to surround the place. On our own we should be too vulnerable.'

'And what if I am wrong? What if this warehouse turns out to be empty?'

I shook my head. 'You do not believe you are wrong, do you?'

Holmes hesitated before replying, but I knew the answer. 'Of course you don't,' I continued rapidly. 'This is no time for tackling it alone, Holmes. What if you are captured again or killed? What then? You must bring in the official police. You promised to keep the Inspector in the picture.'

Holmes shook his head. 'I never actually agreed. I only nodded my head when Lestrade made the request – the order.'

I felt my anger rising at this flippant response. 'That is merely semantics, Holmes. However much you like to act on your own, this case is too big, and the outcome too crucial, to indulge yourself in this way.'

'Watson, what you do not seem to realise is that it is important to approach this matter with extreme stealth. An army of clod-hopping constables arriving on the scene would soon result in confusion and mayhem – providing a convenient smoke screen for our main antagonist to escape. A man on his own – two men if you like – could achieve so much. Stealth and discretion will win the day, not brute force and ignorance.'

I could see that Holmes had a point, but I was still convinced that for him to act as a solitary agent was taking too great a risk. I expressed this view warmly, pointing out that there was still a danger that the Baroness could retain some hypnotic control over him once he was close to her again. I could see that this final point struck home. It was something that he had not considered. He closed his eyes, dropped his chin on his chest, and remained deep in silent thought for some five minutes. At length he rose, walked to the window, and gazed out. He then consulted his pocket watch.

'Holmes?' I said.

He gave me a sharp glance as though he had just remembered my presence. 'You have made some valid points, Watson,' he observed quietly, 'but I am entrenched in my belief that I should go without police involvement. However – ' He held his hand up to prevent me from interrupting him. 'However, I can see the benefit of a compromise.'

'Compromise? What do you mean?'

'I mean that I shall still go to Rotherhithe on my own, leaving you behind, but, at a time to be arranged by us, you will contact Lestrade at the Yard. Tell him the whole story, making sure to stand well back until he has finished exploding, and then accompany him and his army of constables to Solomon Wharf in Rotherhithe.'

'I still don't think you should you go alone. It is so very dangerous.'

'Danger is part of my trade, Watson,' Holmes responded briskly. 'Now, do you agree with my suggested compromise?'

'Apparently I have little choice.'

Holmes raised an eyebrow. 'Apparently?'

After some hesitation I nodded. 'Very well.'

'Good man,' my friend grinned, and clapped me on the shoulder. 'I knew I could rely on you. Now, it is nearing eight o'clock. Allowing time for me to change into my own clothes, and the cab ride to Rotherhithe, I should be at the Eagle Printing factory some time after nine. If you contact Lestrade at ten that will allow me approximately two hours before you and he arrive with reinforcements.'

'I will not fail you.'

'Thank you.'

Within ten minutes, I was shaking my friend's hand as he stood on the threshold of our sitting-room, ready to depart.

'For goodness' sake, take especial care tonight,' I said, clasping his hand all the tighter.

He nodded. 'I will. I will.' A grim smile passed fleetingly across his face and then he was gone.

As I returned to my chair by the fire I felt an overwhelming sense of unease. A thought began to nag at the back of my mind that I should not have allowed Holmes to go on this perilous mission, and that it was foolish and weak of me to agree to his compromise. I wound my watch and checked the time. It was a quarter past eight. Perhaps I should ignore Holmes's arrangements and take a cab directly to Scotland Yard. But, however strong this urge was, I knew I could not respond to it. I had given my word to Holmes and I had never before broken it at any time in our friendship. I was not about to start now.

I tried to take my mind off the matter by picking up a novel, but the words paraded before my eyes without meaning or sense. Constantly my mind strayed back to the Baroness and the giant rat. Any wall I attempted to construct in order to shield my mind from such gloomy thoughts was torn down before it had been fully built. In frustration I tossed the book aside. My hand wavered over the decanter, but I pulled it away. More than anything I would need a clear head tonight.

I began pacing the floor, occasionally glancing out of the window. The lamps were lit all along Baker Street, sending their pale amber pools of light down onto the pavement below. I checked my watch again. It was just after eight-thirty. I was tempted to shake it in case it had stopped, but I observed the tireless second hand gliding around the face as normal. Holmes had only been gone some fifteen minutes!

I resumed my seat and, with tingling nerves, waited.

Some time later natural tiredness came to my rescue and, with the help of the warm fire, I began to nod. I was propelled into sudden, clear-headed wakefulness by the sound of heavy footsteps hurrying up the stairs. I had just risen to my feet when the door burst open and Mycroft Holmes entered. He was red-faced and perspiring profusely, while his chest rose and fell like a wheezy bellows. In his left hand he clutched a newspaper. It took him some moments before he caught his breath well enough to speak.

'Where is he?' he cried, before slumping down into the nearest chair. 'For Heaven's sake, where is he?'

The Enemy's Lair

Mycroft Holmes gazed at me with his piercing blue eyes. 'Come, Watson, it is a simple enough query,' he said irritably, his words still escaping in wheezy gasps.

'He has gone in search of the Baroness,' I replied simply, not really knowing how much I should reveal.

Mycroft's eyes bulged in anger. 'I knew it! I knew it! I can never trust my brother to play the game by anyone's rules but his own. He was to report to me if there were any developments in this matter.' He threw his arms up in frustration. 'And has he? No, he has not. Instead, he is out there, somewhere, risking his own life and placing us all in jeopardy simply because he is not a team player.'

'He thought it for the best.'

'Of course he did. The best for *him*. You know, Watson, you are partly to blame for this. You are his closest friend; surely you could have persuaded him, convinced him of the error of his ways?'

'Believe me, I tried . . . ' I began lamely. I had never seen Mycroft in such a flustered temper before. Usually he was a calm, collected man with an aura of confident self-possession, but now he seemed decidedly shaken and emotional.

He looked at me hard for some moments; then his features softened and something of the old composure returned. 'Of course you did, Watson. My apologies to you. I, above all others, should know that once Sherlock has an idea in his head not even the great Jehovah can persuade him to act differently. And I am sure he believes he is acting in the best interests of all. I simply wish he had contacted me. Instead, I had to find out from one of my men that "Mr Holmes is back in his old quarters". There have been developments, you see.' He held up the newspaper he had been clasping in his hand since his arrival. 'She has been in contact.'

At this statement I felt the cold, clammy chill of fear in my heart. 'May I see?'

Mycroft unfolded the newspaper and handed it to me. 'Half-way down the personal column – a message from The Piper,' he said matter of factly, his voice having returned to its normal pitch and delivery.

I soon found the relevant message. It read: 'Due to the release from our charge of a certain party we now find it necessary to take action sooner than anticipated. The money, in gold ingots, must be ready for delivery tomorrow night. Time and place to be notified later. No further action must be taken until twenty-four hours after delivery to ensure safety. The Piper.'

'She has us chained like a bear at the stake, Watson. Any attempt to foil her operations now could precipitate disaster.'

'Do you mean that you have decided to pay the money?'

Mycroft ran a large handkerchief over his damp forehead. 'I have just spent two hours at Number Ten, discussing the matter with the Prime Minister and some members of the cabinet. The risks are too great to call this woman's bluff. There is no light in our own investigations as to her whereabouts, and we had not heard from Sherlock. On balance, the government cannot see any other alternative.'

'But this is monstrous. You have no guarantee that once the Baroness has the gold she will not carry out her threat anyway.'

Mycroft nodded gravely. 'I know. If only Sherlock had managed to come up with a definite lead – '

'But he has.'

'What!'

'He has discovered the location of her centre of operations.'

'Then why in the name of all that's wonderful did he not tell me?' He gave a sardonic laugh and answered his own question. 'I know: he wanted to act alone.'

I nodded. 'But I was to inform Lestrade at ten o'clock.'

'I think you had better tell me the whole story, Doctor.'

*   *   *

As I was relating the day's adventures to Mycroft, Sherlock Holmes had arrived in the vicinity of Solomon Road in Rotherhithe. He paid off the cabby and affected to enter a public house on the corner, but he simply merged into the shadows by the doorway until he heard the clip clop of the cab horse fading into the distance. Then he was out on the street again making for his destination.

Solomon Road was a long, bleak industrial thoroughfare; there were no houses or shops to be seen. High factory and warehouse walls towered above him on either side of the narrow road. He found himself the solitary pedestrian in this gloomy environment. It was a dark night, with the pale moon held prisoner behind a large bank of ragged clouds, and there was a fine veil of drizzle hanging in the air.

After five minutes of walking he came to the Eagle Printing Co., which was surrounded by a tall wooden fence topped by rolls of barbed wire. The fence, covered by bill posters advertising various products, was punctuated mid-way along its stretch by a pair of stout, solid iron gates, which bore the name of the company in a curved iron sign above. The gates were locked and chained with a heavy padlock. Extracting a small bull's-eye lantern from the folds of his coat, Holmes examined the lock: it was crusted in rust. It was obvious to him that the gates had not been used since the factory closed down and, therefore, there must be another entrance, probably concealed.

Sherlock Holmes walked past the gate to the furthest extremity of the fence that ended by a grain warehouse, which was also in darkness. He looked back along the length of the fence and saw nothing that suggested a means of entry. Slowly and cautiously he retraced his footsteps. He had just passed the gate when something caught his eye on the roadway, which was shiny from the fine rain. Mud had collected in the gutter along the road, making a soft slope up from the cobbles to the pavement. Imprinted in the mud at one point, at right angles to the pavement, were two narrow grooves about five feet apart. Holmes afforded himself a brief smile. These were marks made by carriage wheels, and yet they seemed to lead up to the fence. Holmes reasoned that, however impossible the idea of a carriage passing through a solid wooden barrier, there must be some element of truth in the observation.

Once again he retrieved his lantern and examined the fence. It looked bland and innocent enough but, when he leant his weight against the rough timbers they did seem to sway and give a little. He flashed the lantern further up the fence, its beam falling on a poster for Hornung's Rejuvenation Elixir. Holmes could see at once that this poster was fresher than its neighbours. It bore none of the grime and browning print of the other bills posted along the fence. It obviously required closer inspection. However, the poster was situated just above head height and therefore was difficult to reach. Holmes looked around and spied a wooden box on the other side of the road. He retrieved it and stood it by the fence. Standing on the box raised his height about another two feet. Now he was almost on a level with the poster. He did not need the aid of the lantern to see that there was in fact a little door about six inches square at the corner of the poster – just big enough to push one's arm through. The small hinges and edges were cunningly disguised by the illustration on the poster.

Gingerly, Holmes pressed on the little door and it swung back. He peered through. In the gloom beyond he was just able to make out a large brick building with the letters Eagle Printing Co. painted in white. He felt a tingle of satisfaction as he recognised the lettering as that he had seen while under hypnosis. He allowed himself a gentle smile, but this quickly disappeared as he realised there was no sign of light, or noise, from the building. Surely the Baroness could not have moved her base of operations again? Whatever the situation, he would still have to investigate.

He pushed his arm through the aperture and soon found what he expected to be there. His hand came into contact with two metal chains and a pulley system. Within moments he had identified the slacker of the two chains and had begun to tug on it. Slowly a portion of the fence began to fall away, swinging back like a gate. He pulled the chain sufficiently to create a small gap, which would allow him entry into the grounds beyond. Once inside he hesitated. Should he leave this hidden gate slightly ajar to aid his speedy exit if required, and also to provide Lestrade and his troops with a hint as to how to enter this fortress? If he did, and it was spotted by one of the Baroness's men, then it alerted the enemy that there was a spy in the camp. This eventuality would reduce drastically his chances of success. On balance, he decided to close the gate.

Sherlock Holmes took a risk by switching on his bull's-eye lantern to illuminate his path towards the main building. The beam picked out a track across the wasteland with its overgrown weeds, discarded drums of printing ink, and other debris. At the side of the building he spied a fire escape, which led up to the roof. Without hesitation he clambered up and hauled himself on to the flat roof. From here he had a clear view of the surroundings. Behind the building he saw the curve of the Thames and, moored virtually below him, was a ship. He lay down, with his head hanging over the end of the building, so that he could study the vessel. He felt sure that it was the *Matilda Briggs*, although the name was different. He could just make out the freshly painted letters, *Gypsy Sprite*. There were some lights aboard, but no sign of movement or people.

He pulled himself back and examined his surroundings. At the centre of the roof was a raised door, which obviously allowed entrance down into the building. On examining it he discovered, as expected, that it was locked. However, the wood was wet and old and after two blows with his boot, Holmes had managed to split the wood around the lock enough for him to wrench open the door.

He then waited, his heart thumping with excitement: waited to see or hear if his exertions had roused anyone below. He heard nothing. Retrieving his pistol from his coat pocket, Sherlock Holmes descended a rickety staircase into the building: the enemy's lair.

The Giant Rat of Sumatra

With bated breath, Sherlock Holmes slipped down a short wooden ladder and landed nimbly on a rickety metal gallery, which clung precariously to the walls of the factory, running a circuit of the building some twenty-five feet from the ground. There was a narrow stairway down to the ground floor situated at the corner on Holmes's right.

Peering over the gallery rail, he could see directly below him the huge, rusting steam engine, which once upon a time had run the great printing presses. These were now absent, but shaded markings on the stone floor indicated where they had stood. A large pipe ran from the base of the engine and disappeared into the far wall, en route to the chimney. The cavernous building was illuminated by a row of electric lights strung on makeshift hooks secured to the girders, which criss-crossed the factory just below the gallery. A small generator hummed quietly in the shadows by the door. Apart from the illumination, the place had an air of dereliction and decay. However, what galvanised the attention of Sherlock Holmes and caused his heart to beat faster was a large rectangular object placed in the centre of the building. He had seen it once before. It was a large cage some six feet high and eight feet long, the front of which was covered by a sheet of heavy sacking in order to conceal the contents. But Holmes knew, with heart-stopping certainty, what lay behind that innocuous brown sacking: it was the rat – the giant rat of Sumatra.

Here it was then. He had been correct in his deductions. The mutant creature, which threatened the lives of thousands of people and, indeed, the stability of the city, was but a few feet away from him. So tantalisingly near and yet so far. The cage was guarded by two men who sat on a packing case nursing rifless in their laps. They were smoking cigarettes and chatting idly in soft voices, neither taking much notice of the precious item they were guarding. Holmes knew that these two fellows had to be dealt with in some way before he was able to progress further. If he were able to reach the cage unhindered he would then have a chance to put a bullet through the brain of the monstrous rodent. Once the rat was dead, he could deal with the guards.

Holmes surveyed his options and the lie of the land. Within seconds he had lit upon a course of action that might just work. It was dangerous and audacious but, if the fates were in his favour, he believed he could bring it off. In any case, taking risks, even life-threatening ones, was an accepted professional hazard for the consulting detective. Throwing off his outer coat, he manoeuvred his way around the gallery. The rusting metal structure swayed precariously and creaked at times, as though refusing to bear his weight. Each time the walkway groaned in protest, he stopped and flattened himself against the wall, in case the noise attracted the attention of the men below; but they seemed completely unaware of the intruder in the shadows above their heads.

It was with some relief that Holmes came into a position directly over the girder that ran from north to south across the building, passing, at one point, some twelve feet above the cage. Slipping off his shoes and stuffing them into his jacket pockets, he clambered over the rail and, with great care, lowered himself down onto the girder. In doing so he dislodged a scattering of dust and flakes of rust which fell in a silent shower on to the floor below. Holmes froze and held his breath, his eyes fixed on the faces of the guards, but they still remained engrossed in their conversation, oblivious of his presence.

The girder was just less than a foot wide. Crouching like a chimpanzee, his toes pressing firmly down to maintain a grip, while his fingers grasped the rough edges of the girder, Holmes inched his way along its length, slowly and silently, never taking his eyes off the guards. It took the detective some five minutes to reach the section of the girder that was directly over the rat's cage. At that moment, without warning, one of the guards stood up. He flung his arms wide and yawned noisily. In doing so he threw his head back, with his mouth agape and eyes shooting upwards to face the roof. His actions were so quick and spontaneous that Holmes had no time to react. It was too late to try and lie flat on the girder: any sudden movement would have caught the guard's attention immediately. Instead, Holmes became rooted to the spot, not moving a muscle, praying that he blended in with the shadows.

The yawn over, the guard stretched his arms wide once again, and ruffled his hair. He showed no signs of having seen Holmes. At length he resumed his seat and pulled a hip flask from his pocket. He took a long swallow before passing the flask to his companion. Holmes waited a few moments for the two men to resume their desultory conversation before he made his next move. Holding his breath to steady his nerves, he slipped over the edge of the girder until he was hanging from it like a trapeze artist in the circus. His fingers gripped the top of the girder tightly, but he was aware that they were beginning to slide in the dust. Flakes of rust dropped down on to his face. Holmes was now at his most vulnerable: suspended in mid air above the rat's cage, with the bottom half of his body illuminated by the harsh spread of light from the dangling electric lamps. He was fully aware that he made a ridiculously easy target. It only required one of the men to glance up and he would be seen. Then it would need only seconds for the fellow to raise his rifle to his shoulder and fire. It would take a very incompetent marksman to miss such a target at that distance. Sweat ran in rivulets down the side of the detective's face. He felt the creeping onset of a paralysing fear take hold of his body. He knew that he had to act quickly or his nerve would fail him.

Suddenly one of the men broke out in a raucous laugh that echoed eerily around the cavernous warehouse. Holmes took this as his cue. Releasing his grip from the girder, he dropped some six feet on to the roof of the cage. Although he was in his stockinged feet, the noise of his landing resounded dully in the lofty chamber, sounding like the distant beat of a drum. In an instant, the two guards were on their feet, rifles at the ready. Their relaxed demeanour had vanished; their bodies were now tense and alert. Looking about them with quick nervous glances, it was clear that they could not locate the source of the noise.

'What the hell was that, George?' cried one.

'Dunno. Where'd it come from?' his partner replied.

'I reckon it was over by the door.'

'You could be right. Let's go take a look.'

Holmes, who by now was lying flat on the cage roof, had further problems. The impact of his landing there had caused the rotten wood to sag and splinter. With the weight of the detective now pressing down on it, the roof began to split wide open, eventually giving way altogether. Holmes found himself slipping inexorably through a jagged aperture like someone sinking into a quicksand. Within seconds he was crashing down into the body of the cage. He landed somewhat shocked but unhurt on the straw-laden floor. Near him, in the gloom, was a large inert presence. Automatically, Holmes wrenched his gun from his inside pocket.

Outside, beyond his sight, the guards, having heard the disturbance, were rushing back to the cage. Within seconds, the taller of the two whipped back the tarpaulin. Light flooded in. On seeing Holmes crouched there like a cornered animal, the guard's face cracked open with a laugh. 'Look here, George. Look what we got: a new exhibit,' he cried with glee. And then his smile disappeared completely to be replaced by a strange puzzled expression. The guard's face crumpled with pain and his eyes rolled wildly in his head. With a strangled gasp, he clutched his chest where Holmes's bullet had struck him. For a moment he swayed like a drunkard, a kind of disbelief and wonder mirrored in his misting eyes, and then he fell to the floor, the rifle clattering away from him on the stone flags.

His associate dropped to his knees, but before he was able to lift his weapon for use, Holmes fired again. This time he only winged his adversary, but the fellow gave a guttural moan, spun round, and dropped face downward in a swoon at his comrade's feet.

Holmes's heart was pounding against his ribs as he glanced over to the corner of the cage where the giant rodent lay. It was a ghastly sight with its huge bulk covered in matted, rusty-coloured, shaggy fur. The mouth was agape and its enormous, treacherous yellow teeth were fully exposed as though in a silent snarl. Indeed, everything about the creature seemed silent; and the vicious, red, bulbous eyes stared at Holmes in a vacant sightless fashion. The rodent did not move at all. Its great sides were still. There was no heartbeat within that monstrous body. Moving closer, it became quite clear to Sherlock Holmes that the giant rat of Sumatra was dead.

An Encounter in Solomon Road

'This is typical of Sherlock Holmes! We should have known better than to let him handle this case without close supervision.' The face of Inspector Giles Lestrade was pale and grim, and his eyes flamed with anger.

We were travelling at high speed through the darkened streets of the city on our way to Solomon Road in Rotherhithe. Our cab was the lead vehicle in a convoy, which also included two police wagons full of constables and several plain-clothes detectives. As well as Lestrade, Mycroft, and myself, the fourth occupant of the cab was a young inspector by the name of Lanyon. He remained silent for the whole of the journey, his features betraying no emotion whatsoever.

'I know my brother can be difficult,' observed Mycroft defensively, 'but he always places the interest of the case as a prime priority.'

'Only if it suits him,' snapped Lestrade in response. The pressure of this investigation had dissipated his natural politeness and deference. It was clear that he was not about to accept any mitigating claims for the strategies of Sherlock Holmes. Lestrade's fury had shown no signs of abating since Mycroft and I had arrived at Scotland Yard to inform him of recent developments. I had taken it upon myself to explain the thinking and purpose behind my friend's actions that evening, an explanation that was met by a spluttering eruption of anger. In a voice that echoed around the walls of his office, he informed me that he felt he had been betrayed and treated with disdain by the 'high and mighty Mr Holmes'. In all honesty, I could not defend my friend against these accusations. Since Lestrade had stormed out of his office to rally his men in preparation for our journey, he had not trusted himself to address me and pointedly averted his gaze when I attempted to speak to him. I realised that the wisest course of action was to sit quietly and hope that, by the time we reached our destination, Lestrade's sense of duty would conquer his ire. Observing Mycroft's tight-lipped stare, I deduced that he had decided upon a similar course of action.

The carriage rattled at breakneck speed through the damp thoroughfares of south London and, far sooner than I thought possible, we arrived at our destination. On Lestrade's instructions the cab stopped and we alighted.

I glanced at my watch. It was a little after eleven. Holmes would already have had about two hours in which to carry out his investigations. I just hoped that he had been successful and that he was free from harm.

'Lanyon,' snapped the Inspector, addressing his colleague, 'inform the rest of the men to wait for my signal – three sharp blasts on the whistle – and then they are to come a-running, weapons at the ready.'

Without a word Lanyon scurried off to the first police van some six yards behind us to impart his superior's orders.

On his departure, Lestrade turned to us. 'Now, we'd better stroll down Solomon Road and see what we can sniff out, yes?'

Mycroft and I muttered our assent and the three of us turned down the dark and dreary thoroughfare that was Solomon Road. There were two or three street lights dotted along its length, but their feeble yellow shafts of illumination spilled little further than the base of the posts. However, as the three of us moved down the road at a steady pace, we observed a figure leaning against one of the lamp-posts, some distance ahead of us, apparently smoking a cigarette. The red tip glowed brightly in the dim rays. Although the character was but a mere silhouette, it was clear from the stance and attitude of its pose that the fellow was relaxed and unconcerned by our approach.

'Watch this cove,' whispered Lestrade under his breath. 'This may be some sort of trap.'

As we drew nearer, I began to suspect that the Inspector was correct in his assumption, for it occurred to me that this man – and I now could see that it *was* a man – was actually waiting for us. As we drew near, he lit another cigarette and, for a moment by the flickering light of the match, I observed his features clearly. He was in late middle age with a grey walrus-type moustache, heavy eyebrows of the same hue, blotchy skin, and sharp, piercing eyes. A greasy, flat cap was pulled low over the face. He viewed us with a mixture of amusement and disdain.

'Evenin' gents,' he croaked in a husky voice, turning to face us. His accent was pure cockney.

'Good evening, sir,' replied Lestrade warily.

'I've been waiting for yer, 'case yer wondering why I'm here on my lonesome in the middle of nowhere.'

'Waiting for us?' Lestrade was unable to keep the surprise out of his voice.

'Mr Holmes told me . . . '

'Holmes!' cried the policeman. 'Of course, Holmes had to be involved in this. What did he tell you?'

'To show you how to get in to the warehouse. He thought you'd have difficulty like if you didn't have a guide. I'm yer guide.' He almost bowed.

'Where is Sherlock Holmes?' I asked.

The fellow lifted his head and looked me up and down before speaking. 'Search me – and then again I'd rather you didn't.' He laughed a rasping, coughing laugh. 'Look maties, I'm here to do a job. I've been paid me sovereign so I'll perform me duty, but I ain't up to no interrogation. This chap named Holmes who I met in The Angel Inn asked me to meet you and show you in so – are you with me, gents?'

Lestrade turned to Mycroft, whose features were a mixture of emotions. 'Perhaps we should go along with this fellow,' the policeman said.

'We have little option,' came the reply.

'Good men,' croaked the stranger. 'Now I won't be a jiffy.' So saying, he shuffled to the fence, leaned heavily against it with his shoulder, and pushed hard. A portion swung back, creating a gap of about three feet. 'There you are. Off you go. Mr Holmes'll be waiting for you inside the building.'

'Who are you?' I barked, still uneasy at this arrangement.

'Nah that would be tellin',' he said with a grin, on his face. 'My part's done and I'll wish you gents a very good night. Mr Holmes promised me there would be no further fuss, and he's a man of his word.'

'We'd better let him go,' said Mycroft gently, placing his hand on Lestrade's arm.

'I suppose so,' said the inspector, adding with some sarcasm, 'if only for your brother's sake.'

Our strange gatekeeper had already begun to make his way down the street, limping as he went.

'No great villain there, I'm sure,' I observed as we watched him disappear into the gloom.

'It wouldn't surprise me if it wasn't Holmes himself in one of his disguises,' muttered Lestrade, still bristling with suppressed anger.

'I hardly think so,' responded Mycroft, lighting his lantern. The policeman and I followed suit and, without further conversation, we passed through the gap in the fence into the grounds of the Eagle Printing Works. All seemed to be in pitch blackness and the silence was oppressive. This was broken momentarily by the wailful moan of a ship's siren from up the river.

We made our way across a stretch of rough ground and reached what was obviously the main entrance of the defunct factory. In a recessed archway there was a large double-fronted door which bore the name of the company. This proved to be locked and bolted.

'How can Holmes meet us inside if the door's locked?' asked Lestrade with a sneer.

'There must be some other way in,' observed Mycroft. 'A side entrance, perhaps.'

'Maybe,' said Lestrade, 'but we haven't got all night to search around in the pitch black for it. I think it's time I got my men down here. Half a dozen hefty constables will soon make mincemeat of that door. You stay here, gentlemen, while I summon my men.'

Mycroft nodded and then held up his hand in warning. 'May I suggest that you do not use the police whistle, which I see you searching for in your coat pocket, Inspector. If there are any villains inside the building the less warning we give of our presence the better, eh?'

Lestrade said nothing, but withdrew his empty hand from his pocket and let it hang limply at his side. He gave Mycroft a brief nod and headed back to the fence and Solomon Road to rally his men.

'How on Earth did Holmes get into the building – that's if he did?'

'He is an unconventional and canny fellow, Watson, as you well know. Entering the premises of your enemy by the front door is not to be recommended – unless of course you have an army of bulky constables. There will, I am sure, be a side or back entrance somewhere, or a vulnerable window; although my money rests on the fire escape that I noted on our way round the building. I think that would be my brother's favoured route.'

'Shouldn't we try it?'

Mycroft chuckled. 'Imagine Lestrade's fury to find us gone. No, no. We must remain part of the Inspector's brigade now. Whether Sherlock has been successful in his endeavours, we shall find out soon enough, but I am sure that striking out on our own up a shaky and rusting fire escape would not really help matters – however they stand.'

'You are right, of course. However, I do think it might be prudent to have your revolver ready.'

'It has been ready since we stepped out of the cab. But don't mistake me for my brother, Watson: I may be able to match him, and even beat him, in the intellect stakes, but I am not a man of action or as recklessly brave as he is. I don't mind telling you that at this moment I am quite terrified.' I gazed at my companion and, although his broad face was half in shadow, I could see in his furrowed brow and the erratic blinking of his eyes that he was telling me nothing but the truth: he *was* frightened. I could think of nothing to say that would reassure him. In the situation in which we found ourselves there were no certainties. Indeed, fear was the only intelligent emotion. We lapsed into silence.

However, it was not long before we heard the shuffling feet of the army of constables. Into our faint circle of light Lestrade and Lanyon ushered about a dozen young uniformed policemen.

'See what you can do to that door, lads,' instructed Lestrade.

Six of the men stepped forward and, forming themselves into a kind of human battering ran, they hurled themselves at the door. At first they met with solid resistance.

'And again,' cried their leader, a red-faced fellow with a strong Welsh accent, whose coat bore a sergeant's stripes.

The constables duly charged the door again with more vigour, and this time their efforts were rewarded by a creaking and groaning response from the woodwork.

'We've got it on the run,' cried the sergeant, who led a third and a fourth charge. Each assault was more successful than the last until at the fifth effort there was an almighty cracking sound and the door crashed open with ease, surprising the constables so much that they stumbled forward, the Welsh sergeant actually landing on the floor at the base of the heap.

Lestrade turned to Mycroft and myself. 'There is no need for you to go any further, gentlemen. After all, this is a police matter, so if you'd care to wait here . . . '

'Nonsense, Lestrade,' said I. 'I am involved in this affair just as much as you are, if not more. I fully intend to see it through to the end.'

Mycroft responded in a similar fashion. 'Surely, I don't have to re-mind you that I am the Government's representative on this mission. I have no intention of abandoning my duty.'

Lestrade's taut features suddenly softened for the first time that evening and a brief smile touched his lips. 'Very well, gentlemen, let's investigate.' He flung his arm in an extravagant gesture towards the doorway.

As we moved forward he issued instructions to Lanyon. 'You cover our backs and bring the rest of the men behind us. Make sure their guns are at the ready. But there is to be no shooting unless our lives are in danger.'

Passing through the portals of the warehouse, stepping carefully over the shattered remains of the door, we passed into the main body of the building, a vast shell of a structure illuminated by a string of electric lights suspended from the rafters. I stopped in my tracks when I saw in the centre of this industrial cavern a large wooden cage. Immediately I knew it was the cage I had discovered on the *Matilda Briggs*. Stepping a little closer, I peered through the bars. My heart almost stopped at what I saw. It was the giant rat. We had in fact found its lair. Holmes had been right.

Lestrade's attention was focused on two inert figures, which lay face down some distance from the cage. 'What on earth have we here?' he murmured, almost to himself rather than to us. He turned quickly to his colleague. 'Lanyon, check those two bodies, but don't get too near that cage.'

The young detective, gun in hand, raced over to the figures and knelt down beside them in turn, checking their pulses. As he did so, he snatched the occasional glance at the cage and its contents. His grim expression relayed his feelings. 'This one is still alive, sir,' he said, leaning over the body nearest us. 'The other one's dead. Both have been shot.'

I gazed around this empty factory building for a sign of life, but there was none. Had Holmes been here? Was he responsible for these shootings? And what about the rat?

While I pondered these puzzles, Lestrade addressed his men. 'Right, gentlemen, spread out. Comb the building thoroughly. Work in pairs and report back to me as soon as you see anything.' The constables needed no further instructions. They dispersed at speed and began their work. With a satisfied sigh, Lestrade turned his attention to us once more. 'Right, Mr Holmes, Dr Watson, let's have a look at this cage, shall we?'

It was an awesome sight: the great beast slumped in the corner of the cage, its bulbous, red eyes glinting in the light, while its ferocious, yellow fangs were exposed as in a static snarl. At first I didn't realise that the monster was dead. I thought it may have been sleeping or drugged. But, after scrutinising the full horror of the creature, I realised that there was no movement at all. The thing wasn't breathing.

'What in God's name is that?' gasped Lanyon, who had joined us by the cage.

I answered his query. 'It *was* the giant rat of Sumatra. And it's dead.'

'Thank the Lord for that,' observed Mycroft. 'I had prepared myself for seeing this monstrous thing, but it is more horrendous than even my mind could conjure.'

'I wonder how it died?' asked Lestrade. 'There is no sign of a wound as far as I can see.'

'Once we have finished our business here, this place must be sealed off and the government's medical team brought in to perform a post mortem,' said Mycroft turning his back on the cage. As he did so, I noted a look of sudden shock contort his features and, in desperation, he scrabbled for the revolver in his pocket. I swung round and saw the cause of his alarm. The wounded man, who had been ignored by us all, had recovered consciousness and was aiming his rifle in our direction. Mycroft jerked his gun from his pocket but it fell from his anxious fingers to the floor. Our would-be assailant grinned with pleasure as he cocked the trigger. Thankfully, his wound had made him slow. 'Get down,' I cried to my companions, as I aimed my pistol and fired. My bullet tore through the fellow's shoulder, causing him to cry out in pain and throw his arms in the air. The rifle fired and the bullet ricocheted off the roof and smashed one of the electric lights above our heads, sending down a small shower of minute glass fragments.

'Well done, Watson,' cried Mycroft, retrieving his own gun from the floor. 'You saved one of our lives then.'

'Indeed, doctor,' said Lestrade, 'a splendid piece of work. I never knew you were such a marksman.'

Before I had time to respond to this praise, the Welsh sergeant came bounding up to us. 'Sir, we've opened the doors at the back of the building, same method as before, and moved out onto the wharf. There's a ship out there and it looks like it's just been set on fire. There is one of the crew in the water now.

'Unless I am very much mistaken that will be the *Matilda Briggs*,' said I.

'I'll join you in that assumption, Watson. Quickly, sergeant, take us to it,' cried Lestrade.

As we emerged once more into the cool night air, the dark blue sky was tinged with orange. Down at the end of the wharf, where a group of the policemen was standing, silhouetted against the vibrant yellow light of leaping flames, I saw the ship, which I recognised immediately as the *Matilda Briggs*. It was fully ablaze, bathing the wharf and surrounding area in a kind of rosy aura. As we drew nearer we could feel the fierce heat of the conflagration rolling towards us. In the dark waters, several sailors who had jumped ship were swimming to the dockside, only to be picked up by the waiting police officers. They surrendered to the embrace of handcuffs without any fuss, their shiny, wet faces registering various degrees of relief at having escaped the doomed vessel.

We elbowed our way to the edge of the wharf some fifteen feet away from the Baroness's ship, which was now starting to list in the water as the fire ate into its seasoned timbers. I wondered if she were on board, trapped below deck at the mercy of the raging fire. If she were, should I feel sorry for her? It was a question I could not answer.

With a loud crack and a shower of sparks, the main mast, like a giant burning cross, snapped and crashed into the river on the far side of us. Steam rose to mingle with the billowing smoke, which began to drift towards us. Most of the deck was now shimmering with flames. We watched mesmerised as, little by little, the voracious blaze took possession of the ship.

And then, suddenly, I saw a man emerge from the rippling wall of fire and venture onto the prow. He staggered forward, desperately trying to avoid the fierce, yellow tongues that reached out to devour him. He waved his arms at us and there was a cry, which was subsumed by the crackling, throaty roar of the blaze. I recognised this man – this man whose race against the fire seemed almost futile. It was Sherlock Holmes.

CHAPTER TWENTY-ONE

Into the Pit

With some urgency, Sherlock Holmes put on his shoes and, using the dead carcass of the rat as a monstrous stepping stone, reached up to the roof of the cage and hauled himself out through the gaping aperture. Nimbly he dropped to the ground. Holmes carried out these functions in a mechanical fashion, while his mind was astir with thoughts, questions, and emotions.

Ostensibly, he was relieved to discover that the giant rat was dead, but this relief was tinged with other concerns. How had the thing died? Was the event an unexpected one, or was it part of the Baroness's plan? And where was the brood of baby rats that ultimately carried more of a threat than their mutant mother? Also, Sherlock Holmes was never at ease with his conscience about having to kill a man, even if it was in self-defence. He preferred natural justice to deal, as he believed it eventually did, with all law-breakers.

He examined the two bodies. One indeed was dead. From the position of the fatal wound, he deduced that the bullet must have penetrated the heart and that the man would have died instantly. The other assailant had a stomach wound but, although unconscious, was breathing regularly. He would have to trust to Fate, and to his own constitution, as to how he fared; the detective had no time to minister to the enemy's ailments.

Initially he was somewhat surprised that the noise of gunfire had not roused more of the Baroness's men, causing them to swarm into the building, but, on reflection, he reasoned that the thick walls and the boarded windows would have successfully muffled the sounds. This also indicated that, apart from the two guards, the building was empty. The rest must be aboard the *Matilda Briggs*. It was on this cursed ship that he felt he would reach the heart of the mystery. Searching the guards, he found a key ring holding two large rusty keys attached to the belt of the dead man.

Slipping his own revolver into his pocket, and picking up the discarded rifle, he made his way to the rear of the building. He soon found the door leading to the wharf. As expected, it was securely locked, but one of the purloined keys gained him access to the outside world again. He slipped through the door and locked it behind him.

For a moment he stood still, breathing in the coolness of the night, the fresh, comparatively untainted air. This helped to refresh his body and eradicate from his mind some of the darkness that had been placed there by the recent unpleasant experiences inside the factory. Then, keeping to the shadows, he crept slowly to the end of the wharf where the *Matilda Briggs*, now re-named *Gypsy Sprite*, rested in the grey waters of the Thames. At first, two lanterns on the main deck appeared to be the only source of illumination on the ship, but on closer scrutiny Holmes noticed a dull amber light emanating from one of the cabins.

Keeping to the shadows, the detective manoeuvred his way down the wharf towards the ship. He spied a bulky fellow on guard. He was lolling by the gangplank, smoking a pipe, and appeared both bored and inattentive. Noiselessly, Holmes slipped behind him and brought down the butt of the rifle on to the back of the sailor's head. With a quiet, weary moan he slipped to the floor unconscious, his pipe falling from his grasp and tumbling over the edge of the wharf. There was a tiny splash as it hit the water below. Holmes rolled the body away from the light and quickly threw a tarpaulin over it to hide it from view. Within seconds Sherlock Holmes was on the deck of the *Matilda Briggs*. He was very tempted to make his way towards the lighted cabin, but there was one other location he wanted to inspect first: the hold where the Giant Rat had been kept. Surely it was here that the brood of baby rats was now stowed.

He knew the geography of the *Matilda Briggs* reasonably well, for it was on board the ship that he had first encountered Baroness Dubeyk after he had been kidnapped. He had been brought aboard, drugged, and then hypnotised. He remembered sitting opposite her in her cabin and, while his mind was befogged by tiredness, pain, and the drugs, he fell victim to her powers. He was trans- fixed by her mellifluous voice and magnetic dark eyes. She lured him into a vulnerable hypnotic state. A lifetime of reticence, a barrier that had been secure against emotion and involvement, had disintegrated under the sharp power of the woman's influence. He had surrendered fully to her suggestions – suggestions which then became his beliefs. Strong values had been overturned. It was as though he had been taken to another window on the world and shown bright new views with fresh vibrant colours. He shuddered even now to think of the experience. He had been beaten by this woman and, had it not been for Watson and Signor Salvini, he would still be under her control. The thought of this brought a cold, clammy sweat to his forehead. For a moment his head swam with dangerous, untenable ideas. He felt like a recuperating invalid who sensed illness reasserting itself. Was he weakening because he was close to her again? This could not be! He would not allow it to be so. He dragged himself to the ship rail and gulped in draughts of cold night air, clearing his mind of all thoughts of the Baroness and failure.

With purposeful strides he made his way to the hold. The hatch was open as though in welcome. Surely he was not expected? With stealth, he stepped down the narrow stairway and passed through one of the double doors into the hold. It was lighted by one lantern hanging from a beam at the far end of the cramped, claustrophobic chamber. The lantern provided enough illumination for him to see the cage. He stepped closer, gagging at the stench which emanated from it. His gaze fell upon its occupants: the Giant Rat's progeny. The cage was filled with the infant rodents, as large as small dogs. They were bigger than the creatures he had seen at The Bridge of Dreams, which were obviously a prototype brood. These were the finished article. There were about two dozen of the creatures spilled out across the floor of the cage; but, on closer inspection, Holmes saw that most of them lay still, their obscene snouts open in silent cries. The rats that were conscious writhed and whimpered quietly in prolonged death throes, their eyes oozing pus and their squirming, obscene bodies blotted with pustules. Now it was clear to him: the plague had been visited upon its perpetrator. In some grand reversion of nature, the disease was destroying its own agents.

For some moments the detective stood mesmerised at this scene snatched from a canvas by Hieronymus Bosch. He was not unaware of the irony of the situation. Without anyone's intervention the Baroness's plan had foundered by natural means; or certainly by the dark process of Nature which, when all life is threatened, steps in to prevent wholesale destruction. No giant rats would now threaten London with the plague; this foul corruption had turned on its own creator. Creator or creators – for, indeed, both these mutant beasts, and the foul disease that they carried, had been created artificially for a startling criminal scheme. But the malefactors had been foiled by their own creation.

Standing by the cage, his mind awhirl with this realisation, Sherlock Holmes found himself laughing. His body shook with strange merriment. He knew it came from fatigue, light-headedness, and relief, but it also stemmed from a cutting appreciation of the irony of the situation.

His thin reedy laugher echoed in the dingy hold.

'I would much appreciate it if you would be kind enough to share the joke with me.'

The voice, sharp and incisive, came from the corner of the hold near to where the oil lamp hung. Holmes froze immediately on hearing it and his finger curled around the trigger of the rifle. He knew the voice, although he had met its owner only once before.

'Come now, do not be shy. Share the joke.' The voice came again, speaking in a muffled, careless fashion as though its owner were drunk or very tired.

Holmes turned slowly to face the speaker, whom he could now see vaguely in the shadows beyond the oil lamp. He appeared to be sitting on a high stool.

'I believe you are quite capable of understanding the cause of my merriment, Karswell. Despite your cleverness, and that of your mistress, a force greater than yourselves has scuppered your machinations,' said Holmes evenly, moving towards the shadowy figure of Dr Simeon Karswell.

Now it was the doctor's turn to laugh. It was a high, unstable, humourless sound. 'How grand,' he chuckled sarcastically. 'A force greater than ourselves, eh? Please don't bring God into the arena, Holmes. He isn't involved at all. He just sits on his cloud and watches us humans make a mess of things. No, no. Forget a force greater than – whatever. It was medical naïveté or ignorance that did for us, the Baroness and me. There is a simple old saying about playing with fire – ' He gave a harsh and bitter laugh. 'Well, I certainly got burnt.' Karswell pulled himself forward so that the lamp illuminated his face.

Holmes gave an intake of breath as he caught sight of Karswell's features. They were marked by a series of livid, dark spots, some of which were breaking open. His mouth was enlarged because of swollen gums and this was the reason why his voice sounded strange. There were tears in his eyes.

'You have no need of your gun, Mr Detective. I shall be dead within eight hours. I am competent enough to diagnose that. I have the plague, you see; I have the plague.' He gave the weird chuckling laugh of one whose mind is unhinged. 'I am afraid I grew careless,' he continued. 'I got too close and one of the creatures bit me. I thought it was dead. It was dying but it had enough energy to strike out. I treated myself immediately, but it was too late.' He closed his eyes and squeezed the tears down his ruined face. 'Too late.'

Holmes was lost for words. He knew this man had provided the knowledge and expertise the Baroness had needed to put her diabolical scheme into operation, but he would not wish this fate on any man.

'Divine intervention, I suppose you would call it. I call it damned carelessness! So we all die: me, the giant rat, and all her chickens at one fell swoop.'

'And the Baroness?'

'Oh, not the Baroness, Mr Holmes. I thought you would have known by now, clever fellow that you are, that she lives a charmed life. The Baroness has escaped without so much as a smear of dirt upon her dress.'

'She was your partner?'

Karswell shook his head. 'I was her minion. She sought me out because of my medical knowledge, my knowledge of diseases, and my weakness for gambling. It was ridiculously simple for her to lure me into a situation where I had no option but to do her bidding.'

'To develop these mutant rats and infect them with a plague bacillus.'

'You have a way with words, Mr Holmes. That is a concise but somewhat harsh and simplified version of the truth.'

'But you could have refused. What is financial ruin compared to the destruction of the lives of many innocent people? For Heaven's sake, you are a doctor. You have taken the Hippocratic oath. Your moral duty is to save life – not destroy it.'

'Could I have refused? In the same way that you yourself refused her?'

Holmes could not reply to this taunt. He should have realised that anyone who got close to the Baroness no longer had complete control over their own actions. They became her puppets and acted accordingly. He thought of Stamford, and how his whole behaviour had changed and become alien to his own natural character. He had been enlisted by Karswell to help him in his experiments with the rats on the promise that his debts would be settled and he would be paid handsomely for his services. Ignorant of what he was getting himself into, he agreed. And then he met the Baroness and his will no longer remained his own. In reality there were no villains in this case save the Baroness. The rest had been her slaves, including, for a time, himself.

His thoughts were interrupted by Karswell who, in attempting to stand, cried out in agony with the pain of the effort. Instinctively Holmes moved towards him. 'Keep your distance!' cried the dying man. 'I am now as lethal as any of the rats.' He chuckled again, a wheezy, gargling noise that rattled his chest. 'I am the last threat now, Holmes. With the Giant Rat and her little babies dead, I am the only threat left. Not much to worry about now, is there: a dying, diseased man. Let me show you.' So saying, Karswell lurched forward and grabbed the oil lamp to hold it up to his face, but his grasp failed and the lamp fell to the ground. It smashed at his feet, and the trapped oil and flames, now released, stretched out across the floor, hungrily catching hold of all in their path. The tinder-dry timbers yielded easily to fire and, within moments, the chamber was ablaze. At the centre of the roaring conflagration was Karswell. Holmes saw him as a frozen silhouette, framed by the vibrant yellow flames. And then with one last gargling cry, he collapsed, disappearing from sight in a shower of sparks and a fiery orange curtain.

Without Holmes realising it, the fire had circled around him and already the exit to the hold was ablaze. He knew that if he did not act quickly he would meet a similar fate to Karswell. Dropping the rifle and pulling his coat over his head, he ran the gauntlet of the tunnel of flames and clambered on to the deck. Gulping for air, he sensed a presence behind him. Turning quickly, he was just in time to catch sight of a sailor's fist flying in his direction. He had no time to react. The fist connected with his chin and his head exploded with bright lights. Stumbling back, he crashed onto the deck, banging his head on some hard object. For a moment, he felt a dull pain and experienced blurred vision. Then Sherlock Holmes lost consciousness, while the fire was already reaching up from the hold in a bid to take possession of the *Matilda Briggs*.

When Holmes regained consciousness, moments later, the whole vessel was ablaze. Only the prow had not been fully conquered by flames. Protecting his exposed flesh as much as he was able, he raced down the deck in a desperate zigzag pattern towards his goal. His speed allowed him to brush past the vicious tongues of fire without harm. Clambering up the smouldering steps, he reached the prow just as a sheet of flame sprang up before him. Without hesitation, he jumped through it as one might pass through a curtain.

On reaching the rail at the very front of the ship, Sherlock Holmes saw a group of figures down on the wharf below him. Was he dreaming? Was that Watson? Mycroft? Lestrade? The heat blurred his vision. He cried out and waved to them. The sudden crash of burning timber behind him prompted his next action. Without hesitation, he dived from the prow into the dark seething waters of the river.

The Final Deception

'I really am perfectly all right, my dear Watson. Please do not fuss. I am somewhat wet and I have a few minor burns to my hands. That is all. There is nothing that a change of clothes and a stiff drink will not cure.' So saying, Sherlock Holmes turned and made his way towards his bedroom. 'I will be with you shortly,' he called over his shoulder. 'In the meantime, Watson, be so good as to offer our guests some refreshment, and pour me a particularly large brandy, there's a good fellow.'

After hauling Holmes out of the water and watching the *Matilda Briggs*, still ablaze, sink ignominiously into the river, we had returned to Baker Street along with Mycroft and Lestrade, who had left Inspector Lanyon in charge of the mopping up operations. Holmes had refused to recount any of his adventures that night until he was 'seated before my own hearth in a set of dry clothes'.

As the door slammed behind my friend, Lestrade, who was now much more relaxed than he had been at the outset of our expedition, allowed himself a dry chuckle. 'He is a remarkable man,' he said, shaking his head in amusement, 'I've got to admit that. His behaviour drives me to distraction at times but he is quite, quite remarkable.'

Mycroft cast me a conspiratorial sly wink as if to note this radical volte-face. 'I think there was talk of brandy,' he said cheerily, to cover up the awkward silence following Lestrade's unexpected eulogy.

'Certainly,' I said, collecting the decanter and a tray of glasses.

Within ten minutes Sherlock Holmes had rejoined us. His hair was neatly sleeked back, his features were composed, and his whole demeanour was that of a man who had not a care in the world. Slipping on his old mouse-coloured dressing-gown, he picked up the brandy I had placed on the table for him and dropped into his chair by the fire with a contented sigh. We waited for him to begin.

'As you will have gathered, gentlemen,' he said at length, after lighting his pipe, 'the threat of the giant rat has been removed. London is no longer in danger.'

'Amen to that,' muttered Lestrade.

'I think the time has come, Sherlock, for you to tell us what happened tonight,' said Mycroft.

'Of course. It is a strange story but easily told. Watson, you may wish to make notes of this account while it is fresh in my mind.'

I nodded and reached for my notebook and pencil.

'No doubt Watson has told you something of how I discovered the hiding place of the rat.'

Our visitors nodded their heads.

'Then let me pick up the plot from the moment I reached Solomon Road this evening.'

For a good half-hour we sat enthralled as my friend recounted his exploits, from his discovery of the hidden entrance to the Eagle Printing Company, to his conversation with Simeon Karswell, and his escape from the blazing ship.

After he had finished his tale, Holmes replenished his glass while the three of us mulled over the information we had learned and its implications.

'You are quite sure that there are no further nests of these mutant rats in the metropolis?' asked Mycroft.

Holmes nodded his head. 'I am certain. There is no evidence to suggest there are. I am confident that Karswell would have mentioned them. And, even if there are, the creatures will be dead by now anyway.'

'So we really are safe?'

'Yes.'

Holmes's response brought a broad smile to his brother's features.

'But what about the Baroness? Are we to accept that she has escaped scot-free?' It was Lestrade who posed this awkward question.

Holmes stared into the fire for some moments before replying. 'You can keep a watch on the ports, but it is probable that she has left the country already. It is too hot for her now in Britain: she will seek pastures new.'

'So we have lost her!'

'For the present, I am afraid we have.'

'Well, that takes the gilt off the gingerbread for me in this matter, Mr Holmes. To know that woman is still free – wherever she is – still at liberty to concoct other devilish plans – ' The inspector shook his head sadly.

'It certainly would have been neater, and provided a more satisfactory conclusion to the case, if she had been caught in our net; but that was not to be,' said Holmes.

'If only I could have got my hands on her – '

'Well, you nearly did tonight, Lestrade, but you let her go.'

'What's that?'

A faint flicker of amusement touched Holmes's lips. 'On our way back to Baker Street you mentioned the old fellow that I had set on to show you where the secret entrance to the printing works was.'

'That's right.'

Holmes leaned forward towards Lestrade. 'I did not employ any such character.'

Lestrade's face crumpled in puzzlement and then his jaw dropped open in shock. 'You don't mean to say that – that old geezer – ?'

'Was the Baroness. Indeed. Remember she had been an actress. What more secure way to escape than dressed as a man? She knew that I was on her track, and it was only a matter of time before the police arrived.'

'But why did she stop and help us?' I asked.

'No doubt it amused her to do so; and it also gained her precious time. While you and your troops were busy storming the print works, she was securing her escape.'

'Well, I'll be blowed. I could have reached out and clamped the darbies on him – her.'

'She is a clever and resourceful woman, but thankfully, through our efforts, and those of Mother Nature, her machinations have failed.'

'And that is what we really must be thankful for,' observed Mycroft, raising his large bulk from the chair and stretching. 'Now I, for one, am ready for my bed. It has been a long, weary day, but thankfully, due mainly to you, Sherlock, it has been a blessedly successful one.' He grasped his brother's hand and shook it warmly. He was followed in turn by Lestrade. 'Earlier tonight I was cursing you to the heavens, Mr Holmes, but I reckon you've come up trumps again.'

My friend flashed a warm smile at the policeman.

Within minutes Holmes and I were alone once more in our Baker Street rooms. He tapped out his pipe on the hearth and placed it on the mantelpiece. Pulling back the curtains he peered out, gazing at the sky. 'Early signs of dawn, Watson. The sky lightens from the east. Can you forego your bed for a few more hours yet? There is still one more chapter in this case before we can close it.'

Some fifteen minutes later, as we emerged from our quarters into a silent Baker Street, the pink blush of morning was already seeping into the sky.

'Cabs are scarce at this early hour. I fear we shall have to make our way down to Oxford Street in order to catch one,' said Holmes, taking my arm.

Holmes's prediction turned out to be correct. Indeed, we had nearly reached Marble Arch before we were able to secure a hansom.

'A long and profitable drive for you, my man,' Holmes cried to the bleary-eyed cabbie, as he held out a handful of sovereigns.

At the sight of the gold coins, the driver's whole demeanour perked up. He touched his battered old topper in a kind of salute. 'Where to, sir?'

'Somewhere near Beckenham in Kent.'

'Blimey!'

'Are you game?'

The cabby eyed the coins, which Holmes still displayed.

'I'm game, sir.'

'This is not one of my water-tight deductions, Watson,' explained Holmes, once our journey had commenced. 'However, I have based my theory on all the evidence I have at my command and my limited knowledge of the Baroness. I have told you many times that I never guess – and certainly that is the case. However, this comes very near.' He gave a dry laugh.

'You think you know where the Baroness is?'

Holmes shrugged his shoulders. 'I prefer to wait and see.'

'And our destination?'

'In my short but illuminating acquaintance with the Baroness, I came to realise that she is a cold, loveless woman. There is no room in her icy heart for compassion, friendship, sympathy, or love. She sees people merely as counters to be moved around a board at her will. The pleasure she received from her blackmail threat, using the giant rat, came more from the power it gave her, not over a group of individuals this time, but over the Government of Britain and the population of this great city. The promise of great financial rewards meant little to her. And yet – and yet – even the stoniest heart has its weakness. There was one thing she loved, she doted upon, wasn't there, Watson?'

'The panther!'

'The panther, her beloved pet, which she buried with all the loving dignity she would afford her own child. It was a wild, dangerous creature like herself. And she loved it.'

'So we are going back to Crescent Lodge.'

'In Surrey.'

We found the door of Crescent Lodge unlocked. Clutching our revolvers, we entered the house, our footfalls echoing in the deserted hallway.

'Someone has been here recently,' whispered Holmes, indicating traces of damp mud on the hall floor. 'And certainly the police would not have left the door open after they raided the place yesterday.'

We moved further into the house. It was clear that Holmes was making his way to the conservatory. The building was eerily quiet. It seemed as though the house itself was holding its breath. The only sounds we could hear were our footsteps and the rustle of our own clothes. On reaching the conservatory door, I saw Holmes hesitate, something I cannot recall him ever doing before in this fashion. I knew why. He was fully aware that if the Baroness were here, he would have to battle with her fearsome power again, and even now he was unsure whether he had the strength to counteract it. With grim determination, he opened the door and we entered.

At the far end of the conservatory, by the window which looked out upon the lawn, out to where the panther was buried, sat a woman. She had her back to us and did not move on our entrance. As we advanced she remained immobile, still gazing out at the creature's grave.

Gently Holmes placed his hand on her shoulder and she slowly turned to face us. It was a great shock to see that this woman was not the Baroness. Indeed, I had never seen her before. She was a fresh-faced young lady in her mid-twenties. Momentarily Holmes's face registered surprise and dismay, but then quickly retained its normal composure.

'Mr Holmes?' said the young lady in the sweetest of voices.

'I am,' replied my friend.

'I have a letter for you.' From the folds of her dress she withdrew a long white envelope which bore the name of Sherlock Holmes.

He took it, opened it, and read the letter inside. As he did so, he emitted a strange moaning sigh. Long after reading the letter, he held it in his hand staring at the tidy handwriting as if it would tell him more than it did. Then he passed it to me. It read:

My dear Mr Sherlock Holmes

First let me apologise for the disappointment you must feel at not finding me here waiting for you. The prospect of such a meeting seemed to me to be tinged with too much danger and risk. In my encounter with you I have realised that you are far too dangerous and resourceful an antagonist for me to come too close to. That is why, when you read these words – some time on the morning following your visit to the Eagle Printing Company if I am correct in my assumptions – I shall be safely on the Continent making my way to . . . who knows where? I felt certain you would deduce, as you would describe it, that I would return to Babaska to pay my last respects. However, you did not provide me with enough time for that luxury. Practicalities must always override sentiment. So I organised this girl to deliver my final floral tribute and this message to you. (She is an innocent out of work actress and knows nothing of me or the real nature of her errand. For her it is just another part.)

Have no fear, I shall not return to your country. My time there has not been successful. You have seen the last of me. You are a remarkable man, Sherlock Holmes. What a pity that we were not on the same side. We should have made an unbeatable team.

Very truly yours

EMMUSKA DUBEYK

'What an incredible woman,' I muttered, joining my friend at the window where he was staring out at the panther's grave. Placed there was a large bunch of red roses, the morning dew still glistening on their vibrant petals.

'Indeed. I can only echo her sentiment: "what a pity that we were not on the same side." '

'What an amazing case this has been, Holmes.'

Epilogue

Despite the efforts of Scotland Yard liaising with police departments on the Continent, no trace of the Baroness could be found. It was as though she had disappeared into thin air.

A week after our final visit to Crescent Lodge, Holmes and I were invited to dine at Downing Street, where we received the grateful thanks of the Prime Minister for the part we had played in the affair. By this time Holmes was involved in another investigation and was somewhat distracted for the whole evening.

I saw Alice Mellor just one more time. After a month's leave, she returned to Bart's and one afternoon we took tea together in a café near the hospital. She still looked tired and nervous, and it was clear to me that her involvement in the case had placed a great strain on her nerves. She seemed ill at ease with me and I began to feel a kind of guilt for, indirectly, it was I who had helped to cast this shadow over her life. She told me that she was considering retiring and going to live with her daughter. I learned later that, in fact, she remained on the staff of the hospital and performed her duties with accustomed diligence and fortitude.

I did all I could to place the whole affair at the back of my mind. However, I knew that one day I would write it down, if only in an attempt to exorcise those dark fears that sometimes come to me in the night. In those nightmares I am trapped once more in the hot, stuffy darkness of the hold; I hear the scuttle of claws and smell the foetid stench of breath; and I am once more face to face with the Giant Rat of Sumatra.

THE TANGLED SKEIN

And now I pass on to another thread which I have extricated out of the tangled skein.

DR JOHN H. WATSON
The Hound of the Baskervilles

FOREWORD

When Mr Davies approached me to write this foreword, I must admit I felt rather dubious about *Holmes v. Dracula*. As all readers of Sir Arthur Conan Doyle's stories will know, the great detective's services were called upon to investigate a Vampire scare in Lamberley, Sussex ('. . . south of Horsham . . .') which turned out to be nothing more bloodthirsty than a jealous young son, who inflicted a wound upon his baby step-brother's neck, which looked like the marks of teeth. But Bram Stoker's *Dracula* is a very different kettle of fish – or perhaps I should say, cauldron of leeches!

I need not have had any doubts. Mr Davies has combined most cleverly the creations of two famous authors, and written a stunning yarn, which holds our interest and attention from the very beginning, when the scene is set in those much-loved rooms at 221B Baker Street, with a good old London 'pea-souper' pervading the streets.

Although there is a smattering of quotes lifted straight from the original stories, Mr Davies's tale is more than a mere pastiche of The Canon, and his vivid descriptive passages of action make one long to see 'the film of the book'!

There was an article in the Daily Telegraph recently, written by Adrian Berry, in which a Professor Frank Tipler predicted that we shall all be resurrected before this earth's remaining 20,000 million years – give or take a week or two – are over. The common view among physicists, apparently, is that everything that *can* happen *must* happen. Tipler is Professor of Mathematical Physics at Tulane University in New Orleans, and a former senior research fellow at Oxford; he cannot prove his theory yet, but his present knowledge leads him to believe it is completely logical.

Holmes's logic and practical nature make it hard for him to accept the evidence of vampirism, but there are many cards up Mr Davies's sleeve, which he plays in a most ingenious way before Holmes is finally convinced by Professor Van Helsing and his knowledge of the subject. It was intriguing to read the proposition in the newspaper and the fiction of *The Tangled Skein* anent two very arguable topics.

If I hadn't known the latter was the work of a contemporary writer, I would've sworn it was a long-lost MS of the Master Story-Teller which had been unearthed.

What greater praise can I give to anauthor who is, obviously, on the threshold of great things . . . ?

PETER CUSHING O.B.E.
Whitstable, Kent
January 1992

AUTHOR'S NOTE

How Dr Watson's red leather journal came into my hands is a long and complicated story. Suffice it to say that the notes which I have fleshed out, and adapted into a novel, are very controversial. However, experts have agreed that the handwriting in the journal is certainly that of Dr John H. Watson, biographer and friend of Mr Sherlock Holmes, the world's first consulting detective. Watson himself did not witness the events related in Chapters Four and Six. Therefore, as accurately as I could, I have pieced together from his notes an account of these incidents and recorded them in the third person. Whether the events that are related actually happened, or were the fanciful creation of Watson the frustrated storyteller, no one can now tell. It is, I believe, for the reader to decide.

DAVID STUART DAVIES
January 1992

For Kathryn

PROLOGUE

The events related in *The Tangled Skein* follow closely on the heels of one of Sherlock Holmes's most celebrated cases, recounted in *The Hound of the Baskervilles*. Certain references in *The Tangled Skein* will have greater relevance if the reader is acquainted with the major points of the Baskerville case.

In the autumn of 1888,* Sherlock Holmes is visited by Dr James Mortimer of Grimpen, Dartmoor, a family friend of Sir Charles Baskerville whose mysterious death occurred some months before. Mortimer tells Holmes and Watson of the legend of the Hound of the Baskervilles, a terrible supernatural beast which tore the throat out of the wicked Sir Hugo Baskerville in 1648. Since that time the phantom hound has haunted the moor, terrifying the Baskerville descendants. Mortimer is certain that this hound is in some way responsible for the death of Sir Charles, and he feels that the heir to the Baskerville estate, Sir Henry, newly arrived from Canada, is in danger.

Holmes dismisses the existence of a phantom dog as a fairy tale, but agrees to help Sir Henry. The baronet proves to be a responsible and courageous young man who is not in the least daunted by the legend. A letter warning him to keep away from the moor proves insufficient to deter him from taking up his inheritance. The message, however, assures Holmes that human villainy is afoot.

The detective claims that he is too busy to accompany Sir Henry to Baskerville Hall on Dartmoor, and so sends Watson in his place. At the Hall, an isolated, cheerless house, Watson meets Barrymore the butler, who, having inherited a large sum of money under the late Sir Charles's will, was one of Holmes's initial suspects. The day after his arrival Watson encounters John Stapleton, a naturalist who lives at nearby Merripit House. Together they hear a low moan echo across the moor, and Stapleton assures the doctor that it is the cry of the Hound of the Baskervilles. But the Hound is not the only creature

* Sherlockian experts disagree over the dating of the Baskerville case, but W.S. Baring-Gould gives the year 1888 in his biography of Sherlock Holmes, and the details in *The Tangled Skein* seem to verify this date.

roaming the moor: a convict is hiding there, and Watson glimpses a strange, solitary figure standing on Black Tor.

When Watson tries to run this figure to earth, he discovers signs of habitation in one of the neolithic stone huts on Black Tor. The mysterious figure turns out to be Sherlock Holmes, who has been down on the moor all the time observing events from a distance. He has already come to the conclusion that Stapleton is the murderer. He is the son of Rodger Baskerville, the younger brother of Sir Charles, who was believed to have died unmarried in South America. Stapleton's plan is to kill Sir Henry so that he, himself, can inherit the Baskerville estate. The reconstruction of the phantom hound is his ingenious means of murder.

Holmes slowly fixes his nets and, using Sir Henry as unwitting bait, causes Stapleton to release the Hound, which turns out to be a huge creature – a cross between a bloodhound and a mastiff – treated with phosphorus to make it look more frightening. Although the dog manages to attack the baronet, Holmes is able to shoot the beast before it seriously injures Sir Henry.

Stapleton attempts to escape by crossing the great Grimpen Mire to safety, but the moorland mist is thick that night and he misses his footing. 'Somewhere . . . down in the foul slime of the huge morass which sucked him in, this cold and cruel-hearted man is forever buried.'

CHAPTER ONE
The Mysterious Visitor

'Vampires!'

Sherlock Holmes gave a snort of disgust, and, throwing down the morning paper, strode to the window to stare out at the thick wall of mist which pressed against the panes of our Baker Street rooms.

It was a cold, raw morning in the late November of 1888, and the mellow autumn was already giving way to winter's harsh grasp. The fierce gales of the previous week had robbed the trees of any remaining leaves, leaving the London parks with a stark, skeletal look. And now, like a great yellow scarf, a thick fog had wrapped itself around the city, as if to protect it from the icy onslaught.

It had been a gratifying autumn for my friend Sherlock Holmes. He had successfully completed three cases, including the Baskerville affair. Indeed, only the previous afternoon Sir Henry Baskerville and Dr Mortimer had called upon us, and Holmes had discussed the case of the phantom hound in detail with them. He had been in sparkling form, as he always was when talking of his investigations to an eager and admiring audience.

I had been dismayed to see the change brought about in Sir Henry by his ordeal on the moor. The pale, sunken cheeks and the dark, restless eyes told all too well that he was still haunted by the trials he had undergone. Both he and Mortimer had been in town for some weeks making preparations for a world cruise which, it was hoped, would restore the baronet's shattered nerve.

Once again the sombre portals of Baskerville Hall were to be without a master. Barrymore, the faithful butler whose family had served the Baskerville family for several generations, had finally given notice and, with his wife, had gone to Plymouth with the intention of running a small guest house there. Therefore the great hall had been closed up, and would remain so until Sir Henry returned.

With warm smiles and firm handshakes, we wished our friends *bon voyage* as they left to make the final arrangements before sailing.

After their departure, Holmes and I spent an enjoyable evening, with dinner at Marcini's followed by a visit to the Albert Hall to hear the splendid singing of the De Reszke brothers in Meyerbeer's *Les Huguenots*.

Holmes had been in a relaxed mood, communicative and witty throughout, but seated at the back of my mind was a distinct feeling of unease. I had not shared rooms with Sherlock Holmes for so long without being aware that in this volubility there were danger signals. I realised that with the completion of three cases there was no longer a demand for Holmes's singular talents, and it would only be a matter of time before boredom and frustration set in, unless some new, intriguing problem presented itself. In many ways my friend was like a child who takes delight in the special charm of an unusual and challenging puzzle. Once the puzzle has been solved and the challenge removed, the child will only be placated by being given another mystifying toy. With Holmes, once the case had reached a satisfactory conclusion, the only way to prevent his slide into the murky depths of depression, where the cocaine bottle seemed to provide his only relief, was to present him with another toy – another crime to tax his incredible brain.

As we sipped brandy nightcaps together around the dying embers of our study fire late that night, Holmes had been extremely garrulous, touching on subjects as diverse as medieval mystery plays and flaws in the present foreign policy. In the morning, however, there had been a marked transformation in his behaviour: he had grown sullen and uncommunicative. It was as though on waking he had suddenly realised that there was no problem demanding his attention.

His cry of disgust with which I began this narrative was, in fact, the first time that morning that he had addressed me personally.

'Vampires?' I repeated, mystified by his outburst.

'In the paper,' he snapped, gesturing towards the discarded *Times*. I picked up the newspaper and scanned the page Holmes had been reading. In the bottom right-hand corner, I found the article to which he referred. It ran thus:

VAMPIRES: A REALITY?

In his opening lecture to the Royal Society last evening, 'Minority Religious Cults in Eastern Europe', Professor Abraham Van Helsing of Amsterdam University referred to his belief in the existence of what he termed 'the cult of the undead', beings who are more commonly known as Vampires.

Van Helsing assured his audience that these creatures do exist and that he had encountered them personally. 'Ignorance and disbelief are their strongest protection. As long as the civilised world refuses to accept their existence, this unholy cult will continue to grow,' he asserted as the audience became agitated and unruly. Many members of The Society walked out in disgust, while others jeered and hurled insults at the visting lecturer.

Eventually order was restored, and the lecture continued without further reference to Vampires.

'It does seem rather strange,' said I, casting the newspaper aside, 'that so eminent a scholar should make such a rash statement in public.'

'Rash statement!' Holmes snorted, indignantly. 'Why, the man has made a complete fool of himself. It is easy to see how these superstitious beliefs are carried on from generation to generation among the remote peasant communities, but here we have a man of science claiming the authenticity of such fairy stories. It should be clear, even to the most elementary of scientific brains, that the explanation of such beliefs lies not in the supernatural, but in the acceptance of weird folk tales as factual occurences. For the simple mind the line between reality and fantasy is blurred, but the educated brain should reject any such nonsense without hesitation.'

He shook his head sadly. 'It comes to a pretty pass, Watson, when the mind of man has to conjure up hobgoblins and walking corpses to provide his villainy. We have enough evils in our world, without summoning those from the other.'

'However, there are certain areas of the unexplained about which one must keep an open mind,' I said.

Holmes gave a derisory chuckle.

'An open mind is the last thing one should have when dealing with the unexplained. A questioning and suspicious mind is a necessity if one is not to swallow such supernatural poppycock. How would I have reached a satisfactory solution to the Baskerville case if, for one instant, I had accepted the notion that such a thing as a phantom hound actually existed?'

'I know the hound we dealt with was real enough, but what of the one in the legend?'

'Legend is myth, Watson, originating from tales told around the camp fire. Ghost stories to frighten the children, not data with which to create a logical basis for action.'

Holmes threw himself into the chair opposite me, his features brightening as he warmed to his subject.

'The world of the occult is accepted only by those whose imagination has mastered their intellect. The educated romantic, such as Van Helsing appears to be, is the most dangerous creature of all, for his acceptance of such lunacy gives it credence in the eyes of the gullible public.'

'But one hears of so many bizarre incidents which cannot be explained rationally that I cannot help feeling we should not totally reject the idea of the supernatural.'

'Cannot help feeling!' cried Holmes, echoing my words. 'Feelings are emotional traps: unreliable and feminine. Great heavens, Watson, I believed you had been in my company long enough to realise that facts, incontrovertible facts, not feelings, are the only reliable aids to decision-making.' He gave a wry chuckle. 'Oh, my dear fellow, you have too much of a romantic soul ever to be a successful reasoner. That is why I am able to baffle you from time to time with my little deductions. When the heart interferes with the head, it clouds all issues.'

'Really, Holmes . . . ' I began in protest, but his attention had suddenly been arrested by a loud knocking at our street door below, and he held up his hand to silence me.

'I believe we are about to receive a visitor,' he said gleefully after a moment, rubbing his hands together. His dark eyes sparkled at the possibility of receiving a client, and his diatribe on belief in the supernatural was apparently forgotten.

Footsteps on the stair were followed by a knock on our door. Holmes frowned. 'It seems there is no client after all. Come in, Mrs Hudson.'

Our housekeeper entered. 'Good gracious,' she said, 'how did you know it was me, Mr Holmes?'

'To the trained ear, footsteps are as identifiable as fingerprints, Mrs Hudson, and you have one of the daintiest steps in London,' replied Holmes.

Mrs Hudson blushed.

'But Watson, I see we have had a visitor after all, and he has left us a gift.' Holmes pointed to the package our housekeeper was holding.

'You are right as usual, Mr Holmes. A gentleman just delivered this for you; and he was most particular that I give the package into your hands personally.'

'Did he now? Surely you informed the gentleman that I was at home?'

'Oh yes. I told him that he could see the job done properly by handing it to you himself, and that all he had to do was come up to your room.'

'He refused?' I asked.

'Well, he said he was in a hurry and he felt sure he could rely on me to carry out his wishes.'

'Which you have done,' smiled Holmes, taking the package from Mrs Hudson and placing it on the table.

'What did the fellow look like?' I asked.

'Unless I am mistaken,' said Holmes, 'it would be difficult for Mrs Hudson to pass an opinion, as he had his hat pulled down over his eyes and his muffler held well up around his mouth.'

'That's right, Mr Holmes, he was well wrapped up, and he certainly did not seem too well,' said our landlady.

'You are perhaps referring to his laryngitis?' said Holmes.

'Something like that, I expect; whatever it was, it made him speak in a hoarse sort of way.'

Sherlock Holmes gave a satisfied nod.

'But how did you know that, Mr Holmes?'

He smiled indulgently. 'One of my little guesses, Mrs Hudson. It is certainly the weather for coughs and colds, and it is not unusual for a delivery man to catch one.'

I was far from convinced by this glib explanation and, after Mrs Hudson had left the room, I questioned my friend further. 'Holmes, I know you never guess. So how did you know that the visitor had laryngitis and wore a hat and muffler in the manner you described?'

Holmes ignored my query and stared pensively at the parcel for some moments, tapping it lightly with his finger. At length he spoke. 'Tell me, Watson, why should a man who has a package to deliver not take the trouble to mount a flight of stairs to ensure it reaches its destination safely?'

'He said he was in a hurry.'

'Fiddlesticks! If this package is of such importance, as the labelling suggests – "Urgent and Personal" – surely he could have taken the time to do his job properly? No, Watson, there is something here that is not quite what it seems. His reluctance suggests that he did not wish to come face to face with me for fear I would recognise him.'

'Oh, come now, Holmes,' I protested, believing my friend was seeing shadows where none existed.

'He made absolutely sure that even Mrs Hudson could not get a good look at his face, thus making it impossible for her to give me an accurate description of him.'

'And the laryngitis . . . ?'

'An attempt to disguise his natural voice.'

I laughed. 'Really, Holmes, I do believe you are making a melodrama out of a molehill.'

'Melodrama? No. Speculation? Yes. It has been my experience that when there is no data to work on, speculation is an admirable substitute. It helps one sort the probable from the impossible.'

'But you do have some data to work on,' I said, pointing to the package.

Holmes beamed. 'As always, Watson, your common sense is invaluable. This may tell us all we need to know about our strange visitor. Kindly pass me the jack-knife from the mantelpiece, and we shall see what this mysterious package contains.'

CHAPTER TWO
The Package

The package was oblong – about one foot in length and five or six inches in depth. It was wrapped in thick brown paper and tied around with strong black cord. The words 'Urgent and Personal' were printed in bold capitals in the top left-hand corner and 'For the attention of Sherlock Holmes, Baker Street' was written in a spidery hand across the middle.

Using the jack-knife with which he transfixed his correspondence to the mantelpiece, Holmes cut the cord and slowly removed several layers of wrapping paper. The whole operation was carried out with the utmost care, as though he were in danger of damaging some delicate object inside.

'As I thought,' said he at last, when the wrapping had finally been discarded.

'Don't tell me that you knew it was a book.'

'Not even liberal packaging can conceal the peculiar shape and density of a Messrs Chapman and Hall first edition.'

'If you knew it was just a book, why did you treat the thing as if it were a bomb about to go off?'

Holmes gave a wry smile. 'Because I suspect this is far more than "just a book".'

Not fully comprehending this cryptic remark, I stared at the large brown volume for some moments in an attempt to discover what Holmes considered so unusual about it, but I failed to do so.

'There appears to be no note indicating who sent it to you,' I said at length.

'I never expected one.'

'Perhaps there is an inscription or dedication inside.' I moved to open the book, but Holmes grabbed my arm.

'Don't touch it, Watson. At least not until I have had a chance to scrutinise it closely.'

Taking his convex lens, Holmes crouched down by the table and examined the spine and case without actually touching the book.

'Curious and enlightening,' he murmured, more to himself than to me. At length he stood up and gave a dry chuckle.

'What is it, Holmes?'

'The title of the book. One of Charles Dickens's most popular works: *Great Expectations*. However, my close examination of this tome leads me to believe that its contents have little to do with the adventures of young Pip and his strange inheritance.' He tapped the top of the book gently with the jack-knife. 'Yes, without a doubt this volume has been chosen principally for its thickness. *A Tale of Two Cities* would have been far too slim.'

I shook my head. 'I must confess I am completely baffled by all this.'

Holmes gave me a tight-lipped smile. 'All will be revealed very soon, Watson, but for the moment would you be so kind as to move over to the window.'

Knowing my friend would have a good reason for such a request, I did as he asked. Holmes then placed the book in the middle of the table and, standing at arm's length from it, delicately lifted the hardback cover with the tip of the jack-knife. There was a sudden, loud, violent snap and a short, silver stiletto blade shot from the inside of the book and embedded itself in the ceiling.

Holmes gave a cry of delight. 'Splendid,' he said, gazing up at the treacherous missile. 'You can come away from the window now, Watson. The danger is over.'

I rushed to examine the book: the middle had been cut out and a clever spring mechanism inserted.

'Fiendish, eh, Watson? The spring is set so that when the book is opened it thrusts a knife directly into the heart of the reader.'

'How on earth did you know this before you opened the thing?' I asked.

'To be honest, Watson, I did not. I was unsure what devilment it housed, but I knew this volume was not the innocent gift it was meant to appear. The manner of its delivery and the anonymity of its origin had already raised my suspicions. On inspecting it closely, I observed faint traces of glue along the edges of the pages, and when I tapped the top of the book it sounded hollow. It was therefore clear to me that the pages had been stuck together in order for the centre to be hollowed out. The mutilation of a great work of literature is not, as yet, a criminal act, but it is certainly a devious one. For what purpose had this disembowelling proced- ure been carried out? Obviously to allow for the insertion of some device which had to be operated by the raising of the book's cover.'

'Why so?'

'Because after the book was opened, the device would have been exposed. I was not sure what form of unpleasantness to expect when I did open it, and that is why I asked you to move to the window – out of the immediate danger area.'

'Well, it is fortunate that I did not get my hands on the book first. I would simply have opened it.'

'That would have disappointed my would-be assassin greatly. Remember, the book was expressly addressed to me.'

'Yes, by Jove,' I said, suddenly grasping the full implication of the situation. Holmes was not a stranger to murderous attacks, but this was the first time* one had been made in such an underhand and devious way, and in what I had previously considered to be the security of our Baker Street rooms. It seemed now that we were not even safe by our own fireside.

'Have you any idea who sent the thing?' I asked.

'I have many enemies,' said Holmes, closely examining the trick mechanism in the book, 'but few who are capable of presenting me with such an audacious and deadly gift. A foe with a twisted sense of humour also.'

'Sense of humour?'

'I said the volume had been chosen principally for its size – it needed to be quite thick to incorporate the device – and yet I feel sure the title was not selected at random.'

'*Great Expectations*?'

'Indeed. The sender wanted me dead: those were his "great expectations". Happily, they remain unrealised.' He gave a grim smile.

'That kind of humour suggests a touch of madness to me.'

'You are probably right, Watson.'

'Who is it? Who is this maniac?'

'It is clear that the mysterious delivery man is our culprit. As to his identity – I have strong suspicions, but I shall need further data before I can be absolutely sure. One thing is certain, however: his reluctance to hand the book over to me in person indicates that he and I have met before, and it was the fear of recognition which prevented him from coming face to face with me.'

---

* This assassination attempt predates the one made in 'The Empty House' by some six years. On that occasion, Holmes was shot at from the building across the street from his study.

'What do you intend to do next?'

'Nothing,' said Holmes casually, flinging himself into his arm-chair.

'Nothing?' I repeated incredulously.

'There is no need to check me back as though I were an invoice, Watson. I said "nothing".'

'I cannot understand you, Holmes,' I replied, somewhat indignantly. 'I must say, I find it astonishing that you take this attempt on your life so calmly, and now you appear to be content to let the villain escape.'

'My dear fellow, you misinterpret my intentions. I assure you our mystery murderer will eventually be brought to justice, but for the present I see no reason to put the hounds on him. It will not take him long to discover that his little plan has failed and, if he is the man I take him to be, he will soon resume his mischief.'

'You mean he will try to kill you again.'

'Certainly. The mind that conceived such a deft and cunning means of murder as this lethal contrivance will not be deterred by one failure. In this case, Watson, the roles are reversed: I am the fly. Therefore, I will wait for the spider to come to me – as in time, he must.'

CHAPTER THREE
The Telegram

I confess I was somewhat dismayed by Holmes's casual attitude to the threat hanging over him. Although I knew that in matters of crime detection he was seldom wrong, I felt he was being most remiss in not attempting to track down his would-be murderer.

While he lay back in his chair, casually smoking a cigarette, apparently content, I grew restless. Surely something positive could be done, should be done, rather than just calmly waiting for the next blow to be struck. I examined the battered copy of *Great Expectations* again. While doing so, an idea came to me and, acting on impulse, I took myself out on the pretext of visiting Bradley's for a supply of tobacco. Holmes hardly seemed to notice my departure.

Once out in the bitterly cold, foggy air, I made my way to Charing Cross Road, where I began enquiring at all the bookshops specialising in first editions in an attempt to discover if such a copy of Dickens's *Great Expectations* had been sold within the last week or so. The response was unanimously negative.

Frustrated and disheartened, I returned to Baker Street as the fog grew thicker and the gas lamps were being lit. Holmes greeted my return in a cheery but sarcastic manner.

'Well, have your investigations revealed any further clues?' he asked smugly as I joined him by the fire.

'Investigations?'

'Oh come now, Watson, you are not going to cling to your pretence of visiting Bradley's I hope? That will not do at all. A man who has a tobacco jar overbrimming with his Arcadia mixture, and a bulging pouch, which, incidentally, he leaves down the side of his chair, is not in need of fresh supplies. It was not difficult to deduce that your errand lay elsewhere.'

'If you must know I have been trying to find out more about this fellow who is out to murder you.'

'I thank you for that, but I am afraid I could have told you that nothing would be gleaned from visiting bookshops in the Charing Cross Road.'

'How do you know where I have been?'

'A simple deduction, I assure you. I knew you were unhappy about my decision to wait for fresh developments to present themselves and, before your rather hasty exit, I observed that you had been re-examining the book. Therefore it was clear to me that you were considering carrying out some investigations of your own. The only real path open to you was to try and trace the shop from which the novel had been purchased. Having done this, you would be able to obtain a description and possibly other details concerning our man. Charing Cross Road is the nucleus of antiquarian booksellers in this area. You have not been gone long enough to try elsewhere.'

I nodded, smiling. 'You are correct, of course; and after all that, I can offer you no further information.'

'My dear Watson, I could have saved you the trouble of venturing out in such inhospitable weather if you had confided in me regarding your errand.' He picked up the copy of *Great Expectations*. 'This book has not been purchased recently. Notice how scuffed and dented the leather binding is, and the dirty marks on the inside cover. No bookseller worth his salt would have let the volume leave his shop in that condition. He would have restored the leather and spruced up the whole appearance before putting it on his shelf for sale. It is safe to say that this book has been part of someone's private collection for a long time, someone who is educated, who was once affluent, but who has now come down in the world.'

'How can you tell that?'

'The book, when new, would have been very expensive – see the fine leather and the costly gold blocking – and almost certainly one of a set. It is my experience that only affluent individuals purchase such expensive volumes, and only educated ones hang on to such possessions when their circumstances are reduced.'

Holmes saw the question in my glance and continued. 'The book, although a prized possession, has recently been stored in dirty and damp conditions. A brief sniff at the remaining pages will give you all the evidence you need regarding the damp storage. You know, Watson, sometimes the nose can be more informative than the eye.'

'Is the owner of the book our man?'

'Ah, here we wander into the realms of conjecture, which I am reluctant to do at present. My potential assassin could have been given the book recently, or could even have stolen it. This area of the mystery is still in shadow – a shadow that will remain until our spider makes his next move.'

*   *   *

Holmes had not long to wait.

It was in the late evening of the same day when he received the telegram. Holmes had spent the time since tea curled up in his mouse-coloured dressing gown, smoking pipeful after pipeful of the strongest shag tobacco as he stared into the fire. As I observed him through the dense clouds of grey smoke, I knew from the penetrating gaze that came from those hooded eyes that he was inwardly deliberating over the morning's event.

It was shortly after ten o'clock when the telegram arrived. Holmes read it to himself, gave a derisory snort and tossed it over to me. 'What do you make of that, Watson?' he asked.

I read the communication, which ran thus:

LONDON POOR NEED ALL YOUR HELP. THEIR PLIGHTS
DESPERATE. ARE YOU ONE TO HELP LONDON POOR?
                              THE GARDEN S OCIETY
                                                                  C

'Hmm. Seems like some crank organisation to me,' I observed.

'I agree, old fellow. I do not believe you will find any legitimate charity wasting funds sending expensive telegrams appealing for contributions.'

'Who sent it then?'

'I am not sure . . . yet. Is there anything which strikes you as being particularly odd about the telegram?'

'Well,' said I, glancing at it once more, 'the syntax is a little strange and the "S" of "Society" seems to have been oddly placed.'

My friend rubbed his hands together in glee. 'Excellent, Watson. We shall make a detective of you yet.'

'Possibly,' I replied tersely. 'Are there any points I have missed?'

'What do you make of the letter "C" placed in the bottom right-hand corner?'

I studied the telegram again. It was clear to me that Holmes saw more in this message than met my eye. For some moments I puzzled over the oddly situated letter. 'It is almost like a signature,' I said at length. 'It could well be a clue to the identity of the sender.'

'Splendid!' cried Holmes in that infuriatingly patronising way of his.

'Perhaps,' I continued, 'it is the sound of the letter rather than the letter itself that is important.'

'Ah, you mean "the sea," suggesting some nautical connection?'

I gave a brief nod, determining from my friend's tone of voice that I was on the wrong track.

'A worthy suggestion, but I think you are gracing this message with more subtlety than it possesses. However, my dear fellow, you are not totally wrong, for although the letter "C" does not directly indicate who sent the telegram, it is a key to its content. I can see by your frown that I had better explain myself.

'This oddly-phrased telegram is a coded message, and the letter "C" placed in isolation at the end is the key to the code. Now "C" is the third letter of the alphabet, so if we take every third letter we should be presented with a new and very different message.'

We studied the telegram together.

'Every third letter? That makes the first line N N O E which does not make sense to me,' said I.

'Nor me,' agreed Holmes.

'Perhaps it is every third word,' I suggested.

'You have got it! Excellent, Watson. Every third word it is.'

Holmes quickly scribbled down his translation of the telegram. 'That's more like it. The message now reads: "Need Help Desperate One London Gardens".'

'London Gardens?'

'Yes. That explains why the "S" from "Society" was attached to the word "Garden".'

'Ingenious.'

'Not, perhaps, ingenious enough.'

'What do you mean?'

'This is a plea for help, but why go to the bother of such a cumbersome method of sending it?'

'To prevent a certain party or parties from knowing you were being called in.'

'Possibly, but the code is perhaps too elementary. The sender wishes to intrigue me with his *cri de coeur*, hence the code, but at the same time he needs to be certain I will have no difficulty in reading his hidden message so that I can go to the stated address tonight.'

'You suspect a trap?'

'It is possible. I sense the hand of our mysterious package man again.'

'What will you do?'

'I intend to play knight errant.'

'Then I will go with you.'

Holmes shook his head. 'No, Watson. On this occasion it is imperative that I go alone.'

'You may be placing yourself in great danger.'

'It is most likely, but I must go unaccompanied.'

'Have I ever failed you?'

Holmes gave a thin smile and placed his hand on my shoulder. 'My dear Watson, as I have told you before, there is no one I would rather have at my side in a moment of crisis. However, tonight's little excursion calls for action on my part alone.'

'I see,' I said.

'And,' added Holmes, pointing his long forefinger at me, 'on no account must I be followed.'

'If you insist.'

'I must insist. Your presence could ruin everything.'

'Very well,' I agreed reluctantly.

'Good man. Now there is not a moment to lose,' he cried, throwing off his dressing gown. Within minutes he had gone.

I knew that it was as much for my safety as his own that Holmes had insisted on going alone to meet his unknown adversary, and that indicated clearly how dangerous and risky he believed his mission to be. It was with a feeling of great unease that I watched from the window of our rooms as my friend disappeared into the night, swallowed up by a giant whirl of yellow fog.

CHAPTER FOUR
London Gardens*

Despite the charm of its name, London Gardens was a down-at-heel area in Kentish Town. Having managed to hail a hansom cab at the end of Baker Street, Sherlock Holmes alighted a quarter of a mile away from his destination so as not to announce his arrival. The streets were silent and empty except for the occasional flurry of a small pack of rats on the move. They scampered silently across the damp pavements like a dark, moving stain.

The fog was not as thick as in Baker Street, and a stiff breeze blew the yellow smoke in eddies around the tall, dark figure of the detective. At irregular intervals the darkness was illuminated by feeble gas lamps throwing down pallid circles of light around their bases. Holmes kept to the shadows.

Far across the city Big Ben began chiming midnight. Moving cautiously towards his goal, Holmes observed the buildings growing shabbier. Wafting on the cold night air was the odour of decay. Suddenly he paused, his senses alert, his nerves tense. In the hushed silence of the street he thought he could detect some slight, indefinable noise. Moving forward a little, he listened again, straining to catch the faintest sound. There was no mistaking it this time: it was the soft, rhythmic shuffling movement of someone's feet.

He was being followed.

Without warning, Holmes spun round and faced the darkness behind him. He heard a startled gasp and through the fog glimpsed the vague outline of a man, his right arm raised as though ready to strike him down. As the figure lunged forward, Holmes quickly sidestepped, just missing the vicious blow as it fell. The assailant staggered and grunted some inaudible comment.

Holmes moved slowly back towards the nearest gas lamp to lure the man into the light. The creature that gradually shambled into the rim of illumination was a sorry sight indeed. It was a man of

* From Dr Watson's notebook

indeterminate age. The unshaven blotched face and bloodshot eyes were more animal than human. The thin body was hung with rotting rags held to his emaciated carcass with string. In his limp grasp he held a weapon: a short, stout piece of wood.

'Didn't mean no harm, Guv,' he croaked, the words escaping in tortured gasps.

'Since when has a broken skull been harmless?' snapped Holmes.

The man flung the piece of wood away. 'Didn't mean no harm,' he repeated dully. 'Just desperate, Guv, that's all.' He staggered further into the light. 'I ain't eaten since . . . ' His haggard face clouded for a moment, and his brow furrowed: he obviously could not remember. 'I ain't eaten . . . ' he said again, shaking his head in vague bewilderment.

Holmes considered the wretch before him. Was he really what he appeared to be – one of the sad specimens of human debris that inhabit the unfashionable areas of London, living off what scraps of food he could find, often turning to crime as the only means of survival – or was he in some way connected with the mysterious telegram and the assassination attempt made that morning?

The man shuffled a few steps nearer to Holmes, his hands outstretched in a gesture of supplication, and with him came the stench of the sewer. Holmes studied the vacant eyes, the rotting teeth, the running sores, the cheeks sunken with consumption and malnutrition: these were not counterfeit. This broken creature was no impostor.

A silver coin flashed in the air.

'Thank you, Guv.'

'Now, on your way,' snapped Holmes.

'Heaven bless you,' the creature mumbled as he shuffled backwards and melted once more into the darkness.

Holmes waited some moments before crossing the street and approaching the six dreary and dilapidated houses bearing the name London Gardens. Once proud, fashionable residences, they were now woefully neglected with crumbling façades, overgrown gardens and dirt-smeared windows. The houses were all in darkness except the first, Number One, the address to which he had been summoned so dramatically. In an upstairs room of this house there was a flickering light, and silhouetted against the drawn blind was the figure of a man.

'Waiting,' murmured Holmes, 'in the centre of his web.' He was almost certain he knew the identity of his would-be assassin, but so slender were his threads of evidence and surmise, he deigned not to speak the name, even to himself.

Taking a revolver out of the folds of his coat, Holmes braced himself for action and walked up the path towards the front door. As he did so, he noted a single line of muddy footprints and was able to estimate by the length of the stride that they were made by a slimly-built man of about five feet eight inches in height.

The door opened with ease and he entered the house. By the dim light of a street lamp which filtered through the bleared window panes, he could see the interior was in a worse state of decay than the outside. There were no carpets or furniture to indicate that habitation had once taken place there. The walls were covered with dark blotches of mildew and here and there great strips of wallpaper had become detached and hung down, exposing the cracked plaster beneath.

The house was silent.

Holmes stood in the hall for some time while his eyes grew accustomed to the murky gloom. Gradually, the grotesque shadows thrown by the unsteady gleam of the street lamp lost some of their menace. Moving on tip-toe Holmes began to check the downstairs rooms to ensure that they were empty before he ventured upstairs. He was fairly certain that his adversary was alone, but in this kind of situation one could not be too cautious.

While he was in the room that had been the kitchen, a sudden noise in the pantry arrested his attention. Gripping his revolver tightly, he pulled back the pantry door slowly to reveal two large rats feasting off what looked like the remains of a dead cat. Holmes's intrusion did not deter the rodents from their feast.

The remaining rooms offered up nothing more than thick layers of dust and rotting woodwork. Now it was time to search for the lighted room. Stealthily Holmes climbed the stairs and, on reaching the landing, he paused. Down a short passage to his left, he observed a ghostly, flickering yellow light emanating from the crack under the door at the far end. For a moment a thrill of excitement surged through his body and held him motionless. He knew the extent of the danger in which he was placing himself by entering the room, but his professional career had always depended as much on his ability to face his own fear as on his unrivalled brilliance as a detective.

As he reached the door, the floorboards creaked, as if in warning to his adversary. For a minute he listened intently. There was no response to the sound at all. Everything was still and silent. Quietly he dropped to one knee and peered through the keyhole. As far as he could see the room was bare except for a table near the window, seated at which was the motionless figure of a man. Holmes could not make out the man's features, as the light of a small lamp standing on the table threw them into silhouette.

'Now is the moment,' thought Holmes, and with dramatic suddenness, gun in hand, he burst into the room.

'Good evening,' he said smoothly, addressing the darkened figure. He knew immediately that he had made a mistake but, before he was able to do anything about it, he felt a searing pain at the back of his head. For a moment there was a flash of blinding light, and then darkness overwhelmed him in ebony waves as he sank unconscious to the floor.

CHAPTER FIVE
Miss Lydgate's Warning

As I watched my friend disappear into the night, responding to his mysterious summons, I determined to stay up and await his return. I was well aware that sleep would not visit me until I had heard of his night's exploits and so, after placing more coal on the dying embers of the fire, I settled down with a whisky and the latest edition of *The Lancet*. Despite an interesting article by Charcot on the use of hypnotism as an anaesthetic I could not settle to reading. My eyes skated over the words while my mind kept returning to the dramatic events of that day: the murder attempt and the cryptic telegram. Were they really connected, and if so in what way?

The more I pondered these matters the thicker the fog surrounding them grew. Eventually I reached the point where none of the issues was clear any more. I had just begun to consider the existing evidence once again when my thoughts were interrupted by the impatient ring of our doorbell downstairs. Glancing at my watch, I saw that it was after midnight, and realising that Mrs Hudson would have retired some time ago, I rushed to answer the door myself. As I opened it, a young woman virtually fell into my arms.

'Mr Holmes,' she gasped, her breath coming in short bursts. 'I must see Mr Holmes.'

'I am afraid he is out on a case at the moment,' I said, supporting her arm as I led her into the hall.

'I must see him,' she continued as though she had not heard me. 'I have to warn him.'

'Warn him?' I said, my grip on her arm tightening.

She paused a moment, eyeing me with some suspicion. 'Who are you?'

'I am Dr Watson, a close friend of Sherlock Holmes.'

'I must see him, Dr Watson. He is in great danger.'

'You had better come upstairs out of the cold and tell me all about it,' I said grimly.

Some moments later the young woman sat perched on the edge of a chair facing the fire, a glass of brandy clasped in her trembling white hands. Her pale, delicate features, illuminated by the firelight, bore an unhealthy pallor, and her face was streaked with city grime. Her rather sad demeanour did not, however, disguise her beauty. She had a naturally dignified bearing, and her dark brown eyes were singularly sensitive and spiritual. I noticed too that her clothing, although old and shabby, was of good quality.

She took a sip of brandy and shivered.

'Pull yourself nearer the fire, my dear,' said I.

'It is not the cold that makes me shiver, Dr Watson. It is fear.'

'What exactly are you frightened of?'

'Him. Grenfell!'

'Grenfell?'

'Yes, if that is his real name, which I doubt,' she said with some animation, her eyes sparking with emotion.

'You said that you had come to warn Sherlock Holmes – was it against this Grenfell?'

At the mention of Holmes she glanced frantically around the room as though to catch sight of him. 'Sherlock Holmes . . . yes. Where is he?'

'As I told you before, he is out at the moment.'

'Then it is too late.'

'Perhaps if you would start at the beginning. I am not as clever as my friend at working out riddles.'

She looked at me, her face pale, her eyes moist with tears, and nodded. 'My name is Celia Lydgate. I am twenty-five years old.' She gave a bitter smile. 'Yes, I know I look much older; that is the legacy of the life I am forced to lead. I have not always looked like this, Dr Watson. Once I was quite pretty and had clean and beautiful clothes to wear.' She took another sip of brandy and stared into the flames. 'That was when my father was alive. He was Aubrey Lydgate, the artist.' She waited a moment to see if my face showed recognition of the name, but I had never heard of the man.

'He was not a great painter,' she continued, 'but he made a good living from his portraiture, good enough to provide a comfortable and happy home for the two of us.'

'Your mother . . . ?'

'She died giving birth to me. My father became both parents to me. He was a very wonderful man, doctor.' There was now a tremor in her voice, and I could see that she was fighting hard to keep control of her emotions. 'Two years ago our house caught fire in the middle of the night. It was a habit of my father's while working on a painting to sleep in the studio at the top of the house. He was caught there by the flames. He . . . he could not escape. The fire brigade could not get to him. There was so much smoke . . . so much heat. I could hear him . . . I could hear him screaming . . . '

The young woman broke off, buried her face in her hands, and sobbed quietly. I leaned over and touched her gently on the shoulder. 'Try not to distress yourself,' I said softly, aware as I spoke how impotent my words were. However, they seemed to rally her somewhat and, after a moment, she raised her head, wiped the tears from her face with her sleeve, and continued her narrative.

'My father perished in the fire which destroyed our home. I managed to salvage a few prized possessions, some books and jewellery, but the rest went up in flames: all my father's unsold canvases, everything. And so I found myself totally alone in the world without money, family or a home.'

'What about friends?'

'I had none. My father was my only friend. He was the only one I wanted.'

My heart swelled with pity for this frail, unfortunate woman.

'I had run the house for my father,' she continued. 'I even helped him in the studio, but I had never trained for any occupation, and so was ill-equipped to face life on my own. In order to live, I was forced to sell my jewellery piece by piece. That is why you see me as I am. For the last two years I have only just managed to survive, living in cheap lodgings, taking such charity as I could.'

She paused again and a change came over her features: the soft-set jaw suddenly stiffened, and the light in her eyes hardened. 'I had thought my life was bad enough, but that was before I met John Grenfell; then it became Hell. For some time I had attended a charity mission near Shooter's Hill, close to my lodgings. It is just an old mission hall that doles out prayers, free bread and soup. It was there that I met him – just under a month ago. Curse the day I set eyes on his evil face! To begin with he acted in such a gentle fashion towards me; and, Lord knows, I needed some gentleness in my life. He was the first man since my father with whom I was able to talk. He told me that, like myself, he had come down in the world due to bad luck and enemies. It was only a temporary state of affairs, he said. Oh, he treated me with such kindness at first . . . ' She gave a harsh chuckle. 'I fell in love with him, Dr Watson. That was my fate: to fall in love with a demon.'

She smiled, but there was an emptiness in that smile, and there were tears in her eyes. I offered my handkerchief; she took it and wiped the tears away.

'Pray continue, my dear,' I said. Sympathetic as I was to this wretched young woman's predicament, I could not help worrying about Holmes, and was eager for her to reach the point in her narrative which would tell me the nature of the threat to his life.

'Before long John Grenfell moved into my lodgings. In my innocence it seemed a natural thing to do. We were two outcasts in a harsh world, and it was only natural that we should cling together. We became lovers.' She paused and looked me in the eye. 'Does that shock you, Dr Watson?'

'Miss Lydgate, I . . .'

'I am afraid nothing shocks me anymore. Poverty brutalises all sensitivity. After living in a shabby wilderness for nearly two years without any of the normal human comforts, I was only too eager to take what affection was offered me.' She gave a cold, derisory laugh. 'I soon realised my mistake. It did not take long to find out what a cruel and vicious man had claimed my heart. He would beat me, Dr Watson. At the least provocation, he would beat me.'

Despite my own experience of the darkness that can lie deep in the heart of man, I never failed to be dismayed and angered when I encountered it. 'He shall not touch you again,' I said softly, leaning close to her and placing my hand on her arm.

'But you do not know the cunning of the man. As his true nature became all too painfully apparent to me, I realised that some deep hatred was stoking his anger, pushing him towards madness. And then I discovered by accident that he was working on a plot, some fiendish device to hurt someone. He tried to keep it from me, but one night when he was deep in drink his boastful temper got the better of him, and he told me he was plotting the death of Sherlock Holmes.'

'Please go on, Miss Lydgate,' I urged, my mind already seeing the sinister possibilities that lay ahead.

'He bears Sherlock Holmes some terrible grudge and is determined to destroy him. Grenfell worked on some mechanical device which he placed inside one of the books he took from my beloved collection. I did not find out what the mechanism was for, but I knew that its purpose was harmful.'

'There lies your book, Miss Lydgate.' I pointed to the discarded volume lying on Holmes's chemical bench. 'The device inside was designed to propel that into the heart of the reader,' I added, indicating the blade in the ceiling.

'How horrible!'

'Fortunately, the plan was a failure.'

'But Grenfell intends to kill Mr Holmes tonight.'

'What!'

'He told me this evening that he intended to lure him away from Baker Street and kill him. He threatened to kill me too if I told a soul about it. I was bound and gagged in my own room in case I tried to foil his plans. It took me hours to break free and I came here as fast as I could – but now it is too late. Mr Holmes has gone and Grenfell will have him at his mercy.'

'It would take a clever man indeed to get the better of Sherlock Holmes,' said I; but despite the note of confidence in my assurance, I was filled with a chilling sense of unease. 'Have you any notion how Grenfell intended to trap my friend?'

She shook her head.

'Miss Lydgate,' I said, jumping to my feet and grabbing my coat from the rack, 'I know where Holmes has gone. If he is in real danger as you say, then I must be on hand to help him. In the meantime, you must remain here and await our return. You will be perfectly safe under our roof. Do you understand?'

'Yes,' she replied quietly.

Within minutes, suitably muffled against the cold and foggy air, I was hailing a cab to take me to London Gardens. As it rattled through the black, empty streets, I sat in the dark recesses of the cab clutching my revolver, hoping that my journey was not necessary and that Holmes had gauged the full measure of the danger involved in this exploit. Whoever this Grenfell was, he was certainly a cruel and vicious villain who would show no mercy if Holmes fell into his clutches. Try as I might, I could not eliminate from my mind the foreboding that Holmes really did need my help – and that I might be too late.

CHAPTER SIX

The Spider [*]

The shock of cold water splashed in his face brought Sherlock Holmes back to consciousness. At first his vision was blurred and his mind fogged with pain from the blow to the back of his head. Gradually awareness returned, and he was able to take stock of his situation. He was lying on the floor, his wrists and ankles tightly bound. Standing over him was a man holding an oil lamp, his face masked by shadow.

'Good evening to you, Mr Sherlock Holmes. I am so very glad you were able to respond to my summons,' he said silkily. Holmes recognised the thin, reedy voice, and his suspicions were confirmed. He now knew for certain who had sent him the deadly volume, and who had lured him into this trap.

'I certainly did not intend to address you from this rather un-dignified position, Stapleton.'

Holmes's captor gave a wry chuckle. 'So you knew?'

'Not for certain. Not until now. I was, I must confess, never quite happy with your disappearance on the moor. I believed you to be too cunning a fellow to allow yourself to be sucked down into the Grimpen Mire. The signs that you had done so seemed to me to be rather too obvious, a little too clear-cut. I seemed to detect your hand in pointing the way to that conclusion. It was altogether far too convenient a demise. I never mentioned my doubts to Sir Henry or Doctor Watson, of course. There would have been little point. Your plot had failed and any suggestion of your survival would have left a rather ragged end to what was an otherwise successful case. However, I sensed that you and I should meet again. Dangerous and resourceful adversaries are not as easily disposed of as you attempted to have me believe.'

Stapleton gave what was almost a polite laugh and brought his grimy face, framed by lank flaxen hair, into the circle of light cast by the lantern. No longer was this the urbane naturalist whom Holmes

[*] From Dr Watson's notebook

had encountered on Dartmoor. The detective could see from the man's unkempt appearance and soiled clothes that he had been living in rough conditions for some time.

'I am flattered by your words,' Stapleton said. 'It is always a pleasure to have one's abilities fully recognised. Doubly so when they are acknowledged by the great Sherlock Holmes.'

'Oh, I fully recognise you for what you are,' replied Holmes, pointedly.

'You are a clever devil, Holmes, but despite all your cleverness it is I who now hold the whip hand. I watched you on the moor the morning after the death of the hound. I watched you search for me. Had I a gun then, you would be a dead man. I made a vow that day to settle my score with you, Mr Meddling Holmes. If it had not been for your interference I would have been master of the Baskerville estate now – not a fugitive from the police, running, hiding, skulking in cheap lodging houses like a criminal.'

Holmes responded with a grim smile. 'But you are a criminal, my dear Stapleton,' said he smoothly. 'A mean streak of criminality runs right through you. It was your overpowering greed that drove you to murder Sir Charles Baskerville and attempt to destroy Sir Henry – greed for something that was not yours.'

'It could have been mine,' cried Stapleton, the words echoing dully around the empty room. 'I spent months in poverty planning the whole thing carefully, down to the smallest detail.'

'I will admit that your re-creation of the hound as a means to murder was ingenious. Too ingenious, perhaps.'

'What do you mean?'

'If you had tried a less sensational method of killing the Baskerville family, I may never have been intrigued enough to investigate the matter, and your scheme would have proceeded unhindered.'

Stapleton considered Holmes's words and nodded. 'You are right, of course,' he agreed reasonably. 'I could have chosen a more mundane demise for the Baskervilles – poison perhaps – but where would have been the challenge in that? If one is going to commit murder one should construct the most fiendish and original means of doing so.'

'Hence your nasty package this morning.'

'Yes.' Stapleton's eyes sparkled with merriment, and his mouth split into an unpleasant grin. 'Rather a singular gift, wasn't it?'

'I am sorry I could not oblige you and allow the blade to lodge itself in my heart,' Holmes replied, and then added with emphasis, 'It is a pity you had to ruin one of your prized volumes for such an unsuccessful venture.'

'It was not mine; it belonged to her.' The words were out before he could check himself.

Holmes felt a glow of pleasure: Stapleton had taken his bait. From the tightened muscles around the chin and his sudden rapid eye movements, Holmes could tell that Stapleton was annoyed by his unguarded response.

'She must have been upset at your desecration of one of her precious books,' prompted Holmes gently, but his captor failed to take this further lure.

'Inquisitive to the last, eh, Holmes? Attempting to gather more pieces of the puzzle with a view to tracking me down? Don't waste your breath. You will not be leaving this room alive.' For a fleeting moment Stapleton's face darkened with rage.

'Then why are are you frightened of telling me about the woman?' asked Holmes.

Stapleton hesitated before replying. 'I am not frightened,' he said smugly. 'Let's say that it will give me great satisfaction to think that my careless remark will taunt your curiosity to the end.'

Realising that further questioning regarding this unknown woman would be fruitless at present, Holmes changed the subject. 'When you passed my rooms this afternoon you must have been very disappointed to observe that I was still hale and hearty.'

'You saw me?'

'No, but I felt sure you would return to see if your little toy had performed its allotted task. I did a certain amount of pacing up and down by the window to provide you with the information you needed.'

'You will agree, Holmes, that my second device was more successful.'

The detective gave a brief nod.

'After my first attempt on your life had failed, I realised that to ensure success next time we had to meet face to face, and that the encounter had to take place on my territory. I knew that the only way to lure you away from Baker Street was to send you a puzzle which would so delight and intrigue you that it would relax your caution. I was not naive enough to believe you would not see through the pretence of the coded message. Indeed, I was counting on it, as I knew that you would not be able to resist the challenge of a trap. And like a moth, you flew to my flame.'

Holmes could see Stapleton's face in the shadows, trembling with excitement. 'Interesting simile,' he remarked languidly. 'I used the one of spider and fly with Dr Watson.'

Stapleton smiled. 'Highly appropriate. Tell me, Holmes, how does it feel to be trapped in my web?'

Sherlock Holmes shifted his position slightly to ease the pain of the bonds, which were biting into his wrists. 'I feel somewhat uncomfortable at the moment. However, I have only myself to blame for my predicament. I did not for an instant reckon on your using an accomplice as a decoy to sit at that table, while you hid behind the door to cosh me as I entered.'

Stapleton suddenly threw back his head and gave a strangled cry. It was not immediately obvious to Sherlock Holmes that this was the commencement of a fit of laughter. Stapleton's strange outburst gave way to a prolonged high-pitched whine of merriment. It was the laughter of a madman. At length the crazy laughter subsided as he brought his wayward emotions under control.

'An accomplice?' he cried, wiping tears of laughter from his eyes. 'My friend sitting at the table?'

His face still bore a terrible grin, and his querulous voice clearly indicated that his hilarity was only just being held in check. With a swift, violent movement he pulled the helpless detective from the floor into a sitting position. Holmes gritted his teeth as the ropes bit deeper into his wrists.

'Let me introduce you to my accomplice, Holmes.'

Stapleton swung the oil lamp over to the table, illuminating the dark, silent figure which was sitting there. With a sinking heart, Holmes saw that what he had taken for Stapleton's helpmate was in fact a dummy. The expression of chagrin on the detective's face prompted another outburst of grotesque laughter from Stapleton.

'Who would have thought it!' he crowed. 'Sherlock Holmes, master detective, fooled by a dummy! Not a very commendable way to end your career, I'm afraid.'

'It is a brilliant device,* and you are to be congratulated on it, but I can assure you that I have no intention of ending my career just yet,' asserted Holmes.

---

* Holmes himself was later to use the device of a dummy as decoy in the cases of 'The Empty House' and 'The Mazarin Stone'. The idea obviously came from this encounter with Stapleton, although no reference is made to it in the accounts of these cases.

'An idle threat. The last straw, my dear Holmes, at which a drowning man clutches. And by heaven, Mr Detective, you are a drowning man.' Stapleton gave a smug leer before taking a battered old hunter from his pocket and consulting it. 'Fascinating though this conversation is,' he continued, pocketing the watch, 'I am afraid I shall have to terminate it. My cab is almost due and I do not want to keep the driver waiting. So this is farewell, Sherlock Holmes. I cannot tell you how pleased I am that my quest for retribution has met with so swift and satisfactory a conclusion. I would have found it a great inconvenience to pursue you for long – the Baskerville title still eludes me, and I intend it to be mine. It shall be mine.'

Despite the quiet, almost reasonable way in which Stapleton made this claim, Holmes could see from the fanatical set of his grimy features and the erratic roll of his eyes that this most clever of criminals was rapidly losing whatever shreds of reason remained in his disordered brain. It would be impossible now for him ever to inherit the Baskerville title, and yet he seemed oblivious of this fact. The detective could see that these twin obsessions – revenge on Holmes, and his installation as the master of Baskerville Hall – had caused Stapleton to lose touch with reality.

'I am sorry I will not be here to watch you shuffle off this mortal coil, but I shall obtain as much pleasure from reading your obituary in the papers. I do hope the press does you justice.' He walked to the door. 'Now I really must go. Please do not get up. Oh, of course you can't. How foolish of me. Never mind, I will make sure that you do not get cold here on your own.'

With these words he threw the oil lamp into the far corner of the room, where it smashed against the wall. Instantly a spill of flame shot across the floorboards, licking at the rotting timber.

'That should keep you warm!' With a screech of laughter, Stapleton rushed from the room.

The hungry flames spluttered and stretched, and within seconds half of the room was ablaze. Holmes struggled desperately to release himself from his bonds, but they were too securely fastened. Stapleton had been very thorough.

Billows of choking smoke and the pungent smell of burning wood began to fill the room. As every second passed, long orange tongues of flame reached closer towards the helpless figure of Sherlock Holmes.

Conflagration

The midnight streets echoed with the clatter of hooves as the hansom cab plunged through the fog towards London Gardens. At my instructions the driver did not spare the horses and before long I reached my destination. Alighting from the cab, I was in time to see another speeding off in the opposite direction at breakneck speed. As it swept by, I just managed to catch a glimpse of the pale, exultant features of the passenger before the cab disappeared into the night. The face struck a familiar chord in my memory, but at that moment I was unable to place it.

After instructing my cabby to wait for me, I sped towards the row of six dingy and apparently derelict houses. It was then that I saw flames leaping out of an upstairs window of the first house.

'Great heavens!' I exclaimed. 'Holmes!'

I ran up the path and into the house. Already the hall was filled with a rolling cloud of dense smoke through which I could see the fierce glow from upstairs. With difficulty I clambered up the staircase, calling out at the top of my voice: 'Holmes! Holmes! Are you there, Holmes?'

Above the roaring and crackling of the fire, I heard a faint muffled cry which seemed to come from the room at the end of the landing: the heart of the inferno. I brushed the streaming perspiration from my brow with my coat sleeve and strove to reach the room.

My progress was impaired by the intense, searing heat which pressed upon me from all sides, and the blinding, suffocating smoke. The bannister rail was now fully ablaze and orange tongues of flame darted back and forth along it, infecting all they touched with their fiery contagion. I was conscious that my coat was being singed in several places, and my feet began to sting with the waves of heat that lapped around my shoes.

Eventually I reached the threshold of the room, which was now almost totally consumed in a ferocious yellow blaze. I saw amidst the conflagration the body of a man beyond rescue being devoured by the inferno. My heart sank.

'Holmes!' I cried hoarsely.

It is strange that at moments of shock or crisis, time appears to stand still. For minutes, it seemed, I stared at the burning corpse while through my mind flashed images from my past life with Sherlock Holmes, memories which are forever etched there. As I watched helplessly, the merciless flames were consuming my dearest friend, the best and wisest man whom I have ever known.

In reality this contemplation took but a few fleeting seconds. My reverie was broken by a noise behind me. I turned sharply to see, huddled behind the door like a cripple, the figure of Sherlock Holmes. My heart leapt with joy.

'I'm certainly glad to see you, old chap,' he croaked, weakly.

I gave a cry of amazement. 'What has happened?' I asked urgently.

'There is no time to talk now. Cut me loose quickly. We must get out of here.'

I nodded and, acting as swiftly as I could, cut my friend free of his bonds with my pocket knife.

'We must make a dash for it.' Holmes pointed to the landing, which was now almost fully ablaze.

'I'll go first,' I yelled above the roaring inferno and, pulling my coat over my head as protection, ran as if all the devils in Hell were after me. The scorching yellow tentacles of flame leapt out as I swept by. I did not remain unscathed, for soon my hands began to blister in the searing heat.

Holmes was close at my heels and, as we reached the bottom of the staircase, it and the landing collapsed behind us in a thundering crash of white-hot wood, sparks and triumphant orange fire. The conflagration had now taken complete possession of the premises and the flames danced to new heights, caressing their prize. It would not be long before the roof succumbed to the blaze.

As Holmes and I emerged breathless into the blissfully cold night air, both our coats were on fire. Throwing them off, we stamped out the scorching flames.

'Come, Watson,' cried Holmes, 'we are not safe here: the whole house will disintegrate into the fire at any moment.' He pulled my arm. 'Quickly, across the street to safety.'

On the opposite pavement a group of people who had materialised out of the night was standing transfixed, mesmerised by the fire. We joined them and moments later, as Holmes predicted, Number One,

London Gardens surrendered fully to the conquering inferno with creaking and splintering groans of protest.

From our safe vantage point across the street, Holmes patted me heartily on the back. 'Watson,' he gasped, gulping in the cool air, 'in future when I instruct you not to follow me, I trust you will disregard my orders.' He smiled. 'You saved my life tonight, old fellow.'

'I had good reason to ignore your instructions, Holmes.'

'The old intuition, eh, Watson?'

'Something more definite than that. I was warned that you were in danger.'

'Warned?' I could see that my friend was completely taken by surprise by my revelation. 'By whom?' he asked.

Briefly, but including all the relevant details, I told him of Miss Lydgate and recounted her story. Holmes listened intently, his face betraying no emotion; he made no comment until I had concluded my account. 'Very enlightening indeed. And now this young woman awaits our return at Baker Street?'

I nodded.

'Then let us waste no further time and return there at once.' So saying, he strode down the street to my waiting cab and jumped aboard. I followed and gave the bewildered cabby our destination. Holmes remained silent on our journey home and, despite my promptings, would reveal nothing of the events which had led up to his being trapped in the burning building.

On reaching Baker Street, he hurried up the stairs ahead of me and flung open our sitting room door.

'Aha!' he cried. 'The lady has flown.'

'Gone?' I asked incredulously.

'I am afraid so,' said Holmes, indicating our empty quarters. 'It seems that Miss Lydgate has more confidence in Grenfell's abilities to win through than ours.'

'You mean she was too frightened to stay?'

Holmes nodded. 'From what you have told me, it is clear that this brute Grenfell has her completely in his power. She was taking the greatest of risks in coming here tonight. She knows full well that if this villain ever suspects that she was in any way instrumental in effecting my escape, he will kill her.'

'Good grief, do you mean she has gone back to him?'

'So it would appear. Where else could she go?'

'The poor girl. Holmes, we must do something about this. We must rescue her.'

'All in good time, Watson. First let us have our hurts seen to, and then I for one am in need of a drink.'

I saw from Holmes's expression that it would be useless to argue with him; once his mind was made up, nothing I could say would change it. So, reluctantly, I fell in with his plans, and treated our hands for minor burns. Apart from these, we were none the worse for our narrow escape.

Half an hour later Holmes and I were sitting around our rekindled fire holding a post mortem on the night's events. Holmes's nature was tempered with such resilient steel that, observing him stretched out languidly in his dressing gown, puffing on his old clay pipe, it was difficult to believe that only a short time earlier he had been very close to losing his life in a blazing building.

'The girl's story fits in nicely with my deductions concerning the copy of *Great Expectations*,' he remarked with an air of satisfaction.

'Did you suspect there was a woman involved?'

My friend gave a brief laugh. 'The word you use is apt: I did "suspect", but I had too little data to be sure. I knew that the man I believed to be the mystery assassin had an almost hypnotic power over women, and he would not go for long without wishing to exercise it.'

'Who exactly is this fellow Grenfell?'

'You will know him better as Stapleton.'

'Stapleton? The Baskerville murderer?' I gasped. 'But he's dead!'

'Far from it. He is very much alive.'

'But I thought he was at the bottom of the Grimpen Mire?'

'That is where the evidence pointed, and I thought it best to let the world believe that story, though I was never fully convinced.' Holmes then recounted all that had happened to him between his leaving Baker Street that evening and my timely arrival in the burning room.

'So the body which I thought was yours was in fact a dummy?' I said at the conclusion of his account.

'Indeed, Watson; the very device which initially put me off my guard. You see, I was so certain that my adversary was a lone wolf that I never contemplated the use of such a cunning decoy.' He gave a gentle chuckle. 'It must have been very pleasing for Stapleton when I stepped into the room and addressed the dummy.'

'He was waiting, hidden behind the door?'

'Yes, ready to knock me out, which he did quite successfully. I was well and truly duped. You can set this down, Watson, as one of my less successful ventures.'* He leaned forward and touched my arm. 'And if it had not been for you, old friend, it would have been my last.'

These words of thanks, so sincerely spoken, touched me, and I was lost for a reply. Holmes covered my embarrassment by pouring us both another drink.

'We must save this poor young woman from Stapleton's grasp,' I said as Holmes handed me my glass. I well remembered how he had ill-used Beryl Stapleton, his wife.

'Our first prority must be rest: a night's sleep.'

'But surely there is no time to lose?'

'A tired brain is an inefficient one, Watson. We need to be fresh and alert to deal with someone as clever and dangerous as Stapleton.'

'But what of the girl?'

'She will be safe until morning at least. It will be some hours before Stapleton learns that his second attempt on my life has failed. Until then, she will not be in any real danger. Stapleton is an evil man, but he does not kill without purpose.'

'So you intend to go to bed,' I said sharply, unconvinced by my friend's assurance and making no attempt to keep the indignation from my voice.

'Yes, Watson, and I advise you to do the same; and then in the morning we can carefully review the situation and decide what our next move should be.'

---

* Watson records that at a later date he suggested to Holmes that this adventure should be presented as a codicil to the Baskerville case, but Holmes was dismayed at this suggestion, and taking into consideration the subsequent events, expressly forbade Watson to publish the story.

CHAPTER EIGHT
The Mission

I was annoyed by Holmes's apparent insensibility to the fate of Celia Lydgate, but realised there was nothing I could do to change his mind, so reluctantly I retired for the night. However the smarting pains from the burns on my hands, and the thought of the poor young woman being ill-treated by Stapleton, forbade sleep to visit me and, after a few hours of tossing and turning, I rose and dressed.

It seemed to me that Holmes's main concern was the capture of Stapleton, the rescue of Miss Lydgate being incidental to this, and I realised that while my friend was making plans and setting his traps, she could come to great harm. Stapleton might even kill her! The contemplation of this convinced me that immediate action was necessary and, as Holmes was reluctant to take steps to come to the girl's rescue, it was up to me to do so.

It was still dark when I set out from Baker Street. In the east, a faint lightening of the sky was the only indication that morning was almost here. My plan was to try and find the old mission where Miss Lydgate and Stapleton had met. There I hoped I would be able to trace the whereabouts of their lodging house.

I was lucky. The old driver of the cab I picked up in Marylebone Road knew of the mission at Shooter's Hill and, thirty minutes later, I was standing outside the stark, crumbling building. Dawn was now breaking over the city. The fog had disappeared and it was a clear, crisp morning. An orange sun shimmered over the roof tops, tipping them with fiery light. Already the fretted patterns of frost around the edges of the windows were melting.

A group of ill-clad wretches clustered around the door of the mission, stamping their feet and blowing on their hands in a weary attempt to get warm. As I approached they solicited me for money, and I could not fail to be moved by this ragged and impoverished tableau. As I dispensed a few coins I studied their thin pauper faces to see if Stapleton were among them. He was not. I was about to pass through the tall oak door into the mission when one of the wretches grabbed my arm. 'It ain't no use you goin' in there yet, guv'nor,' he croaked balefully. ' 'E don't serve vittals 'til eight. 'E'll only kick you out.'

Ignoring him, I pushed the door back and entered the building. It stank of sweat and other less definable but nonetheless unpleasant odours. A short corridor led me into a large, lofty hall filled with long, coarse wooden benches; at the far end was a raised dais on which stood a placard bearing the Lord's Prayer.

'Out you! No soup until eight.' The voice, light, cultured but full of authority, came from the shadows on the dais.

'It's not soup I'm after, sir; it's information,' I said loudly, addressing the unknown speaker.

A tall figure emerged from the gloom and came down the hall towards me, taking long purposeful strides as he did so. 'And who might you be?' he asked.

'I am Dr John Watson.'

'A doctor, eh? Well, we could certainly use the services of a doctor here. I am Matthew Boulton. I run the mission. "Soup and a sermon: food for the body and the soul".' He pointed to the benches. 'God's work is not always clean and pleasant.'

He was a thin, heavily bearded man with a ruddy complexion, wearing a rough tweed suit which bore many marks of the owner's neglect.

'I believe you can help me,' I said.

'Oh?' There was a note of caution in his voice.

'I am a friend of Celia Lydgate.'

'Celia Lydgate?'

'You know the girl?'

Boulton's eyes narrowed. 'Is she in some kind of trouble?'

'She could be if I do not find her. I assure you I only wish to offer her my help,' I said, trying to allay his obvious suspicions.

'You are the second person to make that claim within the last hour.'

'Someone else has been here making enquiries about her?' I asked in surprise.

'Yes,' he replied slowly.

'Have you any idea who it was?'

He shook his head. 'Not really. Perhaps you can tell me, Doctor, what all this is about. Such enquiries about one of my flock obviously arouse my curiosity. Poor Celia has been coming to this mission for almost a year without anyone bothering about her, and now suddenly, within the space of a few hours, two men arrive claiming they want to offer her help.'

I grabbed his arm. 'You have to believe me. This girl is in danger. It is imperative that I find her.'

He made no attempt to shake himself free of my grip, but stared fiercely at me.

'Why should I believe you? How do I know you don't mean Celia some harm?'

'I can only give you my word, Boulton. I am working with Sherlock Holmes, tracking down a wanted murderer, and we have good reason to believe that Celia Lydgate will be his next victim. Now will you please tell me where she is?'

I spoke with passion, and I could see that my outburst had some effect on Boulton. He eyed me keenly for a moment before replying.

'Sherlock Holmes . . . the detective?' he said.

I gave him a vigorous nod.

'Well,' he said at length, 'I can only tell you what I told the other man. Celia has not been to the mission for some days now, but I last heard that she was lodging in McCauley Street.'

'Do you know the man she lives with: John Grenfell?'

'I have seen him a few times with Celia, but we have never spoken.' He shrugged his shoulders. 'That is all I know.'

'Thank you,' I said, turning to go. Then, realising that I was missing an opportunity to obtain some vital information, I questioned Boulton further. 'This other man who came asking about Miss Lydgate – what did he look like?'

'He was elderly – aristocratic – grey hair – about your build. He wore a monocle and had a large moustache. He seemed a little deaf: kept asking me to repeat things. Quite a toff really.'

'Did he say who he was?'

Boulton nodded. 'Said he was an old friend of Celia's father and had only recently heard of her plight. He claimed to have been searching for her for some months.'

I thanked Boulton for his information and, after enquiring for directions to McCauley Street, hurried there without delay. I had no idea who the character was who had been enquiring about Miss Lydgate, but, knowing what I did of her circumstances, it seemed that he told an unlikely tale. I had the unnerving feeling that this stranger posed yet another threat to this unfortunate young woman's life.

I soon located McCauley Street and discovered it to be a long, rotting line of tall, red-brick terrace houses; grimy symbols of squalor that tried to hide their secrets behind paint-peeling doors and ragged curtains. My investigations led me to seven of these properties advertising 'Cheap Lodging Accommodation', before I came to the one for which I was searching.

I knocked hard and waited. The faded net curtains at the downstairs window twitched, and about a minute later a thin, scraggy female face thrust itself through the narrow gap of the opened door. The harridan's suspicious eyes bulged from their sockets, and her rotting teeth were revealed as she snapped at me, 'What is it?'

'I'm looking for Miss Celia Lydgate.'

'Another 'un?'

My heart sank. 'Someone else has been making enquiries about her?' I asked, although I already knew the answer.

'Someone 'as,' came the brusque reply. 'And 'e paid me a sovereign for my trouble.' The crone grinned: it was a nasty, avaricious grin.

I pulled out a sovereign and handed it to her. 'Perhaps you can provide me with the same information you gave the other gentleman?'

'She's popular all of a sudden, ain't she? You're not the police, are you?'

I shook my head.

'Nah, course not.' She grinned again. ' 'Oo ever 'eard of a copper partin' with a sovereign? All right, mister, come on in.'

She pocketed the coin in her grubby apron and ushered me into a dingy hallway. The obnoxious smell of dampness and stale cooking fat assailed my nostrils.

'She ain't in, o' course. Been out all night.'

'What about the man she lodges with: Grenfell?'

Her eyes narrowed. 'What are you suggestin'? I run no bawdy 'ouse 'ere. The man's 'er brother . . . that's what she told me anyway. You're not 'ere to cause trouble, I 'ope?'

'No, no, of course not. I am an old friend of Miss Lydgate's family. I am solely concerned for her welfare.'

'Funny, that's what the other bloke said too.'

'This was a grey-haired gentleman with a large moustache and wearing a monocle?'

'That's right. A . . . gent 'e was.' She gave a derisive sniff as though to inform me that I did not fit into that category. 'I suppose you want to see 'er room?'

I said that I did, and begrudgingly she led me up two flights of uncarpeted stairs to a drab little room on the second landing.

' 'E came back before it got light, packed 'is stuff and 'opped it,' the landlady said as she showed me into the room.

'Grenfell . . . her brother?'

She nodded. 'Yes. Slung 'is 'ook. Good riddance too. I never took to 'im. Treated 'er badly an' all. I 'eard 'er cryin' many a time.'

So, I thought, Stapleton has slipped through our fingers yet again; and there was no knowing where he would go to ground. This was a serious blow indeed.

'Have you seen Miss Lydgate since last night?' I asked, eager for some positive news. The old crone shook her head.

I glanced around the small room, which was illuminated only by a grimy, narrow window at the far end. Faded net curtains, furred with dust, hung before it, providing another barrier for daylight to filter through. The room was sparsely furnished, but on the cheap dresser near the bed stood a row of fine leather volumes: a set of Dickens's novels.

'You might as well 'ave a good look round while you're 'ere, get your money's worth. The other bloke did.'

I looked carefully about me, but soon realised there was little I could learn from these surroundings that I did not already know. It was clear Stapleton had run to a new earth, and he was far too clever to leave behind any clues which could indicate his whereabouts. The girl had not yet returned for fear of what he might do – it could be that she never would return.

However, I questioned the landlady further concerning the mysterious gentleman who had been one jump ahead of me all morning. Unfortunately, she was able to add nothing new to what Matthew Boulton had told me at the mission. With these few details, I left the old woman still clutching the sovereign and headed back to Baker Street.

As I sat in the cab looking out of the window at the great city not yet fully awake, I pondered over my investigations. Although I had received no large prize for my efforts – I still did not know the whereabouts of either Stapleton or Miss Lydgate – my detective work had not been altogether fruitless. I had discovered where they lived, and there was a distinct possibility that the girl would eventually return there. More importantly, I had not only discovered that there was another man involved in the case, but also had a fairly accurate description of him. It had not been an idle venture, and I looked forward to placing these facts before Sherlock Holmes.

Climbing the familiar seventeen steps up to our rooms, I could not help smiling at the thought of seeing my friend's face when I told him what I knew. My smile vanished when I opened the door, for there, seated by the fire in the wicker chair, was a well-dressed, grey-haired man of some sixty years. He wore a heavy walrus moustache, and his monocle twinkled in the firelight.

CHAPTER NINE
A Bizarre Crime

As I entered, the man looked up. On seeing me, his face creased into a smile, causing the monocle to drop from his eye. 'Good morning, Doctor Watson,' the fellow said, in a friendly and effusive fashion. He raised an arm and beckoned me forward. 'Come and take a seat by the fire and warm yourself, my dear fellow; it is still bitterly cold out.'

The voice was unmistakably that of Sherlock Holmes, but the appearance betrayed not one hint of this fact.

I had seen my friend adopt a clever disguise many times, but none, I think, so totally deceiving as the one he now wore. Although the voice was amiable and familiar, the face from which it emerged bore none of the identifying characteristics of the lean and ascetic Sherlock Holmes of my acquaintance. Luxuriant grey hair fell casually over the forehead, while a large drooping moustache and full cheeks had changed the shape of his face completely, shortening the head and broadening the gaunt features. His fine, aquiline nose had been altered in such a way that it now appeared to be quite short, with a bulbous tip. This effect was accompanied by a series of deep-set lines about the eyes, and a ruddy complexion successfully completed the ageing process. It was a transformation of which even the great Irving* himself would have been proud.

It was only when I recovered from my amazement at this brilliant disguise, that it dawned on me that the mystery man in whose wake I had followed all morning was Holmes himself. My surprise was replaced by anger.

'Sorry to shock you like this, Watson, but as you are no doubt aware, I have been busy making enquiries.'

'What happened to the good night's sleep?' I snapped.

* Watson refers here to Henry Irving, one of the foremost actors of the period, who was later knighted for his services to the theatre. At the time of this case, Irving was in charge of the Lyceum Theatre, where Watson may have seen him in his production of *The Bells* playing a part which required him to transform his natural appearance greatly.

'I obtained sufficient sleep for my needs,' he replied somewhat lamely.

'You led me to believe that you had no intention of making any further moves in this case until the morning.'

'It is already morning.'

'I feel cheated, Holmes. You might have let me in on your plans. You treat me as though you do not trust me.'

'My dear Watson, I assure you that I have every faith in you. I beg that you will forgive me if I seemed to play a trick on you, but in truth I did it for your own sake, as well as that of the case.' While he spoke he sat before a mirror at his desk and began to remove the disguise. 'I knew that if I made enquiries in the persona of Sherlock Holmes, Stapleton would soon get wind of it, thus placing the girl in even greater danger. Hence the old family friend.' He threw up his arms in a dramatic gesture. 'You needed the rest and I needed to act alone.'

'If only you had told me. I may have spoilt it all now because I have been following the same trail of investigation.'

Carefully removing the grey wig from his head, he said easily, 'I know of your enquiries, Watson. I observed you in McCauley Street.'

'I never saw you.'

'Of course not. However, Watson, you are to be congratulated on your train of reasoning, and in the the light of the information I gleaned this morning it is safe to say that your investigations have been harmless. Stapleton had already fled well before we set out on his trail. No doubt after leaving me to be consumed by fire, he made his way to another hideout. He is a cunning and cautious man who leaves nothing to chance.'

'What about Miss Lydgate?'

'It is my belief that she will turn up at her old lodgings once she has realised that Stapleton has gone for good. I have already arranged for the place to be watched.'

'By the police?'

Holmes laughed. 'Great heavens, no. By a much more reliable force than the police: the Baker Street Irregulars.* I've got young Watkins to organise it. I shall be informed immediately the lady returns to McCauley Street.'

---

* The Baker Street Irregulars were a gang of street urchins whom Holmes organised into a kind of unofficial police force. In *A Study in Scarlet* he said of them: 'There's more work to be got out of one of those little beggars than out of a dozen of the force. The mere sight of an official-looking person seals men's lips. These youngsters, however, go everywhere and hear everything.'

'What if she does not?'

'Then further enquiries will be necessary; but it is certain that her usefulness to Stapleton is at an end, and consequently she has little to fear from him.'

'And what of you? Do you think that he will make further attempts on your life?'

'Without a doubt. His mind is a cruel, calculating instrument and his decline into madness has only increased his fanaticism. His twin obsessions are my destruction and his installation as Master of Baskerville Hall. By some process of his twisted logic, he believes that the latter will result from the former. Stapleton will not rest until I am dead.'

Holmes, his disguise now fully removed, walked over to the mantelpiece, retrieved an envelope, and handed it to me.

'I found this on our doormat on my return this morning,' he said, taking up his pipe.

I opened the envelope, which was addressed to Holmes. It was empty. 'There doesn't appear to be anything inside.'

'Tap the contents out onto your palm.'

I did as my friend suggested and a small black object fell into my hand. It was a dead fly. 'What does this mean?' I gasped.

Holmes lit his pipe and threw the spent match into the fire before responding to my question.

'It means that Stapleton knows I am alive,' he remarked casually. 'This communication is a warning that the game is still afoot – the game of spider and fly.'

'This man is a devil . . .'

'And a devil with great persistence. But we shall have him, Watson. It is only a matter of time before our spider becomes enmeshed in his own web. Now, I think we both deserve some nourishment. We have had an exhausting and challenging night and I see from the fresh dressings that your burns are still causing you some discomfort. May I suggest that one of Mrs Hudson's fine breakfasts will reduce most of your ills, and set us both up to face the labours of the day?' He lay back in his chair, smiling, puffing contentedly on his pipe.

Within half an hour, Holmes and I were tucking into a sumptuous breakfast spread. Holmes had an ambivalent attitude to food. Often, in the middle of a complex and challenging case, he would abandon regular meals and treat food merely as a fuel to keep the body functioning. At times like that, it seemed, his sense of taste

disappeared, for I have seen him, when deeply involved in an investigation, smother his meat or fish with honey to help increase its
energy value. On this morning, however, it was plain ham and eggs
that my friend devoured hungrily.

'Mrs Hudson can always be relied upon to provide an invigorating
feast,' said he, drawing away from the table and seating himself by
the fire. 'Ah, Watson, I fear we are to be denied our quiet post-
prandial smoke. There is a visitor on the stair.'

I believe that I have excellent hearing, but I had heard no noise to
indicate that we were to receive a caller. However, moments later
there was a discreet knock at our door.

'Come in, Lestrade,' cried Holmes.

Our sitting-room door opened and there on the threshold was the
rat-faced Scotland Yard man, with his bowler hat in his hand and a
bewildered expression on his face.

'Now, how the devil did you know it was me, Mr Holmes?'

'Elementary, Lestrade. Who else do I know who wears size twelve
police boots, knocks in that peculiar staccato fashion, and is likely to
call on me so early in the day?'

Lestrade looked disconsolately at his feet.

'Come in, Lestrade,' said Holmes. 'Take off your coat and sit by
the fire. There is still some coffee in the pot. I see you have had little
opportunity for breakfast this morning.'

'Yes, you look as though you have been up all night,' I remarked as
I took Lestrade's coat and hung it on the rack.

'Hardly that, Watson. The smooth chin and the fresh spots of
blood round the collar bear witness to a hurried shave, while the
evidence of the reasonably uncreased suit and clean boots suggests
they have been donned recently. I would say that our friend was
called from his bed early this morning by some urgent matter at
the Yard.'

'You're right, Mr Holmes,' said Lestrade with some surprise.

Holmes gave an appreciative laugh and rubbed his hands together.

'Four this morning when I was summoned,' continued the policeman after taking a sip of his coffee. 'There's been a horrible crime. A
bizarre murder. The sort of thing that appeals to you.'

'Not only bizarre, Lestrade, but also baffling. It is really only
crimes in the latter category which bring Scotland Yard officials
running to my door.'

Lestrade nodded humbly. 'Bizarre and baffling,' he agreed.

Holmes sat back in his chair with a beatific smile on his face. 'Let me have the facts,' he said.

'Have you read the recent newspaper reports about the "Phantom lady" on Hampstead Heath?'

'I remember reading something of the matter. A mysterious woman has been luring children onto the heath and then wounding them.'

'That's it, Mr Holmes.' Lestrade took a crumpled newspaper cutting from his jacket pocket and handed it to my friend.

'*The Westminster Gazette*,' observed Holmes, scrutinising the type.

'Yes. That report appeared two nights ago,' said Lestrade.

Holmes flapped the cutting in my direction. 'Be so good, Watson, as to read it out to us.'

I took the cutting and read the following:

THE HAMPSTEAD HORROR
ANOTHER CHILD INJURED
THE PHANTOM LADY

We have just received intelligence that another child, missed last night, was only discovered late in the morning under a furze bush at the Shooter's Hill side of Hampstead Heath, which is perhaps less frequented than the other parts. The child has the same tiny wound in the throat as has been noticed in other cases. It was terribly weak and looked quite emaciated. It too, when partially revived, had the common story to tell of being lured away by the lady in white, 'the phantom lady'.

'Presumably,' said Holmes, 'there have been further, more serious developments since this report. Last night in fact.'

'Indeed there have,' affirmed the Scotland Yarder. 'Quite near to where the child was found, at about three o'clock this morning, a local constable discovered the body of a young woman.'

'Dead?' I asked.

'I'll say, doctor. Dead as a doornail, with terrible wounds at her throat. According to the police surgeon nearly all the woman's blood had been drained away.'

The Body in the Morgue

I must confess that I gave a deep involuntary shudder at Lestrade's chilling statement. The policeman paused dramatically to observe my friend's reaction. Holmes's face remained motionless, but I, who knew him well, could detect the bright glint of excitement in his eyes.

'Were there any other marks on the body apart from the wounds at the throat?' he asked at length.

'None,' came the reply, 'and there were no signs of a struggle either.' Holmes raised and eyebrow but remained silent.

'Which probably means,' Lestrade continued, with an air of self-satisfaction, 'that the murdered girl knew her killer and was caught unawares by the attack.'

'Possibly,' said Holmes, 'or that the murderer possessed great strength.'

'Then you don't think this crime was committed by a woman – "the phantom lady"?' I asked.

'It is difficult to say, Watson. Before we wander into the realms of surmise, let us deal with what evidence we have. Now, Lestrade, has the victim been identified?'

'Not as yet, Mr Holmes. There were no signs of identification about her person.'

'What about her clothes? You checked the makers' labels?'

'Well, no, I'm afraid I did not.'

Holmes gave a derisory snort. 'And the body? I trust you left it exactly where it was?'

Lestrade hesitated a moment and then shook his head.

'What!' cried Holmes in disbelief.

'We have had the area cordoned off, but the body has been taken to the police morgue at the Yard.'

Holmes, his face ablaze with anger, hit the arm of the chair with the flat of his hand. 'Lestrade! Lestrade! How many times have I told you to leave things exactly as they are at the scene of a crime until I have had an opportunity to make a thorough examination. It is the most elementary of procedures.'

'You can still examine the spot where the body was found.'

'My dear Inspector, the possibility of finding any significant clue after dozens of large boots have been tramping over the ground is infinitesimal.'

Lestrade looked suitably deflated and at a loss for words. I remember Holmes telling me on a previous occasion that, although he regarded Lestrade as the 'pick of a bad bunch' at Scotland Yard, he nevertheless considered him to lack initiative and the capacity for original thought.

On seeing Lestrade's dejection, Holmes's stern features softened. Jumping from his chair, he threw off his dressing gown and retrieved his frock coat from the rack. 'Watson and I have a busy morning ahead of us, Lestrade. We have pressing detective work of our own, but this singular murder interests me. I think we can spare the time to view the corpse, eh Watson?'

I nodded grimly. I could not help feeling there was a danger that my friend would be sidetracked into fresh investigations when the Stapleton-Lydgate case still needed his urgent attention.

Holmes, who could read my mind, said, 'Not to worry, old fellow, all will be well. Now, Lestrade, let us waste no more time.'

A beaming smile filled the police inspector's face. 'Very good, Mr Holmes,' he said.

* * *

The police mortuary which adjoined the main headquarters of the Metropolitan Police in Great Scotland Yard was a forbidding structure. If there is such a thing as the smell of death this place possessed it. It had settled there like an invisible dust, dulling the edge of all sound in the dark and gloomy building. On entering by a stout, studded door one was immediately conscious of being in another realm, one in which the living were outnumbered by the dead.

First of all, Lestrade ushered us into a small office where the desk sergeant entered our names in a large visitors' book, and then we were led off down a long, echoing corridor into a chill, windowless, dimly-lit room, the stone floor of which was splattered with dried bloodstains: indelible mementoes of numerous gory crimes.

At the far end of the room, thrown into murky shadow by the flickering gas jets, stood an old porcelain sink which bore the chips and cracks of time. The battered tap dripped with a regular, insistent rhythm, breaking the oppressive silence. On the wall to the left of the sink was a tall, glass-fronted cabinet containing a wide range of surgical instruments, and a short bench containing specimen jars. In one such jar, suspended in fluid, was a large solitary eyeball. Illuminated by the greenish glow of the gas, the thing seemed to be staring directly at me.

The only other item in the room, placed below the central gas fitting, was a long, narrow table on which the corpse lay covered by a blood-spotted sheet. Attached by rough twine to one of the toes of the body was a label giving what details were known about the deceased. As the three of us gathered round the table, our huge shadows spread up the rough walls and spilled onto the ceiling.

'I have never seen anything like this before. The loss of blood was tremendous.' Lestrade spoke softly, as if subdued by the grisly atmosphere that pervaded the room.

He pulled back the sheet, revealing the face of the dead woman. I gave a gasp of horror. My reaction came not solely because of the ghastliness of the wound, which indeed was a dreadful sight, but because I recognised the face which, now sunken, leathery, and white with the pallor of death, stared up at me with cold unblinking eyes.

'Holmes,' I cried, 'this is Celia Lydgate!'

'What! Are you sure?'

'There is no doubt.'

Holmes's eyes narrowed, and for some moments he stared into the middle distance, deep in thought.

'You know this woman then, Dr Watson?' Lestrade asked.

'Yes', I said and, receiving a reluctant nod of approval from Holmes, gave the policeman a brief account of our adventures over the previous twenty-four hours.

'Blimey,' he exclaimed when I had finished. 'So Stapleton is still alive and free.'

'I am afraid so,' I replied, 'and now he has added another foul murder to his list of crimes, eh Holmes?'

My friend, who for some time had been in a brown study, his chin sunk upon his chest, now turned abruptly to face me, his features gaunt and serious. He shook his head. 'I doubt it, Watson. I doubt it very much. This method of murder is not Stapleton's style at all.'

'Perhaps this killing may be a kind of bait to lure you into another trap.'

'That remains a possibility, I grant you – but a remote one. This girl's murder followed so closely on the heels of his last attempt to destroy me, and before he could have learned of my escape, that I believe we can eliminate him as a suspect in this case. You do not look convinced, Watson. Then answer me this: how would Stapleton have known that Miss Lydgate was crossing Hampstead Heath in the early hours of this morning?'

'She was obviously returning to her lodgings.'

'Agreed. But he could not possibly know that she had even left there until he returned to McCauley Street. He had tied her up, remember. By this time he would have been so overwhelmed by the sense of his own success at eliminating me, that the absence of the girl would not greatly concern him. She was no longer of any use to him anyway, and certainly she played no part in his long term plans.'

'I suppose you are right,' I agreed, reluctantly.

'I am inclined to believe that what we have here is one of those strange tricks of fate where the threads of one case have become entangled with the threads of a new and completely separate one.'

'You mean whoever killed Miss Lydgate was someone who had no previous connection with her?'

'That is what the evidence suggests to me.'

'So,' said I, 'you believe the murder was committed by a maniac without reason or motive?'

'I did not say that. The cause of death is perhaps the most baffling aspect of this case. What do you make of the wound, Watson?' He indicated the gash at the corpse's throat.

I leaned forward for a closer look. The flesh had been torn quite violently; there were tiny pieces missing. Globules of dark congealed blood had hardened around the jagged aperture, giving it the appearance of a small vicious mouth.

'This is beyond all my experience,' I confessed.

'What could have made such a wound?'

I shrugged. 'I really do not know, Holmes. It looks as though the flesh has been torn by the claws or teeth of some wild animal, but that could not be the case.'

'What about the teeth of a human?' my friend asked softly.

'Well, yes, I suppose it would be possible. Great heavens, you're not thinking that it was done by this phantom lady? You cannot think she was responsible for this savagery?'

'I don't know, Watson, but she does remain the prime suspect.

This murder presents some unique features which at the moment are most puzzling, and will remain so until we have further data.'

'But surely a woman would not have enough strength to over-power her victim and inflict such a terrible wound,' cried Lestrade.

'An ordinary woman, no. But a woman incensed, a woman with murder in mind – it is possible. I am reminded of Katherine Elliot, the Battersea Strangler, who not only strangled two of her husbands, but also dragged their lifeless bodies down three flights of stairs to bury them in the cellar.'

'What baffles me, Mr Holmes, is why anyone should want to drain off a body's blood.'

'And what they did with it,' Holmes added, taking out his convex lens and examining the hands of the corpse. 'Those are the baffling elements of this bizarre crime.' He moved further down the body with his lens, muttering and nodding to himself as he did so. He spent some time scrutinising the hands, feet, and face of the victim. Eventually he returned to where Lestrade and I were standing. He wore a grim expression. 'I am afraid this body tells us little but the obvious: the attacker, whose height is about five foot eight, killed swiftly, after initially putting the girl at ease – maybe by means of hypnotism.'

'Well, it is obvious that the killer acted quickly, but how can you be sure of the height and those other details?' asked Lestrade bluffly.

'The height is relative to the positioning of the wound. The killer would have to be approximately the same height as the victim to inflict a wound at that angle. As for Miss Lydgate's unpreparedness for the attack: there is only one wound – there are no other marks or abrasions on the body – which clearly shows that the killer needed to strike just the once; and yet the situation of the wound necessitates the attack being made from the front. Usually with victims who are physically attacked in such a way, one finds particles of dried skin or traces of clothing under the fingernails, scraped from the assailant in the struggle. There are none in this case, indicating that there was no such struggle. And finally, note her eyes: this girl was violently attacked and killed and yet her pupils, set in death, are quite normal, not in the least dilated as one would expect.'

Lestrade bent over the dead girl's face to look at her eyes.

'The picture you present, Mr Holmes,' he said, 'is one of this young lady calmly accepting her fatal assault.'

'That is how it appears to me.'

The policeman took off his hat and ran his fingers through his wiry hair. 'I must confess I am at a loss what to do next.'

Holmes thought for a moment before replying. 'I expect you have detailed a body of your men to patrol the Heath tonight.'

'Indeed I have.'

'Then call them off.'

'What?' The policeman's features clouded with bewilderment.

'Call them off, Lestrade. There is nothing more likely to prevent our killer from going on the prowl again than a bunch of heavy-footed constables stomping around the place.'

Lestrade stared indignantly at my friend, but seemed lost for words.

'You think the murderer will try to kill again so soon?' I asked.

'I think so, Watson. There appears to be no motive for this crime, or at least if there is, it is hidden from us at present, and therefore we cannot rely on a rational pattern of behaviour. This fiend may kill at any time.'

'But if I call off my men, that will give the maniac complete freedom to strike again,' said Lestrade.

'Not exactly. Tonight Watson and I will be on the Heath. We shall keep watch to prevent such a possibility. I believe we have more experience in dealing with unexpected midnight encounters than a whole troop of constables.' Holmes turned to me. 'Of course, that is providing you are willing to accompany me, Watson?'

'When you like and where you like,' I replied firmly. 'But what about Stapleton?'

'This new investigation must take precedence over our concern for him. He only wants *me* dead. The creature who killed this girl has no such limitations. We must devote all our energies to capturing this vicious killer before he, or she, is able to claim another victim.'

CHAPTER ELEVEN

The Phantom Lady

And so it was, as the midnight hour approached, that I found myself with Sherlock Holmes, hidden in a small copse on the Shooter's Hill side of Hampstead Heath, close to where the body of Celia Lydgate had been discovered.

It was a crisp, bitterly cold night, and a keen frost was just beginning to whiten the Heath. Holmes was stern and silent as he gazed out at the expanse of grassland. The full, bright moon, which hung suspended in a starless sky, illuminated his chiselled features: his brow was furrowed in thought and his thin lips were drawn in suppressed excitement.

'This is a dark business,' he had remarked, just before we left Baker Street. 'I sense great evil behind this macabre murder, perhaps a greater evil than we have yet encountered. Really, Watson, I have qualms about taking you with me tonight.'

I interrupted him with a wave of my hand. 'After the events of last night, you try and stop me.'

My friend gave a grim smile. 'Good old Watson,' he said.

I had spent the afternoon relaxing, catching up on some of my lost sleep. Holmes, on the other hand, restless as ever, had been out on several errands. However, as we stood together in the icy dark, ready to face whatever challenges our nocturnal vigil would offer, my friend showed no signs of fatigue, belying the fact that this was his second night without sleep.

'Are you sure we are doing the right thing by staying in one spot, Holmes?' I whispered, the words emerging in a vaporous cloud of frosty air. 'Perhaps we should split up and patrol a larger area.'

Holmes gave me an urgent glance. 'On no account must we leave each other's side tonight. Rest assured, our murderer is out there – on the prowl for another victim. Neither of us knows quite what to expect, what power this fiend has, and alone in the dark we should be very vulnerable against a killer who knows this area well.'

'But how can you be so certain that he will return to this particular part of the Heath?'

'It is a calculated risk, I grant you, but while you were catching up on lost sleep this afternoon, I made some pertinent enquiries. I was able to ascertain that all the attacks made on the children in the last three weeks took place within a quarter-of-a-mile radius of where we are now. I examined the ground where the girl's body was found and, as I suspected, the police boots had destroyed any signs or tracks that would have given us further data. However, some thirty yards away, I did discover a set of very interesting footprints, preserved and hardened by the frost.'

'In what way interesting?'

'They were the naked footprints of a woman.'

'Good heavens, the phantom lady!'

'We shall see,' said Holmes evenly.

A sharp breeze had started up, and I gave an involuntary shudder. 'I wish I had remembered to bring my hip flask,' I murmured. 'A nip of brandy would be most welcome now.'

'Sssh, Watson,' Holmes hissed. 'Listen.'

I stood very still and strained my ears. At first I could not hear anything unusual and then, softly, above the noise of rustling leaves, I heard what had arrested Holmes's attention. It was the sound of a woman singing, faint to begin with, but then, carried by the breeze, it grew louder, more insistent. I felt my body stiffen and my nerves tingle as the sound began to fill the air around us. There were no words, just a melodic, hypnotic humming. In some inexplicable way the sound seemed to be coming closer.

Suddenly Holmes gripped my arm. 'Look,' he said in a hoarse whisper, the words escaping through clenched teeth. I followed the direction of his eyes, which were set in a rigid, fixed stare. My blood seemed to freeze within me as I saw, but a little distance from us, the figure of a woman.

'The phantom lady,' I gasped. The creature was aptly named, for she had the chilling appearance of some unearthly wraith, loosed from one's wildest nightmares to haunt this bleak spot. She was dressed in a long, white, amorphous gown which clung to her as she glided slowly towards us.

As this weird apparition drew near, I could see her features distinctly in the bright moonlight. Her face, the colour of pale ivory, held a wide, cruel mouth, and two lifeless eyes which stared unblinkingly from deep, dark sockets.

Although we were well hidden, this creature seemed to sense our presence, and with the stiff awkward movements of some ghastly clockwork toy, she turned towards us, her eyes glinting in the moonlight like two black pearls. Those eyes were enticing, alluring, desirable, and I found myself held by their penetrating gaze. When, as a medical student, I first witnessed the dissection of a corpse, I was totally repulsed by it and yet, transfixed by the horror, I was also fascinated by what I saw. It was the same now with those cold, soulless eyes.

As her gentle humming and hypnotic gaze began to captivate me, a sense of ease and relaxation swept through my body. I no longer felt the sharp chill of the night; all tension and fear left me. The humming wrapped me in a warm, protective cocoon, while the eyes drew me forward. Without fully realising what I was doing, I moved from the cover of the copse and began walking towards the strange apparition. Towards those eyes: those deep, dark, soothing eyes. I knew I would find safety there, comfort and shelter from the cruel blows of life. In those eyes I saw eternal salvation.

'Watson, for God's sake!'

Holmes's strident cry pierced the warm mist that surrounded my senses and, like someone waking from a dream, I became aware of my own vulnerability. I stepped back in horror as the phantom lady moved towards me, her face strangely still, but now the mesmeric veil had been lifted from her expressionless, dead eyes, and I saw only evil and cruelty. Instinctively, I drew my revolver.

'Stop where you are!' I heard myself calling, my voice finding its way with difficulty from a dry throat.

At my cry her face darkened with rage and, observing my gun, the full, red lips pulled back in a feral snarl. In doing so, her teeth glistened in the moonlight, and a wave of warm, fetid breath swept over me. I staggered back with revulsion, but before I knew what was happening, this harpy rushed forward and grabbed me by the arm. With a screech of anger, she swung me round and threw me flying to the ground. I had not been prepared for such a vicious attack, nor for the phenomenal strength with which it was carried out. So great was the creature's power that, on releasing her grip of me, I landed like a child's discarded doll some five feet away. As I crashed down on the hard earth, my gun slipped from my grasp and spun off into the darkness. I was winded and disoriented for some moments before I was able to move and then, scrambling to my knees, I reached out blindly, my hands roaming over the frosty ground in a desperate search for my pistol.

A noise from the copse made me glance up, and I saw Holmes emerge from the shrubbery and approach the creature. She extended her arms in a beckoning gesture of embrace, and emitted a soft, throaty chuckle, the sound of which made the hairs on the back of my head stand on end.

'Come,' she called to Holmes, in a voice that was musical yet compelling. To my horror I saw that he began to obey her instructions.

'Don't look at her eyes!' I yelled, my lungs bursting, but already I could see that my cry was in vain. Holmes tried to avert his gaze, but found himself locked by the force of those devilish eyes. I could see by his mechanical movements that he was totally in her power.

'Holmes!' I bellowed, trying to break the trance under which she held him. 'Holmes!' I cried again, and this time his eyes flickered in faint recognition of my voice. At my third call of his name he shook his head as if in some desperate attempt to dislodge the creature's hold on his mind. He grimaced, but I could see by his glassy stare that he had failed: his will was not his own.

When she was within arm's reach of him, she closed her eyes momentarily, as though in pleasurable anticipation. When she opened them again, they were blood red.

'Come,' she said again in her weird, musical voice, and grabbed Holmes's arms, her white, talon-like fingers clutching the sleeves of his coat. I saw my friend, fully under her incredible influence, obey the command. I was astounded by the extraordinary hypnotic power she wielded: so strong that it was able to take control of such a fiercely independent mind as that of Sherlock Holmes.

I peered frantically into the darkness around me looking for my gun, but without success. I was unsure of the exact nature of the danger which threatened my friend, but instinctively I knew that his life was at risk. As my hand searched in vain over the frosted ground, I was overwhelmed by a sense of despair. I glanced up again and saw the creature's arms about to encircle Holmes. His body was now quite limp, and he offered no resistance as she held him in an embrace. Pulling him towards her, the creature grasped him by the throat and, lowering her head towards his neck, opened her mouth wide to reveal a sweep of vicious white teeth, with two needle-sharp canines. For a split second the image of Celia Lydgate's wound flashed into my mind. I was petrified with horror as I realised that this fiend was about to savage Holmes in the same manner.

The Cult of the Undead

The events of the next few moments are forever seared in my memory. They seem to me now, as they did then, to be scenes from a nightmarish melodrama in which I was an unwilling participant.

Emitting a gurgling hiss, the phantom lady lowered her head towards Holmes's throat. I was lying some distance away, transfixed with horror, utterly incapable of action. Then, with a suddenness that gave my already straining heart a jolt, another person joined this grisly scene. Emerging from the shadows came the dark figure of a man. He was about six feet tall, dressed in a long, black, double-breasted coat with a heavy fur collar. In his hand he carried a silver object which glinted in the moonlight. As he raised it before him, I saw that it was a crucifix. With great sense of purpose, he held it in front of the creature's face. The change in her countenance was immediate and dramatic. With a guttural cry, she pulled away from Holmes, releasing him from her embrace, her face convulsed with terror.

Taking swift, powerful strides, the stranger followed as the creature staggered backwards with agonised moans of fear and, catching her, he thrust the crucifix forward, pressing it firmly to her forehead. She dropped to her knees, shrieking in agony, her arms flailing wildly in the air. Pulling herself free of her attacker, the girl squirmed along the ground in retreat, and I could see clearly that the cross had left a dark imprint on the smooth white skin of her forehead.

She crouched in terror, mesmerised by the stranger, her breath escaping in short agonised bursts. So great was the change in her, so pathetic a picture did she now present, that I almost began to feel some sympathy for her.

'In the name of God, be gone,' intoned the stranger, holding the silver crucifix before him as a medieval knight would brandish his shield. The phantom lady stumbled backwards a few feet and disappeared into the blackness of the night.

While all this was happening, Holmes had been standing dazed and motionless, but now he suddenly broke free of his trance. In an instant he seemed to take stock of the situation and, seeing the creature take flight, he made to follow her. However, the stranger stepped in front of him and held him back.

'Let her go, my friend,' he said softly. 'There is no catching her now, and she will do no further harm tonight.'

Confusion clouded Holmes's face. I do not remember ever seeing him as shaken as he was that night. I shared his bewilderment, for what I had witnessed seemed to be the stuff of mad dreams.

'You are Sherlock Holmes,' said the stranger in a quiet, steady voice which bore the faint trace of an accent. Turning to me, he added, 'And you must be Dr Watson.'

'You have the advantage,' said I, pulling myself to my feet.

Holmes, with something of the old authority in his voice, said, 'I believe, Watson, that we are in the company of Professor Abraham Van Helsing of Amsterdam University.'

The man nodded curtly.

Van Helsing. The name echoed down the corridors of my memory. Van Helsing! Of course, I thought, the article in *The Times*.

I felt a cold, clammy grasp on my heart as I said in a hoarse whisper, 'Vampires!'

* * *

'I realise that to the the practical, scientific mind such as yours, Mr Holmes, vampires – dead beings that leave their graves at night to suck the blood of the living – will seem to be the creations of carnival charlatans, or the inhabitants of grotesque fairy stories. But it is the fault of our science that it desires to explain all; and when it is unable to do so, then it says there is nothing to explain. I see from your expression that, despite your experience tonight, you still have difficulty in believing.'

It was an hour later, and the three of us were in our Baker Street rooms. Holmes and I were seated by the fire, while Van Helsing paced the floor as he addressed us in his soft, passionate voice.

Van Helsing was not unlike Holmes in appearance: he was older and less tall, but possessed the same high forehead, lean features and a strong, aquiline nose. His hair, long and flecked with silver, fell across his face as he talked; and it was a nervous habit of his to push it back with his hand. A straggly grey Van Dyck beard adorned his chin, as if placed there as an afterthought. But the most startling aspect of his appearance was his piercing blue eyes, which shone out from his tired face with the eagerness of youth and the fervour of intense dedication.

Holmes, who had been listening carefully to Van Helsing, gave the Dutchman a brief smile. 'You cannot expect the scepticism of a lifetime to be eradicated in one evening, Professor,' he said. 'Nevertheless, I must confess that I am more ready to listen to your theories after tonight's episode than I was a few days ago. Eh, Watson?'

I nodded.

'Perhaps you would give us further details of this "cult of the undead", as you call it, and how you came to be so fortuitously on hand tonight.'

'Certainly.' Van Helsing sat in the wicker chair, staring into the flickering fire for a moment as though to gather his thoughts before beginning his strange narrative.

'It may help you to regard vampirism as a sickness, partly physical, partly spiritual. The vampire by its "kiss" takes blood from the living for its own survival. Blood gives life. As the Bible says, "Blood is life". Gradually the victim grows weaker, as though suffering from a wasting disease which is often diagnosed as chronic anaemia. Eventually he dies, and then after a few nights he too rises from the grave, seeking the precious life-giving force. So the cult grows, infinitely slowly, but it grows.

'The vampire rests during the day, its unearthly life held in suspension, and it issues as a living form only at night. Just as evil cannot survive the light of goodness and reason, so it is with the vampire if brought into contact with the purifying touch of daylight.

'Their resting place is the coffin, which must either lie in its original grave or tomb, or contain a layer of earth from the creature's native soil. The coffin is carefully and often ingeniously concealed, for during the day the undead is at his most vulnerable. Often the vampire will recruit the help of a human to protect it during the hours of daylight. This person is usually a mother who hides an infected son or daughter, a servant either hypnotised or so devoted to his master that he is unaware of the evil consequences of his actions, or some disciple of the Devil who carries out his allotted tasks with the hope of one day being initiated into the unholy cult. Without the help of these mortal accomplices it would be far easier to track down the vampire to its lair and destroy it.'

'You think that the creature we encountered tonight was one of these undead?' I asked.

'I do not think it, Doctor, I know,' came the Professor's emphatic reply. 'Her appearance alone would have indicated as much. The long gown which she wore was undoubtedly a shroud. She exhibited all the characteristics of the undead. They have lean, cadaverous features with skin the pallor of death. They are cold to the touch and their breath is fetid like that of all carnivores. The vampire is repelled by Christian images and all things holy. As you witnessed for yourself, the phantom lady fled when confronted with the symbol of our Lord, the crucifix.' He paused to take a black cheroot from his leather cigar-case.

'The physical attack of the vampire follows a definite pattern,' he continued, after lighting the cheroot. 'It begins when the victim, through the hypnotic force of the vampire, is lulled into a sense of peace and wellbeing. An embrace follows, during which the vampire sinks his fang-like canines into the tender region of the throat, causing the blood to flow freely into his mouth. The general point of the attack is the jugular vein. The needle-sharp teeth make a swift incision here.'

Van Helsing tapped the side of his neck with his long forefinger and gave Holmes and me an enquiring glance to observe what effects these fantastic details were having on us, before resuming his narrative with greater earnestness.

'Gentlemen, vampire activity has been recorded in all parts of the world, and I have in my possession records of overwhelming testimony, modern and ancient, from religious and sceptic, from every civilisation throughout the ages, verifying the existence of these vile creatures. However, it is in Eastern Europe where the vampire, *nosferatu*, has secured a strong foothold, and this is due principally to one man – I say man when I really refer to a thing of the Devil: Count Dracula.'

I had never heard the name before, and yet the very mention of it seemed to waken in me some dread indefinable fear.

Holmes, who had sat motionless during Van Helsing's exposition, his hawk-like features set like a mask, now leaned forward. 'Who is this Count Dracula?' he enquired quietly.

'Dracula is the epitome of all that is evil in the world. I am sorry if I sound melodramatic, but I cannot overemphasise the diabolism of this living corpse.'

'Corpse?' I exclaimed.

'Yes. The Count is an undead. Indeed, he is the lord of the undead. In life he was a Transylvanian nobleman, directly related to Vlad Tepesh, the heartless and autocratic ruler of Wallachia in the fifteenth century. Vlad Tepesh was a victorious but cruel warrior who enjoyed the soubriquet Vlad the Impaler due to his vicious propensity for impaling his enemies on great wooden stakes. It is not clear when this family bloodlust became transmitted into the vampire cravings now manifest in the last of the Draculas. There is no accurate record of how old Count Dracula is, but it may be that he and Vlad Tepesh are one and the same man.'

'That is impossible!' I cried. 'That would make him over four hundred years old.'

Van Helsing allowed himself a grim smile. 'It *is* possible, Doctor. Blood is a great preservative. Until recently the Count has lain deep in the labyrinthine fortifications of Castle Dracula high in the Carpathian Mountains, near the treacherous Borgo Pass, only leaving the security of his lair to obtain that life-giving force so necessary for his survival.'

'You say "until recently",' remarked Holmes. 'You mean he is no longer there?'

'My search for Castle Dracula, a search which has taken many years, ended but four months ago. In the great vaults which run under the crumbling structure, I found the bodies of his three brides-in-blood and I was able to destroy them, but of the Count himself there was no trace: he had gone. Searching through the rooms of the castle, I came upon some correspondence dealing with a shipment of large boxes of earth arranged by the Count. Obviously these were a means of his own transportation. The boxes were to be taken to Varna, a port on the Black Sea, in the care of someone called Meinster, who almost certainly is a mortal accomplice of the Count. At Varna the boxes were to be loaded onto a Russian schooner, the *Demeter*. I travelled to Varna and enquired about this consignment of boxes with the port officials. They remembered it well, and also the man in charge of it. They described Meinster as an ugly dwarf with only one eye.'

'And the destination of the schooner?' enquired Holmes.

'London,' replied Van Helsing, quietly.

It was a few moments before the full implication of the Dutchman's statement dawned on me. Then I cried out, 'You mean to say that Dracula is now here in this city?'

'I am certain of it, Doctor,' replied Van Helsing sternly. 'Ostensibly I am in London to give a series of lectures to the Royal Society, but the real purpose of my visit is to track down Count Dracula and destroy him.' He slumped back in his chair as though thoroughly exhausted by his lengthy exposition.

'Another brandy, I think, Watson,' suggested Holmes.

I quickly set about the business of recharging our glasses, for I, too, felt the need of a reviving agent. The night's events and Van Helsing's strange narrative had quite drained my energy.

The Professor gratefully accepted the brandy and gulped it down. Holmes sipped his in a desultory fashion before turning to our guest. 'It was the newspaper reports of "the phantom lady" which led you to believe that there was one of these undead creatures active on Hampstead Heath?'

'That is correct, Mr Holmes. The wounds described in those reports made it clear to me that they were the work of a vampire – a bride of Dracula. Through her, I believed it would be possible to reach the Count himself.

'I have spent every night of the last week on the Heath, waiting to apprehend this "phantom lady". As fate would have it, I was in another part of the Heath when she attacked and killed the young woman last night.'

At this juncture I interrupted with a question concerning a point which had been troubling me. 'Tell me, Professor,' I said, 'why should she attack Miss Lydgate – the young woman – in such a ferocious and violent manner? It was not just a puncturing of the jugular in this case; the flesh was torn savagely. I thought you said the taking of blood was a gradual process.'

'And so it usually is, but in this case the vampire had, most probably, been unable to obtain sufficient blood for some nights and was therefore desperate – as desperate as a starving man for food. Her cravings for the life-force must have reached such an intensity that it was necessary for her to secure a large intake of blood quickly; and so she attacked wildly to acquire her only means of survival.'

'It is horrible,' I shuddered.

'The poor young woman would not have stood a chance. The vampire possesses great strength, especially when aroused.'

'That explains why this creature was able to fling me to the ground with apparent ease.'

'Indeed.' Van Helsing gave me a stern grin. 'I see you are beginning to believe my wild theories, Dr Watson.'

I nodded grimly.

Van Helsing turned to Sherlock Holmes for some similar sign of acquiescence, but my friend's expression remained unmoved.

'You suggest,' said Holmes, 'that the creature we encountered tonight has been infected by Count Dracula.'

'Undoubtedly she is a bride of Dracula, which clearly indicates that he is resting in this vicinity.' Some of the fervour returned to Van Helsing's face and his eyes began to sparkle keenly. 'Mr Holmes, I know of your reputation and of your remarkable powers. There is no man in the world whose help would be more valuable to me than yours. Will you assist me, help me seek out and destroy the propagator of this unspeakable evil?'

Holmes was always susceptible to sincere flattery, and the ghost of a smile which lighted upon his lips told me he was well pleased with Van Helsing's sentiments.

'I certainly owe you a great deal,' he replied. 'But for your timely intervention tonight I might not be here now. I, too, wish to get to the bottom of this bizarre affair, so I will certainly do all I can to help you in your search for Count Dracula.'

The professor smiled delightedly and grabbed Holmes firmly by the hand. 'Thank you,' he said with great warmth.

'As to the actual existence of vampires,' continued Holmes, 'although you put forward a most convincing argument, I am afraid that I shall have to reserve my judgement until . . . we have caught one.'

'I am sure that with your help we shall do that quite soon,' affirmed the professor earnestly.

'I presume I am included in this venture,' said I.

'Of course, my dear Watson. I am afraid I took that for granted.'

'I would have it no other way,' I replied.

'Good, then it is settled,' beamed Van Helsing, pushing back his hair from his forehead. 'We must now decide what our course of action is to be.'

Holmes lit his old clay pipe, and for a moment his face was shrouded in puffs of pungent black smoke. Emerging from this fog, he addressed our visitor. 'According to your theory, if this so-called "phantom lady" we encountered tonight is a vampire, she will need a resting place during the day.'

'A graveyard,' I suggested.

'Exactly, Watson. A graveyard, indeed. Make a long arm, my good fellow, and pass me the Ordnance Survey map of the Hampstead area.'

I did as I was asked, and Holmes, spreading the map out over his lap, scrutinised it closely for some minutes. At length he gave a cry of satisfaction.'

'What is it, Mr Holmes?' asked Van Helsing eagerly.

'I believe I have something here, my friend.' He pointed at the map, and Van Helsing and I followed the direction of his bony forefinger. 'Look, gentlemen, a private graveyard not more than two miles from where we were attacked tonight. Observe how secluded it is: nothing but open land and a small wood to three sides of it.'

'An ideal resting place,' agreed Van Helsing.

'But what can we do, Holmes?' I asked. 'We cannot go around opening every grave to see if this creature is resting inside.'

'My dear fellow,' said Holmes smiling, 'I have no intention of doing any such thing. It is a simple matter to check the register of burials to ascertain if a young woman has been buried there within the last month. That should, I suspect, narrow the field down somewhat.'

I nodded, annoyed at my own dull-wittedness.

'Now gentlemen,' said Holmes, casting the map aside, 'I propose we try to get as much sleep as we are able tonight, and then in the morning I will carry out this simple investigation.' He turned to Van Helsing. 'I suggest we meet for lunch, when I shall report my findings, and we can then plan our campaign.'

'Excellent idea, Mr Holmes,' agreed the Dutchman. 'Perhaps you and Dr Watson will dine with me at my hotel? I am staying at the Northumberland.'

'Fine. Does that suit you, Watson?'

'Yes, admirably,' I replied.

The Powers of Darkness

I slept soundly that night, but towards dawn I drifted into the realm of dark dreams. I found myself trapped in a cave filled with weird subhuman cries. For a fleeting moment I saw Stapleton's grinning face leer out at me from the shadows before it disappeared in a burst of yellow flame. Malevolent eyes winked in the darkness and strange, slimy, claw-like hands clutched at me. Enormous bat creatures swooped down towards me, their foul, leathery wings scraping my face. I was paralysed with fear and unable to raise a hand to protect myself as one of these creatures began to bite my neck. I could feel the small, vicious mouth tearing the flesh of my throat, and the warm blood as it trickled down from the wound.

Eventually my mind could take no more of these nightmare sensations. I was propelled into consciousness with a startling suddenness which I punctuated with a short cry. I lay there in the grey half-light for some moments, my body covered in cold sweat, before slipping once more into a peaceful, untroubled doze.

It was late when I eventually rose, to discover that Holmes had already gone out on his errand. I ate a solitary breakfast, and then read through the morning papers while awaiting his return.

Lestrade called around eleven o'clock to enquire about our night's vigil. It had been decided, for the time being at least, that the true details of our encounter with the phantom lady, and Van Helsing's vampire theories, should be kept to ourselves. Lestrade was an unimaginative soul at the best of times, and for him to be told that our quarry was a vampire would prompt him to question our sanity rather than provide us with a useful ally. Therefore, acting on Holmes's instructions, I told Lestrade that our night had been uneventful.

The policeman's emotions fought with themselves as to whether to receive this news with pleasure or regret. Eventually a smug expression settled itself on Lestrade's sallow features. 'Well, Mr Holmes can't win 'em all,' he remarked with a grin. 'I had better put my men back on the job tonight. I'll let Mr Holmes know if there are any further developments.' And with a dry chuckle he left.

It was just before noon when Holmes swept into our rooms. 'Good day, Watson. You slept well, I trust,' he cried cheerily, throwing his coat across the wicker chair.

I could see by his exultant expression that he had obviously had a successful morning's work. However, it was one of my companion's annoying little traits that he was loath to communicate information until he felt that the right dramatic moment had arrived. This was partly due to his own masterful nature, which loved to dominate all those around him, and partly because of his sometimes over-developed sense of the dramatic. On this occasion he responded to all my enquiries about his morning's exploits with a wave of the hand and a beatific grin.

'Come, Watson,' he said at last, 'all will be revealed over lunch.' He glanced at his pocket watch. 'And, by Jove, we shall be late if we don't hurry.'

*   *   *

The Northumberland Hotel was a large, imposing building trapped down a quiet street between the noisily thronged thoroughfares of Trafalgar Square and the Strand. The restaurant was quite full when Holmes and I entered some twenty minutes later. The air was filled with the discreet chatter of diners, and a blue veil of pungent cigar smoke hung in the atmosphere. It was a large room with dark, mahogany-panelled walls, illuminated by a series of crystal chand-eliers. Red velvet drapes cascaded down from the ceiling by the tall windows. Seated at a table by one of these windows was Van Helsing who, on seeing us enter, rose to his feet and beckoned us with a napkin.

We exchanged greetings, and ordered lunch from one of the scurrying waiters. Then both Van Helsing and I turned to Holmes to await his report.

'Well,' he said at last, 'the pieces of this puzzle seem to be falling into place to suit your theory, Van Helsing. I examined the register of burials at Bellmount Private Cemetery early this morning and discovered that less than four weeks ago the twenty-year-old daughter of Sir Ralph Markham was buried in the family vault there.'

'Sir Ralph Markham. I seem to know that name.'

'Indeed you do, Watson. He is the celebrated naval expert attached to the Admiralty.'

'Ah yes, of course,' said I.

'The girl is certainly about the right age,' murmured Van Helsing.

'After picking up this titbit of information, I took it upon myself to pay a visit to the Markham household – a fine villa, not three miles from Bellmount. As I suspected, Sir Ralph was at the Admiralty on business, but I was able to gain an interview with Lady Markham. She is a delicate lady of some forty years whose fine features clearly show the strain and grief she has suffered following the loss of her daughter.

'I presented myself as Donald Fraser, a medical research consultant from St. Bartholomew's Hospital.' At this point in his narrative, Holmes briefly addressed us in a lilting Aberdonian accent to give us a flavour of his adopted persona. 'I asked the lady if I might put some questions to her about the death of her daughter. She agreed, although I could see it was painful for her to speak of the girl. I can tell you, gentlemen, I felt wretched at having to do such a thing, but I knew the information she could give me would be vital to our investigation.'

Holmes leaned closer to us with an air of confidentiality and continued in hushed tones. 'This is what she told me. Her daughter, Violet, had been attending an academy for young ladies at Coombe Tracey in Devon – a location with which Watson and I are familiar.'

I nodded, remembering our brief sojourn to Coombe Tracey during the Baskerville case.

'While at this academy, Violet Markham contracted "a strange disease". At first she was treated by the local doctor, a man called Collins. However, he was unable to effect a cure, and so a specialist friend of Sir Ralph's visited the girl. Likewise, his ministrations were unsuccessful.'

'What form did this "strange illness" take?' asked Van Helsing.

Holmes's eyes glittered with intense excitement as he replied, 'The symptons were of anaemia; and yet, despite many blood transfusions, she gradually grew weaker. Eventually the girl was brought home. She died within six hours of reaching there. The doctors were not only puzzled by the actual cause of her death, but also by two small wounds on Miss Markham's neck.'

'The seal of Dracula!' exclaimed Van Helsing excitedly, in a hoarse whisper. 'Holmes, it is all there: the mysterious loss of blood, the gradual weakening of the victim, the tell-tale puncture marks on the neck. These are the classic vampire symptoms.'

'The facts seem inescapable,' agreed Holmes, reluctantly.

'You really believe this girl was infected by Count Dracula himself?' I asked.

Van Helsing gave a firm nod.

'Then the trail leads us to Coombe Tracey, where the girl first showed signs of her illness.'

'Watson is correct,' said Holmes. 'The evidence clearly indicates that Dracula is no longer in London but has sought the safer environs of the Devonshire countryside, and it is there that we must attempt to track him down.'

Van Helsing touched Holmes's sleeve. 'Before we take our investigations further, we have a gruesome but necessary duty to perform. We must visit Violet Markham's grave at sunset and destroy the creature which now inhabits her body.'

I shuddered at these words. 'How does one destroy a vampire?' I asked, hardly believing the fantastic nature of my enquiry.

'There are many methods set down in the ancient *grimoires* for the destruction of an undead being, from burning to immersion in running water. Such measures are outside the realms of my experience. However, I have been responsible for the elimination of several vampire colonies in the Carpathians. There are two forms of *modus operandi* which I have found totally effective. A silver bullet fired directly into the heart will exterminate one of these creatures; or a stake fashioned from the wood of an ash tree driven through the heart also releases the taint of evil. Both these acts must be followed by the decapitation of the victim.'

I was shocked, not only by the gruesome acts that Van Helsing described, but also by the cold, dispassionate way in which he described them.

'It is a messy and damnable business, Doctor,' he said, observing my disturbed expression, 'but so very necessary. Our task is an urgent one and it must be carried out today, before this vampire has a chance to walk again and do more harm.'

'Why must this task be performed at sunset?' asked Holmes, unable to keep the note of scepticism from his voice. I knew that he still had not come to terms with the fantastic nature of this affair and, while all the evidence had corroborated Van Helsing's theories, they were so alien to Holmes's scientific and practical nature that he found acceptance of them almost impossible.

'Sunrise or sunset are the most effective times for the destruction of a vampire. They are the most mysterious parts of the day when the powers of good and evil hold equal sway and the balance is more easily tipped.'

'But surely,' I interrupted, 'logically, during the hours of daylight would be a better time?'

'Logic has but a small foothold in the affairs of the supernatural, Doctor.' He gave me a gentle, indulgent smile. 'However, one can apply a certain kind of logic to this situation. Do not believe that during the hours of daylight the powers of evil are impotent. They are merely on the defensive and therefore at their most alert. It would be far more dangerous for us to enter the crypt in bright sunshine than at the times I suggest. Please trust me, Doctor; my knowledge is based on practical experience.'

I nodded dumbly. Through the window I could hear the faint bustle of the Strand, the rattle of the traffic, the cries of the street vendors, the simple noise of humanity as it carried out its daily business, and yet I felt completely cut off from the real world out there. Although I did accept all that Van Helsing had told us, it seemed so far removed from reality. I glanced around at our fellow diners, who were happily indulging their appetites, oblivious to the dreadful truths of which the three of us were cognisant. Surely, I pondered, this is some monstrous dream and soon I will wake up in my chair by the fire in our Baker Street rooms, my comfortable, predictable world restored to me.

My thoughts were interrupted by the arrival of the waiter with our lunch. None of us felt like eating and we lapsed into silence as we tackled our food in a desultory manner. The thought of the task which lay ahead preyed too much on our minds for us to be considerate to our stomachs.

As I toyed with my meal I wondered, with a deep sense of uneasy presentiment, what untold horrors we would encounter before this dark business was brought to a conclusion.

* * *

The day was on the brink of evening and the slate-grey November sky was turning to a dull blue as Holmes, Van Helsing, and I entered the grounds of Bellmount Cemetery through a narrow wooden gate, the hinges of which creaked in protest at their lack of use.

It was a bleak spot: the fading light turned the gravestones into menacing silhouettes, and a sharp breeze blew through the bare branches of the trees overhanging the cemetery along two sides, and teased small piles of rotting autumn leaves.

Holmes and I had spent the afternoon preparing mentally for the abhorrent task which lay before us, while Van Helsing had been engaged in more practical preparations, the result of which he carried with him in his large medical bag.

Somewhere in the adjacent wood an owl hooted. 'He senses the closeness of night. Soon it will be fully dark and the powers of evil will hold sway,' observed the Dutchman quietly.

'Good things of day begin to droop and drowse;
  whiles night's black agents to their prey do rouse,'

said Holmes. 'As you know, Professor, I am not a superstitious man, but I believe there is something in what you say. By far the greatest number of crimes are committed at night: darkness is the criminal's greatest ally, giving him cover and protection.'

The owl hooted again.

'That bird is certainly impatient for the night,' I murmured.

'He is anxious to go hunting – and he is not the only one,' said Van Helsing. 'Come, Holmes, lead us to the Markham vault.'

We lapsed into silence as we followed Holmes, dark lantern in hand, across the graveyard. Many of the headstones were crumbling, and lodged at drunken angles, while the neglected plots had been conquered by weeds: it was a startling reminder of how soon the dead are forgotten.

'There it is,' said Holmes, holding his lantern aloft, its feeble rays falling on a small, squat building tucked away in the corner of the graveyard.

As we approached the vault, I glanced at my two companions: both wore expressions of grim resolution. We descended a small flight of steps leading to the entrance. This was barred by a rusty iron gate which, to my surprise, swung open easily. Van Helsing and Holmes exchanged knowing glances.

The stench of death reached our nostrils as we walked inside. Mice and rats, disturbed by our entry, scurried around our feet. Recessed in the flat ceiling was a small, round, stained-glass window, which threw a faint coloured circle of light onto an oak casket set on a stone slab in the centre of the vault. On two of the walls several stone shelves jutted out, supporting the cobwebbed caskets of dead generations of Markhams. The meagre illumination from Holmes's lantern filled the chamber with a sepulchral glow, which cast our distorted shadows, grotesque familiars, awkwardly against the walls and onto the ceiling.

It was, however, the coffin before us which held our interest. It showed none of the signs of age borne by the others, and, as Holmes held the lantern near, we observed on the lid the brass plaque which bore Violet Markham's name.

Placing his bag on the floor, Van Helsing quickly and nimbly removed the lid of the coffin, revealing its occupant. Although I had prepared myself for the sight which met our eyes, I still could not repress a shudder at what I saw. Lying there, wrapped in a blood-spattered shroud, was the young girl who had attacked us the night before. Her eyes were closed, but the lids pulsated with the rapid movements of the pupils beneath. Her ghostly white features were in repose, and yet they bore the mask of cruelty. Apart from the dark scar in the shape of a crucifx on her forehead, her skin was smooth and unblemished, the lips full and of the rich red hue of health. At one corner of the mouth lay a fine trail of dried blood.

Van Helsing leaned over the girl and raised the upper lip to reveal the canines, larger and sharper than normal. They were more like animal fangs. 'It is with these that she gains access to her victim's blood supply,' he murmured.

Holmes and I stood gazing with horrid fascination at the thing in the coffin. Never in all our adventures together had we witnessed anything like this.

Suddenly the wind picked up outside and the gate of the vault banged shut. The noise seemed to galvanise Van Helsing into action. 'Come, we must act swiftly,' he said briskly. 'Soon it will be time for her to walk again.'

I watched spellbound as the Professor took from his bag a large hammer and a wooden stake about a foot in length and sharpened to a fine point at one end. 'Give me light, Holmes,' he said, and my friend held the lantern closer to the coffin.

I moved forward into the dim circle of illumination. 'Is there no other way?' I asked.

'Please try to understand, Doctor. This is not Violet Markham you see before you. It is only a shell, possessed and corrupted by the evil of Dracula. To liberate her soul and give it eternal peace, we must destroy that shell for all time.' The Dutchman shook his head. 'There is no other way.'

So saying, he placed the point of the stake over the heart of the thing lying in the coffin and raised the hammer ready to strike. With startling abruptness, the creature's eyes sprang open, blazing with a crazed, feverish stare. The cruel mouth twisted into a bestial snarl.

Van Helsing tried to avert his gaze from those smouldering eyes, but in vain: he was caught by their compelling power. The hammer blow faltered and he staggered back from the coffin.

Holmes acted quickly. With great speed and agility he leapt forward, thrusting the lantern into my hands, and snatched the implements from Van Helsing's limp grasp. Leaning over the coffin, he raised the hammer as the creature began to rise. He thrust the stake down onto its breast and struck it with all his might. She slumped back, her body shuddering as though in the throes of a fit. Holmes struck again, and a hideous screech issued from the red lips as the stake sank deep into its unnatural heart. The air reverberated with her terrified cries as the body shook, quivered, and twisted in wild contortions, the sharp white teeth champing together and the mouth frothing with crimson foam. Blood gushed around the stem of the stake, spreading a dark pattern across the shroud.

Holmes struck the wooden stake a third blow. Slowly the writhing grew steadily weaker, the teeth ceased to champ, and then those cruel eyes closed for the last time.

Finally the body lay still.

Holmes dropped the hammer and stumbled to the threshold of the vault, where he stood, breathing deeply. With unsteady legs I joined him and gulped in the fresh, cold night air.

After some moments, Van Helsing came to us. 'You have done a very brave thing, my friend,' he said quietly, placing his hand on Holmes's shoulder. 'Come now and look.'

He led us back to the coffin and, taking the lantern, held it over the girl's face. We gazed down on an unblemished countenance which was at peace, and free from any trace of evil or cruelty. A slight smile now touched her lips. Van Helsing indicated the girl's smooth forehead: the dark shadow of the crucifix had disappeared. 'You see, the taint of evil has been lifted. She is no longer one of the undead. You have given her eternal peace. However, there is one final task to perform: the head must be severed from the body.'

Passing the lantern back to me, he delved into his large bag and produced a medical saw. Neatly, and with the precision and dexterity of a surgeon, he performed the gruesome operation.

'God will now have mercy on her soul,' he murmured, as he finally closed the coffin lid.

'I owe you an apology, Professor.' Holmes spoke in a voice that sounded tired and strained. 'I doubted your word from the beginning, and I fought against my own reason when the facts began to fit your theories concerning the undead. I see now that I was wrong. I can assure you, I no longer harbour any doubts.'

Van Helsing gave a weary, tight-lipped smile. 'I know how you felt, my friend. I travelled that same road of disbelief myself. At first I clung to the old rationale despite evidence to the contrary. Now you, too, are a member of that very select club of believers and, as such, you will find this of great interest.' He took from the pocket of his overcoat a slim, black notebook and handed it to Holmes. 'It contains all my notes and data relating to the undead.'

'Thank you,' said Holmes, taking the book and slipping it into his own pocket.

'Come now, let us leave this place; the smell of evil is still strong in my nostrils.'

We emerged from the vault into the dark night. As we moved away, Van Helsing said, 'Now, my friends, one piece of our work is completed, one that was most harrowing, but there remains a greater task: to find the author of this sorrow and stamp him out forever.'

'I promise you, Van Helsing,' declared Holmes passionately, 'that I will help you track down this Count Dracula and destroy him, whatever the consequences may be for myself.'

Return Visits

The experience in the vault had been a thoroughly exhausting one and, when Holmes and I returned to Baker Street later that evening, we were drained of all energy. Throwing off our coats, we sank into our chairs and sat in silence for some time, lost in our own thoughts, gazing at the cheerfully blazing fire that Mrs Hudson had kindled to welcome us.

We had parted from Van Helsing at his hotel after planning the next stage of our enquiry. Both men acknowledged that an urgent investigation of the academy for young ladies in Coombe Tracey was necessary. It was here that Violet Markham had first contracted her 'strange illness' and, as Holmes asserted, this place was now our only link, tentative though it might be, with Count Dracula.

'There is no time to lose; the trail may already be growing cold. It is over four weeks since he obtained blood from Violet Markham; by now he will have found a new victim to sustain his unnatural life.'

Van Helsing had pressing lecture engagements for the next few days, and so it was decided that Holmes and I should continue the investigations on our own, keeping in touch with the professor by telegram. We were to travel down to Coombe Tracey by the early morning train. Holmes, who was predisposed to be a lone wolf while on a case, was more than satisfied with this arrangement.

Van Helsing had passed his bag containing the various 'prophylactic and destructive paraphernalia' into Holmes's keeping. 'It will be of service,' he said simply, and added as we left him, 'God be with you.'

After some time, Mrs Hudson bustled in with hot tea and buttered muffins. 'I thought you would be wanting a little something,' she smiled, placing her tray on the table.

'Mrs Hudson, my dear, this is marvellous,' I cried, rousing myself from my brown study.

'Go on with you, Doctor. There's nothing marvellous about tea and muffins. It is just ordinary fare.'

'It is because tea and muffins are so ordinary that they are so welcome, Mrs Hudson,' said Holmes. 'Watson and I are somewhat out of touch with the ordinary at the moment.'

With a bewildered shrug, our housekeeper left us to our small repast.

Holmes drank his tea quickly, leaving the muffins untouched; he then filled his old cherrywood pipe with some of Bradley's harshest shag and settled down to study Van Helsing's notebook. I realised that there was little chance of conversation with him that evening, so I too lit my pipe and tried to relax.

I hoped a bowlful of my rich Arcadia mixture might soothe my tense nerves, but it had little effect. Eventually I put my pipe down, lay back in my chair, and closed my eyes, but in the darkness there flashed before me images of the horrid events I had witnessed in the Markham vault. With my medical experience I was no stranger to the sight of blood, but the memory of the strange crimson stain which seeped from the wound across the creature's shroud made my flesh creep.

However, fatigue eventually got the better of my imaginings. Within a couple of hours, tiredness and the warmth of the fire lulled me towards sleep – that 'balm of hurt minds'.

From time to time I was conscious of a clock in the distance chiming the hours, but all else was lost to me until I was jolted into tingling alertness by a sudden exclamation from my friend.

'What a fool I am. I have been as blind as a beetle,' he cried, leaping to his feet and casting his pipe onto the mantelpiece.

'What on earth is the matter?' said I, glancing at the clock and nothing that it was just after eleven.

'No time for explanations now, Watson. Grab your coat. Our night's work is not yet done.'

Without hesitation I followed my friend's instructions and moments later we were hurrying along Baker Street in search of a cab. Holmes, who had given me no indication of the nature of our errand, carried with him Van Helsing's large medical bag.

When a hansom cab came into view, Holmes leapt into the road, almost into the path of the horses.

'Scotland Yard as fast as you can, driver. There's an extra shilling in it for you.'

We had hardly climbed aboard before we were racing through the cobbled streets.

'What is this all about, Holmes?' I asked, when I had my breath back. 'Why Scotland Yard?'

'Think, Watson, think! Tonight we have witnessed with our own eyes actual proof of the vampire's regenerative cycle, but we have failed to put that knowledge to use.'

I shook my head. 'I am afraid I do not know what you mean.'

'The girl, Celia Lydgate, was killed by that thing we destroyed tonight, and so the infernal process continues. She too has now been infected, has become an undead and will, unless we can stop her, rise up, thirsting for blood.'

'Great heavens!' I exclaimed, as the full implication of Holmes's words struck me.

'Let us hope we are not too late and that the creature still lies dormant.'

The cab swung into Great Scotland Yard and pulled to an abrupt halt. Holmes paid the driver and we hurried into the mortuary. Our sudden entrance disturbed the elderly desk sergeant who was sitting by the grate with a metal poker, stirring the coals listlessly. With a sigh, he left the poker resting in the glowing heart of the fire, and shuffled to the desk to attend to us. 'What is it, gentlemen?' he mumbled wearily, buttoning up his uniform.

'The body of the girl murdered on Hampstead Heath last night – is it still here?' asked Holmes with great urgency

'Just a moment, sir. I'll have to check the book.'

'Quickly man,' snapped Holmes, his fingers drumming on the desk.

The policeman frowned at my friend's impatience, and appeared to be about to make some critical remark, but then thought better of it. 'On the Heath last night, eh?' he muttered, more to himself than us, as his finger travelled down a column of entries with what seemed infinite slowness. At last it stopped. 'Yes, sir. The corpse is still here. It will be taken away for burial in the morning.'

'We need to see the body immediately.'

'See it? Oh, I'm afraid that's not possible, not without written authority. You will have to get a warrant . . . '

'There is no time for that,' Holmes interrupted. 'My name is Sherlock Holmes, and I am assisting Inspector Lestrade on a very important case. It is vital that I see the body at once.'

At the mention of my friend's name, a sudden change came over the old sergeant. 'Oh, I didn't realise it was you, Mr Holmes. I had no idea. Of course I know of your work; we all do at the Yard. Anything to help with your investigations,' he said effusively, taking a large key-ring off the wall. Without further delay, he led us to the room we had visited the day before.

'Now then, which is it?' the old sergeant muttered as he fumbled with the collection of keys. 'It's either this big one, or this rusty varmint here.'

Holmes gave a deep sigh of frustration, his features taut with the fury of impatience.

'Ah, this is the one,' the policeman crowed at last, as he finally turned the key in the lock.

None of us was ready for what occurred next. It happened with such speed and violence that even as I recollect them now, the events appear to me in a blurred and somewhat disjointed fashion. No sooner had the door been unlocked than it was wrenched open from the inside, swinging back to meet the inner wall with a loud crack. Never in the insane imaginings of a disordered brain could anything more appalling, more chilling, more terrifying be conceived than the twisted form and nightmare face that now confronted us on the threshold of the room. The chalk-white flesh clung to the skeletal features; two fierce eyes blazed like liquid fire; and the ruddy mouth gaped in a bestial snarl, revealing the treacherous points of two sharp fangs which protruded over the lower lip. The body was draped in the faded green sheet in which it had been wrapped when we had last seen it.

This was Celia Lydgate back from the dead.

For a brief moment she stood before us, swaying in an ungainly fashion like a tired marionette, and then her arms lashed out wildly, the claw-like fingers tearing at the face of the sergeant. With a strangled cry he fell to the floor in a faint, blood streaming from a deep gash on his face.

So utterly taken aback were we by the sudden and violent appearance of this dreadful apparition that she had brushed past us and was running down the corridor to freedom before Holmes and I could recover our senses. Holmes was the first to move and, with me at his heels, he hared off in pursuit. The vampire, released from her prison, had made a remarkably speedy escape, but Holmes managed to catch up with her as she neared the sergeant's office. He launched himself at our quarry and they both crashed to the floor, but so great was the strength of the frenzied creature that she was able to toss Holmes to one side and struggle to her feet again.

Unhurt, Holmes gave chase once more and caught up with her in the sergeant's office as she made her way towards the door and freedom. I managed to dodge past her and engage the large bolts, thus sealing up this means of escape to the outside world.

With a cry of rage the girl retreated behind the sergeant's desk, uncertainty clouding her demonic features. Quickly, Holmes vaulted over the desk, landing directly in front of her.

'There is no escape,' he cried breathlessly.

She snarled her defiance and advanced on my friend, but he held his ground.

'No escape,' he called again, taunting the undead thing, almost as though he were willing her to attack him.

With a deep guttural laugh she drew close to him, her fangs glistening with saliva and bared ready for attack. Holmes, however, remained steady and unflinching. Then, just as she was upon him, he leapt sideways with lightning speed and grabbed the poker from the glowing fire. The vampire darted forward in a desperate bid to prevent him, but she was not quick enough this time. Holmes took his moment. Brandishing the red-hot poker, he lunged forward and, with all his might, thrust it into the creature's breast. An immediate and sickening smell of scorching flesh assailed my nostrils, making my gorge rise. The vampire's mouth stretched wide in a strangled cry, but no sound escaped. Like a drunken mute, she stumbled forward, her frightened eyes blinking erratically as she made desperate attempts to wrench the poker from its resting place. Her efforts were in vain. The body twisted awkwardly and finally collapsed to the stone flagging. For some moments she continued to thrash about wildly like a wounded insect, until gradually she grew weaker and the body surrendered to the floundering spasms of the death throes. And then finally, all movement ceased.

We stood, staring with horrid fascination at the mutilated body, but then it began to change. The face, now in repose, regained its natural beauty, the manic stare fading from its eyes. Even the lines of anguish, which I had seen etched on her features when she visited Baker Street, were gone. Celia Lydgate had found peace at last.

* * *

Sherlock Holmes chuckled. 'I should certainly like to see Lestrade's face when he learns of last night's happenings in the mortuary.'

I grinned and nodded.

'Being told by one of his men that he was attacked by a dead woman is not likely to bring about a happy start to the day.' Holmes chuckled again. 'I can hardly begin to conceive what wild theories he will try to construct to fit the evidence.'

'Indeed,' I agreed. 'What about the poker lodged in the corpse's heart and the decapitated head?'*

'I think these bizarre little details will keep our friends at Scotland Yard well and truly foxed for many a day. I am glad we shall be out of London for a time, and therefore unavailable to provide explanations and solutions to their problems. If we were to reveal the truth of the matter, it would, I fear, place our sanity under grave suspicion. I do not believe the day has yet arrived when Scotland Yard is prepared to add vampires to its wanted list. Therefore our pastoral sojourn is most fortuitous.'

After a very early breakfast, Holmes had sent one of the Irregulars round to Van Helsing's hotel with a note, informing him of the events which had taken place in the mortuary. We caught the seven o'clock Devon Express from Paddington, and it was while we were seated in a first-class carriage *en route* to Coombe Tracey that this conversation took place.

Holmes, his eager face framed by his ear-flapped travelling cap, was in fine spirits, despite the horrific occurrences of the previous night. I knew from past experience that this sense of elation was due to his old bloodhound instinct. He was again on the track of a dangerous quarry, and once more the game was afoot.

As the pale wintry sunshine began to dispel the greyness of the dawn, we left the dingy suburbs of London behind. The journey was a swift one and soon, over the chequered quilt of fields and the low curve of a wood, there rose in the distance a dark melancholy hill with a strange jagged summit, dim and vague like some landscape in a dream.

'I had not thought I should set my eyes on the moor again quite so soon,' remarked Holmes.

'The very sight of it makes me feel uneasy,' said I.

'Places, like people, have distinct personalities, Watson, and the moor is no exception: it is rough, wild, and forbidding. It takes not kindly to the hand of man; it will not be tamed. I wonder how many souls have perished in the slimy clutches of its bogs and mires.' He leaned forward and for some moments, lost in thought, stared out of

---

* Although there is no direct reference to it in the notes, it would seem logical that Holmes allowed the medically experienced Watson to carry out the decapitation of Celia Lydgate, and that is why it is Watson who makes a pointed reference to it here.

the carriage window at the bleak moorland. Then, sitting back, he said quietly, 'If evil is able to inhabit locations, surely here is one of its camping grounds.'

It was not long before the train pulled into the small station of Coombe Tracey and we alighted into the sharp frosty air.

'Your first task, my dear fellow, is to engage rooms for us in the village. I seem to remember *The Grey Goose* in the square as being a passable hostelry. You make the appropriate arrangements and wait for me there,' said Holmes, walking briskly to the ticket barrier.

'And what do you intend to do in the meantime?'

Holmes responded with one of his infuriating smirks. 'Just seeing how the land lies,' he said cheerily.

*   *   *

The Grey Goose turned out to be a fine old Tudor inn which dominated the small village square. The whey-faced landlord was only too happy to provide Holmes and myself with accommodation. After laying a fire in the sitting room and giving me a resumé of the trials and tribulations of running a country inn, he left me to warm myself in front of the blazing logs.

Holmes arrived an hour later. His face was stern.

'Well?' I asked impatiently, eager to know what my friend had been up to.

'I have every reason to believe that we are hot on his trail, Watson,' he said as he sat opposite me, stretching his hands towards the flames.

'You mean . . . ?'

Holmes nodded and supplied my unspoken words. 'Count Dracula.' Like a curse, the name seemed to send a dark shadow across the room, across our lives.

'What leads you to this conclusion? What have you discovered?'

'I have been making some enquiries about The Gardner Academy for Young Ladies.'

'You have been inside?'

Holmes shook his head. 'I learned all I wanted to know by making some observations at the rear of this establishment, and then from certain discreet enquiries amongst the tradesmen of the village. You know, one day I will write a monograph on the usefulness of tradesmen and shopkeepers in the detection of crime. They are veritable mines of information, and quite often more observant and perceptive than the official police force. Incidents and details which would be ignored by a man of Lestrade's vision are noted mentally and filed away for future use by the local cobbler and fishmonger.

'By chatting with various tradespeople this morning I have learned more about Silas Gardner and his academy than a whole day of research would have revealed to me. Gossip, Watson, is by far the most expeditious means of obtaining information.'

'But what exactly have you learned?'

Holmes smiled at my impatience. 'Here, then, are some of the fruits of this morning's labours. The academy is a kind of finishing school where wealthy parents send their daughters to acquire such talents as are supposed to enhance their potential in the marriage market.'

'There are many such establishments on the Continent,' I re- marked.

'Indeed, and this home-grown variety is rare; but apparently the academy has a high reputation in the circles from which it draws its clients. The establishment was set up ten years ago by Silas Gardner and his wife, who seemingly had a weak constitution and died some three years ago. Gardner carried on with the help of his spinster sister, Mary. Apart from these two, the academy has a teaching staff of three with a full complement of ten students.'

'Not very many.'

'The number maintains the academy's claim of exclusivity. How- ever, when it became known that Violet Markham had contracted some kind of incurable disease while in residence at the academy, several parents withdrew their daughters, presumably frightened that the same fate might overtake them.'

Holmes looked thoughtful for a moment. I waited, expecting further revelations, but instead he rose to his feet, rubbing his hands together. 'Come, Watson,' he said, 'let us dine. The Devonshire air has given me an appetite. After lunch we shall pay a call on Mr Silas Gardner; but for the moment let us put thoughts of this dark affair to one side and consider our stomachs.'

The Academy

Holmes refused to be drawn into discussing the case any further until we had dined, and so our conversation turned to lighter matters. After a simple, though satisfying, lunch of cold ham, creamed potatoes, and custard pie, washed down with a glass of local cider, we set off for The Gardner Academy for Young Ladies.

'It is but a ten-minute walk from the inn,' Holmes assured me as we set off at a brisk pace. He was as good as his word, for within the allotted time we reached our destination. We had walked to the edge of the village where the road deteriorated into a rough dirt track which disappeared round a curve as though swallowed up by the moor. On the brink of the moorland, like a stately appendage to the village, stood a large Georgian dwelling set back from the road and separated from it by a small but thickly shrubbed garden. The building extolled the smart precision and symmetry of Georgian architecture, but the worn and scarred stonework told how it had borne the brunt of the harsh weather and the destructive moorland environment of fierce winds and howling storms.

On one of the large square gateposts a brass plaque was affixed:

THE GARDNER ACADEMY
FOR YOUNG LADIES

Principal: Silas Gardner M.A. (Cantab.)

Holmes and I made our way up the short, leaf-strewn path and rang the bell. We heard its ring echo through the house, but it was some moments before the door was opened by a small, timid maid.

Holmes scribbled a single word on his calling card and handed it to her. 'Give this to your master and tell him that Sherlock Holmes and Doctor Watson wish to see him.'

Dumbly the girl nodded and showed us into the hall where we were asked to wait. With a feeble curtsey she scurried off up the staircase to relay the message.

'Obviously a local girl with little notion of the demands of her position,' commented Holmes.

I nodded. The girl's ruddy complexion and Devonian accent clearly indicated that she was a local.

'Yet she tells us there is trouble in this house,' continued my friend.

'How is that?' I asked.

'The signs of crying round the eyes, the hesitant manner. She gripped my card so tightly that she nearly crushed it: indications that she was unsure how her master would react to her allowing two strangers into the house. Even the most inexperienced of maids does not rush upstairs at that rate unless something is wrong. She exhibited fear, Watson, a fear which is generated by uncertainty, which in turn, I would suggest, is the result of her master's vacillating behaviour. The kind of behaviour that is the product of much worry.'

I smiled. 'Your deductions may rely too heavily on feminine behaviour which you, yourself, have described as being notoriously unreliable.'

Holmes gave a short laugh. 'You could be right, Watson. We shall see.' He stood pensively for a moment. 'How quiet it is,' he said, almost to himself.

While we awaited the maid's return, Holmes strolled about the hall, scrutinising the walls, floor, and furniture.

Eventually the maid reappeared. 'The master will see you, gentlemen. Please follow me.'

She curtseyed once again and led us up the broad staircase, across the landing, and down a long, dimly-lit corridor which I judged to be parallel with the rear of the house. Halfway down the corridor, Holmes stopped abruptly and, with the practised air of a bloodhound, began sniffing the air.

The poor maid, quite bewildered by my friend's strange behaviour, prompted him with a small cough. 'It's this way, sir.'

'Yes, yes,' Holmes replied distractedly, and we continued to the end of the corridor, where the maid tapped gently on the door facing us. 'It's the two gentlemen to see you sir,' she said, her voice hesitant and nervous.

The door was opened by a large, untidy-looking man. He stared out at us with eyes bloodshot and bleary from lack of sleep. 'Right, girl, be about your business,' he cried hoarsely. With a stifled sob, she disappeared back down the corridor. Gardner waved his arm stiffly, beckoning us into the room.

Once inside, he slammed the door shut and leant with his back against it as though for support. His appearance was one of personal neglect. A thin grey area of stubble around his chin indicated that he had not shaved for several days, and his clothes were creased and dishevelled.

Facially, everything about Silas Gardner was exaggerated, from the large ears that stuck out at right angles, to the bulbous nose which overhung a wide and fleshy mouth. Indeed, had not his expression been one of pained consternation, I might have found this apparition rather a comical sight.

He eyed us with a wild stare for a few moments before speaking. 'What do you want?' he demanded in a peculiar, hoarse voice. 'And what is the meaning of this?' He held up Holmes's visiting card, on which I could clearly see the word 'blood' scribbled in my friend's hand.

'I should sit down if I were you, Gardner,' came Holmes's calm reply. 'You ought not to get over-excited after a transfusion.'

The white, drawn face grew even paler. 'How the devil . . . ? Who told you?'

'No one told me. My observations inform me that you have been giving blood in a transfusion.'

'How do you know?' repeated the puzzled Gardner, slumping into a chair.

'You are receiving visits from Dr Collins of Grimpen. No, do not bother to deny it. Despite your attempts to keep his visits secret by arranging for him to arrive by means of a circuitous route, using the little-frequented cart track at the rear of the academy, his calls have not escaped the eagle eyes of the village busybodies. Acting on their reports I, myself, witnessed his arrival here this morning at eleven o'clock precisely. Now tell me, Gardner, why the secrecy? Is it that you do not want it known that you have another mysterious and apparently incurable illness on your hands?'

'I don't know what you mean.'

'Oh yes you do. Another girl is suffering as Violet Markham suffered.'

At the mention of the girl's name, Gardner gave a strangled gasp.

'She became ill here too,' continued Holmes. 'I know all the facts concerning her death.'

'That was an isolated case.'

'Until another of your students exhibited exactly the same symptoms. The doctor is treating her for chronic anaemia, but despite daily blood transfusions she seems to be getting worse. You are giving her blood yourself. That is easy to deduce – your weakened physical condition, the stiffness of your right arm, and the tell-tale spots of blood on your cuff reveal that much.'

'It's not true,' cried Gardner, but the lack of conviction in his voice betrayed the emptiness of this assertion.

'Stop prevaricating, man!' exclaimed Holmes angrily. 'You are treating a sick girl here. Outside in the corridor there is the distinct smell of disinfectant, which has been used in large quantities, no doubt in an attempt to prevent the spread of this unknown disease. You have sent the rest of your students and teaching staff away early for the Christmas holidays to protect them, and to prevent the news of this fresh attack leaking out. You dare not dismiss the maid in case suspicions are aroused in the village, so you treat her badly in the hope that she will quit of her own volition.'

With a cry of despair, Gardner threw his head into his hands. 'Yes, yes, you are right,' he sobbed bitterly. He lifted his face, full of anguish, towards us. 'What else was I to do? After Violet Markham's death four girls were taken from the academy. Various plausible reasons were given for the move by their parents, but it was quite obvious why they were going. They feared their daughters would meet the same fate as the Markham girl. Mr Holmes, it has taken me many years to build up this establishment and its high reputation. Daughters of the nobility are sent here to receive the finishing touches to their education. Am I supposed to let everything go for the sake of one sick girl? I have done everything I could for her – I have even given her my own blood.' He gave another choking sob. 'What in Heaven do you want from me?'

'Nothing,' replied Holmes gently. 'We have come to help you.'

Gardner stared uncomprehendingly at us for a few moments and then, wiping the moisture from his eyes, asked, 'How do you know all these things?'

'The bare facts – the early holiday of your staff and students, the secretive visits paid by Dr Collins – I learned this morning in the village. Gossips need little priming. However, the interpretation I have put on these facts is purely my own, based on a set of elementary deductions. It is my profession to do such things.'

Holmes laid a comforting hand on Gardner's shoulder. 'And now perhaps if you were to give us the full details of this affair, we might be able to set about helping you.'

Holmes's words seemed to give the man some sense of reassurance. 'Very well,' he said with a sigh of resignation, dabbing his

eyes with a handkerchief. 'It is as you surmised: another of my
students, Catherine Hunter, has been taken ill. She has all the symptoms that poor Violet Markham exhibited: emaciation and a general
wasting away. During the day she seems to recover a little of her
strength, but every morning we find her weaker. It is as though the
night sucks the energy from her.'

I felt a chill hand on my heart as I heard these words. Holmes gave
me a guarded look.

'As you say, Mr Holmes, Dr Collins is treating her for chronic
anaemia,' Gardner continued. 'But he is not convinced that this
is the real cause of her illness. He believes it to be a previously
unknown wasting disease akin to anaemia, but much more virulent.'

'Was it Collins who first treated Violet Markham?' asked Holmes.

'Yes. He is Dr Mortimer's *locum tenens* at Grimpen. When he
first arrived in this area, he called to introduce himself and to see
if his assistance was required. As it happened, Violet had been com-
plaining of feeling a little off colour, so I asked Collins to look at
her. He spotted the seriousness of her complaint and ordered her
straight to bed. He fought hard for Violet's life. The other so-called
specialist, who was called in later by the parents, could do no more
for the girl than Collins had. In fact, it was Collins who warned
against her move to London. He said the journey would be too much
for her – and it was.'

'And when Miss Hunter became ill you called on Collins again
because of his previous experience?' I asked.

Gardner nodded.

'And not being the village doctor there was less chance that news
of the illness would leak out,' observed my friend.

'What of the girl's parents?' I asked.

'Catherine's mother is dead and her father is the overseas manager
of a large firm of chemical manufacturers, based in Prague. I have
hesitated in contacting him, hoping that at any time the girl's condition might improve.'

'Does she show any signs of recovery?' enquired Holmes.

'She does not,' replied Gardner bitterly.

'I think it is time that Watson and I saw the girl.'

'Oh, I cannot allow that, Mr Holmes. Dr Collins insisted that she
was not to be disturbed before his visit tomorrow morning.'

Holmes gave a sigh of impatience. 'Gardner, I believe we can help
you. I believe it is within our power to rid the district of the source
of this disease. I believe we can save this young woman's life. But

to enable us to do these things we must have your full and un-questioning co-operation. Refuse us that and you are doomed to have another dead girl on your hands.'

Gardner's face blanched.

'We are not solely working for your benefit, or the girl's, but for mankind,' continued Holmes. 'If this foul disease is allowed to spread, the results could be calamitous for this country. We are here to prevent this; you must place your full trust in our abilities.'

Uncertainty clouded Gardner's features. The lack of sleep and the loss of blood had dulled his reasoning powers. His eyes flickered, registering his vacillating thoughts. Gradually, he lowered his head and shook it slowly from side to side.

'Mr Holmes,' said he softly, 'I am at my wits' end. I will do anything to make Catherine well again. You offer me a straw of hope – I must grasp at it.'

'More than a straw, I think,' rejoined Holmes.

'Very well, I will do as you say.'

'Good man. However, let me make it clear from the outset that my instructions must not be questioned and must be carried out to the letter. Is that understood?'

Gardner nodded dumbly.

'Good. Now let us see the girl. Have no fear. My friend, Watson, is an experienced doctor and there is no man to whom I would rather entrust the health and safety of a daughter, if I had one.'

It was with some doubt still lingering on his face that Gardner led us to the sick-room, a journey which required us to retrace our steps down the corridor to the spot where Holmes had stopped to sniff the air. I, too, now noticed the faint odour of disinfectant hovering there.

The sick room was long and narrow, having a french window at the far end which opened out onto a small balcony, beyond which I could glimpse the grey sweep of the moor. A warm fire glowed in the grate; a grandfather clock ticked noisily in one corner. Placed centrally in the room was a small four-poster bed whose occupant lay still with only her pale, drained face appearing above the covers.

Sitting in a chair by the fire was an elderly, grey-haired woman, who rose as we entered. She was tall and wiry, with sharp, intelligent features.

'This is my sister Mary,' said Gardner by way of introduction. 'These two gentlemen have come to help us, my dear.'

The woman eyed us with suspicion.

Holmes stepped forward. 'Miss Gardner, I am Sherlock Holmes and this is my friend and colleague, Dr John Watson. I believe we are able to assist you in curing your ailing student.' He gestured to the sleeping figure of Catherine Hunter.

'Sherlock Holmes – the detective?'

Holmes gave a gentle bow.

'But how can you help us?'

Before Holmes had a chance to reply, Silas Gardner interceded. 'Best not to ask too many questions, Mary. Mr Holmes has pledged to give us his help and, from what we know of his reputation, we must take him at his word.'

'I assure you, Miss Gardner,' said Holmes, 'that Watson and I will do all in our power to cast this dark shadow from your lives.' The steady sincerity of his words visibly moved the woman, who had obviously been sharing the strain and worry with her brother. She could only respond with a tight-lipped smile and a nod.

'Is Miss Hunter attended here at all times?'

'My brother and I share duties. Silas sits with her in the morning and I usually sit with her in the afternoon and early evening, though she makes no demands on us. She has been in a deep sleep for nearly two days now.'

'She is left unattended at night?'

Mary Gardner nodded. 'Why, yes. We leave a lamp burning in the room, and a bell is set by her bed in case she wakes and requires assistance, but we have not felt the need to keep an all-night watch on her. Besides, Dr Collins said it was not necessary.'

'It is imperative that this girl be watched at all times, and most diligently during the hours of darkness,' said Holmes.

She frowned. 'I do not understand . . . '

'Please, Miss Gardner, no questions. I beg you to take my word. Watson and I will watch tonight, for I believe the crisis is near. Now if you and your brother would be kind enough to leave us alone while we examine the patient . . . '

They both exchanged worried glances, and then, with some reluctance, Gardner led his sister to the door, where she turned and addressed my friend. 'I have been praying for help, Mr Holmes. Not just for ourselves, you understand, but also for that poor girl who is not yet old enough to have tasted the fruits of life. I hope you are the answer to my prayer.'

'I hope so too, Miss Gardner. I hope so too,' replied Holmes.

After they had left the room, Holmes and I moved to the bed.

Catherine Hunter appeared to be in a deep sleep, but I realised that her situation was far worse than that: she was in a comatose state. Her face, framed by a tumble of raven hair, was a deathly white mask. All colour had gone from her lips and gums, and her cheekbones projected prominently. Her breathing was shallow and her pulse was desperately weak.

'She is very near death,' I said after my brief examination. 'We may be too late.'

Holmes gave a sigh of despair. 'The poor creature. Is there no hope?'

'A little. It depends somewhat on the tenacity of the girl, how strongly she fights to stay alive. But it is essential that she does not lose any more blood.'

Holmes turned her head gently to one side to reveal the incontrovertible proof that she was the victim of a vampire. Just over the external jugular vein were two small punctures in the skin, darkened by slight bruising and tiny specks of congealed blood.

'The fiend has been feasting here,' exclaimed Holmes hoarsely. From his pocket he produced a small silver crucifix and placed it around the girl's neck. 'This at least will afford her some future protection.'

Holmes then began to examine the room in great detail with his lens. He moved noiselessly, sometimes stopping, occasionally kneeling, and once lying close to the floor to scoop up a small pile of dust into an envelope. He carefully scrutinised the french windows and the small balcony beyond while chattering to himself constantly, keeping up a running fire of exclamations, groans, whistles, and little cries, suggestive of encouragement and hope. His mind was so absolutely concentrated on the matter before him that he seemed completely to forget my presence.

I waited patiently until he returned to my side, his face flushed and darkened with exertion, but his features wreathed in a glow of satisfaction.

'What have you learned?' I asked.

'Mainly a confirmation of our suspicions. The girl has been receiving a night-time visitor who gains access through the french windows. There are no signs of a forced entry, therefore he must be admitted by the girl, no doubt under some kind of hypnotic compulsion. The visitor is a tall man, over six feet tall, and of European origin.'

'How can you be sure of this?'

'There is a thin layer of mud on the balcony spilt from a small shrub pot out there. The visitor's shoes have carried traces into the room, leaving a faint impression of a heel mark. The distance between each gives the height. The mud on the balcony also shows his origin. There is one very clear set of footprints out there, obviously made while he was waiting to be admitted. The maker's trademark stamped into the heel of the shoe is recorded in the mud which has set hard with the frost. Indistinct though it is, it is just possible with my lens to make out the letters B-U-K-O-V.'

'Bukov?'

'Obviously Bukovina, a town in the heart of the Carpathians, situated at the head of the Borgo Pass.'

I was gripped with a mixed sense of excitement and dread. 'Dracula!' I cried. 'It must be him.'

'Yes, Watson,' affirmed Holmes, unable to disguise the elation in his voice. 'However, the most surprising find is this.' He took the envelope from his pocket and emptied the contents onto the palm of his hand: small fragments of dried mud.

'What is so special about it?'

'These small pieces of mud are also from the intruder's shoes, and yet this is not mud picked up from the balcony. It is far darker, suggesting that it comes from a region where the soil lacks oxidation.' He rubbed the particles into a fine dust. 'This is moorland mud and, more particularly, it is from the area around Black Tor, a locality with which I became extremely familiar when I camped out there during the Baskerville case. There is an unusually large quantity of felspar and mica crystals in the ground, and these few dry fragments indicate that they are from that area.' He clenched his fist tightly around the powdered mud and raised it triumphantly. 'You realise what this means?'

'That Dracula is hiding somewhere out there on the moor,' I said.

'Yes, Watson. Or to be more precise at Black Tor. Indeed, one of those old neolithic stone huts would make an excellent resting place.'

'Then we have him!' I exclaimed.

Holmes gave a short laugh. 'Good old Watson, forever the optimist. No, my dear fellow, we do not have him yet. Our nets are closing in on him, but we must play a steady game and not become over-confident now – the stakes are too high.'

'What is our next move then?'

Holmes consulted his pocket watch. 'There are enough daylight hours left to allow us to visit Black Tor. It may be there in that desolate spot that we can bring this dark business to a close.'

CHAPTER SIXTEEN

On the Moor

Within an hour Sherlock Holmes and I were seated in an antiquated wagonette, rumbling over the rough track which meandered its way across the moor. The request to borrow the carriage, and our sudden departure, had perplexed Gardner further. His pallid face had gazed blankly at Holmes while my friend had tried once more to reassure him that all our actions were directed at saving Miss Hunter's life.

'Be assured,' said Holmes, as he climbed into the driver's seat, 'that Watson and I will return before evening to watch over the girl during the hours of darkness.'

Gardner nodded dumbly. We left him standing by the gate of the academy, a tall, stooping figure with nervously clenched hands.

'I am afraid this affair has broken him,' remarked Holmes, after we had lost sight of the academy.

'If only we could tell him the full facts of the matter,' I said.

'They would not only confuse his already tired and bewildered mind, but push him over the threshold into madness. Remember, we have undergone a dreadful initiation into our belief in the undead, but we can hardly expect Gardner to share or understand this belief. Therefore we must persist with the illusion that the girl is suffering from a rare kind of disease. The truth must remain our terrible secret.'

I gave a murmur of agreement and then lapsed into silence. Holmes gently but firmly guided the horses over the rough and bumpy track. Steadily rising, we passed over a narrow bridge and skirted a noisy stream which gushed down, foaming and roaring amid the boulders. A dull greyness touched the moorland as the sparse foliage relinquished its autumn colourings to the neutral grip of winter.

It was a sharp, bitterly cold day with a cruel wind which pierced the thick folds of my coat. Holmes, however, did not seem to notice the cold. As he manoeuvred the vehicle along the increasingly difficult route, he was lost in thought, his brow drawn into two hard lines.

Soon the familiar shape of Black Tor loomed into view. Over the wide, gloomy expanse of moor there was no movement or sound except for the eerie moan of the wind. And then suddenly a curlew, disturbed by our approach, rose from the bracken and soared aloft into the slate-coloured sky, swiftly becoming a dark speck on the horizon. The departure of this solitary creature seemed to reaffirm the loneliness and enmity of the moor.

Below Black Tor's imposing silhouette, we had to leave the wagonette and make the rest of our way on foot. Holmes tied the horses to a stunted tree and then, from the back of the carriage, took Van Helsing's bag.

'This will be our best route,' he said, indicating a faint trace of a path through the bracken, leading up to the Tor. Holmes strode ahead of me up the rocky slope, his long legs clearing the rough terrain with ease.

Halfway to the summit, he waited for me to catch up with him, and for a few moments we stood together and gazed around us. Without speaking, Holmes pointed westwards and, following the direction of his finger, I saw the Baskerville estate, the grounds, outbuildings, and hall, which seemed to blend itself into the mottled grey sweep of the moor. The mullioned windows of the hall, like dark empty eye sockets, stared blackly out at us.

Further east one could observe the deceptive green patches of fertility which I knew to be the Grimpen Mire. One false step into this great swamp-land meant death to man or beast. I remembered how I had seen one of the moor ponies wander into it, how it had struggled vainly, writhing in a desperate attempt to keep its head above the foul ooze, and how its terrified cries had echoed across the moor. Slowly, with a dreadful inevitability, the green slime had lapped over its head, sucking it down into the depths of that huge morass. I shivered at the memory.

Having rested awhile, we continued our climb. A thick, grey mist settled in the gulleys and clung to some of the higher spots, where sharp outcrops of rock peered out like malevolent gargoyles.

On reaching the summit we saw down below us, sheltered in a large dip, the circle of neolithic stone huts. It was in one of these that Holmes had dwelt while spending his time on the moor during the Baskerville case.

Holmes, with myself close on his heels, rushed down into the cup-like hollow where the remains of the ancient dwellings were situated. Kneeling down, he scooped up a handful of soil. He examined the dark earth under his lens and then, with a sharp cry of pleasure, cast it away into the air.

'Exactly the same type as that left by our visitor!' he exclaimed, his voice sounding unnatural as it broke the brooding silence of that bleak and lonely spot.

'Then he is here – somewhere in this vicinity?'

'Dracula has been here, of that I am convinced,' said Holmes. 'Whether he is still here is for us to discover.'

So saying, he began to make his way among the granite boulders which littered the floor of the hollow, heading for the one stone hut which still retained sufficient roof to act as a screen against the weather. I joined him by the opening which served as a door.

'This would make an ideal refuge,' he murmured, as he examined the ground by the entrance. 'And there appears to have been recent activity here. Some coming and going.' Suddenly his eye lit upon a small, shiny, black, round object in the soil. He scooped it up and gave it a cursory glance, before placing it in his pocket without comment.

Cautiously we entered the old stone hut.

It was empty.

Holmes opened Van Helsing's bag, took out a candle and lit it. A flickering yellow glow filled the dark recesses of the hut, making the areas of dampness on the rough stone glisten like frost. Fixing the candle on a short outcrop of rock, he proceeded to examine the interior of the ancient dwelling. Kneeling down at the far end of the hut, he gave a sharp cry of excitement. 'Look, Watson. Fresh earth! The ground here has been disturbed recently.'

'What do you mean?'

'Compare this area with the rest of the hut,' he snapped impatiently. 'The earth there is hard and compressed, while here the top soil is loose and fine as though it has been turned over by a spade.'

Snatching up the candle, he held it closer to the ground. 'See – this area is about seven feet by four: the size of a large coffin.'

The implication of my friend's remark filled me with dread.

'We should have brought a spade with us,' continued Holmes, 'but there is no time to go back for one now. Come, Watson, we must use our hands to dig.'

With these words he crouched down and began scooping away the loose soil. Before joining him in his labours, I stood for some moments, stunned by my friend's singular request. Of all the wild and macabre situations in which I had found myself accompanying him on his investigations, this must have rated as the most bizarre. By the light of a guttering candle we both knelt on the ground, scooping the earth away with our hands.

'I am glad that Lestrade cannot see us now,' I remarked quietly. 'He would surely clap us behind the bars of some mental institution, convinced that we had lost our reason.'

Holmes gave a wry chuckle.

Our efforts were very soon rewarded. We had removed about eight or nine inches of soil when Holmes struck something solid. Bringing the candle nearer, he cleared the ground further to reveal an area of rough dark wood.

'It is a coffin,' exclaimed Holmes. 'Come, we must clear the lid.'

With bated breath, I joined my friend in scraping away the soft soil until we could determine the familiar shape of a burial casket beneath us. I shuddered as I realised how close we might be to the end of our quest. It was clear that Holmes believed that Count Dracula could be at rest within this very coffin.

While we worked, the wind outside increased, sending fierce, errant gusts into the hut. The candle flame flickered erratically, causing our huge shadows to gyrate madly along the dark granite walls. The moan of the wind and the irregular illumination, combined with the task in which we were employed, increased the sensation that I was losing touch with reality. The call of the wind and the dancing shadows lulled me towards this illusion, until Holmes, with some force, grabbed me by the arm and shook me. It was enough to make me cast these impressions from my mind, and I resumed digging with greater industry.

In ten minutes we had fully exposed the lid of the coffin. Out of breath after our exertions, we stood gazing down at the ominous casket. My nerves tingled and I suddenly realised that I was very frightened. I glanced at Holmes. His face bore an expression of unease, but his jaw jutted forward with stern resolution.

'Are you ready, Watson?' he asked quietly.

I responded with a tight-lipped nod.

Taking a hammer and wooden stake from the bag, he laid them down on the soft earth.

'Let us try raising the lid,' he said.

The lid of the coffin appeared to be resting on the body of the casket and did not seem to be secured in any way. It was, therefore, with remarkable ease that we were able to lift it and cast it to one side.

With a thudding heart, I stared down with apprehension and expectation.

The coffin was empty.

I must confess I felt a warm rush of relief, my nerves releasing their tight grip on my senses. Holmes, however, gave a groan of disappointment.

'What does this mean?' I asked.

'It means that I have severely underestimated Count Dracula's cunning,' Holmes replied angrily.

'Then he has not been here?'

'Oh, indeed he has.'

Holmes swung the candle directly over the empty casket. I could now see that lining the bottom was a thin layer of pale, dry soil.

'Native earth,' explained my friend. 'A necessary requirement for a vampire's resting place.'

'But if this is Dracula's coffin, where is he? He cannot have risen yet; it is still daylight.'

'If we knew where he was . . . ' Holmes began sharply and then, after a brief pause, he adopted a more patient tone. 'Remember, Watson, that once a vampire's coffin has been discovered and destroyed, he is doomed, for he must lie in his own native soil during the hours between cockcrow and sunset. It would appear that Dracula has been cunning enough to provide himself with several such refuges, so that if one is discovered and desecrated, he will have access to others.'

'You mean Dracula has other similar resting places scattered about the region?'

'Precisely. It is a diabolical form of insurance. We have just been unlucky enough to unearth one of his unholy sanctuaries which is not being used at present. Remember, Van Helsing told us how Dracula had arranged for a consignment of boxes to be transported to this country.'

I stood listening to the words of my friend with gathering depression. If Dracula had, as Holmes was suggesting, a whole series of hidden coffins in which he could rest during the hours of daylight, then the task of seeking out and destroying this fiend was an almost impossible one.

My glum expression betrayed my thoughts, for Holmes said, 'Take heart, old fellow, Count Dracula will not leave this area while Catherine Hunter lives. He means to have her as his bride and will not depart until his conquest is complete. Therefore, as long as the girl is in our charge, we hold the ace card in this game. We have that which he desires and therefore he must eventually come to us. I had hoped to destroy this creature while he was at his most vulnerable, taking his unholy rest, but now I am convinced that a confrontation is inevitable.'

I shuddered.

'We must prepare ourselves both physically and mentally for the encounter. It will be the most dangerous of our lives.'

'What is our next move?'

'We must return to our charge. We have a vigil ahead of us. It would be foolish to suppose that Dracula will not try to take final possession of the girl tonight. We must be there to stop him. However, before we return to the academy, I will sterilise this resting ground.'

Taking a silver crucifix from the bag, he dropped it into the coffin where it lay on the Transylvanian soil, glinting in the sombre candle-light.

'At least there is one less refuge for him now: he will not be able to lie here again.'

It was only mid-afternoon when we emerged from the old stone hut, but already the day was surrendering itself to the coming dusk. The light was fading and the faint blush of evening haloed the darkening contours of the moor. Holmes strode ahead again, pausing at the edge of the Tor to allow me to catch up with him. His tall, spare silhouette, with his sharp features framed by the close-fitting travelling cap, turned to face the rolling expanse of the moor, and for some moments he stood still and silent. I sensed that he was preparing himself for what he realised was the greatest challenge of his career.

As we made our way back to the wagonette in the gathering gloom, I felt as though the dark powers were already straining to take possession of the dying day. One thing of which I was certain was that the coming night would see us once more in battle with those evil forces.

CHAPTER SEVENTEEN

Enter Dracula

Before returning to the Gardner Academy, we called at the small post office in Coombe Tracey, where Holmes sent a telegram to Van Helsing informing him that, although our investigations were bearing fruit, as yet no crisis had been reached. Holmes did not go into further details.

'I feel, at the moment, that we can deal with matters quite satisfactorily without the need to bring Van Helsing all the way down to Devonshire,' he remarked.

I remained silent. I knew that the real reason Holmes did not wish the professor to come was that he wished to handle the case on his own. In our long career together I had never known my friend seek the fame or glory which naturally accrued to him. For Sherlock Holmes, the game was all. However, he always guarded jealously the privilege of carrying out investigations in his own way, without help or hindrance from others. It was the same in this case: respectful as he was of Van Helsing and the arcane knowledge he possessed, Holmes still desired to tackle this most dangerous affair on his own.

The light was almost gone when we arrived back at the academy. Gardner was greatly relieved to see us return and offered us the hospitality of his table. Much to my chagrin, Holmes declined the offer, saying that we must take up our positions in the sick-room immediately. However, Gardner's sister, taking pity on my hungry glances at their tea-time spread, brought us in some food on a tray.

'While you were out, Mr Holmes, this came for you,' she said, holding out a long white envelope to my friend.

'How was it delivered?'

'The maid found it lying on the mat shortly after you had left.'

Holmes took the envelope and pocketed it. After Miss Gardner had left, I said, 'Surely you will not leave the letter unopened?'

'I already know who it is from and the message it contains. However, you may open it yourself if you wish to satisfy your curiosity.'

He passed me the envelope and, tearing it open, I saw there, lying between the thin walls of white paper, a dead fly.

'My God! Stapleton!' I exclaimed.

'Still playing his games.'

'Then he must have followed us down here.'

'Or we followed him.'

'What do you mean, Holmes?'

'Nothing of consequence.'

'How did you know the envelope contained another warning?'

'No great deduction, I assure you, Watson. Despite the disguised handwriting, I recognised the tell-tale loops on the letter "L". It is obviously Stapleton's scrawl.'

'What will you do?'

'I have little choice. Stapleton's presence down here is a nuisance, I grant you, but at present nothing must divert my energies from the case in hand. Until Stapleton's threats take on a more palpable form, I must ignore them.'

I saw the sense in these words. To try and pursue two elusive quarries could easily lead to double failure – but at the same time I had severe misgivings about Holmes's apparent lack of concern for the warnings. However, I knew there was little point in discussing the matter, so I settled down to the small repast.

After we had eaten and the remnants of our meal had been cleared away, Holmes locked the door of the sick-room. It was now dark outside. The sky, sprinkled generously with stars, held a pale, watery moon whose beams, streaming through the french windows, bathed the room in a faint ghostly light. Holmes lit the lamp by Miss Hunter's bed.

'We will just keep this one alight, Watson. I do not want to frighten away our prospective visitor by giving ourselves too much illumination.'

Putting his hand into Van Helsing's bag, he pulled out a short, round silver flask.

'Keep hold of this,' he said, pressing it into my hand.

'What is it?' I asked.

'It contains holy water. According to Van Helsing's notes, it is paricularly effective in fighting evil. Water blessed in the church is believed to be the essence of spiritual goodness, and when brought into contact with the corrupted body of a vampire it purges by cauterising the flesh.'

My brows rose in wonder.

'Difficult to believe, I realise, but we know from experience that we can trust Van Helsing in these matters. We are fighting on a different plane now, Watson, and we must use the weapons of that plane.'

I nodded gravely and pocketed the flask.

We drew chairs to either side of the fireplace and were soon lost in our own thoughts. Sherlock Holmes sat with his head sunk forward and his eyes bent upon the red glow of the fire. After a while he lit his pipe and, leaning back, watched the small puffs of blue smoke as they chased each other up to the ceiling.

In my mind I attempted to retrace the strange series of events which had occurred over the last few days: the varied threads of the tangled skein which had led us to this sinister vigil.

I have no recollection of falling asleep, but I remember one moment noting how low the fire was getting and how loud and insistent was the ticking of the grandfather clock, and the next Holmes shaking me by the arm to wake me.

'What is it?' I gasped, shocked at being pulled so sharply from my slumbers. Holmes silenced me with a finger at his lips and nodded in the direction of the bed where Catherine Hunter lay tossing and turning in a disturbed manner. Her eyes remained closed but her eyelids fluttered erratically and, as she struggled under the covers, she emitted a series of unearthly guttural sobs.

'How long has she been like this?'

'It started slowly some twenty minutes ago and she has been growing steadily more agitated since midnight.'

'Midnight!' I exclaimed. 'I must have been asleep for some time.'

A grin momentarily touched my friend's stern features. 'About four hours, but do not let it worry you.'

Suddenly, with a sharp exhalation, the girl gripped the bed covers and sat bolt upright, her eyes shooting open in a trance-like stare and her breath escaping in short, tortured gasps.

I motioned as if to go to her, but was held back by Holmes. 'Leave her, Watson,' he murmured. 'We must not interfere now. He is almost here.'

Far out in the night came the howl of some solitary beast roaming the moor. Looking out through the darkened panes I saw that the moon was wrapped in a bank of dense cloud, and that the stars had deserted the sky. The world beyond the french windows had become a sinister, black void which seemed to press in on us. A gust of wind rattled the windows and the lamp flickered uneasily until, on the verge of being extinguished, it flared vigorously into life again.

The girl, staring fixedly into the night, tried with clawing motions to tear the crucifix from around her neck but, as soon as her hands touched it, she snatched them away again with a yelp of pain. As she did so I observed dark scorch marks on the tips of her fingers. The evil powers were taking control of her body and there was apparently nothing we could do.

Holmes, his neck muscles taut with apprehension, stood in front of me, watching the girl's behaviour intently. In his hand he gripped a silver crucifix.

Again the wind buffeted the french windows as though trying to gain entry, and they bowed visibly with the force. It seemed as though the whole room trembled with the power of the blast. This time the lamp lost its battle to stay alight and, with a final valiant flicker, it went out. Now our only source of illumination was the glow of the fire.

The girl's face, bathed with a rubescent tint from the vibrant embers, took on a truly demonic appearance. Pulling herself to the edge of the bed, she twisted her head vigorously from side to side, saliva drooling from her mouth, while she set up a constant stream of garbled utterances. It was as though she were answering some command we could not hear.

'I can't! I can't!' she wailed in anguish, after failing once more to tear the crucifix from her neck. And then despair turned to anger as she beat her fists on the bed. 'I can't! I can't!' she repeated, spitting the words out in a fit of fury.

The wind shrieked like a banshee as if in reply to her cries. I could feel the fear swelling inside me, but it was not the normal sense of apprehension and danger that I had experienced many times on exploits with Holmes; this was far worse because it was fear of the intangible – the unknown. I could see from Holmes's expression that he, too, felt this terrible sense of unease.

Suddenly our wait was over.

There was a tremendous crash as the wind, like some invisible battering ram, charged the french windows with such force that they burst open. I felt the fierce, icy blast as the cold air roared into the room, scattering papers and cushions, sending ornaments spinning from the mantelshelf, snatching volumes from the book case, and dashing them to the floor. The girl was flung backwards onto the bed, her dark hair streaming out behind her. It was as if some giant unseen hand, bent on destruction, were sweeping across the room. Our chairs overturned and the extinguished lamp toppled over and smashed on the floor. Yet we stood our ground, bracing ourselves against the onslaught.

Pulling herself forward, the girl clambered to the end of the bed, her face full into the wind, her eyes wild with anticipation.

Just as suddenly as it began, the wind died away and the air was still. We stood amid the damage and disturbance, apprehensive and still. It was then with a heart-jolting shock that I realised that a figure had emerged from the darkness outside and was standing by the french windows on the threshold of the room. On seeing this apparition, the girl uttered a sharp choking cry and slumped on the bed in a dead faint.

The figure was that of a very tall man clad from head to toe in black; there did not appear at first glance to be a speck of colour about him anywhere. His face was indistinct in the dim light, but I could discern two very dark, piercing eyes and a hard, vicious mouth.

Gliding rather than walking, he moved into the the dim area of illumination cast by the fire, his long cape billowing out behind him. The man's features were now clearly visible: his pallid face was angular with a thin, high-bridged nose and peculiarly arched nostrils; thick dark hair swept back from his lofty domed forehead; his ears were pale and pointed; the chin was broad and the cheeks were sunken and skeletal. The dark, ruddy lips parted and two sharp, white fangs protruded over the lower lip.

This was Count Dracula.

He turned his fierce gaze on Holmes, his lips sweeping back in a feral snarl, the needle-sharp canines flashing in the firelight. Until this moment Holmes had, like myself, been standing motionless before this unholy spectre loosed from the grave, but now he stepped towards the figure, holding the silver crucifix before him.

'You are expected, Count Dracula,' he intoned in a firm, authoritative voice. 'Come no further: the dead are not welcome here.'

At first a mocking grin touched Dracula's lips but, on seeing the crucifix, his face grew stern with fear, the nostrils quivering with passion and frustration.

'Who is it that meddles in the affairs of Count Dracula?' The rich, dark, chilling voice echoed round the room.

'An enemy dedicated to your destruction. My name is Sherlock Holmes.'

The cruel lips swept back into a smile. 'You poor fool,' he mocked. 'Do you really believe you have the power to destroy me? Many have tried to bring about my demise, Sherlock Holmes, but none has succeeded. Pit not your puny wits against me.'

'You have your weaknesses,' replied Holmes, thrusting the crucifix nearer to Dracula.

The vampire's face turned dark with rage. 'These superstitious trinkets will not protect you,' he cried, and, averting his gaze, took a powerful swipe at my friend's arm, knocking the crucifix to the floor. Holmes leapt after it but, before he could retrieve it, Dracula was upon him, his long powerful fingers at my friend's throat. With one mighty movement, he thrust Holmes to the floor. Malicious glee spread across the fiend's countenance as he loomed over the prostrate body of my friend who, try as he might, was unable to release the Count's grip on his throat.

'Watson, the holy water,' croaked Holmes, his face paling as the life was throttled out of him.

Fumbling desperately, I pulled the small silver container from my pocket and released the cork.

At the mention of holy water, Dracula's attention switched to me. Relinquishing his grip on Holmes, who now lay at his feet, apparently unconscious, he took a step in my direction. I found myself flinching as I stared into those indescribably evil eyes and saw the white fangs flash. With great resolve, I raised the container and aimed the contents at the Count, who instinctively held up his arms to protect himself. The holy water splashed on to the palms of his hands, scorching the flesh.

With a howl of agony, Dracula flailed his arms around wildly in an attempt to shake the holy water from his hands, but it was too late: the blessed droplets had already left dark, rutted scars in the flesh. He stumbled back, his eyes blazing with fury and pain.

Holmes, who by now had regained his feet, saw his chance and snatched up the crucifix, holding it firmly in both hands. He advanced on the vampire, driving him to the open french windows. As the black figure began to blend once more with the outer darkness, he stopped, thrusting an accusing finger at Holmes. 'You will suffer for this, Sherlock Holmes. I shall have my revenge,' he cried defiantly. Then, pulling his cloak around him, he dissolved into the night.

For a moment I remained motionless, partly with shock at the suddenness of the action, and partly with relief that the ordeal was over. Holmes closed the french windows and leaned with his back against them, his face drawn and tired.

A moment later there was a loud knocking at the door, and we heard the voice of Silas Gardner calling to us. 'Mr Holmes! Dr Watson! What has happened? Are you all right?' he cried out frantically.

'Yes, everything is under control,' Holmes replied calmly. 'There is nothing to worry about. Go back to bed.'

There was a pause, and then Gardner called again, 'Are you sure?'

'Yes. Now go to bed,' snapped Holmes impatiently.

'Very well,' came the reluctant response.

When Gardner had gone, I examined the girl, who had collapsed unconscious on the bed. I found that despite her fevered state, her pulse was stronger than it had been and, once she was back under the bedcovers again, she seemed to slip into a more relaxed and peaceful sleep.

'Well, Watson,' said Holmes, after we had quietly tidied the room and resumed our seats by the fire, 'we have at last come face to face with Count Dracula. He was all that Van Helsing told of him and more.'

'Indeed. A demon from hell,' I agreed.

'We have never had an adversary who was as powerful or as totally malevolent as this creature.' He glanced across at the girl. 'Through our efforts tonight we have foiled Dracula's attempt to take more of her blood and, as a result, she has a chance of survival. But he will not give up easily: for him blood is life. He has marked this girl to be his undead bride, and he will do all in his power to consummate this foul union.'

'Well, at least we have won the first round.'

'But it is only the first round: there will be others. We must not let this small victory put us off our guard, for now it is not only the girl's life which is in danger.'

'What do you mean?'

'The moment we tangled with Count Dracula we became marked men. Recall his parting cry: "I shall have my revenge". That can only mean one thing: he intends to destroy us, Watson.'

CHAPTER EIGHTEEN

The Widening Circle

We continued to watch over Miss Hunter for the remainder of the night. Holmes suggested that I should try to snatch a few hours' rest in the chair, but my nerves were too shaken to allow sleep to over-power them. Although I believed we would not be troubled again that night, I found my eyes constantly wandering to the french windows, attempting to penetrate the darkness beyond.

Around four in the morning the wind stirred once more, carrying with it flurries of snow. The large flakes spattered softly against the glass, and for over an hour I watched the curtain of snow as it swirled past until eventually it stopped, leaving each pane with a new smooth, white frame.

The first light of dawn brought with it a deep sense of relief. As the orange rays streamed into the room, my whole body relaxed from the tension it had been under all night. The sunlight provided the assurance that, for the time being at least, the immediate danger was over.

I went to the window to gaze out at the new day, yawning and stretching as I did so. The blizzard had erased colour from the world and left a landscape covered in a thick white crust which sparkled in the sun.

Somewhere in the distance a vigilant cock crowed the arrival of another dawn and, as it did so, Catherine Hunter stirred in her slumbers and emitted a low sigh. It was the first sign of life she had showed since her collapse in the night. I took her pulse and, to my surprise and joy, I found it to be almost normal. Her features, too, were relaxed, and there was a slight blush of colouring to her cheeks.

Opening her eyes, she gazed at us quizzically.

'Who are you?' she asked in a faint whisper.

'Have no fear, Miss Hunter, we are here to help you. I am Sherlock Holmes and this is Dr Watson.'

'You have been very ill, my dear, but you are on the mend now,' I added.

'I had a dream,' she said softly in a distracted fashion, her young, pale features clouding over at the thought of it. 'A dream. There was a wind, a great wind; it was all about me. And there was a man . . . he had a cruel face.' Her eyes opened wide in a frightened stare. 'He came for me. He . . . came for me. He came . . . ' The girl's voice rose in anguish, beads of perspiration breaking out on her brow as she relived the terrifying events of the previous night. In her agitation she made a valiant attempt to sit up, but she was too weak, and slumped back onto the pillow.

'He came for me. He came for me,' she repeated, closing her eyes tightly as if to drive this dark memory from her mind. Tenderly, her slender fingers caressed the two puncture marks at her neck.

I mopped her brow and said, 'Lie still for a while, my dear. You are not strong enough to move about yet'.

She turned to me, her face a mask of fear. 'The man . . . he . . . ' She broke off and began to sob quietly.

Holmes took her hand in his. 'It was all a bad dream, Miss Hunter. All that is behind you and the bad dream will not return. We shall see to that. You must forget about this nightmare and concentrate all your thoughts on getting well.'

Despite my friend's claims to misogyny, he certainly had a way with women. Many times I have seen him, by means of a sympathetic attitude and soft words, calm the most distraught of female clients in our Baker Street chambers. When I have commented on this, he has always sneered at my observations, assuring me that any action he takes towards a client is of a purely practical nature. 'No one, Watson, can give an accurate account of his or her problems when on the verge of hysteria.' Nevertheless, his charm was effective, for when he had finished speaking to Miss Hunter, the signs of worry had left her face and a smile was on her lips. 'Thank you,' she whispered.

'Now, how is your appetite?' enquired Holmes in his more usual businesslike tone.

'I am rather hungry,' Miss Hunter admitted.

'Good. Well, Watson, do you think we could persuade Miss Gardner to provide our patient with a little something to eat?'

'I am sure we could,' I grinned.

A small breakfast of scrambled eggs and hot sweet tea was prepared by Mary Gardner, who was overjoyed to see that the girl had re-gained consciousness.

'I do not know what magic you have woven, Mr Holmes, and I do not care,' she said, holding her wiry frame erect, 'but thank you.

Both of you,' she added, turning to me and squeezing my arm in gratitude. Words failed me, as they apparently did Holmes, and so we responded to these kind words with a simple nod.

The girl made a brave attempt at tackling her breakfast, the first food she had taken for over three days, and after she had eaten what she could, I gave her a sedative to help her sleep soundly.

Half an hour later, after a shave and a change of linen, we were breakfasting with Gardner in his study. He too, like his sister, was delighted at the girl's improved condition, but requested, in forceful terms, a full explanation of the commotion made during the night.

Holmes remained calm. 'Believe me, Gardner, when I say that I cannot at this time go into details of what happened last night. We are not yet out of danger and I must ask you to continue to trust us and ask no further questions.'

Gardner brought his podgy fist down on the table. 'But why is there need for this secrecy?' he cried, angrily.

'It is in the girl's best interest,' replied Holmes, quietly but firmly. 'I know it must be difficult for you to accept our instructions without question, but you can see that there is already a vast improvement in Miss Hunter's condition, and surely that is your major concern.'

'Yes, yes,' agreed Gardner, nodding his head vigorously. He then fell silent, although it was clear from his petulant expression that he was still unhappy about being kept in the dark.

'Now, gentlemen, if you will excuse me,' said Holmes, pulling away from the table and throwing down his napkin, 'I have to leave you for a short time. There is a certain matter I need to attend to in the village. Will you keep an eye on Miss Hunter until I return, Watson?'

'Er . . . yes, of course, Holmes,' I replied, somewhat taken aback at Holmes's announcement. I felt dismayed, for it seemed that once again I was not to be allowed into my friend's confidence. I was tempted to remind him of the London Gardens business, but thought better of it.

'I will be back in about two hours, old chap,' he assured me as he pulled on his ulster.

After his departure, Gardner, believing that I was a more vulnerable vessel than Holmes, attempted to elicit information which my friend had denied him.

'Surely you can tell me, Dr Watson, what is wrong with Catherine Hunter?'

'I can tell you no more than Holmes,' I replied firmly, indicating quite clearly that the matter was closed. Resigned to our conspiracy of silence, he abandoned further efforts to coax information from me.

At this point Gardner's sister bustled into the room to clear the breakfast dishes away because, as she informed me, the maid had failed to report for duty that morning. At this interruption I took the opportunity to excuse myself and returned to my charge.

I found Miss Hunter in a deep, relaxed sleep. Pleased but fatigued, I settled in a chair by the fire. In order to prevent myself from falling asleep, I picked a slim volume from the bookcase and began reading. The book contained a selection of Clark Russell's fine sea stories, and I was soon absorbed in his world of high-masted schooners, devastating hurricanes, and shipwrecks.

Some time later my nautical preoccupations were disturbed by a tapping at the door. I unlocked it and Gardner entered, accompanied by a tall young man with broad but rather hunched shoulders and a blotchy, moon-shaped face, topped by a brush of unruly blonde hair. He was introduced to me as Dr Collins.

'I am very pleased to meet you, Dr Watson,' he said in a thin, reedy voice. Quickly, I attempted to make some deductions about him as Holmes would have done had he been present. I followed my friend's methods to the best of my ability. Some facts were obvious. It was clear that Collins had only recently become a full-time medical man, and that he was probably in his first practice: his black medical bag was shiny, and hardly used. He probably did most of his visiting by wagonette as his shoes were clean. He was a bachelor; his shirt cuffs were frayed, and there was a button missing from his frock coat – a state of affairs no young wife would tolerate.

I could read nothing of his character from the sallow, blotchy features from which two pale blue, expressionless eyes peered out at me. The thin-lipped mouth held an ambivalent smile.

Gardner spoke again. 'I have explained to Dr Collins that you and Mr Holmes have – ' he hesitated, searching for a suitable phrase, ' – er, have taken over the case, but he requested that he might see his patient before he leaves.'

'If that is acceptable to you, Dr Watson,' Collins added.

I was unsure how Holmes would respond to this request, but I felt that I could not prevent a fellow doctor from seeing his patient, so I acquiesced.

'I must confess that I am amazed at the news of Miss Hunter's improved condition this morning,' announced Collins earnestly. 'I feared for her life yesterday. I have to admit her illness has me completely baffled.'

'This is your first practice?'

'My first full practice. I left medical school last year and worked for some time as an assistant at a surgery in Bloomsbury.'

I was pleased to learn that some of my deductions were correct.

'And of course this practice is only mine until Dr Mortimer returns. I am only his *locum*.'

I nodded.

'May I see Miss Hunter now?' he asked, peering over my shoulder at the girl on the bed.

'Yes, of course, but she has been given a sedative and must not be disturbed.'

We moved to the bed and Collins uttered a gasp of surprise at the change in his patient. 'This is remarkable!' he exclaimed. 'Have you given her another transfusion?'

I shook my head.

Collins took the girl's hand. 'Why, her pulse rate is virtually normal. May I ask what kind of treatment you have been giving?'

Before I had chance to respond to this question, it was answered by Sherlock Holmes. I had not seen or heard him enter the room and, by the look of surprise on their faces, neither had Collins nor Gardner.

'I am afraid, Dr Collins, that at present we are unable to discuss either the cause or treatment of Miss Hunter's illness.' He came forward and joined us at the bedside. 'I am Sherlock Holmes,' he said, extending his hand.

'I am pleased to meet you, Mr Holmes. Silas has told me of your involvement in this matter. I must confess that I more readily associate your name with the diseases of society rather than those of the body.'

'Sometimes the two cannot be separated. You are pleased with the progress of your patient?'

'Indeed. She has made a dramatic recovery. On my last visit I had little hope that she would survive another day.'

'Or night.'

Collins's brow creased in bewilderment at my friend's cryptic remark, but Holmes ignored this and continued. 'Have you seen anything like this before?' He turned the girl's head gently to one side to reveal the two small puncture marks on her neck.

'Oh, those,' murmured Collins, moving in to examine them more closely. 'Yes, they have puzzled me somewhat, but they appear to be healing now.' He shrugged his shoulders. 'I took them to be some kind of animal bite: maybe those of a pet cat.'

'Possibly,' said Holmes vaguely. 'Did you notice wounds like this on the neck of Violet Markham?'

Collins was obviously taken aback. 'You know of the Markham girl?'

My friend nodded.

'It is strange, Mr Holmes, but now that you come to mention it, I do believe there were similar blemishes on Violet Markham's throat.' His head tilted back and he narrowed his eyes, trying to search his memory for confirmation. 'Yes, now that I think about it, I am certain,' he said at length. 'By Jove, I completely failed to see that there was any connection. These marks, then, are not merely accidental scratches of some pet, but are in fact symptoms of the disease?'

'Or the cause,' murmured Holmes.

'They were not made by a cat or a dog. I can vouch for that,' affirmed Gardner. 'We do not allow pets on the premises.'

Collins gave an exasperated snort. 'What a fool I have been to miss something so simple when it was right there under my nose. Ah, I am a shortsighted oaf.' His thin voice rose almost to a whine of indignation at his own incompetence.

'Being aware of the recurrence of these marks would not have helped you in any way with the treatment of Miss Hunter,' I remarked in an attempt to console the young doctor.

'True, Dr Watson, but it would have given me a whole new area to research which might have brought me nearer to an understanding of this damnable disease. Surely this is what led you to your discovery? Gentlemen, you must tell me from what fountain-head this disease springs and what caused those strange wounds in the flesh of the neck.'

'I must repeat that as yet we cannot discuss our findings,' said Holmes coldly. 'We are still very much in the dark ourselves with regards to both cause and remedy.'

'But this girl is recovering through your ministrations. You must have discovered the key to the correct treatment. You cannot keep that key to yourselves.' Collins turned to me, his eyes alight with strong emotion. 'Dr Watson, as a medical man, it is your duty to your profession to share what knowledge you possess, small though it be, so that others can act upon it and possibly discover more.'

'My dear sir,' I began, unsure of how I was going to answer his passionate plea, knowing that the truth was out of the question. Holmes, aware of my difficulty, interceded.

'Watson and I have no wish to cling to the scant knowledge we have acquired in our study of this strange malady. Rest assured that as soon as Miss Hunter is recovered to full health, we shall make our findings known to the world at large, but until that time, we shall maintain our privilege of secrecy.'

The words of my friend seemed to have the most odd effect on the young doctor. His mouth gaped and his eyes opened wide in a wild stare, while his hands clasped the sides of his chin. 'My God!' he gasped in a strangled voice.

My first thought was that he was undergoing some form of fit. Silas Gardner, who had been standing quietly in the background during this interchange, rushed forward with a chair for Collins, but he waved it aside.

'What is it, man?' snapped Holmes.

'The marks. The marks on the neck,' came Collins's disturbed reply.

'What about them?' I asked.

Collins ran his fingers through his shock of blonde hair and mopped his brow with a frayed handkerchief while he regained some of his composure. 'I am sorry, gentlemen,' he apologised, still breathing heavily, 'I have had rather a shock. I have only just realised that we have another victim of this disease on our hands.'

We were all momentarily stunned into silence by this revelation. I felt an overwhelming sense of despair sweep over me. Another victim! Once more the circle of evil was spreading beyond our reach.

'You had better explain yourself,' said Holmes shortly, his face grey and stern.

'As I stated earlier, I had not appreciated the connection between the small neck wounds and this illness until you drew my attention to it.' He paused and shook his head sadly. 'Mr Holmes, another of my patients has similar marks at her throat.'

'Who is this girl?'

'Milly White. She is the young daughter of Gabriel White who farms up at Vixen Heights. He came to my surgery early this morning very upset. Apparently Milly had a fainting fit in the night and she has not regained consciousness. I went back with him to the farm to look at the girl. When I arrived, I found that she had regained consciousness but was very drowsy. On examination, I discovered that there was nothing to be worried about. She appeared to be thoroughly exhausted, but this is a common ailment among the farming folk on the moor. They cannot afford to employ labour, so all members of the family are called upon to work long and strenuous hours. I took it that Milly had simply been overworking, nothing more. The White's farm is a large one and quite isolated; there is little else for a young girl to do out there but work. She had scratches and little bruises all over her and, although I did notice small wounds on her neck, I thought nothing of them at the time.'

'But now you realise that the apparent exhaustion and the throat wounds are the identical symptoms to those of Violet Markham and Catherine Hunter?' suggested Holmes.

Collins nodded vigorously.

'Great heavens,' wailed Gardner, slumping into a chair. 'I was beginning to think our troubles were over, but now it seems we have an epidemic on our hands.'

'Epidemic? No, simply the possibilty of another isolated case,' said Holmes. His words were meant to give some consolation to Gardner, but as he spoke my friend's face was gloomy. He turned to Collins. 'I think Watson and I had better take a look at the girl.'

'Would you, Mr Holmes? I would be so grateful.' The young doctor took my friend's hand and shook it warmly.

'We will go now.'

*   *   *

Within half an hour Holmes and I, along with Collins, were seated aboard the doctor's wagonette, headed for the White's farmstead at Vixen Heights. We had left a very sad and gaunt-looking Silas Gardner back at the academy in attendance on Miss Hunter.

I wished to discuss in detail with Holmes the full implications of there being another victim. Was there a second vampire in the area? Or had Dracula, denied his life source at the academy, lusted elsewhere for blood last night? If so, surely we were in-directly responsible for yet another innocent being drawn into the widening circle of evil. However, our conversation was hampered by the presence of Collins, whom, I was sure, Holmes wished to keep ignorant of the true facts, so we were forced to talk of relatively trivial matters.

Collins was in charge of the horses and guided them gently, their hooves making deep imprints in the smooth, snow-covered track up to the Heights. The countryside was spread out around us like a vast, white, rumpled tablecloth gleaming in the sunlight, and the moor had been beautifully transformed; even the jagged summits of the tors were softened by the snow line.

Holmes, who had said very little on the journey, was moved to comment on the scene as we reached one of the high points of the journey, which enabled us to look down on the wide, white expanse of the moor.

'A thin veil of beauty, eh, Watson?' he said thoughtfully. 'The great Grimpen Mire now seems as innocent as the firm ground that surrounds it. It is uncanny how Nature in all her facets mirrors the ways of mankind, for how often are we taken in by the apparently innocent appearance of a person, little suspecting the deceit that lies beneath that unblemished surface.' He gave a tight-lipped smile. ' "All bloodless lay the untrodden snow".' *

'There it is!' Collins's thin, strident voice broke in. He reined the horses to a halt and pointed ahead. On the shoulders of a hunch-backed ridge one could see the shape of a low stone farmhouse.

'We shall have to dismount soon and take to the path,' cried our companion, as he spurred the horses forward once again, their hooves sinking into the snow.

We drove for another five minutes until we came to a broken-down gate across the track. Here we left the wagonette and, with Collins in the lead, Holmes behind clutching Van Helsing's bag, and myself at the rear, we made our way up to the farmhouse.

The snow was quite deep, coming well over our ankles, and made walking difficult. We all managed to stumble a few times before reaching the farmyard of the bleak moorland dwelling. It had been somewhat sheltered from the snowfall by a collection of out-buildings, but nevertheless there was still a fine unblemished carpet lying there.

The place seemed strangely deserted. Silence pressed in on us and I felt a twinge of unease. It was far too quiet. Collins knocked hard on the rough wooden door and called out, but there was no reply. We exchanged puzzled glances.

* A line from 'Hohenlinden' by Thomas Campbell. Yet another indication that Watson was wildly mistaken in claiming that Holmes had no knowledge of literature when he drew up a list of the detective's limitations in *A Study in Scarlet*.

'I don't like this,' said Collins, frowning. 'Perhaps we had better go in.' He stepped back from the door and addressed my friend. 'Would you care to lead the way, Mr Holmes, as you are more experienced with this disease than I?'

Holmes nodded briefly. 'Come, Watson,' he said, and, with a firm push, opened the door and disappeared inside the farmhouse. I followed him.

On entering, I received a great shock: not only was the place deserted, but it was also derelict. The long, low room in which we stood was devoid of furniture and fittings, plaster hung limply from the walls, and large clumps of mould sent out green tendrils across the bare stone floor. Daylight filtered in through small, grimy, cobwebbed windows. The fireplace was filled with soot and rubble, and the smell of damp and decay pervaded the room. It was quite obvious that this farmstead had been unoccupied for years.

I turned to Holmes, but his face registered no surpise whatsoever.

The door behind us snapped shut, and I jerked round to find myself facing the barrel of an Ely No. 2. Looking up I saw Collins's blotchy features wreathed in a malevolent grin. 'Sorry to disappoint you,' he sneered, 'but as you can see, there is no one here.'

Immediately it became clear that there was no White family and, more importantly, that there had never been another 'victim'. These had been conjurations of Collins's imagination, used to lure us away from Catherine Hunter to this isolated farmhouse. Holmes and I had been completely fooled, and had walked straight into a trap. The ultimate purpose behind Collins's devious machinations was not yet apparent to me, but I knew now that he was an enemy and that we were in great danger. I made a slow, careful movement to retrieve my gun from the pocket of my overcoat.

'I wouldn't if I were you,' Collins said coolly, cocking his pistol.

At this, to my utter astonishment, Sherlock Holmes burst out laughing. Unease clouded Collins's features for a moment, but he soon recovered himself. 'It is pleasing to see that the great detective can indulge in lightheartedness, even when he has been completely fooled. It is a very engaging characteristic.'

'I must apologise for laughing at your supreme dramatic moment,' beamed Holmes, 'but I am afraid I shall have to lower the curtain somewhat prematurely on your absurd melodrama.' He spoke in an easy, relaxed manner. 'You see, my dear Dr Collins, I have not, for one instant, been deceived by your transparent charade.'

'What do you mean?' There was now a note of alarm in Collins's voice, and his brows furrowed with trepidation.

'Simply that I knew from the beginning that you were a liar, and that your purpose in bringing us here was to trap us.'

'How could you know that?'

Holmes continued. 'I will not dwell on your claim that you were unaware of the importance or the similarity of the wounds on the throats of Violet Markham and Catherine Hunter. Even a layman, giving only a cursory examination, could not have failed to note such elementary parallels in their condition, and since you were the medical practitioner who attended both girls, your claim becomes preposterous. But, even allowing that I accepted this highly dubious statement, there were many other points which revealed your deceit.'

'Such as?' challenged Collins sharply, half in anger, half in fear.

'Let us begin with your feet.'

Collins gave his feet a quick, puzzled glance.

'They alone told me that you had not visited a lonely snowbound farmhouse this morning. Any visit would not have left your shoes so shiny and the bottoms of your trousers so dry and pressed as they were when you arrived at the academy.

'The snow betrayed you in another way also. It has not snowed since dawn, and it was quite obvious from the undisturbed layer of snow on the path and in the farmyard that not only had there been no visitors today, but no one had stirred from the inside of the building either – most unusual for a busy farming family such as the one supposed to dwell here.

'Even as we caught our first glimpse of the farmhouse back down on the track, it was apparent the place was uninhabited. I suggest that even the hardiest folk would have a fire going, and thus smoke from their chimney, on such a cold winter's day.'

Collins stared hard at Holmes. My friend's exposition had obviously shocked him. 'Well, you are a clever man, I grant you, Holmes,' he said finally, a supercilious sneer forming on his lips as his shaken confidence returned. 'However, you are not quite clever enough.' He thrust the pistol nearer to Holmes. 'You still stepped into my trap.'

'Yes, it is true that I played along with your little game, but you see, I had to: you are my only direct link with Dracula, and I am relying on you to lead me to him.'

Now it was my turn to be shocked. I was aware that Collins was an enemy and meant us harm, but I had never thought of him as a confederate of Dracula.

'I knew that the Count had to have at least one mortal accomplice in this area who must eventually come and try and destroy me.' Holmes nodded to Collins. 'You made a prompt entrance.'

Collins's eyes were blazing and his hand trembled with rage, so much so that I feared he might fire the gun in his fury. 'How did you know I served The Master?' he snarled.

'Never underestimate your opponent, Collins, especially when he is Sherlock Holmes. You left a preponderance of clues to indicate your involvement with Count Dracula. I took the liberty of closely examining your wagonette while you were in the academy this morning. It was a most rewarding exercise. I discovered hidden in the back under a tarpaulin a large spade, which you no doubt used to dig the various hiding places for the coffins you have been secreting around this area for your master. Several traces of mud on the spade told me graphically in which region of the moor you have been at work. I grant you that on its own the spade is hardly damning evidence, but I also found several splinters of rough dark wood of the the kind used in the construction of those infernal coffins which Dracula transported to this country. Watson and I came across one such casket on the moor yesterday, where I found this.' Holmes held out his hand, palm upwards, to reveal a shiny black button. 'Yours, I believe – missing from your frock coat.'

'Very clever. Very clever indeed,' growled Collins. 'You are right, of course; Count Dracula is my Master and I serve him well. I have been chosen, and soon he will allow me to become one of his immortal disciples. He is the omnipotent lord whose power spans the centuries.' There was an unnerving thrill in Collins's voice as he spoke.

'Where is your master now?' asked Holmes calmly.

'He is behind you,' cried our adversary.

Instinctively I swung round, but my gaze came to rest on a still and empty room. Collins giggled hysterically. 'My apologies for frightening you, Dr Watson,' he burbled, an obscene grin spreading across his face.

'Where is Dracula?' asked Holmes once more. His voice was steady and even, but there was in it a hint of menace which sobered Collins.

'Wouldn't you like to know, Sherlock Holmes? Unfortunately, you will go to your grave not knowing. It is my task to kill you.'

Ignoring this threat and the pistol aimed at his heart, Holmes continued to question Collins in his relaxed manner. 'When did Dracula first come to you?'

Delight filled the young doctor's face. 'He called to me out of the darkness. I felt his sweet presence near me. I heard his command. He said he needed me and he took me into his service. He promised me eternal life.'

'You were to be his guardian?'

'Yes.'

'To protect him during the daylight hours?'

'Yes.'

As he spoke, Collins appeared to be slipping into a self-induced trance. It seemed to me that this might be the best time to rush forward and try to overpower him, but Holmes, sensing my intent, gave me a disapproving shake of the head.

'Where does your master lie now?' he asked Collins.

Our captor's eyes glinted brightly once more in the dim light, and the haziness left his features, to be replaced by a sarcastic grimace. 'In a dark warm place, Sherlock Holmes,' he intoned slowly, his whole body flexed and tense. 'He lies deep in the earth. You and your friend will join him soon.'

He aimed the pistol at Holmes's heart and pulled the trigger.

An Unlucky Shot

Involuntarily, I winced in readiness for the sharp crack of the pistol shot, but instead there came only a small, dull click.

Holmes gave a snort of laughter while Collins, bewilderment suddenly stamped on his features, pulled the trigger once more – with the same ineffectual result.

'It is not only your master who is omnipotent, Collins,' grinned Holmes, containing his amusement. 'I neglected to inform you that during my inspection of your wagonette, I also discovered your pistol, which you so very neatly transferred to your pocket on our journey up here. I have removed all the bullets.' Reaching inside his coat, Holmes pulled out six shells and casually let them fall to the floor. 'The game, my dear sir, is well and truly up.'

Shock and anger fought for possession of Collins's emotions. The former triumphed and, for a moment, he glowered wide-eyed at Holmes, until his rage found expression in a violent, frenzied cry. Then, with unexpected abruptness and amazing speed, he snatched up the bullets from the floor and raced to the doorway.

'Damn you, Holmes! Damn you in hell!' he cried vehemently and, picking up a large stone, hurled it with great force at my friend before dashing out into the snow.

Holmes dodged the missile, which thudded harmlessly to the floor.

'Come, Watson, he must not get away. We need him to lead us to Dracula.'

We ran from the farmhouse just in time to see Collins racing at full speed in the direction of the moorland behind the farm.

In pursuit, we bounded across the farmyard and scaled a cragged, six-foot wall. On the other side we sank into fine powdered snow, which had blown into drifts; in some parts it came almost to our waists. It was a struggle to move forward, and our progress was slow. For some moments our quarry slipped from view. All I could see was the white, undulating sweep of the moor. Then Holmes spotted him.

'There he is,' he cried, stabbing his arm in the direction of a moving black speck some two hundred yards ahead of us. We battled on, increasing our efforts, and as we reached higher ground where the snow had scattered more evenly, the going became a little easier. Gradually, we began to gain on our man.

Pulling my revolver from my pocket, I stopped, aimed, and fired. Collins dropped to the ground for a brief moment before resuming his flight.

'Careful, Watson,' Holmes warned. 'We need our fugitive alive.'

Collins reached the cover of a group of rocks and from there, having reloaded his pistol, he returned fire. I heard a loud report, and a bullet whistled past our heads. Holmes and I crouched low while still moving forward. There was another shot, and a bullet plopped into the snow just before us.

'Hold fast, Watson!' exhorted Holmes in a harsh whisper, pulling me to the ground. 'We are coming within his range, and without sufficient cover we are sitting targets.'

For some time we lay bedded down in the freezing snow waiting for Collins to make his next move, but nothing happened: all was still and silent. I knew Collins had four more bullets left, and until he used these, Holmes and I could not attempt to reach him safely. The thought came to me that if I could fire some shots close enough to scare him, this might prompt him to retaliate, thus exhausting his supply of ammunition.

I focused my eyes on the cover of boulders and watched carefully. After a time, I caught a fleeting glimpse of our quarry as he shifted his ground. It was, however, sufficient for me to mark him, and I loosed off a shot in his direction. The echoing noise of the report was followed by a cry of pain.

'I think you have him,' said Holmes, but there was no pleasure in his voice.

I stood up in amazement. I had never expected to hit Collins from that distance and in such a position.

'Get down,' hissed Holmes. 'He may be bluffing.'

I dropped down low alongside my friend and we waited for some minutes, but still no sound or movement came from behind the rocks.

'Come on,' said Holmes, at length, 'we must investigate.'

Still crouching close to the ground, we moved quickly to the cluster of boulders. Cautiously creeping round behind the rocks, we discovered Collins's lifeless body. He was lying on his back, one outstretched hand still holding the pistol, his eyes wide open and staring at the sky. A third dark eye glowered at us from the centre of his brow. A thin trickle of blood ran from the wound down the side of his head, through his blonde hair, and onto the snow, where it formed a growing crimson stain.

Holmes groaned, and his face flushed with anger. 'Watson! Watson! Watson!' he exclaimed, raising his clenched fists and shaking them in frustration.

'I am sorry,' I muttered, inadequately. 'I did not mean to kill him. I only intended to goad him into using up all his ammuntion.'

There was a long, uneasy silence while Holmes fought to bring his temper under control. 'It was not entirely your fault,' he said eventually. 'You were only doing what you thought fit.' He shook his head sadly, adding bitterly, 'If only you had not killed him.'

'It was simply a lucky shot,' I stammered.

'More in the line of an unlucky shot,' observed Holmes tartly. 'It has cost us dearly. We have lost our one real link with Dracula.'

He knelt down by the body and searched the clothing for clues. I stood by, feeling downhearted and helpless. The sky had darkened again and the wind had stiffened, bringing with it the threat of another blizzard.

Holmes stood up and dusted the snow from his coat. 'Anything?' I asked.

To my dismay, he shook his head. 'Nothing that I did not already know.'

My depression deepened and I gave a heavy sigh.

'Come,' he said wearily, taking my arm, 'we must not dwell upon this setback.'

We were about to retrace our steps back to the wagonette when something happened that froze us to the spot. A thin, gurgling noise began to issue from Collins's throat. We stared down in wonder at the dead man to see saliva mixed with blood frothing at his purple lips. And then, through the gaping mouth of the corpse, a voice spoke to us with chilling clarity. I had only heard those deep, rich, measured tones once before, but knew I would never forget them. It was the voice of Count Dracula.

'Do not be jubilant in your minor success, Sherlock Holmes,' the voice said. 'You have yet to learn of my victory. With me, it is a life for a life. I have triumphed again, and I shall not rest until my chosen hold sway over all.'

The Upper Hand

We watched in horror as these words issued forth from the mouth of Collins's corpse. The voice died away, leaving only the moaning wind sweeping across the moor – a sound that also seemed to mock us, our mortality, and our apparently futile aspirations to destroy one who had the power to speak from the grave through the mouth of a dead man. We still did not have the full measure of Dracula's malevolent powers.

'Triumphed again!' exclaimed Holmes, echoing Dracula's words. 'Great Heavens, Watson, you know what this means?'

'Catherine Hunter,' I replied fearfully.

'I fear so. We must return to the academy without delay. There are still a few hours of daylight remaining; let us hope the fiend's threat has no power until nightfall.'

* * *

By the time we reached the wagonette it had begun to snow heavily, and this impaired our journey back to Gardner's academy. The horses grew nervous and jumpy as the flurries of snow swept past them, and Holmes had to struggle with the reins to keep them under control.

I remained silent for most of the journey. I was still depressed at being responsible for Collins's death, and although I tried to console myself with the knowledge that it was brought about more by accident than design, I could not shake off my feelings of guilt. Repeatedly, I turned the whole Collins business over in my mind until I felt impelled to ask Holmes to clear up a point which still puzzled me.

'Holmes, if you knew Collins was in league with Dracula, why did you let him take us all the way out to Vixen Heights?' I asked, shouting my question over the noise of the wind and the rattle of the wagonette.

Without taking his eyes off the road ahead, Holmes gave me his answer. 'Two reasons, Watson. I had a faint hope that he would take us to his master's lair, but failing that, I believed that by allowing Collins to think that he had successfully tricked us, it would be easier to fool him into revealing the whereabouts of the Count's resting place. You know how much more chatty these egomaniacs are when they feel they have the upper hand.

'But do not reproach yourself, old chap. I am as much to blame for Collins's death as anyone. I underestimated Dracula's hold over the man. I should have taken further precautions. However, that is all behind us. I simply hope we are in time to prevent further disaster.'

I did not reply, and we both lapsed into silence.

Although it was not yet dusk, the storm-laden sky was now quite dark, and it was with a great sense of relief that I saw the lights of Coombe Tracey before us. Moments later we were pulling up outside the academy. Holmes leapt from the wagonette and dashed inside. With myself close on his heels, he rushed to the sick room.

Once there he thrust the door open. With a groan of despair, he stood transfixed on the threshold of the room. Looking past him, I saw the cause of his anguish. The bed in which we had left Catherine Hunter but a few hours ago was empty, and she was nowhere to be seen.

'The fiend has her.'

'But how?' I stammered, glancing round the room. There was no sign of a forced entry or a struggle – everything was as we had left it.

'That is what I intend to find out,' he said with a growl. Turning on his heel, he made for Silas Gardner's study and entered without knocking.

The Principal of the academy was at his desk poring over some papers. The only source of illumination in the room, apart from the fire, was the desk-lamp, which threw harsh shadows across Gardner's bulky features. At our brisk entry, he looked up with an expression of sharp surprise.

'Holmes!' he gasped, his eyes widening in wonder.

'Where is she?' demanded my friend.

Gardner appeared totally confused by the question, and merely gazed back at us distractedly.

'Where is the girl, Catherine Hunter?' Holmes leaned over Gardner menacingly, his voice dropping to an ominous whisper.

At last Gardner was able to speak, but what he had to say was disconcerting to our ears.

'You should know the whereabouts of the girl better than I. You sent for her.'

'Sent for her?' I echoed his words in amazement.

'Yes,' he replied slowly, his eyes flickering erratically as grains of uneasy suspicion began to grow in his mind.

'You had better explain,' said Holmes calmly.

'You . . . you did not send for her?'

Holmes shook his head.

Gardner gave a strangled gasp, shaking his head wildly. 'I do not understand. If you did not send for her, who did? What in Heaven's name is going on?' He attempted to leave his chair, but Holmes held him back.

'Tell us all that has happened since our departure with Dr Collins.'

'There is not much to tell,' said Gardner. 'An hour or so after you had gone, a man arrived saying he had a message from you.'

'This man – was he an ugly fellow, a dwarf with only one eye?'

'Yes. Yes, he was. He told me that you and Dr Collins had arranged for Catherine to be taken away from here to undergo special treatment at a private nursing home in Exeter, and I was to admit her into his care so that he could transport her there without delay.'

'You believed him?' I exclaimed with incredulity.

'I had no reason to doubt him,' replied Gardner indignantly. I had to admit to myself that this was true. If I had been placed in similar circumstances with the limited knowledge that Gardner possessed, I too would have found this dwarf's story convincing.

'We roused Catherine,' he continued, 'and, heavily muffled against the weather, she was bundled into the brougham in which the dwarf had arrived. Now for God's sake, Mr Holmes, will you tell me what is going on here? If you did not send for Miss Hunter, as I fear by your reactions you did not, then who was this man and why did he say he was acting on your orders?'

I have seldom seen my friend at a loss for words, but on this occasion he was utterly dumbfounded. What could he tell Gardner? He had avoided the truth for so long that to admit the real facts of the situation now would only confuse and alienate Gardner, and destroy Holmes's credibility completely.

At length he replied, 'There are certain details concerning this affair which I have kept from you, Gardner. Not for any selfish or underhand motives, you understand, but to protect you and your reason.'

'My reason?'

'Indeed. And I must continue to maintain this secrecy.' Gardner was about to interrupt, but Holmes silenced him with an upheld hand. 'I know that it is difficult for you to accept this, but believe me, if I thought that it would help you or Catherine Hunter in any way, I would not hesitate to give you the full facts of this macabre business. Suffice it to say that there are aspects of Miss Hunter's illness which are not purely medical, but involve corruption of another kind: the corruption of the hearts and minds of men. Dr Collins was also a victim of this corruption, and it ultimately led to his destruction.'

'What!' This time Gardner did get to his feet. 'You mean Collins is dead?'

Holmes nodded. 'He was merely a decoy to lure us away from the girl's bedside, so that the real agent of this disease could get his hands on her.'

'You mean the dwarf?'

'No. He is just another servant carrying out orders. The fiend we seek desires to destroy Miss Hunter by infecting her further with his own contagion. It is our task to seek him out and destroy him before he succeeds.'

Holmes paused, and Gardner's face blanched. 'I dare not think,' he said with fear in his voice, resuming his seat, 'I dare not listen to what my imagination is suggesting.' His fingers went instinctively to his neck, gently touching his jugular vein.

'Close your mind to these thoughts and keep the nightmare from your door. Accept and be thankful that you will never really know the dark truths surrounding Catherine Hunter's illness. That is a burden we must carry.'

Gardner remained silent for some moments, the deep furrows on his face gradually easing and the tight mouth relaxing. He nodded as though accepting the wisdom of my friend's words.

'God be with you,' he said in a voice that was little more than a whisper.

'Now we must go. Our hope is a slender one and time is short.'

'I believe he knows everything,' I said to Holmes after leaving the room.

'And so he does, but not in such a way that he can articulate his understanding. It is felt rather than comprehended.' He sighed. 'However, Gardner remains the least of our worries, Watson. Obviously the character who whisked the girl away was none other than Meinster, the disciple of Dracula of whom Van Helsing told us. It was this dwarf who was in charge of Dracula's consignment of boxes which left Transylvania. There is no doubt that at this moment he is hastening to his master with his precious cargo.'

'What on earth are we to do?'

'Dracula now has the upper hand, Watson. We are drowning men, so we must grasp at straws. There is just one weak opening left to us.'

'What is that?'

'Collins's surgery: we may find there some small clue which will give us a lead to where Dracula holds court.'

As we ventured out into the cold night air once more, the dark sky was clear of snow and dotted with stars. However, I felt heavy of spirit. Try as I might, I could not shake from my mind the overwhelming conviction that Count Dracula had triumphed.

The Vital Clue

Collins had been using Doctor Mortimer's surgery, which was situated in the hamlet of Grimpen some six miles from Coombe Tracey, and it was there that we sped after leaving the academy.

As we rode over the white, moonlit countryside, I could not rid myself of the feeling that our errand was a futile one. Surely by now the girl was in Dracula's clutches and lost to us. He would already be preparing to leave the area. Once he was away from the moor, it would be almost impossible to pick up his trail again. I kept these thoughts to myself, but sensed that Holmes knew what I was thinking.

After nearly an hour's ride we pulled up outside Mortimer's surgery, a little grey house standing in an elevated position at one end of the main street of Grimpen. In contrast with the surrounding dwellings, no friendly light blazed through its windows in welcome: it stood dark and silent.

'There is no time for subtlety or decorum tonight,' announced Holmes, after trying the front door and finding it locked. Standing back a little, he raised his foot and brought it crashing down against the door. There was a dry crack as the ancient timber surrounding the lock splintered on impact and the door flew open.

Systematically, and with as much speed as we could allow, Holmes and I combed the whole building for some clue, some indication of where Count Dracula could be hiding. It was an unrewarding task. There was remarkably little evidence of Collins's habitation of the place: a few shabby clothes in the wardrobe, an unmade bed, a number of dirty dishes in the kitchen sink, and a pair of boots thickly coated in dried mud.

For nearly an hour we searched and found nothing of significance. What made our task immeasurably more difficult was the fact that we did not know exactly what we were looking for.

Holmes left the consulting room until last. I thought it the least likely room of all to surrender up a clue to us, but by the time we were scrutinising it closely, I hoped I was wrong in this judgement.

However, after an exacting search, my friend sat dejectedly in a chair, staring morosely at the floor, his face worried and his eyes tired. He was unused to carrying the burden of defeat.

I stood by him, feeling helpless and morosely penitent as I once again began to reproach myself for the death of Collins. Then I saw Holmes lean forward suddenly with a start, staring at the floor by the wall, near to where he was sitting. His eyes flashed with excited expectation, and he dropped to his knees and began examining the carpet closely with his lens.

'You have something?' I cried, my nerves taut with hope.

'I believe I have,' he murmured. 'Do you see these four small imprints in the carpet?'

I knelt by Holmes and followed his pointing finger. By the wall I observed four small round depressions forming the corners of an invisible rectangle some five feet by three.

'What do you make of them?' he asked.

'It appears as though something has been standing there – a weighty piece of furniture.'

'Excellent, Watson. And whatever it was, it had been there for some time. If you examine the indentations closely, you will see that the carpet is much lighter and cleaner than the surrounding area, which not only indicates that the object has stood there for a lengthy period, but also that it has only recently been moved.'

'By Collins, you mean?'

'Exactly. Now, the questions are what stood here and, more importantly, what was the purpose behind its move?'

He surveyed the contents of the room, and his gaze rested upon a tall, heavy bookcase against the opposite wall.

'That's it, my boy,' he cried. 'That's your weighty piece of furniture.' He walked over to the bookcase and studied it for a time; then a broad smile warmed his features and he clapped his hands in delight. 'Of course,' he said gleefully. 'Now, Watson, if you will be so good as to give me a hand to move this monstrosity away from the wall, we shall see if my deductions are correct.'

Each taking hold of either end of the bookcase, we managed, with much effort, to move it some two feet from the wall. Peering behind it, Holmes gave a cry of delight.

'Look, Watson, that is why Collins moved the thing here,' he said, indicating a door in the wall which had been completely hidden by the bulky bookcase. 'He wished to keep that secret, hidden away from prying eyes like ours.'

Squeezing in behind the bookcase, he pushed open the door to reveal a flight of steps which dropped away into darkness. 'They obviously lead to a room under the house.' He laughed. 'The game's afoot, Watson.'

With Holmes carrying an oil lamp from the surgery, we began to descend the narrow stone staircase that stretched into a black void. The lamp sent out such a meagre glow that we were only able to see a few feet in front of us. The air grew noticeably colder and felt like clammy breath on my face.

At last we reached the bottom and found ourselves in what must have been the keeping cellar. Holmes managed to locate two rusty gas mantles and lit them. In the shimmering green flare, we took stock of our surroundings. The cellar contained two wall benches, one of which, fitted with a vice and littered with various tools, appeared to be a carpenter's work bench; hanging on the wall above it was a large wood-saw. The other bench held four large medical jars containing some dark fluid. But it was the centre of the cellar which arrested our immediate attention, for there, laid on the floor side by side, were two coffins of the sort we had found on the moor. One was open and empty save for the thin lining of dry soil in the bottom. The other was closed.

'Another of Dracula's sanctuaries!' I exclaimed.

'Yes,' agreed Holmes. 'We must sterilise these caskets to prevent their further use.' He gave a sharp sigh of annoyance. 'In my haste, I have left Van Helsing's bag containing the crucifixes in the wagonette. I shall have to go back for it.' He took the lamp and bounded up the stairs.

Left alone in the cellar, I suddenly became aware of how intensely cold it was. I shivered and exhaled sharply, my breath condensing into thin white clouds as I did so. Stiffly, I moved to the bench holding the medical jars and, taking the stopper from one, dipped the tip of one finger into the dark, sticky fluid and sniffed at it. I turned away in disgust. It was blood. I could only imagine that these jars formed a kind of emergency supply for the Count. When he was unable to gain access to the warm red blood of the living, he would be forced to renew his strength by quaffing part of this stored supply. The very thought of such an obscene practice turned my stomach, sending me into a paroxysm of shivering.

With a great effort I tried to bring my trembling body under control; and then something else claimed my attention. In the oppressive silence, I thought I heard a faint scratching sound. I listened intently and heard the sound again. Gradually it grew louder. As the noise increased, I was able to locate its source and, to my horror, I realised that it was emanating from the closed coffin.

I drew nearer. There was no doubt about it: the eerie, rhythmic scraping was coming from inside. It was clear that there was someone or, rather, something in there trying to get out. With unnatural calm, I examined the coffin lid and found that it had been firmly nailed down.

It was then that I heard something that all but stopped my heart – something which still haunts my nightmares. It was a voice – a muffled, groaning voice. A voice from the coffin. Numbed with a terrible apprehension, I heard it again, the words feeble but distinct: 'Help me. Help me.' They faded into the chilly silence of the cellar, leaving me staring down in wonder at the rough wooden casket, unable to move from the spot, held there by both fear and curiosity.

'Help me,' the call came once more, louder this time and more insistent. I shot a glance towards the staircase, but there was neither sight nor sound of Holmes. What on earth was I to do? The question thundered in my brain, and I was paralysed with indecision.

'Please let me out.' The cry was pitiful to the ear. There was something familiar about the voice; it was like a ghostly reminder of a past acquaintance. The cadences teased my memory, but I could not conjure either a name or face out of the mists of my memory to identify it.

'Please let me out.' The voice repeated its agonised plea. I visualised the occupant of the box driven to the verge of madness by his confinement, struggling wildly to escape his dark prison. Who was he? Was it a vampire fiend, or some unfortunate innocent who had been trapped there by Count Dracula or Collins? There was such anguish in the voice that I began to be persuaded that it was the latter. Surely, I reasoned, if it were one of their kind, the lid of the coffin would not have been nailed down.

I imagined the captive lying in the stifling darkness, hemmed in by the rough walls, frantically scratching and scraping at the coffin lid in the hope of clawing his way to safety. While he laboured, the meagre supply of foul air that was so precious to him was gradually diminishing. Surely I could not stand by and allow this diabolical torture to continue?

While I pondered these things, my eye lit upon a large chisel lying on the workbench. On a sudden impulse I snatched it up, and began to work the lid of the coffin loose. It was a simple task, and within a short time there were only a few nails remaining to be prised free. As I set about removing these, I saw two claw-like hands appear from either side of the coffin lid, pushing their way to freedom. With mounting terror I watched as the claws grasped the lid and thrust it easily to one side; it clattered to the stone floor some feet away, the noise filling the cellar like a clap of thunder.

The prisoner of the coffin leapt free, and with slow, animal-like movements turned in a low crouch to face me, his hands, torn and bleeding from his frantic efforts to escape, held before him like the curled talons of some monstrous bird. With heart-pounding panic, I realised all too late that I had been tricked. This was no unfortunate, cruelly imprisoned by our enemies; this was a blood-lusting vampire!

I gazed in repulsion at his gruesome appearance: the flaky white features framed by a wild growth of straw-like hair; the area around the mouth coated with white foam; the cruel fangs thrust over cut and bleeding lips; and misty red eyes which, unaccustomed to even the dim illumination of the cellar after their confinement, blinked furiously, the pupils flashing in wild fervour.

My horror grew for, as I stared at this demonic travesty of what had once been a human face, I realised that I recognised it.

The creature began to advance on me. My mind raced. What was I to do? I could not attack, for in its present aroused state, the thing would be far stronger than I. My revolver was useless against a vampire, and I had no other means of protection. As it moved closer, I stumbled back in clumsy retreat, but already I sensed the paralysis of fear numbing my limbs. As the clammy, foul breath of the thing swept over me, I could see the light of victory in its vicious eyes.

And then I heard a noise on the stair. It was Holmes returning. I bellowed at the top of my voice, 'Help! Holmes, help!' At that moment the creature pounced, throwing me to the ground before I was able to cry out again.

The fall released me from the immobilising grip of terror and, acting quickly, I rolled to one side before the vampire could pin me down. I struggled to my feet with the creature clinging to me. Out of the corner of my eye, I could see Holmes.

'Here, Watson,' he called, holding out a crucifix for me.

I stretched out my arm and took it from him, but, as I did so, my assailant jerked me round with such force that it slipped from my tentative grasp and fell to the floor. With a savage cry, he kicked the crucifix and sent it slithering along the ground out of reach. Rough hands were now at my throat, and sickly sweet breath was strong in my nostrils as the demonic face drew closer to my neck. I gulped for air as a dizziness began to overwhelm me. The room seemed to darken and slowly started to spin.

As I fought against this swimming sensation, I heard a sudden sharp crack and the creature released its grip on me and jerked round. The room brightened and steadied. My eyes began to focus once more, and I saw Holmes wrenching the woodsaw from its rack on the wall above the workbench. With a final tug, he pulled it free. The vampire stood still by my side as though mesmerised by Holmes's actions.

'Duck, Watson,' he cried. I obeyed instantly and threw myself to the floor. As I did so, Holmes, holding the saw in the manner of an axe, as though he were about to fell a tree, swung it with great force at the vampire. The saw gave a ghostly whistle as it hurtled through the air. This was followed by a sickening crunch and an obscene, gurgling cry from our enemy. I was rooted to the spot, unable to avert my gaze from the scene before me, which seemed like something conjured up from Dante's *Inferno*. The saw sliced through the pallid flesh of the vampire's neck and completely severed the head, which toppled from the body in a fountain of blood. The grisly object dropped to the ground, where it lay, the lifeless eyes frozen in shock, the mouth gaping open in a silent scream.

The headless corpse staggered a few feet, the arms flailing wildly, and then it sank to the floor, the blood still flowing from the severed neck and collecting in a dark, sticky pool.

Holmes dropped the saw and gazed in disgust at the scene of carnage before him. 'When will this nightmare end?' he said quietly.

I dragged myself to my feet and, after waiting a few moments to steady my nerves, lifted the lamp to illuminate the grisly trophy so that Holmes could see the face. I asked in a voice strained with emotion, 'Do you not recognise this fiend?'

Holmes stared down at the decapitated head, and his eyes widened in amazement. 'Stapleton!' he cried.

Indeed it was Stapleton, the cunning murderer, who for some days had presented a direct threat to the life of Sherlock Holmes. Now here he lay, his death far more grisly than any he had planned for my friend.

'This is our vital clue!' exclaimed Holmes, indicating the head. 'A grotesque one, I grant you, but it provides the information we have been seeking. I now know where we will find Count Dracula.'

The Envoy

'Come, Watson, we haven't a moment to lose,' Holmes cried as he charged out of the house to the wagonette. I raced after him, my mind bursting with questions. How did Stapleton come to be in Collins's cellar? When and where had he become a vampire? Why was his coffin nailed down? How did Holmes now know where Count Dracula was? But the question that was uppermost in my mind as we clambered aboard the wagonette concerned the location of Dracula's hiding place.

On asking Holmes, I could see from his frown of irritation that I had interrupted his train of thought. 'Not now, Watson,' he snapped, as he roused the horses into movement. Reluctantly I resigned myself to Holmes's silence.

As we sped down the main street of Grimpen, past the huddled houses and the small inn, I could not help reflecting how far removed our present errand was from the cosy normality of the lives behind those cheerily lit windows which blazed in the darkness.

Soon we left the small hamlet behind and were once more traversing the lonely moor. The night was clear and crisp and the moon, unhindered by clouds, shone down brightly, causing long blue shadows to lean across the snow-covered countryside. Holmes handled the horses expertly and, despite the slush on the track, sent them racing at high speed, their flanks steaming with exertion and the veins on their necks prominent, like strands of rope.

I sat on the seat beside Holmes, bracing myself as best I could against the frequent violent jolts of the wheels sinking into the treacherous ruts or bouncing over small rocks as we careered along the rough, winding track. My eyes watered at the oncoming blast of icy wind, which lashed my face until it began to smart. At the same time, a combination of the thrill of adventure and the fear of the unknown produced a tingling through my veins and arteries. It was a feeling I had experienced many times before when Holmes and I had set forth into the night on some dangerous exploit. But never had our mission been as dangerous, or the outcome so important, as this.

I glanced at Holmes, his travelling-cap pulled well down, his gaunt features pale and exultant in the moonlight, and I sensed that he too must be experiencing a similar mixture of emotions. I saw the glint of determination in his eyes, and was reminded of the oath he gave to Van Helsing: 'I will help you track down this Count Dracula and destroy him, whatever the consequences may be for myself.' Holmes was aware, as was I, that this business was reaching its climax, and the arena we were about to enter would involve us in a fight to the death. Silently, I prayed for strength.

On reaching the top of a long climb, the ground sloped away before us. Holmes spurred on the horses and we crashed and shuddered down the dangerously uneven track.

I gazed up at the moon. It was full and clear, hanging serenely in the midnight sky. For a moment I thought that I saw something sweep across it; some fleeting movement which darkened its surface for an instant. I looked again but there was nothing to be seen. Whatever it was had disappeared. However, my senses were now alert and I scanned the darkness keenly. And then, from nowhere, there it was again: some small dark shape which darted ahead of us, caught as a blurred silhouette against the face of the moon. Holmes had observed the apparition too. However, he said nothing and concentrated on controlling the horses. He was now finding it difficult to restrain them from galloping at full speed down the tortuous track.

A faint flapping sound came to my ears above the noise of the rattling wagonette and, as it grew louder, the horses became aware of it too. Nervously, they began to shy a little.

'What is it?' I called to Holmes.

He did not reply, but looked intently about him. And then once more we saw the dark shape flit across the face of the moon. This time it moved with less speed and we were able to discern it clearly.

'An owl!' I exclaimed with relief. 'It's only an owl.'

Holmes's features remained stern. 'But it is getting closer,' he said ominously.

He was right. The sound of flapping wings grew louder, and the long-eared owl, emerging from the darkness, swooped over the heads of the horses, causing them to rear in panic. It was a brute of a creature, larger than any owl I had seen before. Holmes grappled with the reins, struggling to keep the horses under control as their hooves flashed and stamped down urgently into the grey slush.

The owl returned, wings spread wide to decrease its speed, and its long sharp talons thrust forward. It hovered for a moment before dropping down and fastening its talons into the neck of one of the horses. The steed gave a high-pitched squeal and shook its head furiously in a frantic bid to dislodge the bird. In a frenzied bustle of flapping, the owl released its grip and soared away, swallowed up by the night. In the moonlight, I saw a series of dark, glistening rivulets of blood trickling down the horse's neck.

Thoroughly unnerved by this sudden and vicious attack, the horses, snorting with terror, increased their pace in a wild, instinctive effort to escape the assailant. The wagonette plunged down the track, occasionally skimming over some obstacle which flung it sideways, causing it to tip violently and run momentarily on two wheels.

While we were being tossed about in this frenzied manner, the owl flashed across our field of vision once more. It turned and swooped to make a further attack on the horses.

'The devil!' cried Holmes and, snatching up the long horsewhip at his side, lashed out at the bird. The tongue of the whip cracked angrily and snaked towards the creature but, just in time, it veered upwards and swept behind us.

Unfortunately the whiplash spurred the horses to greater speed, and I clung tenaciously to the sides of my seat as we rocketed down the slope, now completely out of control. Holmes tugged frantically at the reins but to no avail, as the runaway horses, mouths frothing with foam, rushed headlong into the engulfing darkness. It was only some miraculous instinct that kept them to the track.

The bird returned.

This time it flew directly before our faces, and I could feel the draught of its wings upon my cheek. It swept in a circle around the vehicle and then, with a terrible barking cry, launched itself at us. It swooped directly at Holmes, who dropped the reins to protect his face. With claws outstretched, the persistent predator almost glided into the attack. Holmes uttered a sharp cry of pain as the talons scored through the leather of his gloves. Punching his arms wildly in the air, he fought the bird off, and it took flight again. During this temporary retreat, Holmes lashed out at the owl once more with the whip. This time he caught it on the wing. Feathers sprayed into the night air and the owl plummeted to the ground, where it fluttered in an ungainly fashion in the snow. However, this was but a momentary respite for, glancing back, I saw the creature shake its giant wings to gain equilibrium and then, with a shriek of triumph, soar skywards, apparently unharmed.

By now I had retrieved my revolver from my coat pocket, and I fired a shot at the bird. Unfortunately, it was almost impossible to take a steady aim, and I missed.

Within seconds the determined creature attacked again. This time I was its target. As if flew at me, it opened its powerful, curved beak. Bracing myself, I waited until it was some five feet away and then fired another shot. This time I was successful. A dull red moon of blood appeared on the underside of one wing, but this did not prevent the bird from launching itself at me. I grappled with it, trying to keep the flashing talons away from my eyes. The vicious beak tore at my gloves, eager to reach the soft flesh beneath.

The wagonette shuddered violently and tipped, as once more the wheels hit some obstruction along the track. With this sudden up-heaval, both the bird and I were flung into the rear of the vehicle. I landed on my back, holding the shrieking, flapping creature at bay. I could hear the sharp clicking of its beak as it struggled in my hands. It was then that I saw Holmes above me with the whip. Holding it in the form of a noose, he slipped it over the bird's neck and pulled tight. The owl squawked and struggled furiously, its long wings thrashing in a desperate bid to free itself, but Holmes kept hold of the noose. Gradually the flapping wings drooped, and I felt the body grow limp, but my friend did not release his grip until he was certain that all life had passed from the bird.

I was about to lift myself up, when there was a thunderous crash and the whole world seemed to cave in on me. There was a savage jolt, and I was flung forward. I felt myself falling through the air. Momentarily there was icy, starlit blackness all around me, and then, just before I lost consciousness, I had the sensation of sinking into soft, cold snow.

How long I lay insensible I do not know, but I was eventually roused by the sound of Holmes's voice calling to me, piercing the wall of fog which surrounded my brain.

'Are you all right, Watson?' he was saying, shaking my shoulder in an attempt to wake me.

I opened my eyes and saw his concerned face leaning over me. 'I think so,' I replied hoarsely. 'Let me get up and I will know better.'

With Holmes's help, I pulled myself unsteadily to my feet. Look-ing around me, I saw what had happened. Down by the side of the track, near to where I had been lying, was a deep, rocky crevice. At the bottom of this chasm, some fifty feet below, lay the twisted wreck of the wagonette. Alongside it, in black relief against the snow, were the bodies of our two poor horses. It was clear that we must have struck some large stone on the track which had catapulted the vehicle over on its side, and it had crashed down into the crevice, dragging the horses with it. By some miracle, Holmes and I had been thrown clear, the soft snow breaking our fall.

Dusting the white flakes from my clothes, I nodded to my friend. 'No bones broken,' I said.

Balanced on the edge of the crevice was the inert form of the bird. It was a monstrous beast, measuring well over two feet in length. Its talons were still tipped with blood.

'What a freak of nature,' I said, 'for such a thing to attack us.'

'A freak certainly, but not of nature,' Holmes replied. 'This bird was sent by our enemy. It is simply another creature of the night at Dracula's command. Van Helsing notes in his book that he believes the Count has power over all nocturnal beasts, particularly bats, owls, and wolves. This bird was obviously sent to delay our journey, or even kill us.'

'Then Dracula is aware that you know where he is hiding?'

'Oh yes, Watson. Collins was not overestimating the powers of his master when he called him omnipotent.'

'But how can he know?'

'It would seem to me that Dracula has some telepathic or spiritual link with all the creatures under his command. Remember how he was able to speak through Collins's dead body? If this is the case, then as soon as I destroyed Stapleton, the Count would have been immediately aware of the fact and known that I was close on his heels.'

'And so he despatched this foul envoy,' I said, indicating the dead bird.

Holmes nodded. 'Yes, and it has achieved at least one of its aims: it has delayed our journey. However, not only have we lost time, but also Van Helsing's bag. It lies somewhere down there amid the wreckage, completely out of reach. The only consolation in all this is that we know that we are on the right trail.'

'Then where is Dracula hiding?'

'I thought you would have worked that out for yourself, Watson.'

I shook my head.

'He is at Baskerville Hall.'

'What!'

'I really should have considered it earlier. It is an ideal location for a vampire retreat: a large, empty house surrounded by desolate moorland; a dwelling as ancient as the Count's own.'

'Where does Stapleton fit into all this?'

'It is a long, complicated tale, Watson, and there is not time to tell it now. We must hasten to Baskerville Hall without further delay before this fiend has the opportunity to flee the district and thus be lost to us forever.'

Solemnly, we resumed our journey to Baskerville Hall on foot. Although we kept to the track, rather than risk crossing the moor by a more direct route, the going was far from easy, as the snow was quite deep.

'How long was I unconscious?' I asked, after glancing at my watch and finding that it had stopped.

'For several minutes, I am afraid,' came Holmes's reply. 'I, too, was knocked senseless.'

'What time is it now?'

'Well after one o' clock.'

'Then the girl is doomed,' I cried with a heavy heart.

'We must not give up hope. I agree that the odds appear to be heavily stacked against us. If Catherine Hunter has become one of the undead, it will be through my own incompetence.'

I rallied to Holmes's defence. 'Nonsense, you have done all that was possible.'

'Thank you for your loyalty, Watson, but I should have been more aware of the dangers to the girl. I should have realised that Meinster was in the area and that, in my absence from the academy, he might attempt to snatch Miss Hunter from us.' He shook his head sadly. 'And while I was playing my own games with Collins, I left her totally unprotected. I have seriously underrated the power and ingenuity of our diabolical enemy.'

'And,' said I, as remorseful as my companion, 'if I had not shot Collins, he might have led us straight to the lair of his master.'

'There are a great many "ifs" in life, I am afraid, Watson, but it is my profession to be aware of them. However, we cannot change the past: if Dracula has finally taken possession of Catherine Hunter, there is nothing we can do about it. But the main purpose of our mission remains – the destruction of Count Dracula.'

CHAPTER TWENTY-THREE

The Darkest Hour

We trudged on in silence until we reached the lodge gates of Basker-ville Hall. They were a maze of fantastic tracery in wrought iron; touched now with snow they resembled a magnified section of fine lace. The weatherbeaten pillars, surmounted by the boar's head of the Baskervilles, stood guard at either side of the gateway. Passing through the open gates and by the lodge, which lay in ruins, we moved into the straight, dark avenue of trees leading up to the Hall itself, which stood like a shimmering ghost at the far end. The tall trees, winter naked, stretched their skeletal branches above us, interlacing to form a high vaulted roof through which one caught an occasional glimpse of the bright moon. As the branches swayed in the breeze, they knocked against each other as though in warning of our approach.

The avenue opened out into a broad expanse of lawn now flaw-lessly smooth with snow, and there before us was Baskerville Hall. It remained as I remembered it. The centre was a heavy block of building from which a porch projected. Ivy, frosted and glistening in the moonlight, covered the front section of the hall, with a patch clipped here and there where windows, like dark stains on the face of the house, broke through the silvered foliage. From this central block rose the twin towers, ancient and crenellated and pierced with many loopholes. On either side of these turrets were the more recent additions to the hall: modern wings built of black granite. No light radiated from the mullioned windows; they remained dark and forbidding.

It was clear that recent visits had been made to the Hall, for the snow on the drive was criss-crossed with wheel tracks and there were many footprints by the porch. As we stood there, Holmes put his hand on my arm. 'Watson, I am afraid I have taken your participation in this affair for granted, and now it seems to me that I am about to plunge you into a situation so dangerous that the chances of survival are very slender.' He paused briefly. 'My dear friend, you have acquitted yourself admirably throughout, but I have no right to ask or expect you to accompany me into the house.'

'Nonsense,' I said sharply. 'I have never failed you yet, I hope, and I have no intention of doing so now. It is my duty.'

Holmes gave me a brief, stern smile and squeezed my arm. 'Good old Watson,' he said softly.

Without further words, we approached the large oak door of Baskerville Hall. It was unlocked. On entering the dark, silent house, Holmes and I found ourselves once more in the lofty, heavily-raftered hall. Our footsteps, soft though they were, seemed to echo through the building. Holmes, with nimble, cat-like tread, moved to the table in the centre of the chamber, retrieved a small candelabra, and lit it, the flames washing the room in a sepulchral glow. We gazed around us at the high, thin window of old stained glass, the oak panelling, the stag's head, the coats of arms, and the ancient weapons fixed upon the walls, all dim and sombre in the pale light.

As we surveyed our surroundings, a sound came to our ears. It was the sob of a woman, the muffled, strangled gasp of one who is torn by an uncontrollable sorrow. It seemed to emanate from the very walls themselves, as though it were part of the sad history of this house. With a silent gesture, Holmes pointed towards the minstrels' gallery and indicated that we should investigate. From his coat he took a pistol and, with this in one hand and the candelabra in the other, led the way up the right-hand staircase to the square, balustraded gallery which ran round the upper section of the chamber. Here we stood and listened again to catch the disturbing, moaning cries of the sobbing woman. They seemed to be coming from one of the rooms along the corridor to our left. Holmes pointed in that direction, confirming my impression.

Stealthily we crept along the narrow corridor, the candlelight sending our shadows dancing around us, as though they were in-dependently motivated and no longer allied to our bodies but, in some diabolical way, alien to them.

The haunting sobs grew louder. We paused outside the fourth bedroom. There could be no doubt that it was from this room that the sounds of misery emanated. I felt a cold sweat on my brow as Holmes, placing the candelabra on the ground, opened the door slowly.

The room was lit by the glow of a small fire. Lying face downwards on the bed was a woman, crying into her pillow, her body shuddering as tormented gasps escaped her lips. After a moment, she became aware of our presence and looked up, turning her tear-stained face towards us, furtively peering in the dim light, attempting to identify the intruders. It was the face of Catherine Hunter.

The sad, misty eyes flashed with joy as a look of recognition came to her features, and her expression changed from one of misery to one of hope. Eagerly she rose from her bed and rushed towards us. 'Oh, Mr Holmes, Dr Watson. Thank God you've come,' she cried. 'You have no idea . . . no idea.' She shook her head sadly and began to cry again. 'Thank God you've come,' she said once more, falling into my arms.

I, too, gave silent thanks that we had arrived in time to save this young, innocent soul from the evil of Dracula. I held her to my breast and patted her gently. 'The worst is over,' I said. 'There is no need to cry any more.'

'I'll try,' she whimpered, gazing up at me with moist, pathetic eyes.

'Thank heaven she is safe,' I said, turning to Holmes, who was standing motionless, staring at the girl.

'You will not let that devil come near me again, will you?' she implored, looking deep into my eyes.

I knew she was referring to the Count, and stopped myself from contemplating what awful indignities he had subjected her to. She clung closer to me, her tear-stained face brushing mine. It was then that something in her behaviour began to unnerve me. My body tensed as I felt the draught of her hot breath upon my neck. It had the same sweet, sickly odour I had encountered before. I sensed danger, but it was too late. Before I was able to push the girl away, I felt her lips touch me, and then her sharp fangs pierced my flesh. I gave a cry of revulsion and tried to force her from me, but she clung on tenaciously.

Holmes dashed forward and, grabbing the girl by the hair, pulled her aside. She stumbled back towards the darkened corner of the room. I, too, found myself unsteady on my feet, my mind clouding with nausea. Nervously, I touched my neck. A thin trickle of blood ran down onto my collar. Mercifully, she had only scraped the surface, and had not gained access to the jugular vein.

The girl crouched in the corner like a caged wild animal, snarling and hissing.

'My God,' I cried, clutching the wound at my neck, the horrible reality of the situation suddenly clear to me, 'we are too late!'

'Yes,' agreed Holmes gloomily. 'Dracula has taken possession of Miss Catherine Hunter. Despite her fine performance, calculated to put us off our guard, she is now one of the undead.'

The girl gave a strange gurgle of laughter, causing the hairs on the back of my neck to prickle. 'I am his.' She smiled slowly, revealing her fangs. 'I am his bride.' She hissed, and clawed at the air like a wild cat before advancing towards us. 'You came to save me, but who is going to save you?' Her dark eyes rippled with hypnotic power as she reached out a long, white arm towards Holmes.

'No! Leave them be! They are for the Master!' This sudden, authoritative command, which froze the girl in her tracks, came from behind us. We turned and saw, standing half in shadow in the door-way, the figure of a dwarf.

On short, stubby legs he strode into the room. His head was bald, while the lower region of his face was covered in thick black hair through which his fat red lips were barely discernible. He stared at us with baleful blue eyes, mean and spiteful in their intent. This was obviously Meinster, the Count's servant, who had arranged his transportation to these shores. Fleetingly, the thought crossed my mind that he was indeed a truly suitable mortal accomplice for Dracula, for he was as deformed and ugly physically as was his master spiritually. In his chubby, childlike hands he held a powerful rifle.

He grinned an awful grin before he spoke again. 'The Master is expecting you,' he said, in a sharp staccato rhythm, his voice heavy with accent. In an instant the grotesque smile had gone. 'Down-stairs,' he ordered, the voice emerging from the forest of dark hairs which virtually concealed his mouth. He pointed with his rifle, indicating that we were to lead the way.

Slowly we retraced our steps to the hall, the dwarf and the girl following behind us. I noticed that Holmes had managed to slip his gun into the pocket of his coat unseen.

'What are we to do?' I asked in an urgent whisper.

'We wait,' came the terse reply.

Once in the hall, the dwarf spoke again. 'Dining room!' he barked, prodding me in the back with his rifle. The girl ran ahead of us and, with a giggle of delight, threw open the door.

The dining room was a long, dark, oak-panelled chamber decor-ated with portraits of the Baskerville ancestors, long dead spirits who haunted the place, staring down on the living with serene complacency. In company with this group of silent ghosts was another presence from beyond the grave: Count Dracula. He was standing motionless, like the portraits, with his back to a blazing fire which crackled in the hearth of the inglenook fireplace. His face was as a death mask, but the eyes flickered and blazed with fierce intensity. As we entered, his hard, cruel mouth slowly split into a sardonic smile.

'Why, gentlemen, I had almost given up hope that you would arrive,' he said, smoothly. 'I am so pleased to be able to offer you the hospitality of my temporary accommodation.' His voice was melodious, but there was menace underlying the charm of his mocking courtesy.

From the folds of his cloak he extended his long, slender arm, curling one of his skeletal fingers in a beckoning gesture to the girl, who glided past us and, with a sigh of pleasure, took up her position by the side of the Count.

'You are just in time to toast my new bride.' His lips pulled back over his fangs in a vulpine grin. Here was the smiling, damned villain that Van Helsing had described to us, but there was something about Count Dracula that no words, however eloquent, could convey. It was the aura of absolute evil which radiated from the creature – and creature he was. By returning from the dead and denying his mortality, he had forfeited the right to be called a man.

With a swift, violent movement, he pulled back his cloak and tore open the front of his shirt to expose the alabaster-white flesh beneath. Gently he lifted the girl's head with one hand while, with the other, he ran the sharp nail of his forefinger diagonally across his chest, scoring the flesh and opening a vein. Dark globules of blood appeared along the scar-line and began to seep from the wound.

'Come, my dear, drink.' With incongruous tenderness, he pulled the face of the girl to his breast, his right hand holding the back of her neck while she eagerly lapped the blood which flowed from the wound.

I felt my stomach turn as I was held transfixed by this disgusting and degrading spectacle. Dracula stood erect and unflinching, a malevolent smile on his face as the girl, with murmurs of delight, drank his blood.

It was a scene from Bedlam.

'We are now one, my dear,' he crowed, his voice echoing round the darkened room. 'Flesh of my flesh, blood of my blood, kin of my kin. Our union is in blood, and blood is the life.' He waited a moment in silence and then, without warning, jerked the girl's head away from his chest. Her mouth dripped with his blood, some of it spattering onto the floor.

'Thank you, Master,' she cried ecstatically, her eyes glazing with pleasure as her tongue licked at her lips in an effort to retain as much of the precious life force as she could.

Dracula glared at us in triumph after this obscene exhibition of his mastery. 'It is done. She is mine,' he said simply. My disgust was replaced by fury, and impotent rage flared within me. This creature was playing with us, taunting us with his power, and there was nothing we could do about it. I glanced at Holmes. I could read nothing from his taut, immobile features; I could only guess what he was thinking, facing, as he was, his most formidable antagonist ever.

'I have taken all I want from this region,' Dracula was saying, caressing the girl's hair. 'It is time to leave for pastures new, taking my bride with me. Meinster has arranged for our transportation back to London, and from there – who knows where I shall continue my work? You see, gentlemen, I am on a crusade. I left my home in the Transylvanian mountains with a mission: to spread the cult of the undead. It is my intention to travel the world, creating colonies of my own kind so that the legion of the undead will swell and grow until we hold power over all.'

Holmes and I stood in silence, listening as the Count gloated in contemplation of his own mad dream.

'However, before I depart, I intend to deal with you, Sherlock Holmes, and your meddling accomplice. You have interfered with my plans for the last time. You have destroyed three of my agents, including my new convert, Stapleton. It is therefore only appropriate that I should destroy you also.' His face twisted into an awful grimace, and the vicious fangs flashed in the firelight.

'It is so pleasant to have you here,' he continued, his voice resuming its tone of chilling courtesy. He held out his arms in a gesture of welcome, but as he pulled them back, he closed his open palms into tight fists, holding them close to his face. 'I rarely have the opportunity of talking with my enemies. Of necessity such meetings are brief and without words. You have been a worthy opponent, Sherlock Holmes. For a man who has not lived even one lifetime you are wise. It is many years, centuries, since I have been opposed by such an intellectual equal.'

Holmes gave a curt bow and addressed the Count for the first time. He spoke in a relaxed manner, but I was aware that this was a fabricated ease. I also knew that when he spoke like this, there was definitely mischief afoot. His words gave a lift to my heart. Perhaps,

I thought, the intellectual prowess of my friend could be a match for the black malevolence of Dracula.

'I thank you for the compliment, Count,' said Holmes. 'May I respond in kind, by saying that in my meagre lifespan, one in which I have devoted my energies to fighting evil and injustice, I have never encountered an adversary as thoroughly malevolent, corrupt, or . . . as pitiful as you.'

The gloating smile vanished from Dracula's lips.

'Pitiful?' he cried, his booming voice filling the lofty chamber. 'Pitiful?' he repeated, his features darkening.

It was now Holmes's turn to smile. 'A once noble and victorious warrior forced to live like a common criminal, skulking in the shadows, fearing the rays of the sun, seeking the blood of lesser mortals so that you may cling to the half-life you lead. You claim immortality, Count Dracula, but what a high price you pay for your squalid existence. Indeed, I do pity you.'

As Holmes made this final observation, the Count's eyes flamed passionately, and his nostrils quivered with emotion. 'How dare you feel pity for me,' he snarled, taking a step towards my friend. But suddenly he stopped himself, freezing in mid-stride, and swiftly brought his anger under control. His fury dissipated, he now afforded himself a hollow laugh.

'Sherlock Holmes,' he said icily, in a voice full of arrogant pride, 'I am Count Vlad Tepesh Dracula. I am one who commanded great armies hundreds of years before you were born, and I have survived the centuries. I have conquered death by means of the rich wine of life, which I drink freely as I will. Long after you are rotting in the earth, I shall still be here ruling the night – the Lord of the Undead. What pity you have, Sherlock Holmes, spare for yourself.'

'And yet you fear me,' replied Holmes softly.

'I? Fear you?' The Count gave a snort of derision.

'Then why destroy me?'

'Because you have been an irritant to my plans. I destroy you as one destroys a troublesome insect.'

'So, you do not fear me?'

'The mortal does not exist whom I fear.'

With a swift, dexterous motion, Holmes produced a gun from the folds of his coat and aimed it at Dracula's heart. 'And do you still not fear me?' he asked coolly.

The dwarf raised his rifle and pointed it at Holmes, but Dracula stopped him. 'Stay, Meinster,' he called sharply, and then turned his attention back to Holmes. 'You hope to destroy me with one of man's puny toys? You disappoint me, Sherlock Holmes. I expected you to arrive better equipped to deal with one who sits on the left hand of the Devil. You challenge me with a mere pistol.' He gave a throaty chuckle. 'You will find I am invulnerable to such pathetic aspirations.'

'In this affair I have underestimated you, Count. Now, I think, the tables are turned.' Holmes's voice remained calm and confident; and then I suddenly realised why. I, too, had underestimated my friend in thinking that he would threaten Dracula with an ordinary bullet. My mind flashed back to the luncheon with Van Helsing and I remembered the professor's words: 'a silver bullet fired directly into the heart will exterminate the vampire'.

Holmes cocked the pistol, and on the instant Dracula, sensing real danger, retreated, flinging out his arm in a bid to protect himself. As he did so, Holmes fired, but I knew immediately that the bullet would not reach its target. As if with some uncanny second sense, our adversary realised the gun held a real threat for him and, as Holmes pulled the trigger, the Count darted swiftly out of the firing line.

For a fleeting second I thought that the shot had missed Dracula altogether but, clutching his left hand, he gave a scream of agony. Blood was spurting from the palm, and it was here that my friend's bullet had lodged itself.

In the next few moments so many things seemed to happen at once. We were like characters in a static tableau suddenly galvanised into frantic motion. As soon as the shot had been fired, Meinster raised his rifle again. With his attention focused on Holmes, I was able to pull out my own gun and, without hesitation, I loosed two shots into the dwarf's body. Orthodox bullets had no difficulty in dealing with him.

Meanwhile, the Count was staggering to and fro on unsteady legs, howling like a wounded animal and clutching his damaged hand. The girl whimpered at his side, making desperate attempts to embrace him. As these entreaties grew more demanding, Dracula turned on her with a roar of fury. 'Away with you,' he commanded, spitting the words into her face. This harsh rejection brought hysterical shrieks from the girl, and she threw herself on her knees and clung even tighter to the Count. Tears streamed down her cheeks as she gazed up at Dracula, pleading with him to let her stay by his side.

With a snarl of rage, he grasped the girl with his uninjured hand and cast her from him. Such was the force of his action that she was flung straight against the wall by the fireplace. There was a sharp crack as her head hit the stonework and, to my horror, I saw the girl fall and tumble sideways into the fireplace. As she collapsed onto the burning logs, the voracious yellow tongues lapped hungrily about her, speedily setting her dress alight. The garment seemed to explode into flames. Pain wrenched the girl into a dazed consciousness and, with choking gasps of terror, she tried desperately to drag herself from the fire. I started to the girl's aid, but halted in my tracks as I recollected what she had become. I watched numbly as, her eyes wide in torment, she writhed helplessly, the blaze enveloping her whole body. The sizzling roar drowned her feeble screams, as she was consumed by the tenacious flames.

My most vivid memory of this swift and terrible cremation is of seeing, when the blaze had died down, her blackened skull with its hideous death grin, peering out through the ashes. I felt nothing but pain in witnessing the scene. I remembered only the frail creature I had encountered at the academy; a young innocent girl contaminated by the vile process of vampirism.

While I was held spellbound by Catherine Hunter's grisly demise, Count Dracula had been staggering about the chamber nursing his wounded hand, which had now begun to turn dark purple in colour.

Holmes was watching the Count from a safe distance, with a wary smile. 'The purity of the bullet is beginning to spread,' he warned. 'Soon your hand will wither and decay. Gradually your whole body will be affected by the spiritual goodness.'

'Damn you, Sherlock Holmes,' the vampire cried, his features twisted with fear, as he stumbled from the room.

We followed him into the hall, where he stood gazing desperately about him, dark blood still seeping from the wound. Suddenly his eyes lit upon a pair of medieval axes fixed upon the wall. Taking purposeful steps, he strode across to them. With a sickening sensation, I knew in my heart what he was going to do.

'We must stop him,' I cried.

'No!' exclaimed Holmes. 'Despite the wound, he still has far greater strength than both of us.'

So, as helpless spectators, we watched with horrid fascination as Dracula wrenched one of the axes from the wall and, without hesitation, brought it down with a great blow upon his own wrist, severing the wounded hand.

He stumbled on unsteady legs for a moment, issuing a muffled grunt of pain which gave way to a deep, croaking laugh. He pulled away his bleeding stump, having successfully prevented the goodness of the silver bullet spreading to further parts of his body.

The detached hand twitched violently and then slowly blackened, curled, and withered before our eyes. The flesh faded from the bones, which in turn crumbled into powder. Within seconds all that was left of the severed member was a small pile of grey ash.

Still wielding the axe, Dracula swung round to face us, the light of victory returning to his eyes. 'Damn you, Sherlock Holmes,' he said again, and threw the axe with great force at my friend. So accurate was the Count's aim that, despite Holmes's sudden move sideways at the last moment, the axe only just missed him. However, it pinned part of his coat to the oak panelling behind him. I rushed to his aid, but he had little difficulty in plucking the weapon from the wall and freeing himself. We turned to find an empty hall with the main door swinging open.

'Come, Watson, this is the last act. Dracula is in flight. He will be heading for one of his resting places on the moor. We must follow him there and, at sunrise, we shall be able to destroy this fiend for ever. If we lose him now, all our efforts will have been in vain.'

CHAPTER TWENTY-FOUR

The Moor Claims Another Victim

We emerged from the Hall in time to see the Count disappear down the murky avenue of trees, his cloak flapping behind him. We raced after him but, on reaching the lodge gates, he had vanished from sight.

'Where is he?' I gasped, peering vainly into the darkness.

'Look!' cried Holmes, pointing to Dracula's tell-tale prints in the snow. They left the track and ran across the white, undulating moor in the direction of Black Tor.

'Come, Watson. We must not lose him,' called Holmes urgently, as he set off once more in pursuit of our unholy quarry.

I followed my friend and soon we were both knee-high in wet snow. Our progress was slow and intensely uncomfortable: the snow soaked our clothing and the cold numbed our legs. Gradually we reached higher ground, where the snow had been blown into drifts, leaving some shallow sections almost devoid of snow altogether, thus easing our discomfort and aiding our advance. The sky was lighter now and I realised, with some surprise, that our adventure had lasted almost the whole of the night, and that soon dawn would be breaking over the moor.

We reached an area where the wind had parted the snow, leaving a rock-strewn gully which made its way between two towering white walls. It was here that Dracula's tracks ran out. Holmes sprang up onto a boulder and scanned the shadowy moor. 'Which way? Which way?' he cried impatiently to himself, his head thrust forward as he stared into the gloom. 'Ah, there he is!' he exclaimed at length, pointing to the west of us. I just glimpsed a dark shape disappearing over the horizon. 'He is making for Vixen Heights, beyond the mire. Once there, we have lost him for ever.'

When we gained the top of the next rise, the snow began to deepen again. With heads down, we pressed on as fast we were able. Dracula's prints reappeared and were now easier to follow with the gradual lightening of the heavens. The rosy tint of morning slowly seeped into the sky, washing the moor with a pale red hue.

Then we saw Dracula below us, a dark smudge on the landscape. His pace seemed much slower, as though his strength was fading along with the darkness.

With an incredible burst of speed, Holmes raced ahead of me down towards the Count. He ran as I have never seen him run before. His long legs seemed to skim over the ground, while he gained steadily on his quarry, and within moments it appeared that they were level. My heart skipped a beat as I saw Holmes pounce upon the vampire. There was a brief struggle and both men fell to the ground locked in each other's embrace. As I drew closer, I saw Dracula pull himself free and clamber up a rocky incline. Holmes bounded after him. They stood facing each other, dark silhouettes against the pale sky. Holmes dipped his head and charged at the Count, butting him in the chest. Dracula gave a cry of alarmed surprise and staggered back to the edge of the rocks. He seemed to remain hovering there for some moments before toppling off the ridge beyond my vision.

I rushed forward around the rocks and broke upon a scene I shall never forget. Dracula had fallen some fifty feet into the great Grimpen Mire. Already the foul ooze was pulling him down into its fatal depths, and his struggles to extricate himself only caused him to sink further. Soon he was waist high in the morass and, with arms flailing wildly, he called out in fear and anguish strange words of his native tongue. His black cloak lay spread out behind him like wings, and he resembled some great insect squirming in panic to pull itself from the clutches of the stagnant morass.

Holmes joined me and with care we moved closer to the scene. At our approach, Dracula turned to us with desperate eyes. 'Help me. Please help me,' he pleaded. Despite what I knew of this demonic creature, I could not help but feel a twinge of pity for him, witnessing the pain and anguish in his eyes as with terrible inevitabilty, the mire sucked him deeper into its murky embrace.

Holmes watched in silence.

The sky lightened further and the rim of a new day's sun touched the horizon, spreading its first fragmented rays across the moorland.

'No,' bellowed the Count, thrashing violently in the green slime. He held his still bleeding stump across his face to protect his eyes from the sunlight. It was as though Nature were taking revenge against this creature who had for so long transgressed its laws. Like a freshly minted sovereign, the sun rose above Black Tor, flooding the moor with a rich golden light. The vampire screamed in pain as the destructive rays struck his squirming body.

And then, before our astonished eyes, this fiend from the grave began to decompose. The whole scene appeared as a ghoulish vision from a drug-induced dream. The foul process began with the flesh on the face darkening, withering, and falling from the bone. This was accompanied by a profuse outflowing of a yellowish liquid from around the eyes, which shortly dropped from their sockets. The mouth also disgorged this foul bile, and soon the whole face was no longer recognisable as anything human.

The torso, visible above the surface of the mire, shrank and crumbled. The rotting frame of the vampire disintegrated completely, until all that was left of him was a dark green liquid mass of loathsome putrescence which was slowly sucked down into the Grimpen Mire.

We stood for some moments, staring at the now still and innocent looking surface of the bog, stunned into silence by what we had seen: the cheated centuries catching up and taking their toll on the ancient body of Count Dracula.

Holmes was the first to speak. 'No longer will the earth be plagued by this most evil of creatures,' he said quietly, the beams of the early morning sun bronzing his fatigued features.

Suddenly, from across the moor, came a long low howl of grief. The haunting cry caused us to turn towards Black Tor where we saw, silhouetted against the sun, the shape of a huge dog, baying.

The sight of the hound chilled me to the marrow.

'My God!' I cried.

Holmes gave me a knowing glance. 'It is lamenting the death of a kindred spirit.'

I turned again to Black Tor, but the dark shape had disappeared.

CHAPTER TWENTY-FIVE

Retrospection

On our return to Baker Street, Sherlock Holmes was plunged almost at once into another case. This mystery, mundane in the extreme by comparison with our recent adventure, concerned the disappearance from the home of Lady Rowena Durband of her precious jewel, 'The Star of Krishnapur'. However, the case was sufficiently demanding to occupy my friend for the best part of a week, and thus prevented him from brooding over the death of Catherine Hunter, for which he blamed himself. It was the single thought that had occupied his mind on our return journey to London. He had sat, huddled into his coat, staring morosely out of the carriage window. 'I am responsible for her death,' he murmured from time to time. Despite my protestations to the contrary, and assurances that he had done all in his power to help her, he would not be consoled or drawn into discussing other aspects of the investigation.

Gardner, also, had been profoundly affected by the girl's death. Although I sensed that he had been expecting to hear the worst, when he was told of Catherine Hunter's demise the colour drained from his face, and his hands clutched the arms of his chair until the knuckles grew white with the pressure. Holmes informed him that, despite our efforts, we had been unable to save her from the clutches of the vile disease with which she had been infected for some time and, in order to prevent the threat of contagion, we had been forced to cremate the corpse. He gave Gardner his assurance that the disease had now been stamped out and there would be no repercussions. The troubled Principal only stared back at him with dull, vacant eyes. The death of Catherine Hunter had been the final blow of many that had rained down on Gardner's head in the past months. He was a broken man who saw his life in ruins. All he had striven for – establishing the academy, developing its high reputation – seemed meaningless to him now. This aggravated the guilt that Holmes felt and, say what I might, I could not shift his opinion on the matter.

When we reached Baker Street, we found an irate Inspector Lestrade on our doorstep. 'Where have you been for the past few days?' he asked indignantly, clasping his bowler hat in his hands so tightly I feared he might snap the brim.

'Out of town,' came Holmes's terse reply.

'There is no need to be facetious,' cried Lestrade. 'I want an explanation from you, Mr Holmes. I want to know what happened on the night you visited the police mortuary.'

'Very little,' said Holmes wearily.

Lestrade's eyes bulged and his face flamed with anger, but Holmes managed to calm him down with a patient smile and a few words of apology. 'I am sorry for being flippant, Lestrade,' said he, 'but for many nights, sleep and I have been strangers, and fatigue is making me a little lightheaded. The truth is that I am as much puzzled by the strange happenings at the mortuary as you. I am led to believe that we were the dupes of some confidence trick, or some other such phenomenon. My subsequent investigations have led me up a blind alley, and for once in my life I must admit that I am completely baffled.' Holmes wore a solemn and dispirited expression as he re-layed this information to Lestrade.

His admission of defeat brought a smug beam to the Scotland Yarder's face. 'Dear me,' said Lestrade, puffing out his chest, his voice edged with sarcasm, 'I never thought I would see the day when I would hear the famous detective admit defeat. I thought there was no problem beyond your powers of deduction.'

'So did I,' responded Holmes dolefully.

'Not to worry, Mr Holmes,' replied Lestrade, grinning. 'You are only human – after all.' He clapped the bowler hat to his head, patted my friend consolingly on the shoulder, and left.

'He is a simple soul, Watson,' said Holmes, after Lestrade's departure. 'The thought that I have been beaten will easily take precedence over all other considerations in the Celia Lydgate matter. I suspect we shall hear no more of it.'

He looked pale and haggard, the strain of the last few days etched into his weary features. After a small repast of hot soup, beef and pickle, he spent the rest of the day in bed.

It was that very evening when he received the urgent summons from Lady Durband concerning her stolen jewel. Still fatigued, but unable to resist the challenge, he set out for her Park Lane mansion.

I did not accompany Holmes on this occasion, but stayed close to our fireside, turning over in my mind the details of the recent adventure we had shared.

Holmes's investigations into the Durband mystery required him to leave London for a few days, and therefore he was out of town when Professor Van Helsing called to hear his account of the Dracula affair. Although I was able to give our colleague a general outline of the case, I knew that I did not possess sufficient knowledge to relate the story in full. Van Helsing, while delighted at the outcome, was naturally dismayed at not being able to discuss the matter in detail. I arranged that he should dine with us at the end of the week, on the eve before Christmas, when my friend would be able to recount to him all the events leading up to the destruction of Count Dracula.

By the time Christmas Eve arrived, the weather in London had taken a seasonal turn. It had snowed heavily the day before, and now the metropolis lay snow-capped and ice-bound beyond our window. Within, we kept our fire glowing in the grate, while the wind, bringing fresh flurries of snow, howled fiercely in the streets. Holmes was in much better spirits, having successfully completed the Durband case. He had only just returned from Dover, where he had retrieved the diamond and apprehended the culprit, the twin brother of Lady Durband's footman.

Punctually at seven-thirty, Van Helsing arrived and, after exchanging seasonal greetings, we sat down to a splendid feast prepared for us by Mrs Hudson. There was little conversation as we tucked into the traditional Christmas fare, but after the meal, as we sat around the table and sipped our post-prandial liqueurs, Van Helsing prompted Holmes into discussing the Dracula investigation.

'As we later discovered,' began Holmes, 'Count Dracula's purpose in leaving his ancestral home, after many years spent hiding in its vaults and venturing but a little distance to obtain the blood of the village girls in the Carpathians, was to spread the cult of the undead like a plague across the world. This country was the first stop on his unholy crusade. However, after he arrived in London, I believe he realised that to operate in such a large city would be far too dangerous for him, so he fled to the remoter regions of Dartmoor where he felt he would be able to carry out his plans with less likelihood of hindrance or detection. Meinster, his mortal accomplice, arranged for the transportation of the boxes containing the native Transylvanian soil to Grimpen. One of these boxes also held the body of Count Dracula, of course. It was at Grimpen that Dracula enlisted the help of Collins. He needed someone who knew the area and who could provide him with information and refuge. Being a doctor, Collins was an obvious choice, for not only had he access to supplies of blood, he was also able to cover up the evidence of Dracula's attacks. In treating the Count's victims, it was possible for Collins to allay suspicions of vampirism while at the same time keeping his master informed about his victim's condition and alerting him to any danger.'

'How was Collins persuaded to help Dracula?' I asked.

'He was rather a weak-willed individual, and easily fell victim to the Count's compelling hypnotic powers.'

'Usually in cases like this, the helper is given the promise of immortality for his service,' remarked Van Helsing.

I nodded, remembering that Collins had spoken of such a promise.

'There can be no doubt that Collins told Dracula of the academy at Coombe Tracey,' continued Holmes, 'and when the Count first visited there, he chose Violet Markham as his bride-to-be and began making nocturnal calls to drink her blood. You may remember, Watson, Gardner telling us that Collins called at the academy the very day she began to feel ill – before it was possible for any other medical help to be sought.

'However, despite Collins's protestations to the contrary, the Markham girl was eventually transported home to London out of Dracula's reach.'

'Where she became the phantom lady that we encountered on Hampstead Heath,' murmured Van Helsing softly, as though clarifying the situation in his own mind.

'Her departure must have angered the Count,' I said.

'Indeed,' replied Holmes. 'She had been snatched from his very grasp, but he had no intention of following her back to London, so he chose another of Gardner's students to be his bride: Catherine Hunter.

'Meanwhile, Collins had secreted Dracula's coffins around the area with the assistance of Meinster; and the Count himself moved to the centre of his web: Baskerville Hall.'

'Now tell me, Holmes, how did you deduce that Dracula was at the Hall?'

'It was Stapleton who told me.'

'What!'

'Not directly, of course. I knew that once Stapleton thought I was dead, he would turn his attention to Baskerville Hall. Remember, he

believed he was the rightful owner. If you recall, after we received
the second of his warning envelopes at the academy, I suggested that
perhaps we had followed Stapleton down to Dartmoor, rather than
the other way round.'

I nodded.

'When he left me in the blazing building, he was so confident I
would die that he collected his things from McCauley Street and
caught the early morning train down to Dartmoor, arriving, in fact,
the day before us.'

'But what about the warning we received the morning after the fire?
Surely he would not have sent that if he believed you were dead.'

'That envelope, if you remember, unlike the other, was not addressed. That is because it was meant for you.'

'Me?' I spluttered.

'It was a warning to you not to attempt to avenge my death. I had
told Stapleton about the spider and fly imagery we had used, and his
twisted mind saw the dead fly as a threat that you would recognise
and understand.'

'If that is the case, he misjudged me if he thought such a gesture
would stop me from taking action.'

Holmes gave me a warm smile. 'On his arrival in Coombe Tracey,
Stapleton secured himself a temporary hideout while he scouted the
lie of the land. It was while on such an expedition that he must have
observed me.' He chuckled. 'I imagine he was unpleasantly surprised
to see me again, the man he hated most in all the world, a man he
thought dead.'

'Hence the warning at the academy.'

'Yes. He could not resist letting me know that he was on my trail
again. However, events took a cruel turn for Stapleton. By this time
the extra frustration and disappointment at my survival must have
finally pushed him over the edge, and he lost touch with reality
altogether. I knew that once he discovered that Baskerville Hall was
empty, he would most likely break in and take possession, living out
his mad dream of being master of the Baskerville estate.'

'But not for long, eh, Holmes?' remarked Van Helsing. 'Dracula
would not allow another master into his sanctuary.'

'That is correct. Dracula, on discovering this intruder, wasted no
time in initiating him into the cult of the undead. And it was Stapleton's vampirised form which Watson and I encountered in Collins's
cellar. It was an encounter which told me where the Count was
hiding – Stapleton's refuge: Baskerville Hall.'

'That is clear to me now, Holmes,' I said, 'but why didn't Dracula simply kill Stapleton?'

'We must remember, Watson, that Dracula, despite his animal-like existence, was a cunning and intelligent creature. He saw Stapleton as his disciple. After claiming the soul of Catherine Hunter, the Count intended to travel with her to pastures new, leaving Stapleton to roam the Devonshire countryside in search of blood, creating his own initiates into his foul cult. In a macabre way, Stapleton would have achieved his wild ambition and become master of the moors.'

'If that is the case, why was he nailed down in his coffin?'

'Because Dracula did not want Stapleton interfering in any way with his own activities. There was room for only one active vampire operating in the region, and Dracula ensured that it was he. Collins, no doubt, would have been instructed to release Stapleton once the Count and his bride had departed. Actually, he would probably have broken free of his own accord eventually, so great was his thirst for blood.'

'Had I not released him prematurely,' I added.

'Great heavens, what happened?' cried Van Helsing. Holmes recounted our grisly escapade in the cellar, when he had decapitated our old adversary with the wood-saw.

'What has puzzled me for some time,' said I, when he had finished, 'is why, once he knew we were on his trail, Dracula did not ensure his own safety by fleeing from the area.'

'Perhaps I can answer that for you, Dr Watson,' said Van Helsing. 'Dracula was a Transylvanian nobleman and he had a nobleman's pride, which he carried with him beyond the grave. He certainly would not allow his plans to be foiled by mere human intervention. Your presence was both an irritant and a challenge to him. One potential bride had been snatched from his clutches; he was not going to lose another.'

'That is where he made his fatal mistake: he underestimated his adversary,' I grinned, and glanced at Holmes; but he seemed to be unaware of the compliment I had paid him. For a brief moment his eyes held that glazed, distant look he sometimes had when his mind was far from our Baker Street rooms.

At length he resumed his narrative and gave Van Helsing all the remaining details of the affair, including how he had one of the silver crucifixes melted down into a bullet by the local blacksmith in Coombe Tracey on the morning after our first encounter with

Dracula; and he gave a vivid description of the final moments of our adventure when we had watched the remains of the Count sink beneath the green slime of the Grimpen Mire. Van Helsing sat forward in his chair, his blue eyes twinkling keenly as he listened spellbound to my friend's account.

When Holmes had finished speaking, the Professor was quiet for a moment and then, in a voice brittle with emotion, he said quietly, 'And now that foul creature is no more; I wish I had been a witness to his end. The world has a great deal to thank you for, Sherlock Holmes.'

'I appreciate your compliment,' Holmes replied graciously, 'but whatever success I achieved in this case was with the help of my dear friend, Watson.'

'Of course,' agreed Van Helsing, giving me warm smile.

'However,' said Holmes, 'I would feel more jubilant if I had managed to save the life of Catherine Hunter. I reproach myself for her death.'

Van Helsing and I gave cries of protest.

'You did all that was humanly possible,' I assured him.

The Dutchman leaned forward and touched my friend on his arm. 'I know how you must feel about the death of this young girl,' he said in quiet, even tones, 'but, my friend, you must place it in perspective. Miss Hunter's death is a tragedy, of course, but compare it with what you have achieved. If Dracula had escaped and lived, think how many more young girls would have been corrupted by this vile beast of the night. Consider, those are lives you have saved.'

I saw from Holmes's expression that these words, so earnestly spoken, touched him. He gave Van Helsing a nod of acceptance and appreciation, and almost at once his spirits lifted.

'Now then,' he said briskly, rubbing his hands together, 'that is enough talk of the dead. We have had several weeks of hard work and now it is the festive season, so let us relax and enjoy it. Watson, if you would be so good as to refill our glasses, I would like our guest to try a new brand of cigar I have obtained from Bradley's.'

I did as I was asked, while Holmes retrieved the cigar box from the mantelpiece and offered it to Van Helsing.

'I am sorry, Holmes,' he said. 'I do not wish to be rude to my host, but I am not a cigar man; I much prefer my own little cheroots.' As if to verify this statement, he produced a leather cheroot case from his inside pocket.

'But you must!' cried Holmes, thrusting the box towards Van Helsing, who was rather taken aback by my friend's forceful insistence. 'You must try one.'

'Very well,' agreed the professor reluctantly. As he opened the box, his expression turned from one of polite reserve to one of surprised delight. The box was empty save for a small, shiny object which caught the light as Van Helsing lifted it out.

Holmes chuckled with glee. 'Please excuse my rather theatrical way of presenting you with a memento of our association, but I am afraid I could not resist it.' Van Helsing hardly heard these words as he examined the object carefully. 'It is Count Dracula's ring,' explained Holmes. 'It was all that was left when the severed hand had withered away. I felt it was only fitting that you should have it.'

Van Helsing held the gift up to the light and eyed it with pleasure. It was a simple gold band holding a large, shimmering ruby which had at the centre some dark blemish, which seemed to me to represent the black heart of the fiend who had worn it.

'It is a fine token, my dear Holmes, but I cannot accept it. It was you who played this most dangerous game to the end, and therefore the ring is your trophy.'

'Nonsense,' cried my friend. 'I want you to have it. You have sought the destruction of Count Dracula for many years; here is lasting proof that this most malevolent of creatures has finally been exterminated.'

Van Helsing was about to protest again when he was arrested by the sound of voices singing. The notes of 'The First Noel' drifted up from the street below. We all crossed to the window and looked down to see some half-dozen snow-sprinkled youths gathered around our door, singing with great charm, their faces lighted by the rays of a horn lantern carried by the tallest of the group.

'The season of goodwill to all men,' murmured Van Helsing softly, pocketing the ring. My friend waited until the singers had finished their carol and then, throwing up the window, he dropped some silver coins to them with a hearty cry of 'Merry Christmas'.

'Merry Christmas,' came their cheery reply as they trudged further up the snow-decked street.

Van Helsing left shortly afterwards, telling us that this would be our last meeting before he returned home to see in the New Year with his family. We accompanied him to the street and helped him secure a hansom cab. Thanking us once more, he disappeared from our lives in a swirl of snow.

On our return to our cosy sitting room, Holmes became subdued and somewhat uncommunicative. Then, as I sat by the fire enjoying a smoke, he took up his violin and began scratching out some obscure airs, no doubt of his own composing. The music was harsh and discordant at first, but gradually the melodies sweetened, until at last he was playing a selection of Christmas carols. I closed my eyes, completely wrapped in Holmes's masterly playing: the soothing tunes telling the age-old story of the child Messiah born in a stable. It was comforting to think at this time of Christian celebration that Holmes and I, in our small way, had contributed to the wellbeing of all.

Shortly before he retired for the night, Holmes went to his bed-room and returned with two packages which he handed to me. 'It is past the midnight hour. These are for you, Watson: small tokens for Christmas,' he said.

'Why, thank you, Holmes,' I cried in surprise, and unwrapped the gifts. One was a jar of my favourite Ship's tobacco, and the other was a large notebook, bound in red leather, with my initials stamped in gold in the bottom right-hand corner.

'It is for your chronicle of the Dracula affair,' he explained. 'A story for which the world is not yet prepared, therefore your record of it must be a private one.'

I nodded in agreement. 'And, since gifts are being presented, perhaps you will accept this with my best wishes,' I said, retrieving a small packet from my bureau drawer and handing it to Holmes.

'Thank you, Watson,' he said, discovering my present to be another pipe to add to his collection. 'A meerschaum. I have not as yet tried one of these. I shall look forward to my first smoke in the morning, but for now, I am rather tired, so I shall bid you goodnight.'

I felt restless and far from ready for bed myself, so I poured another brandy and sat for some time by the fire, watching the snowflakes sweep past the window, while I thought over the strange series of events which had led to the dramatic conclusion of our recent adventure. And then, in the early hours of that Christmas Day, 1888, I began to jot down in my new red leather volume the first notes of the frightening tale which I decided to call 'The Tangled Skein'.